The
GHOST
RIFLE

Westerns

by MAX MCCOY

HELLFIRE CANYON

CANYON DIABLO

DAMNATION ROAD

OF GRAVE CONCERN

THE SPIRIT IS WILLING

GIVING UP THE GHOST

The
GHOST
RIFLE

MAX McCOY

PINNACLE BOOKS
Kensington Publishing Corp.
www.kensingtonbooks.com

PINNACLE BOOKS are published by

Kensington Publishing Corp.
119 West 40th Street
New York, NY 10018

ISBN-13: 978-0-7860-4693-5
ISBN-10: 0-7860-4693-7

First Pinnacle paperback printing: June 2021

10   9   8   7   6   5   4   3   2   1

Printed in the United States of America

Electronic edition:

ISBN-13: 978-0-7860-4694-2 (e-book)
ISBN-10: 0-7860-4694-5 (e-book)

For Kim

Great things are done when men and mountains meet;
This is not done by jostling in the street.
—WILLIAM BLAKE

There be three things which are too wonderful for me,
yea, four which I know not: The way of an eagle
in the air; the way of a serpent upon a rock;
the way of a ship in the midst of the sea;
and the way of a man with a maid.
—PROVERBS 30:18–19

PART ONE
THE TOWN

1 *Bloody Island*

Jacques Aguirre was hungry. He was always hungry, even when he had just eaten, and if he wasn't hungry for food, he wanted whiskey, or the thrill of laying money on the turn of a card, and always the attention of women beyond his station. There were other hungers that ebbed or rose according to his spirit—a fascination with clever objects, a thirst for respect, the yearning for freedom—but his essential condition was ravenous.

Even now, as he stood with a heavy dueling pistol in his right hand, muzzle to the stars and the flint ratcheted back, he could not untangle his whiskey-soaked mind from his hunger; his thoughts wheeled back around to food, and the shortbread pies filled with sweet blackberry jam that he had eaten as a child at the sturdy oak table in his grandfather's great stone house across the ocean.

"Ready?" Aristide Rapaille called.

"Always," Jacques said, drunkenly overconfident.

"Then point your piece at the ground," Aristide chided.

"Ha," Jacques said. He lowered the pistol and gave his friend a sly grin.

Aristide was standing twenty paces to the side, his arms

folded in Gallic disgust, his stylish boots planted wide in the sand and mud on the banks of this narrow island in the middle of the Mississippi. Even standing in muck, he had the air of a patrician, and his face with its fine features seemed always to be privy to some hidden joke.

It was not yet spring, but no longer winter; on this first Thursday of March 1822, the island was cold and the willows rippled in the midnight breeze. Beyond the willows and other scrub trees, at the river's edge, the water swirled past, driven by spring rains. The moon was climbing the southern sky, nearing full, blocking out the nearby stars, rendering the island and the river beyond in a muted and surreal palette.

The moon reminded Jacques of an unblinking cat's eye, seeing all but moved by nothing. The thought—and the whiskey in his gut—made him laugh.

"Will you be still?" Aristide scolded.

Aristide turned his head to look at his uncle. The moonlight gleamed and rippled on the slick beaver felt of his high hat. The hat had cost an ounce of gold, weeks of labor for the average tradesman, and was fitting for an individual of Aristide Rapaille's position—son of one of the wealthiest families in St. Louis, friend of former territorial governor William Clark, and owner of the most expensive, if not the best, gun shop in the city. It was at the shop, on Chestnut Street just around the corner from the St. Louis County District Court and Jail, where his friend Jacques spent twelve hours of every day. The difference in stations between them was a scandal for the Rapaille family, for Jacques was not just an employee but an indentured servant.

"Are you ready, *tonton*?"

The uncle, Guy Rapaille, was holding the pistol at an awkward angle, in order to examine the lock in the moonlight. Rotund and bespectacled, with an expensive hat that rose even higher than Aristide's, the uncle was having second thoughts about having challenged a man less than half his age, and far below his class, to settle a manner of honor. Unlike the Rapailles, Jacques had no hat, or fancy vest, and instead of a fine coat with bright brass buttons, his was plain dark cotton with bone toggles.

But here, on Bloody Island, their clothes mattered little. Many before them had come to this broad sandbar between the Missouri and Illinois shores—where dueling had long been outlawed—to settle personal differences. Local attorney Thomas Hart Benton had killed Charles Lucas, another lawyer, here just five years before, settling in honor (if not in truth) which one was the liar.

As Jacques was the challenged, the right to choose weapons belonged to him—and of course he chose pistols.

The pistols had not been made at the shop, which specialized in the new short-barreled, large-caliber, half-stock rifles favored by the free trappers who ascended the Missouri River in search of the finest beaver pelts, from the coldest and highest places in the unimagined West, from which Aristide's hat was made.

The pistols were a boxed pair, made in London by Manton, in .51 caliber with 10-inch octagonal barrels. The stocks were walnut and the furniture was silver, and they were loaded with balls that had been cast from lead taken from the mines in Washington County, a day's ride to the southwest.

"Are you having difficulty with your piece?" Aristide asked.

"Of course, he has difficulty," Jacques called. "Just ask his wife!"

"Please," Aristide said. "No more. This is an affair of honor."

"He has no honor," the uncle said. "Look at how he has mistreated your poor sister, Abella. He should be ashamed, but instead he cracks wise. How can you befriend such a person? He is a jack, a knave—no more than a *picaro*, a rogue."

Jacques had heard the term thrown at him before, across the gambling tables in the dark dens along the Mississippi below the city, or from the wealthier patrons of the shop when he was so bold to address them directly, and from Sheriff Brown when he cautioned Jacques against his libertine ways. He rather enjoyed the sound of *rogue*.

"I am unsure of the flint," the uncle said.

"I loaded the pistol myself," Aristide said. "The flint is seated well, and the pan is primed."

"Might you not have allowed your affection for your friend—"

"No, Uncle."

Jacques muttered and cursed in the language of his childhood.

"In English or French, if you please," the uncle snapped.

"I do not please," Jacques said.

"Nobody can understand that guttural argot," Uncle Guy said. "It is not Spanish, but it sounds Gypsy."

"I am not Romany," Jacques said. "I am Basque, from the ancient city of Carcosa. My native tongue is Euskara, and if you had heard my grandfather sing the ballads of love—well, you would never mistake Euskara for Romany again—or perhaps some lesser language, like French."

"Your impudence will be your death," the uncle said, in French.

"Perhaps," Jacques replied, in English. "But not tonight. Would it be satisfactory if we traded pieces?"

The uncle conceded that it would.

Aristide went about the careful business of swapping the guns, one at a time, turning his shoulders to the moonlight to ease the work. Standing twenty yards away, in the direction of the skiff that had brought them to the island, was Dr. Mason Muldridge, hands clasped in front of him, watching silently.

"This would be simpler, Uncle, had you a proper second," Aristide said, as he handed over the new piece, butt first. "Our good doctor seems ill-suited to such a venture."

Muldridge stared, but said nothing. He had been pulled from his bed and the arms of a well-earned sleep by drunken and frantic pounding on his front door, expecting to attend to some calamity, perhaps the loss of a limb. Because he could not refuse his friend Rapaille, he had made it clear he would take no part other than to care for the injured or pronounce the death of one of the principals.

"Well, it's good that old Muldridge is here," Jacques said. "After this is settled, I could use a shave and a haircut. That was your profession before, was it not? A barber?"

Muldridge took a pinch of snuff.

"This is all forbidden by the Code Duello," Muldridge said. "Never at night."

"Galway rules or Kilkenny?" Jacques taunted.

Muldridge's nose twitched.

"The latter allows nights and every other Easter, seconds to be chosen from among the finer bordellos, and coffee and beignets at dawn."

Muldridge sneezed mightily.

"Leave him alone, Jacky," Aristide said.

"If this were proper, the combatants would be gentle-men," the older Rapaille said, squinting to inspect the pistol's lock. "I lower myself to right a wrong."

"You only lower yourself to make water."

"Jacques!" Aristide chided.

"But does he not look like an old woman?"

"Just what I would expect from a drunken peasant."

"I am drunk," Jacques said. "Blessedly and enthusias-tically and dangerously drunk. But, my sir who is almost my uncle by virtue of my brotherly friendship with our beloved Aristide, my birth is as noble as your own. Ah, I see you are confused. Should I speak slower? Allow me to make it plain: In the Basque country, my family are aristocrats, lords of the land, masters of the sea, and I was their prince. It is only through an unfortunate series of miscalculations involving certain games of chance that has resulted in my temporary servitude. But rest assured, I am your peer, if not your better."

The older Rapaille snorted.

"My better?" he asked. "Surely this bootlick jokes. He cannot even vote."

"Please," Aristide said. "We are all of us Americans now. Let us remember the Declaration of the Rights of Man and to not bring the prejudices and ignorance of the Old World into this new one."

Jacques smiled grimly.

"It seems not all Americans are as equal as others," he said. "It is true that I cannot yet vote, although I am counted as a free man. My status enrages me. And do not forget, my dear friend, that the Rights of Man gave birth to the bastard Corsican, dead but still stinking on St. Helena. Let us all be done with Bonaparte."

"We have the Bill of Rights," Aristide said.

"Ever the optimist," Jacques said. "Why should we expect Americans to fare any better? In time, these declarations too shall be perverted from an instrument of freedom to one of bondage and chaos. But here, standing on an island between and beyond the states, we are truly equal, and I am about to cast a leaden and irrevocable vote with the most democratic of ballots."

The uncle blinked back fear.

"Stand well clear, doctor," Jacques said, waving a hand at Muldridge. "Your skill as a surgeon might be required before the night is out, and it would be a shame if an errant ballot found a home in your breast."

"I beg you," Muldridge called, as he stepped back a few more yards. "Stop this lunacy."

Jacques laughed again, turned, and threw a rude salute to the moon.

"Let us wait," Aristide offered. "Next month Jacky will have completed his term of service and will be a free man. In that month he might sober up enough to regret his loutish behavior and offer a proper apology."

"And allow him to ruin other young women," the uncle asked, "like a dog in rut?"

"Now you call your own niece a bitch," Jacques said.

"And my sister," Aristide cautioned.

Jacques did not hear the uncle's protestations, for he was suddenly awash in guilt for this last bit of cruelty. His affection for her seemed genuine. But how was he to know? He remembered the last time they had embraced, a fortnight ago, in the shadow of the old Spanish Tower that overlooked the river. Abella was a pale and lissome girl, with black hair that cascaded down to her thin waist, with trusting eyes and kind hands, skin that smelled of vanilla, and a mouth that was ripe to be kissed.

"Jacky!" Aristide called once more. "Stay awake!"

Jacques looked up.

"Is the challenged ready?

"I am," Jacques said absently in Euskara. He was still thinking of Abella, for she had promised to meet him again tonight, beneath the Spanish tower. He was glad the moon was full, because it would better illumine her graceful form.

There was a muttering behind him.

"I am ready," he said impatiently. "I am eternally ready."

"In French, if you please." Jacques laughed.

"I do not please," Jacques roared. "I am never pleased! I am hungry, as God is my witness, and I starve for life. Let us get on with it, so that I may continue my pursuits—of good whiskey, blind luck, and bad women. For God's sake, Ari, hand me the flask from your pocket for courage before your uncle's lack of wit and paucity of charm forces me to use my pistol on myself."

Aristide warned him about further insults.

"Does he never shut up?" Uncle Guy asked. "All he does is talk. A torrent of words pour from his mouth, equal parts bile and self-aggrandizement, but not an iota of wisdom."

Jacques waved him off.

"Will you not offer an apology?" Aristide inquired. "This whole business can be avoided."

"I will not accept," the uncle said.

"And I will not offer," Jacques said. But at the edge of his mind there was a softly formed thought that perhaps he should, that he should not always be so ready to court trouble, that the uncle was right, every word in his head tumbled unchecked from his mouth.

"Very well," Aristide said. "Is the challenger ready?"

"I am," the uncle said.

"Then take your ground," Aristide said. "The challenged has chosen the weapons and, and as required by the code, the challenger specifies the distance. How many yards, *tonton*?"

The old man began to speak, then hesitated.

"You must give a distance," Aristide said gently.

"Thirty yards," the old man stuttered.

"Why not a hundred?" Aristide asked. "The result will be the same."

"You will now each count off fifteen paces, in opposite directions," Aristide said. "Then you will stop and turn to face your rival. The signal to fire will be when I drop this." Aristide produced a square of white silk. "No shooting into the ground or the air is permitted, nor is any advance or retreat. You must stand your ground and exchange shots. If, after the first exchange, neither party has received a ball, then the pieces may be loaded and the signal repeated. But in no cases will more than three exchanges be allowed. Understood?"

"Yes," the old man said.

"Of course," Jacques said.

"Then take your ground."

Then the men stepped away from one another, counting as they planted each foot in the sand.

"Un," Uncle Guy said.

"*Bat!*" Jacques returned in Euskara.

"Deux."

"*Bi!*"

"Trois."

"*Hiru!*"

"For God's sake, gentleman," Aristide said. "Be good enough to count in the same language."

"Four." This, in unison.

Jacques reached fifteen first, and he turned as the older man continued, a bit unsteadily.

"Fifteen," Uncle Guy said, finally, and turned cautiously.

"Very well," Aristide said. Then he held out his right hand, the silk square, undulating in the breeze, at shoulder height. The combatants raised and cocked their pistols.

Aristide released the square, and his uncle fired before it had touched the ground. Jacques saw the shower of sparks and tongue of fire from his opponent's pistol. The scene was frozen for an instant in his mind, as when a flash of lightning captures a lingering moment, and by the time he heard the sound of the blast, he felt the air ripple as the ball nipped at his right shoulder.

Outraged, he placed the moonlight-gilded sights of his dueling pistol on the uncle's nose and flicked his finger forward to set the trigger. Suddenly, he was sober. It would take only a few ounces of pressure from his right index finger to reduce the dotard's head to mush. But his hungers did not include bloodlust, so he shifted his aim to the top of the uncle's beaver hat and squeezed the trigger. The pistol thundered and bucked in his hand, and he watched with satisfaction as the ridiculous hat wheeled wildly into darkness.

The old man dropped his pistol and clasped the top of his head with both hands, as if to make sure his skull remained intact.

"Nicely placed," Aristide said.

"Thank you, my friend."

"Are we done?" Jacques asked.

"No," the uncle said. "Reload."

"Very well," Aristide said tiredly, and took the pistol

offered by Jacques. Carefully he tamped down fresh powder and patched ball, primed the pan, and handed it butt first to his friend. But as Jacques grasped the handle, Aristide would not release his hold. Blood, as black as ink in the moonlight, was running down Jacques's wrist and dripping to the sand.

"You have been hit," Aristide said, letting go of the pistol and calling for Muldridge.

Jacques cursed.

"Did you not feel it?" Aristide asked.

"No," Jacques said. "Not until now."

Jacques suddenly felt the weight and awkwardness of the pistol and wanted to be done with it. He slipped the weapon into the outside pocket of his coat, then removed the jacket, noting the hole in the sleeve.

"Take off your shirt as well," Muldridge directed, suddenly competent.

Jacques lifted his left arm while Aristide helped pull it over his head. Because Jacques was a working man, his dress was simpler than that of Aristide; not only was he disallowed a shirt with separate cuffs and collars, he could not afford one, either. The shirt had to be given a little tug, because the fabric of the right sleeve stuck in the warm blood coating his elbow and forearm. There was a light sheen of sweat on his chest and on his ribs, betraying a fear of being shot at that whiskey could not smother. From a silver chain around his neck swung a curious piece, a milled and polished brass disk that was some three inches across, with four curved arms in the center. The design was odd, like that of a cross with curiously lobed ends, facing left. On the outside was a row of teeth punctuated by indents around the rim, with another circle of teeth and indents nestled inside.

"What is the medallion?" Uncle Guy asked, staring at the disk.

"Let me conduct my examination, for God's sake," Muldridge said. He gently touched Jacques's shoulders and turned him gently this way and that in the moonlight, his face inscrutable in concentration.

Jacques could not see the wound, but was alarmed by the amount of blood.

"Well?" Aristide asked. "How bad is it?"

"It will leave a scar," Muldridge said.

"So does amputation," Jacques said.

"For God's sake, doctor, how bad is it?" Aristide pressed.

"No bones broken, or damage to the biceps," the doctor said. "Your arm was bent, holding the barrel of the pistol upright, when Monsieur Rapaille fired. The ball passed through the fabric and gave you a nasty bite. It will leave a scar, nothing more. Keep it clean and pray that it does not fester."

Jacques nodded.

His left hand fluttered upward and instinctively grasped the brass disk dangling from the chain around his neck, his thumb skimming the teeth, as he muttered thanks to both Saint Ignatius and the chthonic goddess Mari.

"Is it a religious symbol?" Guy asked with suspicion. "It resembles Ezekiel's dream of a wheel within a wheel."

"Exactly," Aristide said. He knew the truth, that the pattern in the disk was the *lauburu,* the ancient four-headed cross of the Basque people. But he wanted to deflect his uncle's questions. "It is some pagan symbol, which Jacky's people revere. But such strangeness cannot be accounted for. Best to leave it alone, rather than court the devil."

Uncle Guy crossed himself.

"You are a lucky fool," Muldridge told Jacques. "You

mocked me until you needed attention. What if the ball had shattered your arm, or ruined your hand? What kind of living would you have made then, unable to run a nut or turn a screw? What would an apology have cost you? If your life means so little to you, what about that of the girl, Abella? What of her life?"

"You speak out of turn," Jacques said.

The doctor pursed his lips, holding the words back.

"Then this affair of honor is over," Aristide said quickly. "The challenger has drawn substantial blood. I assume this is enough to represent satisfaction?"

"It is," Guy said, his relief evident.

"I have grown tired of this," Jacques said as Muldridge bandaged his upper arm with a strip of cloth ripped from his ruined shirt. "Now that we are all Americans again, let us return to the public house beneath Tower Hill. We will toast our fine adventure casting ballots of lead on Bloody Island."

2 *The Landing*

Aristide put his back into the oars as the skiff drew near the end of Lucas Street, where the ground dipped gently to the river's edge. This was the broad levee, where the steamboats docked, took on firewood and offloaded passengers and goods, and made repairs. It was edged by storehouses and workshops and businesses decorated with columns and capitals, whitewashed walls, and broad vaulted windows where an occasional candle burned.

The skiff was an eleven-foot boat of the kind that fishermen up and down the river used, with a flat stern and a snub bow, and coils of rough hemp rope in the bottom. They had found the boat tied beneath one of the lesser docks and had borrowed it to make their way to Bloody Island, for it had just enough seats for the dueling party of four. They had been halfway across the river when they discovered the boat leaked; it wasn't enough to cause an immediate concern of sinking, but was enough to swell the coils of rope and damp their boots. So on the way back, Aristide—who was clearly the only viable candidate for rowing—rowed now with purpose, both to cut across the current in order to round the shallow bar that guarded the deeper channel along the levee, and to reduce the amount of time they would have to spend with their toes sloshing in the Mississippi. But Aristide, facing the stern, was having a difficult time steering the boat, because the required maneuvers seemed backward.

"Aller à droit!" Uncle Guy cried out. Then, *"A gauche! A gauche!"*

The wooden bottom of the boat scraped over the sand and gravel of the towhead. There was a chill wind on the water, and it seemed to grow suddenly colder as the boat slowed.

"Pull," the uncle said.

Aristide did, and the boat resumed its forward motion.

"Snag!" Jacques cried.

With a groan the boat lurched up on a submerged tree trunk, pivoted wildly, and then was free. Aristide pulled one oar handle and pushed the other in an attempt to make a line again for shore.

"My God, Aristide," Jacques said. "Have you never rowed a boat before?"

"Not at night or with people shouting directions or with a head still singing with rum. If either you or my dear uncle can do better, you are welcome to try."

"No, thank you," Muldridge said from the stern.

"Thank you, doctor," Aristide said.

The boat was now heading roughly in the right direction, but the faster current in the channel was sweeping it downstream.

"Faster!" Jacque shouted, then laughed.

Aristide cursed and pulled harder.

"Ah," the uncle said, as the levee neared.

Then the boat crossed the eddy line to calmer water, and Aristide lifted the oars from the water as they glided toward a dock. It wasn't the dock they had taken the boat from, but it didn't matter to them.

Uncle Guy rose from his seat in the bow and reached a hand out to grasp the dock. He missed, then caught a plank on the second try and pulled the skiff in close.

"There are steps," Aristide said, nodding at some stones rising from the water to the top of the landing. The boat was close enough that the others could now reach across the gunwale and help pull the skiff along, and soon the bow bumped into the stone steps. The uncle grabbed the end of a coil of rope at his feet and tied a careless knot around a piling, while in the stern the doctor quickly tied an expert clove hitch.

"I am done with this leaky tub," Uncle Guy said, stepping shakily out of the boat and up onto the steps. He kept one foot too long in the skiff, and the imbalance drove one side of the boat dangerously close to the water. Jacques was behind him, with his rough coat over his shoulders, and he put both hands on the old man's posterior and pushed him up. As the uncle finally gained both feet on the steps, the skiff righted itself with a jolt, and Jacques fell, losing his coat, laughing. He was up in a moment, however, but forgot his coat, for he was warm yet with drink and the excitement of the duel. He put one boot on the gunwale and lightly jumped for the steps. But he did not see that his right boot had become entangled in a loop in the rope Uncle Guy had hastily uncoiled to tie up with, and it tripped him just as he made the steps.

Jacques fell heavily on the steps, and as he did the dueling pistol that had been in his right pocket clattered to the stone. Whether the gun had been cocked when he put it in his pocket, or whether the jolt had drawn the hammer back just far enough, Jacques would forever ponder but never know. What was certain was the flash of flame and the crack of thunder as the gun discharged, its barrel pointed back toward the river.

"Jacky?" Aristide asked. "What a peculiar joke."

Jacques glanced back and saw his friend Aristide looking at him with surprise, standing with his hands out as if Christ crucified, his shirt smoldering from the burning patch and a dark-as-ink stain spreading from his right side. Their eyes met, and the last emotion that Jacques ever saw on his friend's face was disappointment. Then Aristide buckled and he pitched into the Mississippi, the motion carrying his body away from the skiff.

Silence descended like a thunderclap. The night wind was suddenly cold on Jacques's bare chest.

"Ari," he said.

Jacques tore off his boots and dove from the steps into the river, swimming madly, calling his friend's name when his head bobbed above water. Aristide was floating facedown, but as the weight of the tail of his coat slipped to one side, he turned, his hair swirling in the water around his face. Jacques thought he should be able to reach Aristide in just a few strokes, but the farther he swam, the more distance there seemed between them.

Then Aristide's body slid beneath a downstream dock, where a dozen silent keelboats were moored. If there were watchmen on the keelboats, they were either passed out drunk or asleep, for nothing moved on their decks. Then the moon was shrouded by some low clouds, portending rain, and it was darker now than it had been on the island.

Jacques stared at the darkness beneath the docks, thinking of the snakes that were surely coiled in the driftwood and tree branches and other trash that collected there. A fear of those hidden places gripped him, and he could not bring himself to search beneath the docks for Aristide's body. Jacques sobbed as he swam back to the skiff, calling for Uncle Guy and the doctor to help search.

Muldridge, who was still sitting in the stern of the skiff, shrugged.

"The river has him now," he said.

"There must be something to be done," Uncle Guy said, but his uncertain tone betrayed his words.

"Not until dawn," the doctor said. "And even then, our task will be to find the body. Such a wound was surely fatal, and if he did survive the gunshot, he would be insensate and drown. His body will likely be carried far downriver."

Jacques pulled himself dripping up onto the bottom step, where the sulfurous stench of black powder lingered. Out of habit, his right hand went to the brass disk around his neck. It was still there. Then he sat and pulled his knees up and rested his forehead on his folded arms. He had killed his best and only friend by accident, but it made Aristide no less dead.

"What have I done?" he asked.

"You have committed murder," Uncle Guy said, "and for this you will surely hang."

"But it was an accident," Jacques said. "You saw so yourself."

"I saw no such thing," Uncle Guy said. "My back was turned. I only heard the shot. When I did look around, I saw my nephew Aristide murdered."

"Then you, good doctor," Jacques said. "You must have seen.'

"My view was blocked by Aristide's back," Muldridge said. "I know only the result."

Jacques turned back to Uncle Guy.

"Please, friend's dear uncle," Jacques implored. "The pistol fell from my pocket when I tripped on the rope you carelessly dragged behind you. This you must know to be true."

"You were drunk and should have watched your step."

Jacques found himself suddenly without words. The silence that followed was excruciating, an indictment unspoken, a judgment implicit. Shame and guilt were unfamiliar emotions, and as hot tears spilled down his cheeks, his stomach churned so that he thought he would retch.

"We should summon Sheriff Brown," Muldridge said.

"Yes," Jacques said, resignedly. "It must be so."

His life had been changed in an instant. No longer would he have Aristide to drink and laugh with, to throw dice and play cards with, to be the brother that blood had never given him. The sheriff would come and he would spend some weeks in the wretched jail in the courthouse downtown and eventually there would be a trial and even though he might be acquitted of murder, he would always be guilty of taking his friend's life.

"Let us not summon the sheriff yet," Uncle Guy said.

He was standing on the dock above them, his dueling pistol held loosely in his hand.

"What do you mean?" Muldridge asked.

"Why go through a trial when we have the means to dispense justice immediately? Trial by jury is unreliable. We understand perfectly the guilt of the accused. Let us not allow his fate to be decided by a dozen chosen from the rabble who are no better than the accused. It would be better to be done with this *picaro* here and now."

"Aristide's death was an accident," Jacques said. "This is murder."

"Guy, he is right," Muldridge said.

"Stand clear!"

"Where am I to go?" Muldridge asked. "The boat is not large."

"Let him do it," Jacques said. "It is no more than I deserve."

"At least allow me to make myself small," Muldridge said, scooting to the bottom of the boat and doing just that.

"Quit whimpering," Jacques said. "I will mount the steps and stand on the dock, facing the firing squad of one."

Uncle Guy hesitated.

"No," he said. "Allow the doctor to pass instead."

Jacques shrugged.

Muldridge rose and clamored forward, exited the boat, then quickly ascended the steps to the dock.

"I am alone now," Jacques said, "waiting for my own Charon to lead me from this dreary coast. But that would be you, dear uncle of the dead, would it not? You will kill me and then—what?—throw my body into the boat and push it into the current? Both Ari and I will be missing for a few days, and then one will be found, and eventually the other, and it will seem that we had a contretemps that turned unexpectedly violent, with results mortal to us both."

"Why do you still talk?" Uncle Guy asked. "Even at the point of a gun, you continue to spew your thoughts at us as incautiously as if you had sneezed with a mouthful of wine."

Jacques shrugged.

"The truth is, I had not considered yet what to do beyond killing you."

"You should," Jacques said. "I have presented you a nearly perfect plan."

"Nearly?"

"The doctor," Jacques said. "What of him? Can you count on his silence?"

"Muldridge is our family doctor," Uncle Guy said. "A man of discretion."

"Please," the doctor pleaded. "Leave me out of this."

"Ah, it is too late for that," Jacques said. "You will allow Uncle Guy to murder me without benefit of judge or jury? Even if you think I deserve it, there will be uncomfortable questions from Sheriff Brown and others. You will keep silent during questioning? Can you lie convincingly? Will your palms not sweat and your eyes not twitch knowing that giving false testimony is one of the most serious of crimes itself?"

"Shut up," Uncle Guy shouted. "Just shut up."

His shout echoed back from the walls of the warehouses. Somewhere, a dog began to bark, and then another. Soon, a chorus of angry canines rose toward the night sky, and a few more lights appeared in the windows of the trying-to-sleep river town.

"There is my jury," Jacques said. "A jury of dogs. They deliver their verdict, and it seems not to be in my favor. Proceed, Uncle Guy. Even you can put a ball in my chest at this distance."

"You talk to buy time."

It was true. Even though a part of him longed to be punished for the accidental killing of his best friend, the greater part sought to live. Jacques knew that if he kept talking—and kept Uncle Guy answering—the greater his chances were of either talking his way out of his own murder, or seizing upon some small advantage that would allow him to escape.

"Give me the medallion," said Uncle Guy.

"You have a sudden interest in paganism?"

"I would deprive you of comfort at the moment of your death."

"Oh, you think it valuable, don't you?"

"What is it, then?"

"Come closer," Jacques said, beckoning. "Press the muzzle against my bare chest and pull the trigger. I long for justice and the forgiveness of that long sleep that awaits. You can take the disk and study it at your leisure when I am dead." He was hoping to lure Uncle Guy close enough so that he could make a grab for the pistol's barrel and wrest it away.

"No, you come up here."

"Very well, Uncle."

Barefoot, Jacques slowly climbed the steps. His pace was as slow as if he were ascending the gallows. At the top step, he looked up at the night sky. The clouds were so thick now that he could see no stars.

Then he stepped onto the dock, finding his footing with careful toes.

They were only ten feet apart, but in the darkness, they were just shadows to one another. Jacques's back was to the river, and the rotund shadow that was the uncle blocked his path to the landing. Jacques could not see it, but he sensed the hammer of the pistol was cocked and that Rapaille's finger was on the trigger. He only hesitated, Jacques knew, because his old and tired eyes were unsure of his target that the dock had been deprived of moonlight.

He heard the uncle take two steps toward him, to improve his aim, and Jacques knew it was time to move or die. He crouched and lunged forward, colliding with the great stomach that preceded Uncle Guy like the prow of a ship, and they both tumbled to the rough planks of the dock while fighting for the pistol. Jacques wrapped both of his hands around the wrist that held the pistol, forcing the barrel away. The old man drove the fingers of his other hand into the soft flesh of Jacques's nose and upper lip, the fingernails stabbing him. Jacques bit one of the offending fingers, hard enough to hear a crack, and the uncle yelped in pain and withdrew his injured hand.

The doctor was ascending the stone steps, but Jacques warned him that he would be next to be bitten. Muldridge obediently sat on the top step.

Uncle Guy cursed and squirmed, but Jacques managed to twist and bring a knee up and press it against the old man's throat, forcing the right side of his face into the rough timber of the decking.

"Let go of the piece," Jacques said, surprised that he could not yet prise the pistol loose.

Uncle Guy, face against the dock, said something that sounded like "no."

"I swear I will crush your windpipe if I must. Let go, Uncle."

More sounds, but none that were words.

Jacques had more leverage now, and he brought more force to bear on Uncle Guy's neck. There was a gurgling sound, and labored breathing, and finally the old man's grip on the pistol began to loosen. Then suddenly Jacques had the pistol.

Jacques got to his feet and pointed the pistol at the uncle, who was alternately coughing and sucking in air. Jacques stepped cautiously past him, a bit closer to the dark rows of warehouses and the rest of St. Louis on the limestone bluffs beyond. With his free hand, he wiped the blood away from his nose and gums.

"Damn you," the uncle said between wheezes. "Damn your children, and all that you and they may touch."

Anger and grief expanded in Jacques's heart until it felt as if the ballooning organ would push his ribs through his chest. His head was ablaze with an unquenchable fire, and he was half surprised to find that his skull cast no light on his surroundings. The dogs keened in the distance, round upon round of hoarse cries of some pain from the beginning of the world, and Jacques stumbled backward, pushing his hands to his ears, the pistol still in his right fist.

"Aristide," Jacques cried. "Oh, Aristide!"

Then he turned and flung the pistol over Uncle Guy's head, beyond the end of the dock, and far across the dark water. It landed with a percussive splash in the Mississippi and was gone forever.

Jacques ran. The bottoms of his feet beat a tattoo on the wooden decking. He slipped, ripping his trousers and bloodying his knee. Then he was up and flying again down the dock in the dark, carrying his hunger and his shame with him. He jumped from the dock, and his feet sank into the sand and mud of the landing, bringing him to hands and knees, with his forehead touching the earth, an involuntary prostration to the crushing and sure consequences of hubris and careless action. Never again, he swore to himself, would he speak without thinking or act without sincerity and deliberation. He was fluent in four languages, and had damned himself in all; he had all the strength and dexterity a man of twenty-three could expect, and had employed these to his ruin; he had had a friend who loved him like a brother, and he had betrayed that fraternal love with fatal carelessness.

Jacques lifted his head, brushed the sand and mud from

his face with a forearm, heard the dogs baying and snarling in the distant night. His right hand clasped the disk that swung from the chain around his neck, holding it tight over his heart. He rose, nearly fell again, and of a sudden, found his feet and was running toward the darkness.

3 *The Grackle*

Jacques slowed when he reached the dark Rue des Granges, the north-south street that roughly bisected the city into the residential on one side and the businesses, government building, and riverfront on the other. He turned south, even though his modest rented room was in the other direction; he suspected that he would never again see the place he had lived these last five years.

Keeping to the deepest shadows near buildings and beneath the trees, he made his way through the city until the Rue des Granges became just a path, and then he followed the path down from the limestone bluffs and into the woods and into a dark bottoms. It was about this time that the soles of Jacques's feet began to howl. He sat on a stump long enough to remove his stockings, wind them as best he could around his feet, and tie them. The result afforded some relief, but was awkward.

The path turned east and then paralleled Mill Creek, below Chouteau's Pond, and eventually, when it found the Mississippi, it became a river trace that led five miles below to an irregular collection of buildings below a hamlet whose formal name was Carondelet; but that was known by all as Vide-Poche, *empty pockets,* for visitors would have their pockets emptied by the unconventional and enterprising residents who lived there.

The ramshackle structures along the riverfront at Vide-Poche were pieced together from whatever had been lost from a raft or keelboat or taken by a flood and brought down the river. Rough plank doors on leather hinges and fine window panes often graced the same façade, and while most of the buildings were unpainted, a few were dashed with gray or blue lead paint, or whatever other hue the river might decide. In rare strokes of luck, a steamboat might be ripped apart by a boiler explosion or their bottoms gouged open by a barely submerged but unseen tree trunk, and richer cargo would be strewn across the river, including sometimes hogsheads of tobacco and barrels of whiskey. The steamboats seldom ventured farther upriver than St. Louis, because the river became too shallow and dangerous, choked with impassable sandbars and other hazards, so typically the boats would dock at St. Louis after having joined the Mississippi at the confluence of the Ohio River, having originated at Cincinnati and other points east; increasingly, however, they had come up from New Orleans.

Jacques knew Vide-Poche well, for despite the taverns and brothels and gambling dens, its main attraction was business. Here he offered a bounty for the metal parts that could be salvaged from steamboat wrecks, of which there was much twisted boiler plate. But he paid a premium for the finely machined rods and cylinders and other driving pieces.

The Aguirre family were generations of bell and cannon makers in centuries past, and clockmakers in the current one; the disciplines were interconnected because they required a mastery of metalworking, from bronze and brass to wrought iron and hammered, or blistered, steel. Wrought iron could not be hardened because the carbon content was too low, and so it would not hold a fine edge, but the Viking and the Saracen blacksmiths had centuries ago learned to use charcoal and burning leaves to slowly impart carbon to their sword blades.

The same steel that made fine-edged weapons also made good mainsprings for timepieces, but watchmakers were bedeviled by the problem of inconsistent iron content in the steel, which made spring tension unreliable. In 1744, it was a clockmaker named Huntsman in Sheffield, England, who first devised a method for producing cast steel, with a uniform carbon content, that made more accurate watches. He did this by using small coke-fired crucibles to heat small strips of hammered steel until it melted—a feat that was generally thought impossible. Melting the steel made the carbon mix uniformly and purged the steel of impurities, which could be skimmed off as slag.

Steel held the promise of better guns, the Aguirre family knew, but a steel rifle barrel was impractical because the tools needed to make and work it did not yet exist. So cast steel was limited to some of the smaller parts that had to perform well and reliably, such as the spring that drove the hammer or the jaws that held the flint. Sheffield was still the best, but there was nothing comparable in America— especially on the edge of the frontier. So Jacques traded with scavengers to bring him his steel.

From this scrap he employed smiths to make rifle barrels that were superior to all others, mixing the steel with wrought iron in the forge. The process reintroduced carbon and impurities, but produced a stronger iron that could, with effort, be hammered and welded into rifle barrels. But the fortified iron was only a necessary part of the puzzle, not the solution. The solution was a secret, held in the disk on his chest, and it was the kind of secret upon which empires are built; he had shared it with only one other person, and now that Aristide was dead, Jacques alone carried the promise—and the burden.

The largest establishment in Vide-Poche was a gambling house and brothel to which was attached a tavern called The Grackle, named for the scavenging and noisy blackbirds that picked through the trash on the midden out back. Jacques never knew The Grackle to close, and the entire concern was glowing like a lamp. The door was open, and Jacques walked in and stood at the bar, desperately needing a drink.

"Aguirre!" a man of middle age with a gray face and an auburn beard called from the end of the bar.

"Craddock," Jacques said.

"Whiskey?"

"Yes, for God's sake."

"Amen," Craddock said, placing a tumbler on the bar and pouring three or four ounces from a gurgling ceramic jug. The bar top was made of puncheon, like the floor, and the splotches of whiskey spilt from the pour darkened the wood.

Jacques took a drink and then surveyed the room. Three card games were in progress at full or nearly full tables, and Jacques knew the men at one of the tables; they called and motioned for him to join, but he shook his head. There was a loud dice game in the corner, and pair of whores lounged on the landing of the stairs that led to the upstairs rooms. They were both twenty years old or less, and one of them was thin with long blond hair and the other was thick in the middle with brown, curly hair. They both looked at Jacques with questioning eyes, but he shook his head.

"Here," Craddock said, offering Jacques a damp rag.

Jacques took the rag and began to wipe his face.

Craddock knew better than to inquire about a customer's injuries, because they had likely occurred in fights over cards or faithless women or other affairs involving remarkably poor judgment. But he could not help but to ask where Jacques had misplaced his shirt.

"Ripped to make bandages," Jacques said.

"Ah, the arm," Craddock said, and waited a few moments for Jacques to volunteer the story. Instead, Jacques took another sip of whiskey. It was bad whiskey, with an aftertaste like lamp oil.

"And your boots?" Craddock dared.

"Lost them," Jacques said. "Went for a swim."

"Glad that is all," Craddock said. "There's a runaway nigger on the loose. They say Sheriff Brown chased him for the last two days with dogs, but hasn't caught him yet. People are afraid for their persons and their families."

"One runaway is hardly the beginnings of another slave revolt."

Jacques felt sympathy for anyone who was denied their freedom, no matter the color of their skin, and he found slavery abhorrent. In Spain, slavery was historically more a matter of religion than it was ethnicity, so he was free of American biases about race.

"I hope the poor bastard gets away," he said.

"That would be unpopular talk in town."

"We are not in town," Jacques said, "but beneath it."

Jacques pushed the tumbler away.

"For God's sake," Jacques said, "something better."

"Your taste has improved," Craddock said.

He took a bottle of bourbon from the shelf behind the bar, uncorked it, and carefully poured a couple of ounces in a tall shot glass. Jacques took the clear glass and held it toward the lamp above, noting the warm amber color. Then he tasted it, detecting good earth and oak and apricot. There wasn't a trace of kerosene in the aftertaste.

"You'll need another dressing on that arm."

Jacques nodded.

"I have a roll of clean muslin," Craddock said. "For upstairs, you know. I'll get you a few strips."

"And a shirt?"

"I might could find one," Craddock allowed. "It is chilly outside, isn't it?"

Craddock went upstairs and in five minutes returned with the muslin bandages, a couple of shirts, and a well-worn jacket.

"The keelboat men are sometimes so drunk they leave their clothes behind," Craddock said. "Last night, we had one walk out the front door and down to his boat shucked as the day he was born. But I wasn't going to be the one to tell him he was creating a public scandal, because the only piece of attire he didn't forget was his belt with a damned big knife in its scabbard."

Jacques took the shirts and inspected them. Both were big enough to fit him, and unremarkable in color and cut. He chose the one that smelled the least offensive.

"Sorry, I could find you no boots," Craddock said.

Jacques shrugged.

"Let me do your dressing," the thin girl said, suddenly beside him. She began to untie the bloody bandage. "You don't mind, do you?"

Jacques said he would allow it.

When the bandage was off, Jacques knew it was apparent to both the bartender and the girl that the wound had been caused by powder and ball. He offered no explanation.

"I'm Chelley," she said. "If you were thinking of asking."

"I wasn't." He knew it wasn't her given name.

"Still, it's good to know what to call one another," she said.

Craddock handed over an onion bottle of cheap rum.

"Be sparing," he cautioned.

"Afraid I'll spill a nickel's worth on the floor?"

"A nickel is still a nickel."

"Said like the Jew you are," she said.

Craddock just smiled.

Leaning close to Jacques, Chelley held the round bottle in her right hand and cupped her left beneath the wound. She hesitated.

"This is going to hurt," she said.

"I know," Jacques said.

She poured the rum over his upper arm. He clenched his teeth but said nothing.

"Dammit, you've poured half the bottle on the floor," Craddock said.

"I'll pay for it," she said.

"No," Jacques said. From his trouser pocket he found some silver and placed it on the puncheon top. "For the drinks."

"Ah," Craddock said, picking up the coins.

"Be sure she gets a Spanish dollar or two."

"The good bourbon is expensive."

Jacques pulled three more silver coins from his pocket. It was the last of the money he had on him, which meant it was the last of the money he had in the world.

"That is quite enough," Craddock said.

"It is more than enough for rags and rum," Jacques said. "But I require a bit more in return for that price."

"What, then?"

"A knife, to start."

"Ah, revenge. A large one like the keelboat men carry, then?"

"No," Jacques said. "Something smaller. And sharp."

Craddock hesitated, then reached beneath the bar and retrieved a slender knife with a nine-inch blade and a smooth handle made of elkhorn. It had a brass bolster and pommel, and the blue metal was an intricate pattern of folded and hammered steel.

"A New Orleans toothpick," Craddock said. "A gambler's knife."

"Damascus," Jacques said, taking up the knife. He gingerly touched the edge of the blade and found it sharp.

"It was something scavenged from the wreck of the *LaFayette* a couple of years ago," Craddock said. "It's useful for prying corks from bottles and sharpening punks and discouraging casual opportunists."

"It will do," Jacques said.

Yes, Jacques thought—it will do to cut patches and coax locks and fight in close quarters, as needed. Craddock tossed a leather scabbard on the bar. It was plain, thick leather, well oiled, and closed with brass rivets.

"It was your men who picked the *LaFayette* clean," Craddock said.

"I remember," Jacques said, putting the knife in the scabbard, then undoing his belt and threading it through the scabbard's loop, positioning it on his left side. "Three killed in the wreck. Sad, but the scrap made particularly fine barrels. Why do you mention it?"

"They are working another wreck now, an unfortunate

boiler explosion on the *Vesuvius* three nights ago. Five dead."

"I read the news," Jacques said. "What's your tack?"

"These pirates you employ," Craddock said. "They are rough men, and they are afraid of little and take what they want. Their leader, Moses Bledsoe, sometimes grows impatient when his purse becomes too light."

"Speak plainly, man."

"These men set out the night before news of the wreck came."

Jacques took another sip of the good whiskey.

"Why mention this to me?"

"You appear in some distress, my friend," Craddock said. "Your kind of distress is caused by others. Bledsoe could eliminate the source of your discomfort. For a price."

"I am my own discomfort," Jacques said. "And beyond relief."

Chelley finished wrapping the clean muslin around Jacques's upper arm, then tied the ends. She smiled and placed her right hand on his, and for the first time he saw that her hand was that of a child, small and soft.

"Should we go upstairs now?" she asked.

Jacques shook his head.

She brought her small hand up to his chin and lifted his face to hers.

"But you have paid."

"For your kindness."

"Alas," she said. "I do not trade in kindness."

Jacques smiled.

"Still, you are charming, even when your spirit flags," Chelley said. "I could try to raise those spirits and relieve whatever crushing burden you carry. I welcome a challenge, especially when it's a handsome one."

"Another time, perhaps," Jacques said.

But he knew there would be no other time. He guessed Uncle Guy had summoned Sheriff Brown from his bed by now, and they had broken down the door to his rented room and then searched the gun shop. Vide-Poche was a logical choice for them to look next, but was just far enough away to delay them by an hour or three.

Jacques was sipping whiskey and thinking about his aching feet when he felt the change in the room. It seemed suddenly cooler, even though the wind had not changed, and the conversation at the tables behind him stumbled and then stalled.

"How are you, Mose?" Craddock asked.

The response was a string of creative expletives that made even Chelley blush. She untwined her arm from Jacques and, without making an excuse, disappeared upstairs.

"Guess some folks don't like my company," Bledsoe said as he walked over to the bar. Jacques glanced casually over and nodded. Bledsoe whistled and took a step back, as if to get a better view.

"What in damnation happened to you?" he asked.

"Damnation indeed," Jacques said.

"Ha!" Bledsoe said. "Ain't that the living truth."

Bledsoe was among the largest men Jacques had even seen, in both height and muscle. His ancestry was uncertain, because he had characteristics of nearly every race. When asked, he said his mother had mated with an alligator and he was the result. His coffee-colored skin was perpetually wind- and water-cracked, his eyes were brown, his hair was mostly brown and in naturally tight curls. His full beard, however, was as red as any Irishman's, which gave him a devilish appearance. From the lobe of his left ear dangled a gold earring, which added a touch of the piratical.

"Pickings was good," Bledsoe said, taking off his slouch hat and throwing it on the bar. "We have four hundred pounds of scrap from the engines and drivers of the *Vesuvius* for you down in the boat. Many fine and brightly polished pieces. Fresh, not a trace of rust yet on any of it, just the way you like it. To be fair, there should be a premium in it for me and my crew for this haul. You can't get this kind of steel west of Wheeling."

"Where's the crew?"

"Down at the river, watching the boat."

"I'll take a look," Jacques said, begrudging Bledsoe for making him speak. He didn't want to talk. But he had to. "If it's as good as you say, I'll pay the price agreed upon, and the premium."

"Two bits a pound," Bledsoe said. "That's the price."

"It wasn't," Jacques said. "I'll not pay a hundred dollars for scrap from which I can only make use of five or ten pounds. The price has always been ten cents a pound."

"Oh, but those short-barreled rifles you make," Bledsoe said. "They are gaining a reputation as second to none, just like me. Take bigger loads of powder, so they shoot harder and farther than other rifles, and more accurate to boot. And they say they ring like a bell when they're fired! It's the magic you brought with you across the ocean, some has it. Whatever it is, ain't nobody else can do it. But you can't make 'em without our scrap. So you have to pay up."

"If my magic is so strong," Jacques said, "why risk crossing me?"

A shadow of doubt clouded the big man's brown eyes.

"Dammit, Craddock, where's my whiskey?" Bledsoe called.

Craddock brought the jug and sloshed a cup half full.

"There you go, Mose," Craddock said. "Whatever you want."

"Where's Chelley?"

Bledsoe drank down the whiskey and motioned for more.

"Don't know," Craddock said. "Asleep maybe."

"I saw her run when I come through the door," Bledsoe said in a voice full of gravel. "I didn't hurt her last time. I was just havin' a little fun, you know?"

"I know, Mose."

Bledsoe turned back to Jacques.

"Why, we're friends," he said. "We're just talking over a little business about the scrap. Besides, I could sell to somebody else. Plenty of gunsmiths along the river."

"They wouldn't know what to do with it," Jacques said.

"Folks can learn."

"Like you've learned?" Jacques said. "Heard you set out before news of the wreck came."

"Well, maybe," Bledsoe said, smiling. His rows of teeth, white and gleaming through the red beard, made him look even more sinister. He drained the second cup of whiskey. "Maybe I just had one of those whatdyacallems, a promenade—"

"A premonition."

"That's it. I had one of those about the safety valve on the *Vesuvius* being disarranged. Came to me in a dream. Doesn't take long for a boiler under steam to blow when the valve is closed. Thought maybe the boys and me could reach her and warn of the danger, but it was not to be. The fate of the *Vesuvius* was sealed."

Not wanting to hear the rest of the conversation, Craddock began to step away under the pretext of doing some chore at the far end of the bar.

"Another," Bledsoe said, pushing the cup toward him.

Craddock filled it.

"Fetch Chelley."

"Like I said, I think she's asleep."

"Find her or I will tear the place apart until I find her."

"Sure, Mose," Craddock said. "It'll take just a minute."

"Leave the jug."

Craddock went upstairs.

"What kind of piss are you drinking?" Bledsoe asked, noting Jacques's glass.

"Whiskey, like you."

"Don't look like the kind of tiger piss I drink," Bledsoe said. "Looks clear and weak. Do you drink it dainty? Hold out your pinky while you sip at it like a bird?"

"Sure," Jacques said. "That's just how I do it."

"Two bits a pound," Bledsoe said flatly.

Then he reached into his greasy pockets and removed a couple of apples. They were red and ripe, about the size of a man's fist. He placed them carefully on the bar, side by side, took a long drink of whiskey, and produced a knife with a gleaming blade that was at least ten inches long, with a heavy hilt and handle for balance. He laughed, flipped the knife up in the air, and caught it easily by the handle.

"I call it Biter," Bledsoe said. "For that's what it does. It just doesn't cut, it bites."

He took one of the apples and began to peel it, the razor-sharp blade trailing an unbroken spiral of red skin.

"Bad for the blade," Jacques said. "The sugar will dull it."

"Biter is oiled and honed regular, don't worry," Bledsoe said, then cut a sliver of apple and popped it in his mouth. He continued the conversation, his mouth full. "Ever kilt a man with a knife?"

"No," Jacques said.

"Now, *that* dulls a knife. In a knife fight, to kill quick, you're generally going for someplace that has bone. The ribs to reach the heart or the lungs, or through the teeth to the back of the head. Sometimes you just have to saw or break your way through. Oh, you can gut somebody, and there's a certain satisfaction in that, but crap and piss and blood and bile is hard on a knife, too."

Jacques finished his whiskey.

"You've never killed anybody, have you?"

"Does it show so much?" Jacques asked, hating him even more.

Craddock came down, pulling Chelley by the hand.

"No," she said. "Please."

At the bottom of the stair, the other whore turned aside to let them pass.

"Come right down and give old Moses Bledsoe a big Empty Purse welcome! If I didn't know better, I'd say you weren't happy to see me. But we can make up for lost time. Remember that game we were playing last time?"

"Oh God, no."

Jacques's hand went to the Damascus toothpick at his belt, but Craddock shook his head.

"Just hush up and let him get on with it," Craddock whispered to Chelley, but he was really talking to Jacques. "It won't take long. Here, let me hold your dress."

Craddock pulled her dress over her head. At that point,

Chelley gave in. She sighed and removed most of her underthings and threw them to the bartender. She stood in the middle of the room, with only a silky thing covering her nakedness.

"Now, that's what I wanted to see," Bledsoe said.

He took the other apple from the bar and tossed it over to Chelley, who caught it in both hands.

"Over there," Bledsoe directed, pointing to a spot along the wall where a group of card players were clustered. "Move that bloody table out of the way and stand up against the wall, like last time."

The card players scattered, taking their money and their hands with them. Craddock dragged the table out of the way. Although Chelley was shaking slightly, she walked steadily over to the spot indicated and turned to face the room. She forced a smile, but it did not hide her disgust with The Grackle and the world beyond it. Then she gave the apple a little polish with the silk undergarment. She took a single bite from the apple, scooping out the white flesh and leaving the impression of her teeth in the crimson skin. She chewed, and wiped a bit of juice from the corner of her mouth.

"Get ready," Bledsoe said. "You know what to do."

Chelley lifted the silk and positioned the apple between her thighs, just above her knees, the fresh bite positioned like a bullseye. The apple wobbled a bit because of her shaking knees.

"Now here's a game," Bledsoe shouted, striding toward the door, knife in hand. "Who's with me? Who will bet against me?"

"What are the odds?" somebody called.

"Five to one in favor of Mose," Craddock said.

"Based on what?" Jacques asked.

"History," Craddock said.

"I cover all bets against," Bledsoe said. "Side bets are allowed among your own selves. Clap your money on the bar and our boy Craddock will keep track of everything, just like we was shooting craps."

Bledsoe stretched, tilted his neck this way and that, and worked his shoulders as if they were pistons. Then he moved the knife from hand to hand, as if he were discovering its balance for the first time. Then he tossed it in the air again, but this time failed to catch it. It came down point-first on the floor between his feet.

"Could that be a bad sign?" Bledsoe asked, then laughed.

There was a flurry of hands and money from the knot of gamblers at the bar. Craddock busily separated the wagers into piles, with a card dealer's exceptional memory of who had placed which bet.

Bledsoe plucked the quivering knife from the puncheon.

"Betting is closed," Craddock said.

Bledsoe rocked back and forth on the balls of his feet.

"You had better close your eyes, little one."

"No," Chelley said, defiant. "It only made me more afraid last time."

Bledsoe drew the knife back, and made an exaggerated throwing motion, but did not release. The gamblers gasped. A trickle of urine rolled down the inside of Chelley's left thigh, but she kept her eyes open.

"Ah," Bledsoe said.

He turned away slowly, as if he had changed his mind. Then he twirled and in an instant the knife shot out from his right hand, tumbling as it went, the blade flashing in the lantern light. Then the blade came down and split the apple and buried itself in the wall behind Chelley. The halves of the apple bounced on the floor as the girl's knees gave way.

The gamblers cheered or cursed and Craddock sorted out the results.

While Bledsoe whooped and held his arms above his head and strode about the room like a lunatic, Jacques made to help the girl up. She refused his extended hand and warned that nobody was to touch her. On the inside of her right thigh was a crescent-shaped trace of blood, made from the knife's last rotation after it had split the apple but before it pinned itself in the wall.

"Am I not the damndest ring-tailed cub of perdition that you ever saw?" Bledsoe bellowed. "When you see me you had better step aside or be ready to go to your Maker. My right hand is steel and the left one is iron and my knife is what split the waters from the firmament on the second day of creation. I breathe thunder and spit lightning, and I am creation's favorite. It was my flaming blade that guarded the way to the tree of life, and here is God's own proof of it. That is why only fools bet against me."

Chelley got to her feet, collected her clothes from behind the bar, and walked with them in her arms deliberately over to the stairs. But as she brushed past the other girl sitting there, she paused, and glanced over her shoulder at Jacques. Their eyes met for a moment, but her expression was unreadable. Then she was gone.

Jacques returned to his spot at the bar.

"Do you want me to fetch your knife?" somebody called.

"I'll kill anybody who touches it," Bledsoe said, joining Jacques. "I'll collect it when I'm ready."

"I am thinking of lighting the blade on fire next time,"

Bledsoe said conspiratorially. "Using a bit of grease? Lighting it from a tallow and then throwing it spinning and flaming to its target. An improvement, you think?"

"You are mad," Jacques said.

"The more people think so, the more they are afraid of me," Bledsoe said, his voice uncharacteristically quiet. "Tell me, friend. Are you afraid?"

"Yes," Jacques said.

"Good," Bledsoe said. He motioned for Craddock.

"Give my friend some more of that weak tea he was sipping before," Bledsoe said. "Let me buy you a drink and we will toast to the uses of fear and enchantment."

Jacques waited until Craddock had poured the drink and gone away again.

"I am afraid," he said. "But not in the way you think."

"How, then?"

"I fear that I see myself in you."

Bledsoe laughed.

"Most men should have such vision," he said, and slapped Jacques on the back. "Now, what of our business?"

"Let us conclude it," Jacques said.

"At two bits."

"Yes, at two bits," Jacques said, and made a motion of reaching for money he didn't have, then paused. He had no interest in collecting the scrap, but he knew there was only one way to leave The Grackle standing, and that was if Bledsoe believed their account had been settled. "But let us make a wager of it."

"Oh?"

"We will cut the cards. Double or nothing."

For anything else, Jacques would have to place money on the table for each hand or throw of the dice, and his pockets were empty. But he might be able to get away with wagering the entire amount unseen.

Bledsoe waved.

"No more games."

"If you feel your luck has run out, so be it."

"I did not say that."

Jacques called for Craddock to bring a deck.

"Then we will add a premium to the bet," Jacques said. "Instead of $100 for the scrap, the price if you win will be $125."

He could see greed stir in Bledsoe's eyes.

"And what if you win?"

"A pair of boots," he said.

"My boots?"

Jacques looked at Bledsoe's feet. They were as large as the rest of him.

"No, not yours," he said.

Bledsoe turned, looking about the room, and as he did so Jacques could see layers of muscle and fat ripple in the back of his neck. With a grunt, Bledsoe pointed at a gambler at one of the tables who seemed a medium-sized person—and who was wearing a pair of calf-high black boots.

"You, get over here."

"Me?" the gambler asked. "I've done nothing to offend."

"Get up from that damned chair and get your sorry tail over here," Bledsoe said. The man, who had the manner of a domestic and the complexion of a sack of flour, stood and walked timidly toward the bar.

"Lift up your foot."

"What?"

"Let us see the sole of your boot!"

The pale man put a hand on the bar for balance and

lifted his left foot, revealing a barely worn leather sole and a heel with shining brass tacks. Jacques placed the bottom of his own foot against the gambler's, then nodded.

"Now the other."

The man did so. The soles were equal in quality.

"Take them off," Bledsoe demanded.

"But they cost a week's wages."

"I didn't ask, did I?"

The man sat on the floor and, crossing one leg over another, tugged off the boot, revealing pink toes peeking through coarse stockings that needed repair. Bledsoe produced a gold half-eagle coin from his pocket and tossed it to the pale man, who trapped it between the palms of his hand.

"That's twice what they are worth," Bledsoe said. "Now leave them."

The man padded back to his card table.

"A five-dollar pair of boots against an additional twenty-five wager," Bledsoe said. "Why?"

"It amuses me," Jacques said, filling Bledsoe's cup from the jug. "And in truth I find myself in need. It is a fair walk up the trace to Saint Louis—at least when one is drunk and barefoot."

Bledsoe laughed.

"Craddock, shuffle the cards," Jacques said. "And do it well."

"I want to see your coin," Bledsoe said.

"And I wanted to see the scrap," Jacques said. "Let's get on with it."

Craddock shuffled, a bit clumsily because he was nervous.

"Aces low," Bledsoe said.

Jacques drank the good whiskey and pretended not to

care, despising himself for how easy worthless talk came to him. But just as Bledsoe had his strength and skill with the knife, Jacques was required to make use of his talents if he wanted to live through the night and escape the hangman's noose. With no gun in his hand, he had to rely on his tongue. And even though his spirit was shattered by the accidental shooting of his friend, he was not yet ready to surrender his own fate to others. In his mind he was reckoning the two paths immediately before him: Either he would win the draw and he would have a set of boots and an easy exit from The Grackle, or he would lose and be forced to drive his toothpick through Bledsoe's muscle and bone to find his heart in an attempt to kill him before he retrieved Biter from the wall and carved him to pieces.

Craddock wove the cards together, and the riffling sound they made was reassuring to Jacques, who had heard it with anticipation so often. Then Craddock brought the cards together and jogged the deck to even up the edges. He placed the deck in front of the men with a flourish.

"Gentlemen," he said. "You may proceed."

"Who goes first?" Bledsoe asked.

"I never cut a deck and I never take the first card," Jacques said.

"Is that supposed to be some kind of strategy?"

"No," Jacques said. "Superstition."

"So be it. I prefer to be first in all things."

Bledsoe cut the deck and placed the top half faceup on the bar.

The ten of spades.

Bledsoe grinned and slapped his thigh as if he had already won.

Craddock called the card, so as to officially note it. Then he reassembled the deck and offered it to Jacques, who tried not to betray his panic. He would have to draw a face card in order to win, and there was less than a one in four chance of that. Why hadn't he insisted on aces high? The odds would have been only marginally better, but fortunes had turned on slimmer margins.

"Get on with it," Bledsoe said.

Jacques smiled and reached for the deck with his right hand, and said silent prayers to St. Ignatius and Mari, all while inching his left closer to the knife at his belt. Despite himself, there was that old familiar thrill running down his spine, the exhilaration of wagering more than he could afford to lose. While keeping his eyes on Bledsoe, he ran his thumb and forefinger down the deck until his fingertips touched the top of the bar. Then he moved his hand back up a fraction and decisively split the deck.

"Ah," Craddock said.

Bledsoe cursed floridly.

"The one-eyed jack," Craddock said. "Jack of diamonds."

Jacques could feel his cheeks flush with relief.

"The boots," Jacques said. "I will have them now."

4 *The Tower*

Beneath the clouded night, Jacques could feel the weight of the old Spanish tower looming over him, a hulking stone monument that marked the reach but not the grasp of Imperial Spain, a rebuff to the British, and an edifice now rendered useless by Jefferson's sweeping Louisiana Purchase of 1803. It was as if the shadow of the Old World was still pressing down on Jacques, threatening to press him suffocating into the earth.

The crumbling round tower was near the west end of the Rue de la Tour, which had been the edge of the city some forty years ago, but now the growing city had closed around it. It was thirty feet around the base and forty feet to its turret, where a battery of six cannon had once overlooked the approaches to St. Louis. The tower had been optimistically christened Fort San Carlos when it had been built, in 1780, and it sat atop an apex of palisades and trenches. It had seen action only once, in the farthest western battle of the American Revolution, when some 300 French traders and Spanish soldiers and some slaves and free blacks had come together to repel a British-led force of nearly a thousand. The British had crossed the river from the Illinois side, and most of their command were from various eastern tribes aligned with the British, chiefly Sac and Fox, Wapashi, and Sioux. The attack faltered in the face of fire from the tower and the trenches, and with it failed British hopes of finding purchase on the western American frontier.

Within the space of a generation—from the end of the American Revolution to the Louisiana Purchase— St. Louis had passed from Spanish, to French, and finally American rule. It had been the site of debarkation for a generation of American explorers, including Meriwether Lewis and William Clark. Now St. Louis was part of the new state of Missouri. Its position on the Mississippi, just below the mouth of the Missouri River and above the Ohio, gave it a waterborne reach that extended from Pennsylvania to the Rockies, and from Minnesota to New Orleans. Still a sleepy river town of five thousand, it was poised in 1822 to become the crossroads of America.

As he sat with his back against the base of the tower, his arms crossed on his knees, Jacques struggled to push thoughts of geography from his mind. Thinking of distance made him unhappy, because he would soon begin estimating how far he was from his grandfather's great stone house across the ocean. His hunger had returned, and what he wanted presently was coffee and beignets.

He did not know what hour it was, because the sky betrayed no stars. He turned up the collar of the ragged coat he had gotten from Craddock at The Grackle, trying to keep the chill night air from his neck, thrust his hands into his pockets, and waited desperately for Abella to appear. In his mind he rehearsed his farewell, explaining how he must flee in the only direction in which the law would not follow—the west. He would promise to return, of course, some day soon when he'd made his fortune and could buy his way free of his bond debt and the murder charge. After all, nothing was impossible with enough gold. He would warn her not to believe anything her Uncle Guy had to say about him, because the old man had never liked him because of his youth and genius. Yes, that's the word he would use, because Abella must trust that his place in the world was assured, because of his talent and vision. This is something he half believed himself, at least on his best days. It was important that Abella believe in him, because otherwise she would not wait for his return. If she had any money on her person, he would ask for it. He would tell her he loved her, and she would yield to him.

Then there was the business of Aristide's death. He would explain that it was an accident, as much her uncle's fault as his own, and they could grieve for Aristide together. The tears he would cry would be real, because he already missed his friend.

Then he remembered the vow he had made to himself while running from the dock that he would curb his speech and always act truly and with purpose, and the thought made his head ache. Once he was free of St. Louis, he told himself, he would begin his new life of truth and moderation. There would be plenty of time for reform. And wasn't the burgeoning desire to give up sin itself a virtue?

She appeared suddenly, moving ghostlike on the path to the tower, her identity hidden by a hooded cape that reached nearly to her ankles. As Abella drew nearer, she pulled back the hood, and the clouds broke and moonlight bathed the scene. She seemed to materialize from the darkness: a slim figure with a cataract of dark curls spilling over her shoulders, hands clasped together, a luminous face with large eyes that even in the moonlight appeared the palest blue. Her face so resembled Aristide's, with its delicate features and high cheekbones, that Jacques felt panic.

"Jacky," she said.

"I'm here," he said, already on his feet.

They ran to each other and he pulled her close and she placed her head against his chest. She smelled of rose water and clean hair and the warm and somewhat milky scent of healthy skin. His hunger grew. He kissed her, tenderly at first and then more insistently, until she drew away.

"We must speak honestly."

Her English had a suggestion of a French accent, making her speech fluid and lyric. She was accustomed to demurring to others, especially men, so her sentences were seldom emphatic. Her hands punctuated her speech with small gestures, sometimes holding the weightless words gently between her palms, and at other times releasing them to float away.

"There will be time for talk later," he said, kissing her neck. "This is the time for passion."

"I waited an hour for you earlier," she said. "I assumed you had forgotten the time because you were gambling and sporting at one of the houses near the river. I see I was right, because you smell of whiskey and worse. What are those clothes you're wearing?"

"The result of a bad night at cards. That's all."

He kissed her again, and Abella surrendered to him for a minute or more, then again pulled herself away.

"You stink of another woman."

"How can you say that, my love?"

"Do you truly love me?"

"Of course," he said, toying with the silver cross that dangled at her throat.

"No, you cannot say it is a matter of course," she said gently, although her angry fists were pressing against his chest. "If you love me you must say it, without qualification or presumption."

"You know that I love you."

"I know nothing of the sort," she said, pushing him away. "You cannot even say it without tempering it. What I know is not in question. What you feel is."

He grasped her hips and pulled her to him.

"I feel you against me and the sap rises."

She slapped his face.

"If you loved me, you wouldn't have left me waiting," she said, jabbing a finger into his chest. "If you loved me, your clothes—or whoever's clothes you wear—would not stink of spirits and the perfume of a certain class of woman."

"I swear I have only been with you."

It wasn't a lie, he told himself. He did not love the others.

"I do not believe you," she said. "What I most want in the world is for it to be true, to believe you love me as I do you, but the danger is that I want it so much that I have allowed myself to believe it without evidence of love. Women need such proof because the consequences of being ruined are grave."

Jacques knew he should tell her he loved her, but something prevented him. Perhaps it was that telling her would be yielding a certain power to her, to surrender his freedom, to commit to live as others did.

"I am here with you, now," he said. "Is that not proof enough?"

"It is proof only that it is convenient for you at the moment, because you are lonely or lustful or lacking something else I can provide," she said. "I take pleasure in you as well, but you seem to need something in addition to our animal pleasures—a validation that you are desirable to all women because you are desirable to me, whom you think beautiful."

"You are beautiful."

"Do you not listen to others, Jacky?"

"How can I hear? All of my senses are flooded by you."

"You lie to me and yet I still love you," she said. "You treat me as trash, and yet I could not deny you to others. But you have cheapened me, as my uncle said you would."

"Your uncle is a fool."

"My uncle speaks plainly. We must talk, and do it now."

"Why?" Jacques asked. "What have you heard? It was an accident. As God is my second, I swear."

Abella stared at him.

"An accident?"

"Oh, my sweet Abella," Jacques said, taking her by the shoulders. "A pistol accidentally discharged. It was only by chance the ball struck your brother."

Jacques could see now from her expression that she had not known.

Her hand went to her mouth and her right eye fluttered. She sank slowly to the ground, her legs folded beneath her. He reached for her, but she slapped his hand away.

"Where is he now?"

"Your uncle did not—"

"I have not spoken to my uncle since yesterday noon," she said. "How badly is Aristide injured?"

Jacques sat on the ground beside her.

"He fell into the river," he said.

"How? What do you mean?"

"We were on the landing, he took the ball, he fell into the water."

"Dear God," she said over clasped hands. "Tell me he lives."

"I cannot," he said.

"Then he is dead."

"I don't know," Jacques stammered. "We could not retrieve him."

"How long ago?" she asked.

"Three hours, perhaps."

"Then he is certainly no longer among us."

Abella wiped tears from both cheeks with a square of cloth she took from her sleeve. She asked why he didn't come straightaway to tell her. He said he was afraid.

"This was after one of your nights of gambling and carousing and only God knows what else you do?"

"Well, yes," Jacques said. "But your uncle was with us, and after some unpleasant words he threw down the gauntlet."

"A duel?"

"Yes," Jacques said slowly, stretching the word out so that it was mostly a hissing sound.

"He challenged you, then. For my honor?"

Jacques nodded.

"The duel was accomplished with only minor casualty," Jacques said. "I was struck in the arm. I will show you the wound, if you care. The accident with Ari occurred upon our return to the landing."

"This pistol that was dropped," she said. "From whose hand did it fall?"

"It fell from my own pocket."

Abella smiled bitterly.

"You have killed my brother," Abella said. "How can

these not be the first words out of your mouth? That my only brother, and your dearest friend, is dead? That he was shot because of your carelessness and fell into the river and is no more?"

"I could find no words."

"That is never the case," she said. "Instead you make me the fool." Then she lapsed into French, alternating between prayers and curses, her sobs low, quiet, and desperate. Jacques attempted an arm around her shoulders, but she violently repelled him.

"There was much for us to talk about," she said as she got to her feet. "But no longer. You have broken me. This grief and heartache are too much to bear. You have always longed for your freedom. Well, you are free now from me."

Then she turned and ran.

Alone now with his outrage, Jacques placed his back against the stone of the tower to keep the world from spinning. How would he survive now? Abella had refused him even the smallest of comfort. And in her anger, she might lead Sheriff Brown or her uncle to the place where she had seen him last.

All now was nearly lost.

He spat in the direction Abella had fled and uttered a Basque curse.

Then he pushed himself away from the stone and began running toward Chestnut Street. He expected the Rapailles' gun shop to be watched, but if he was careful enough, he might gain entrance without anyone being the wiser. In the alley behind the shop was a high attic window with a loose pane that rattled when the north wind blew. He had slept in the attic for the year after arriving in St. Louis, before being allowed to rent rooms elsewhere, and it was a miserable space with an uncomfortably low ceiling that smelled of dust. But he knew he could climb the old maple tree that grew in the alley and, from a stout branch, reach the window. By pressing at the right point on the frame, and then giving it a rap, the sash lock could be slipped and the window opened.

5   The Lauburu

His intent as he descended the narrow stairs from the attic was that he should burn the gun shop to the ground. What a blaze it would make, with the hardwood stocks of the guns as kindling and the casks of gunpowder popping. The blaze might even consume his hated papers of indenture, though their destruction would be more symbolic than actual. But such a conflagration would be an unmistakable message to Uncle Guy:

Va te faire foutre. Fuck you.

But Jacques knew that even he was incapable of such a wanton act of destruction. A fire might not only destroy the shop, but the buildings on either side, as well. For that matter, the entire center of town would be at risk and the many innocents sleeping there. And then there was the regard he had for the row of rifles on the wall behind the counter; many of those guns he had built himself. They were like living creatures to him. As a child, he had seen illustrations in books of a mechanical duck the size of a real duck that could eat grain and pass pellets, and the spectrum of animate and inanimate had been forever blurred. Long after he realized the digesting duck must have been some kind of illusion, there remained in him an almost religious conviction in the promise of the mechanical.

There were times when he knew that things had come to mean more to him than people, and although the thought distressed him, he had to acknowledge that things were generally more interesting and they also made fewer demands. This feeling had not been true when he was a child, but after being forced from his grandfather's home he had found himself among strangers, and his heart grew cold. As the years passed, he became increasingly fearful that human beings, too, were machines—automatons like Vaucanson's duck—but made of flesh and error.

Most of the time he was alone with his work and his thoughts, and it was the rare individual, such as Aristide, who seemed to understand the passion he had for the springs and gears and wheels of his trade. These things were manifestations of the divine, he had often told Ari, and the world itself was a kind of clockwork mechanism. Cards and dice and men and women were pieces of the mechanism, each with its own function, and the mechanism ran well when all was true and balanced. But when things were not in balance, the timing of the mechanism became unreliable and the laws of probability were mere suggestions, allowing for things like throwing craps three times in a row. Something had gone deeply wrong with the mechanical timing of this night, something so out of true that the entire mechanism felt as if it would fly apart, just as his heart threatened to hammer right through his ribs and emerge from his chest. He feared that he himself was the faulty part, cut just inaccurately enough to result in disaster.

He would attempt to contain the size of the tonight's

disaster. The shop would not be consumed by fire, but he would be damned if Guy Rapaille profited from his hard work and innovation while he ran for his life—or swung from the end of a rope.

He reached behind the counter to where he knew Uncle Guy kept a bottle of whiskey to help loosen the purse strings of paying customers. He found a half-empty bottle, uncorked it, and took a long drink. It was not good, but it was not bad, and the familiar warmth of the alcohol spread inside him.

With bottle in hand, Jacques made his way back to the workshop, where he built the guns the Rapailles sold and repaired those of other shops. Rifles in various stages of completion were on benches or in vises, and parts ranging from rough carved stocks in walnut and maple to locks and barrels awaited boring. The barrel blanks were hammered and welded together from the scrap that Jacques provided, and the blacksmith who performed this task often argued about the metals provided, saying that too many shattered like an artillery shell when tested with an extra-strong proof charge of triple powder and two balls. But the results, when they passed proof, were worth the effort.

Every other shop in America bored their rifles by hand, a two-person operation on a special bench that required the turning of a long bit by hand on one end while the barrel was pressed into the bit from the other. That was the way newcomer Samuel Hawken made them at his shop on North Main Street, and it required an expert touch and days to finish. But Jacques had realized long ago that it was the human element that introduced error in the process, and if that error could be removed, a perfectly rifled barrel with a faster twist and greater accuracy was possible. His barrels were also lighter than others of the same length and caliber, and a fully finished rifle weighed a little more than seven pounds, instead of ten and more pounds for other rifles. The savings of three pounds could make the difference, after a long day of hunting, between bringing home meat and going hungry.

Since crossing the ocean on the ill-fated ship *April,* his head had been filled with memories of his family's clockworks, of all the mechanisms and escapements, and when his papers were sold to a gunsmith, he began to think of ways to apply clockwork mechanisms to the production of rifled barrels. The inspiration for the escapement needed came to Jacques in a dream: the critical part would be the shape of the *lauburu,* the Basque cross with four hook-shaped heads.

The question of how to power the rifling machine was the easiest to solve, and required the least precision. Clocks had been driven by water for centuries, and he would use water to drive his machine. A tank of a few hundred gallons produced enough force to power for a day or more a gear drive helped by the inertia of a heave flywheel and controlled by a spinning, centrifugal governor. The drill bit—which would cut eight grooves, not merely six or even seven, as tradition had it, and at a twist of one in forty-eight inches—would be moved into the barrel, and not the other way around, advancing and retreating incrementally thousands of times, and producing a cut that needed little polishing. The heart of the machine was not the bit or the water drive, but the *lauburu*-inspired escapement that controlled every aspect of the drill's movement. In final form, the escapement disc with multiple tracks and teeth directed several functions at once: advancement, twist, the depth of the grooves. The only human interventions needed were periodically refilling the water tank, oiling the bit, and clearing shavings—but in time, these tasks, too, could be automated.

The escapement itself was a machined brass disk the size of a dinner plate, with the same rows of teeth and detents as the miniature that Jacques wore around his neck. The disk was locked in a cabinet when the machine was not in use, because even though someone might be able to reproduce the rifling bench, they would be lost without the secret of the escapement.

Jacques took two more slugs of whiskey, then retrieved the key from its hiding place in a jar on the workbench, unlocked the cabinet, and withdrew the escapement. Then he mounted it on the indexed shaft at the heart of the boring machine, secured it by tightening the grub screw, then reached overhead to allow the water to flow into the drive from the rain tank overhead.

He wanted to see the boring machine in action one last time before he destroyed it. It had taken him three years to make a working machine, and so far it had made only a dozen barrels, but each made for rifles that were superior quality. With each barrel, he measured and tested and shot, and made slight improvements here and there, adjusting the machine's timing or its speed or the throw of a rod. The last barrel the machine had bored had come as close to perfection as anything Jacques had ever seen, and the rifle that it made had sold quickly for the outrageous sum of fifty dollars to wealthy old Clark, who owned the council house down by the river. The Rapailles, of course, wanted more like it. The fact that he had made something that he himself, even after he was free and working for ordinary wages, would likely never be able to afford, felt intolerable.

He drank more whiskey.

The weight of the water collecting in the catch bucket soon was enough to start the drive, and the mechanism slowly came to life, increasing in speed until the governor checked it. Shafts and gears engaged. The barrel in the bench was only halfway finished, and he could not see the bit doing its work, but he heard the singing sound of metal on metal. The boring machine was a huge clock that measured time in thousandths of an inch.

Jacques closed the tap, stopping the flow of water, and watched as the machine whirred to a stop. Then he loosened the set screw and took the *lauburu* escapement from its shaft. Handling it with a certain reverence, he placed it on the bench and wrapped it in one of the rags used for wiping down finished barrels.

Then he turned back to the machine and opened the tap again. The water filled the drive, and the machine's limbs began to move. But without the escapement, things were soon at cross-purposes, and there was the ugly sound of bending metal and breaking wood. Jacques picked up the cloth-wrapped escapement from the bench on his way out of the shop and tucked it beneath his arm. He strode past the rows of new rifles and trade guns without even a glance. None of them had been made by his machine, but by inferior smiths. Even though any one of these rifles would have been perfectly serviceable for any other wanted man about to embark for parts unknown, he wanted none of them. Only one rifle would satisfy him, and he aimed to have it.

He left the empty bottle on the counter for Uncle Guy to find.

As Jacques ascended the stair to his attic exit, the cacophony of the boring machine grew. There was a sharp report as the drill bit snapped off in the half-finished barrel, pieces of the machine were thrown about the workshop, and then the water reservoir burst.

In a few moments he was out the attic window, down the maple tree, and in the alley heading east. The sky was clear now, and full of stars, but it was still quite dark because the moon was down. But he knew the path well, and he followed it toward the river and up onto one of the limestone bluffs above the landing. He unwrapped the heavy escapement from the oiled cloth, and the brass felt cool and substantial in his hands. Then he went to the edge of the bluff and, using both hands, heaved the disk as far out over the river as he could manage. It sailed far out and hit the surface of the water with a sharp smack, leaving a swirling dimple in the surface of the river that glittered by starlight and then was gone.

Jacques shouted into the night:

"Va te faire foutre!"

"Who are you telling to go fuck themselves?"

Jacques turned but saw no one.

"Who is there?"

"Nobody," came the answer.

Now it struck Jacques that the voice was coming from above, and he stared into the branches of the trees around him on the bluff. In the forked trunk of a towering elm, he saw a bit of movement.

"Ah, nobody," Jacques said. "There you are."

"I've been here, the whole time, watching you chuck somethin' out in the water," the voice said. "Was it a gun? Usually when men throw shit into the middle of the night it's a gun or a knife they've just used on somebody. If a woman, it's usually . . . a child."

"Why are you in that tree?"

"My question is why ain't you?" the voice asked. "You're

running from something you done, that's for sure. I know runnin', because I'm a runaway nigger myself."

"Why tell me that?"

"I don't think you're in any position to go set Sheriff Brown on me, because you'd have to explain why the hell you were here in the middle of the night and I would tell him you was throwin' something into the water."

"What do you want?"

"Money, if you got it. Advice, if you don't."

"I have no money," Jacques said. "For God's sake, climb down out of that tree so that we can talk."

There was rustling in the tree and then the man dropped down, landing on his feet. He was taller than Jacques, by four or five inches, but was about the same age. Even in the shadows, Jacques could tell the man had only one eye. A wicked scar ran down his forehead to where his left eye had been, and which was now covered by a cloth patch.

"Howdy," he said. "I'm nobody, but you can call me Shephard Quarles."

Jacques shook his hand and told him his name.

"Well, Mister Aguirre, it looks like it's been a rough night for you."

He allowed that it had.

"Where are you running to?" Jacques asked.

"Haven't made up my mind yet," Quarles said. "Across the river, maybe. I hear they outlawed slavery in Illinois."

"They did," Jacques said, "not that it will do you any good. They have established laws about free blacks—if you don't have papers to prove you're free, and not indentured, then they pack you over for sale here in Missouri."

"Farther east, then."

"It's the same in Indiana and Ohio. You'd have to get all the way to New England to be free."

"Then what's a runaway slave to do?"

"I don't know that I have any advice."

"Hell, you can start by just telling me where I am."

"You're at the edge of St. Louis," Jacques said. "Not an opportune spot for you, I'd think, because it has the biggest slave auction in the state. I'm assuming you didn't come from the north, or else you would have had trouble crossing the Missouri River."

"Could I swim it at night?"

"I wouldn't try," Jacques said.

"So I can't go north," Quarles said. "And I can't go east, and I damned sure can't go south. That leaves one direction. How big across do you reckon the state of Missouri is?"

"About two hundred and fifty miles."

"That's a month, traveling at night," Quarles said.

"With luck," Jacques said. "You'll want to follow the Missouri River, which will take you to the northwestern corner of the state. When you get to Westport, you'll have a choice—continue upriver, which leads to the northern plains, or take the Santa Fe Trail towards Mexico. Black slavery is illegal there, and the Mexicans won't return you. If you take the river, you'll be beyond the states and north of the Missouri Compromise line of 36-30."

"What's that?"

"Latitude," Jacques said. "Thirty-six degrees and thirty minutes north, which is most of the southern boundary of Missouri. North of the line, territory is to be organized as free."

"Then why ain't Missouri free?"

"That was the compromise," Jacques said.

"But on the far side of Missouri, I'm free."

"Free and with a lot of new territory ahead of you," Jacques said.

"New territory," Quarles said. "I like the sound of that."

"You know," Jacques said, "it occurs to me you wouldn't have to travel across the state at night if you had a white man who could say he's your master."

Quarles laughed.

"Look at yourself," he said. "Ain't nobody going to believe you're rich enough to own me. Besides, I'd rather not have a murderer for a traveling companion. They're going to be looking for you harder than they're looking for me, but they'd string both of us up. No sir, thank you all the same."

Jacques knew he was right.

"It's spring and pretty soon the weather is going to be fine, and there will be plenty to eat from the fields and back gardens," Quarles said. "I'll be careful and take my time and sleep during the day. I'll just keep that muddy river always sort of on my right side, so I know I'm going the right direction. That will work, won't it?"

"I don't know," Jacques said. "I've never been west of here. But I think you have a pretty fair plan, considering."

"Considering what?"

"The odds," Jacques said. "I give you one chance in five."

"Good," Quarles said. "I'll take those odds, because I know what the odds are if I stay put. I'm on my way to Canaan's Land now, that's for sure."

"Do you leave family behind?"

"Not a soul," Quarles said. "My dear old mother died when I was just five, and I never knew my pap. So there's nobody left for them to punish for me runnin' off."

"What finally made you decide to go?"

Quarles shook his head.

"I decided a year ago," Quarles said. "But it took me this long to work up the courage. They said I was looking at a white woman the wrong way, and an example had to be set. So they took my eye."

Jacques asked how.

"With a meat hook."

Jacques whistled. It made his left eye hurt just thinking about it.

"I've got to say farewell," Jacques said, turning to the path. "My own promised land awaits. Good luck."

"Good luck to you, cousin," Quarles called. "And remember, if anybody asks—we ain't seen each other."

6 *The Museum*

Coaxed by the tip of the Damascus toothpick, the lock yielded with a raspy click, and in a matter of seconds, Jacques was through the side door and inside the chill darkness of the long brick council building. His head was still swimming with whiskey, so he paused for a moment with his back against the closed door, taking several quick deep breaths. The building smelled of fur and leather and more than a touch of decay. He knew that the rifle would be here, in this monument that Clark had built to his past, displayed with the stuffed animals and headdresses and unidentified fossils that visitors of a certain class were obligated to view appreciatively on their journeys west.

"You have come to kill me."

Jacques did not move, hoping the shadows would protect him.

"I have waited long."

Jacques remained silent in the dark.

"Answer, please," the voice urged. It was the voice of an old man, with a Virginian accent, the kind of voice that, Jacques had noticed, drew respect on the street and deference behind doors.

"I knew you would come stealing, in the dead of some lonesome night, flowing down the great river from the heart of the world. You have already done for Lewis. Well, I am ready to die as well. I welcome the peace of it. Tell me, does the world still wheel about the cedar stave?"

The darkness was like a filthy blanket.

"I have not come to kill you," Jacques said, at length.

"No?"

"Nor do I know what you speak of."

"You disappoint me."

"You're Clark," Jacques said. "I met you, or rather saw you, a fortnight ago. You won't remember. But I recall your voice."

"I cannot remember if I cannot see you."

There was the sound of rummaging among items on a table, then the repeated striking of a flint and a shower of dancing sparks, with some blue among the fiery orange. Then the wick caught and there was the warm glow of a taper. The table was thick with letters and scraps of parchment and items scissored from newspapers.

The flame drew Clark from the darkness, along with gleams from a dozen pairs of glass eyes. The stuffed animals ranged in size from orange-toothed beavers to hulking bears. There were other objects in the hall, mostly artifacts from various American Indian tribes, arranged in displays meant to please and educate visitors. The largest of these was a birch bark canoe, which hung from the ceiling overhead. There was leather clothing and porcupine-quill breastplates, a tarnished suit of Spanish mail, and wild masks and headdresses that must have displayed every feather and type of fur on the Upper Missouri. On one table was a collection of long-stemmed pipes with red pipestone bowls, and on another a variety of grinding bowls.

But predominately the museum was devoted to the tools of warfare, and along with scores of bows and hundreds of flint- and iron-tipped arrows were spears, maces, stone clubs, and tomahawks.

"It's a museum," Jacques whispered.

"Many bring me things," Clark said. "My interests are widely known. But a few of these things I brought back myself from the journey of discovery. Jefferson wanted it all, but I kept a few items of personal interest."

Clark was a tall man of some fifty years who sat uncomfortably in an upholstered chair, a cold clay pipe on the table beside him. Framed with wispy red hair that was turning to white, his face was pale and rouged by time, but his brown eyes were sharp and clear.

"You are the governor."

"Former governor," Clark said. "Now Indian agent. Come closer."

Jacques did, cautiously.

"The gunsmith," Clark said with surprise. "The clever young Basque who makes the best rifles in St. Louis because you sold the souls of your unborn children to Satan for the secret of the perfect rifled barrel. Or at least that's how the story goes. That's the story that was told to me."

"I have no children," Jacques said. "Born or otherwise."

"And your soul?"

"That is another matter."

"It is wise to encourage the story," Clark said. "It has a certain romance to it, perhaps adds an extra measure of value to your arms, and proves fascinating to women."

"You seem to know a fair measure about me."

"Guy Rapaille likes to talk," he said. "And even as I was purchasing the rifle, I saw you watching furtively from the back of the shop, harboring some kind of smoldering resentment. Others profiting so handsomely from your talents."

"Then you understood."

"But such is the lot of those in servitude," Clark said.

"I will be free," Jacques declared.

"So if you have not come to murder me, then what?"

"Only to rob you."

"I have not much silver at hand."

"I have only come for what was once and ever shall be mine."

"Ah, the rifle," Clark said.

"Yes."

"It is a fine piece," Clark said. "I have found none better. But tell me, why does it make the odd ringing sound when fired? It is a bell-like sound, an almost musical note—"

"It is B-flat."

"I'll take your word for it," Clark said. "But why does it ring?"

"Because I wanted it to."

Clark nodded.

"We shall parley, then," Clark said. "Come and sit beside me, and let us talk."

"As equals?"

"As men," Clark said.

"As Americans?"

Clark laughed.

"What is an American?" he asked.

"I don't know, sir," Jacques said. "The answer has vexed me for years."

"Sit down," Clark said.

Jacques cautiously crossed the room and took a seat in a matching upholstered chair opposite the most famous man in Missouri. Clark reached across the table and drew back a jug of Kentucky whiskey, uncorked it, and he sloshed some in a pair of stemmed crystal glasses.

"To your health," Clark said.

"And yours," Jacques returned.

They clinked glasses and drank.

How much liquor had Jacques consumed that night? It was impossible for him to tally. But he was glad for the anesthetic effect of it, because it made not caring for either Abella or Aristide easier. As the good whiskey bloomed in his gut, Jacques became bold.

"Whom do you await, sir?"

Clark smiled.

"My past," he said. "It is what all men who have lived boldly and risked much and broken others wait for in old age—a reckoning made incarnate, a sure hand to wield the unforgiving knife, a blood atonement."

Clark stared at the reflection of the candle flame in the whiskey.

"Long ago I left the only real part of myself in a village near where the Heart River joins the upper Missouri, during a bitter winter that was a dream that seemed like it would never end," he said. "But dreams do end, and I have carried the memory of that winter with me as a stone in my chest, a loss that can never be recovered, a burden that the adoption of my wards has not eased."

"Wards?"

"Toussaint and Lizette," Clark said. "The children of our guide Charbonneau's woman, Janey. At least that is how I knew her. The name she was given by the Hidatsu, to whom she was a Sabine captive, proved impossible for my tongue. Janey is dead now these long years, of fever.

With their father a wastrel, I received the children into my household."

"You are generous," Jacques said.

Clark waved his hand.

"Generosity is measured in sacrifice," he said. "This cost little."

"You have much," Jacques said.

"I threw much away," Clark said, "and have had much taken from me. Captain Lewis was the most troublesome man I have ever known, but I was friends with him from the start, even though he was given to melancholia and entirely ill-suited for military life. But he was strong and stubborn, and a learned man. He often chided me for my poor spelling and rough ways. We argued, but always as brothers. But he was hard for others to take. A member of our own party shot him once, through the buttocks, when we were a just month upriver from St. Louis on our return trip. It was presumed to have been an accident, but I have always wondered if the private who fired the offending round had done so on purpose."

"Such a wound carries a message," Jacques said.

"Yes, the message is that it hurts like hell," Clark said. "Lewis spent a week lying facedown in the canoe until his pride forced him upright. But nature has no sense of pride, or of shame, and the laws of men mean nothing. There is only the eternal wild. It happens suddenly, that one day you are defined and confined by some, and then you pass some invisible line of ground and heart, and you become as nature, living only with consequence."

"How did you enforce discipline?"

"We were equals in the wilderness," Clark said. "Oh, Captain Lewis and I kept up appearances, but Lewis demanded that everybody had a vote in the important decisions, including Janey and my nigger, York. Lewis outranked me, because I was only a lieutenant. When we spent time with the Indians, from necessity or duty, the bonds of the society we knew came unraveled and were replaced by local custom. York was, for all purposes, a free man. He was a favorite of the young women of the tribes, and knew many, a situation that would be punishable by death here."

"What of York now?"

"He returned insolent and sulky," Clark said. "I thrashed him for it, but it did little to improve his mood. He was of no service to me. Freedom had ruined him." Clark paused. "I hired him out to several farmers, but he did no better for them. Finally, I freed him, but I heard the cholera took him."

"And you?" Jacques asked. "Did freedom ruin you?"

"It was the truest freedom I have ever known," Clark said. "It was exhilarating and terrifying at turns, and I came to love both the mountains and the people who live there. Americans have an image of the West as a vast empty canvass upon which we can, through cunning and industry, sketch our destiny, but it is instead a palimpsest—a word I know but cannot spell! The marks we make are only the most recent, competing with traces of older civilizations. There are villages, gunsmith, big enough for several thousand individuals—but which are empty but for skeletons and questions."

Jacques said that was difficult to believe.

"I am unsure," Clark said, "of whether it was fame that did in Captain Lewis, or the memory of the things we had seen. In either case, it took only three years for it to destroy him; when he died, in 1809, at a miserable inn called

Grinder's Stand on the Natchez Trace, it was by his own hand."

"He was not killed by the assassin you fear?"

"He was his own enemy," Clark said. "Even though he was territorial governor of Upper Louisiana, he was hopelessly in debt, and a drunk and a dope fiend. I had no doubt when I heard the news that he had committed self-slaughter, because I had heard him talk of it so often before. My regret is that I could not save him."

Jacques's hand began to shake.

"Are we tasked with saving our friends?"

"Those who are worthy of saving, yes," Clark said. "But they are scarcer than hen's teeth."

"Indeed," Jacques managed. Eager to change the subject, he asked, "Will you return to the Heart River?"

"It has been seventeen winters now."

"It is indeed a long time, but not an eternity," Jacques said. "You could confront your past on your terms, rather than wait for it to come stealing in the night. Perhaps your past fears you as much as you fear it."

"My past is a Crow war chief named Standing Wolf, and he fears nothing."

"Perhaps he no longer lives."

"He is neither dead nor alive," Clark said. "He can change his shape, as it suits him, and his age is contrary. He was old when I fought him on the Heart River, but he will be younger now."

Jacques tried to argue, but Clark shook his head.

"Until you have been there," Clark said, "you cannot know."

"That is true of all things," Jacques said.

Clark smiled.

"You think me mad."

"We are all mad, in our own way," Jacques said. "But I cannot share your delusion that these savages have the power of immortality. That would be surrendering to superstition."

"It is only superstition if it is someone else's religion," Clark said. "Theirs is as rich as ours, and makes a damn sight more sense. The Mandans knew we were coming, because the moss on Oracle Stone with the Sacred Medicine Wheel told them so. When we go to church, we can't so much as get a clue about tomorrow's weather."

Jacques laughed.

"Do you know, gunsmith, what is a man's greatest possession?"

Jacques's instinct was to say wealth, but he doubted a wealthy man would agree, for all men like to think themselves humble. And even great fortunes could ebb and flow on the winds of war and the tides of commerce. Family? An accident of birth. Faith? It was a child's prayer, a fool who was sure the sky loved him, a dog barking in the night.

"A man's greatest possession," Jacques said, "is his freedom."

Clark smiled, reached out, and sloshed more whiskey into the crystal.

"Freedom is important," Clark agreed. "Without freedom, you are nothing. Most men believe themselves to be free, but they are hobbled by invisible chains. These chains are forged willingly by the captive, and keep them forever bound to civil society. To break these chains, one must—"

"Be cruel."

Jacques was thinking of Abella and her soft lips.

"To be bold," Clark said. "To risk much, to court regret, to face an archrival, to endure suffering beyond imagination, to surrender to forces beyond ourselves and our understanding. And, in the end, to return from the adventure with something that has value beyond that of gold—facts."

"Many would say the surviving is better than the knowing."

Clark laughed.

"Many among my men would have agreed with you," he said. "But only one of them did not survive. Sgt. Floyd died of illness early during our ascent of the Missouri. He remains there still, on a hill overlooking the river. He was twenty-two. He comes to me at night, sometimes, still concerned that his family knows he died well."

"It is your imagination," Jacques said. "Forgive me, but the aged are prone to such night terrors. Perhaps you should not stay up so late and drink so much."

"You forget whom you address, sir."

"Ah," Jacques said. "You forget I am a rogue and a thief and care not for station and am full of your whiskey. So you have encouraged my insolence."

"So I have," Clark said. "Whiskey makes friends where wine makes rivals."

"Let us continue to drink whiskey, then."

"It has been good to speak honestly," Clark said. "The opportunities are increasingly few these days."

Jacques allowed silence to fill the space between them. Then:

"Are you not free, my dear governor?"

"I am free only in my memories," Clark said. "My time has run, and I am now bound by old age and reputation. Never again will I taste freedom, never in this life and likely not the next. But for you, gunsmith, the Upper Missouri beckons."

Clark took one of the newspaper clippings on his desk and pushed it toward him. It was a notice from the *Missouri Gazette and Publick Advertiser*.

TO ENTERPRISING YOUNG MEN

The subscriber wishes to engage ONE HUNDRED MEN, to ascend the river Missouri to its source, there to be employed for one, two, or three years — For particulars, enquire of Major Andrew Henry, near the Lead Mines, in the County of Washington, (who will ascend with and command the party) or the subscriber, at St. Louis.

Wm. H. Ashley
February 13, 1822

"There is your freedom," Clark said. "I will write you a letter of introduction."

Jacques pushed the whiskey away and rubbed his eyes with the palms of his hands. He suspected that Clark was toying with him, that he was keeping him there long enough so that Sheriff Brown would burst in and haul him away to the jail in the basement of the courthouse to await trial, conviction, hanging.

"Why are you helping me?"

"Because you must do what I cannot."

"You are William Clark," Jacques said. "Your influence is unlimited."

"Only in our world. Not in his."

"Standing Wolf."

"That's why I bought your rifle," Clark said. "A weapon

to give an old man the advantage of a few dozen yards against an ever-younger opponent. But I will never again make the journey. But you, my enterprising young friend, are hungry for the journey. You do not have to steal your magnificent rifle back, for I will give it to you. But there is one condition: You must promise me that you will find Standing Wolf and kill him."

"How can I promise to kill a ghost?"

"He will be real enough."

"How would I even know this enemy?"

"He possesses a peace medallion," Clark said. "A gift sent with us from Jefferson."

"I heard you took many such medals with you."

"Eighty-nine of them," Clark said. "But most of them were small, hardly bigger than the coins in our pockets. But there were three larger medals, a little more than four inches in diameter, and Standing Wolf received one of these when I believed him an ally instead of a demon. The medallion has the president's face on one side and, and obverse, a pair of shaking hands beneath a tomahawk and a clay pipe. 'Friendship,' it says. You will know Standing Wolf by this sign."

"And I am to kill this ghost."

"Yes," Clark said. "If you can. And take the medallion as proof."

"Allow me to inspect the rifle," Jacques said.

"You will bring the medallion back to me."

"I must have the rifle."

"It is on display behind you," Clark said. "Look for the grizzle bear."

Jacques rose from the chair and walked a few yards down the line of exhibits to the grizzly bear. The tawny-coated bear was portrayed as standing on its hind legs, its head nearly touched the ceiling. One of its legs was caught in a wrought iron, double-spring bear trap chained to a stake, with some red paint around the jaws of the closed trap to signify blood. The bear's paws were reaching out as if to sink its wicked claws into Jacques, and its mouth was open, red tongue lolling between jagged yellow teeth.

A chill ran down Jacques's spine.

The bear seemed at first glance, in the candlelight, to be frighteningly alive. But a careful examination, looking past the teeth and claws, revealed the skull and cape stretched over a wire frame to give it form. The fur on the bear's concave face was tattered, exposing white bone in places, and some soft parts of the snout were missing.

"The size is exaggerated," Jacques said.

"You may have the opportunity to compare one day," Clark said. "The grizzle is a fearsome animal, and shocks the senses like thunder, but other creatures are more likely to kill you. A bear will leave you alone until you cross it, but a wolf hunts in a pack and will chase you down if it thinks you are weak."

The rifle was resting across the antlers of the elk skull, as if left there by a careless trapper. Near the gun was a fringed leather possibles bag and a powder flask made from a yellowed cow's horn. The rifle was as he remembered it, with a river maple half-stock and patch box in the stock that was engraved with a compass rose. When he picked it up, it seemed even lighter than he remembered it. A sense of calm returned, holding the rifle again.

"If there was ever a rifle made to kill a ghost," Jacques said, "this is it."

"You'll need the other things," Clark said. "Take them."

Jacques took the powder horn and the leather possibles

bag that were hanging from the antlers. By their weight, he knew they were full.

"Standing Wolf," Clark said. "You will find him and then you will kill him."

Jacques said he would.

"And take the medallion?"

"Yes," Jacques said.

Clark held out his hand and they shook on it.

"The letter of introduction?" Jacques asked.

Clark shuffled through the detritus on his desk, found a blank piece of paper, and loaded the nib of a pen from a desktop well.

"Now, I can't very well use your real name," Clark said. "So I need to know what you will call yourself from this time on. And you must give me your answer quickly, for I see the rose of dawn in the east through the eastern windows, and you must be on your way before daylight."

Without hesitation, Jacques replied:

"Jack Picaro."

Clark had him spell the name, one letter at a time.

When he had finished scratching out the letter, he signed it with his full name, and added a paraph below, an elaborate flourish to guard against forgery. Then he shook some reddish sand from a shaker on the paper, tapped it with his finger to blot the ink, then blew the sand from the paper and onto the desk. He folded the letter into a square and offered it to Jacques.

"Henry will know my signature," Clark said.

Jacques took the letter and tucked it carefully into his jacket pocket.

"You didn't answer the question about a man's greatest

possession," Jacques said. "We talked much about freedom, but it was not the answer you sought."

Clark smiled.

"A man's greatest possession," Clark said, "is his reputation."

PART TWO
THE RIVER

7   *The Jefferson*

It was summer and the river glistened silver in the sun, the diamonds of light reflecting from patterns of wave and trough and directly into the eyes of the men on the keelboat *Jefferson*. When Jack Picaro finally bedded down at night, on the deck with thirty other men coughing and snoring around him, he saw the undulating patterns of glittering sunlight floating behind his closed lids.

The men were poling the boat upriver, using long ash rods made in St. Louis, and they would walk the narrow-cleated tread that ran down each side of the boat, just below the gunwales, then step off, walk back, and repeat the process. Always, they were fighting the current. They were poling now because the boat was following a shallow channel, and they were so near the southern bank they would sometimes have to duck to avoid tree limbs. They poled when it was shallow enough, and when it wasn't, the men walked and stumbled along the bank and pulled the boat along with a heavy rope called a *cordelle*. Sometimes, when it was impossible to either pole or cordelle because of a deep channel and a treacherous bank, they would *warp* by attaching a line to a snag or other obstruction and winch the boat forward. Rarely, if the wind was coming from the right direction and there were no immediate obstacles, the *Jefferson* might raise a small square sail on the mast and allow the weather to propel them. Their progress was from six to fifteen miles per day, depending on the combination of propulsion that was used; it had taken them a month just to reach Westport Landing, where the Kansas River entered the Missouri in the northwestern corner of the state.

The past weeks of hard service on the keelboat had toughened Jack, turned his skin as brown as leather, trimmed the fat from his middle, and made his calves and biceps bulge. He had soon learned to toe the tread barefoot, because boots or shoes would only increase the likelihood of tripping on a cleat or when stepping down from the tread; his first day of poling he had fallen in the river twice, after having gotten his feet twisted beneath him; but now, barefoot and surefooted, the motion seemed as natural as breathing. The continuous labor on the *Jefferson* had given Jack new muscle.

But poling introduced a mind-numbing stupor, making it impossible to think too deeply on any subject, and Jack soon discovered this was a relief, a kind of rest for a mind that had always turned so fast as to risk flying apart. Still, he was thankful when one of the hunters employed to bring meat to the boat to supplement the infernal diet of white beans would come to him with some small problem that required mechanical expertise.

With Clark's letter in hand—*"if you hyre this man for your compnay you will half no rigrets, fore he is a good gunsmith and relieable"*—Jack had been hired straightaway by the gruff Captain Andrew Henry and placed on the second boat bound upriver. More men would follow, but the objective of this first group was to reach the mouth of the Yellowstone River and to build a fort there. This would be headquarters, from where the company would obtain their beaver furs from the Indians, who would be paid with the trade goods carried in the boats: beads, blankets, muskets, axes, and gallon upon gallon of cheap whiskey. Each boat held enough of these goods to trade for a fortune in fur.

The *Jefferson* was seventy feet long and eighteen feet at the beam, and four feet from the deck to the bottom of the keel. She had been made at Pittsburgh, on commission of General Ashley, and sailed a thousand miles down the Ohio River to the Mississippi, and then to St. Louis. The *Jefferson* had a high and narrow prow, a low-slung cabin that ran nearly the length of the boat, and a fan-shaped steering oar at the stern where the patron, or pilot, stood barking orders at the ship's company. The ship drew only twenty-four inches of water and had thirty tons of supplies and trade goods packed in every conceivable space. It had a thirty-foot mast that rose from the backbone of the ship, up through the deck, and through the cabin. At the prow was a one-pound swivel gun loaded with shot, and at the tip of the mast fluttered the American flag, now with a twenty-fourth star to represent the state of Missouri.

"Jack!" called his friend, Decatur. "Wake up, Jack! Ship your pole!"

In his near-trance state of walking and poling and walking back, Jack had failed to notice that the river had turned and the channel was deepening, and was surprised that his pole no longer touched the river bottom. In the stern the pilot was cursing, because they had no option but to put in and arrange the cordelle, but the sandy bank was littered with overturned stumps and driftwood and other debris that had been deposited there with the spring floods.

The poles were shipped and the current was allowed to take the boat, giving up a few dozen hard-fought yards, while the pilot leaned on the steering oar and urged the *Jefferson* to a clear spot on the bank. But the pilot had misjudged the speed of the current, and the boat jammed up against the branches of a fallen tree, the limbs groaning and popping as the side of the boat crushed into them. Then men were over the side and securing the boat to the tree, which seemed in no danger of being dislodged, and the thousand-foot cordelle was brought out. The end of the cordelle was near the top of the mast, so that it would be high enough to clear obstacles. A bridle rope running from the prow to the cordelle above kept the boat from pivoting around the mast.

Major Henry was aboard the *Yellowstone*, which was a half day ahead, and the *Jefferson* was under the command of a dyspeptic former solder and fortune seeker named Peter Orton. A veteran of the War of 1812, Orton was a native of New Jersey and was more at home marching than dragging a boat upstream. He had been chosen because, as a sergeant in the regular army, he had experience leading men and some familiarity with tactics, which might come in handy in a fight with hostiles. But Orton was nervous whenever the *Jefferson* lagged too far behind the other boat, and especially when they had to put in unexpectedly, because these were the times they were most vulnerable to attack.

Orton climbed the stairs to the top of the cabin, so as to get the best view, and scanned the bank for signs of trouble. But the bank here was a deep cut, at least ten feet of fresh earth, and it was impossible to see what was over the top. Orton had a habit of holding his hands behind his back and rocking on his feet when he could not make a decision, and this he did while the crew waited.

"For Christ's sake," Decatur Jones whispered in Jack's ear. "You'd think he was Napoleon sizing up the field at Austerlitz. Let's go on with it, I'd like to make the mouth of the Yellowstone before the snow flies. Hand me my rifle."

Jack took Decatur's rifle from the upright rack just inside the cargo cabin and handed it to him, butt first. It was an old but serviceable gun in a caliber that was too light for the West—.33 caliber—and Jack did his best to keep it in good repair for his friend. Then he took his own rifle, the .50 caliber he had been given by Clark, and together they went to the downriver side of the boat to wait.

"I'm hungry," Jack said.

"You're always hungry," Decatur said.

The amount of labor required on the boat sharpened Jack's hunger, and the monotonous nature of the work made him bored, which further contributed to the hunger because there were so few things to think about.

"I hope there will be meat tonight," Jack said.

"With luck, there will be. Elk, buffler. Something."

"What I wouldn't give for a pie," Jack said.

"What are the odds of us having pie this far upriver?"

"Once the fort is built, maybe," Jack said. "Surely they will bring flour and a Dutch oven. There must be apples at the mouth of the Yellowstone, right? Perhaps even cherries?"

Jack lapsed into silence, thinking of food. It was still a long time before they were expected to reach their destination, and if their luck held it would be before the snow flies. Then his mind went from food to women, and he wondered if once the fort was built there would be women, and what they would look like. If there were no women, there would certainly be whiskey and gambling to pass the winter.

"Mister Levine," Orton called. "Have you any idea where we are?"

The pilot shrugged. It was his first trip upriver, so he had nothing to base his guess on, other than a map that was a few years old, and already the map was worthless for using as a guide to shoals and other hazards; each spring, the river remade itself.

"We must be nearing the Cheyenne River, but that's just reckoning by how much river I think we've covered," Levine said. "You could shoot our position with the sextant and clock, but that won't get us no nearer than fifty miles either way."

"The sextant and chronometer are in the boat ahead," Orton said.

Hands behind his back, Orton paced the top of the cabin.

They had already entered the vast Sioux territory, but the Lakotas were friendly to the white boatmen and encounters amounted to no more than a few meetings in which pipes were smoked and some trade goods exchanged. Jack had watched the ceremony with interest, noting how much importance the Lakotas placed on proper etiquette. It was bad manners to speak the name of a dead person, for example, and if you told a lie you would be laughed at.

"Ho!" one of the men shouted. "Movement on the bank."

"Look sharp," Orton called.

Then Johnston, one of the hunters, appeared, waving his slouch hat over his head. He and another man, Martin, were carrying a pole on their shoulders, from which swung an elk. Earlier, the *Jefferson* had fired its swivel gun so as to signal its location to the hunters.

"If you want meat for supper," Johnston called, "you'd best not shoot us."

"Stand down," Orton called. Then, to the men, "Did you see any hostiles?"

"No," Johnston said, "But they damn sure saw us."

"How do you know?" Orton called.

"Does the rabbit see the hawk or just feel its shadow?" Johnston said, running a hand through his long blond hair and then replacing his hat, which was decorated with a big turkey feather. "This is Ree country, and they have no love for white children. They was watching us, sure as rain. I could feel them."

The traders and trappers were casual to the point of confusion in their names for various tribes, Jack noticed. They called the Arikara the Rees, but there was also an unrelated tribe to the north that were the Crees. It was the same with the Sioux. The Sioux were a group of tribes, of which the Lakotas were one.

"We was watched," Martin said. He was tall and bald and had a stammer that made him stingy with his words. He was also given to fits of religiosity and always carried a Bible in the pocket of his hunting shirt.

Orton looked displeased but did not argue with the hunters.

Both Johnston and Martin had been a long time on the Upper Missouri, and it was rumored that they had somehow been associated with Lewis and Clark. Although neither would confirm it, they seemed to know several members of the company, and talked sometimes of John Colter and Patrick Gass.

"If these red niggers had their eyeballs on you," Levine said, "why didn't they kill you when the killin' was easy?"

Johnston laughed.

"You're a stupid one, ain't you?" Johnston asked.

Levine glared, but did not object to the insult except to spit over the side of the boat. Johnston was one of the few men among the company he was afraid of.

"Why kill two rabbits when you can get forty," Jack said.

"The boy's right," Johnston said. "They are damned good trackers and they will have followed us back to the boat to see what weakness we present. I'd say you'd better get the damned boat moving, Sergeant Orton, or this might be the last place we ever put in."

"He's right," Martin said.

The boat's second-in-command, Edward Hollister, related in some cousinly degree to Captain Henry, leaned against the swivel gun and shrugged. He was nineteen years old and had affected an army officer's coat—and an air of nonchalance—but without any insignia of rank.

"Perhaps they're just curious," Hollister offered. "We are, after all, civilized men, and as such might present a novelty to the savages. Nay, we might present a model for them as to correct behavior in the pursuit of mutual profit."

"They've seen plenty like us, Eddie," Orton said. "If it wasn't the French, it was the British, and if not the bloody British, then the Spaniards. Even some Russians, maybe. And they will know that we are in pursuit of only one thing, truly, and that is to exploit them for our profit. And they will have learned that if we are thwarted in that attempt, our next impulse will be to kill them. Such is the way of the world."

"It is a sad world, then," Hollister said. "I was only considering the example set for us by Captain Lewis."

"It will take more than a silly air gun to impress them," Orton said.

"The Girandoni was actually a fine weapon," Hollister said. "Fired twenty-two rounds on one charge of air. At least, that's what I heard."

"To hell with the Austrian gun," Orton said. "Give me fire and lead."

"Don't," Martin stammered. "Don't wish."

Orton asked what he meant.

"Martin means give a care to what you wish for," Johnston said. "The Rees have been collecting guns from their enemies for years. He also probably means to admonish you for cussing, but I'll be damned if I have the time to stand here while he spits it out."

Jack had heard of the air gun that Lewis had taken with him on the expedition, and also knew similar weapons were common in Europe. But he had not heard of such a rate of fire. It would be interesting, he thought, to dismantle one and investigate the mechanism that made such repeating fire possible.

"All right," Orton said. "Better get moving. Deploy cordelle!"

Jack threw his shoes around his neck by the laces, stepped off the boat onto the trunk of the fallen tree, and made his way along it, as if tightrope walking, using his rifle for balance. Near the root end of the tree he hopped down in the shallow water and splashed his way to the bank. His toes delighted in the cool water and the soft mud.

Decatur followed and slid down from the trunk into the muddied water that Jack had left behind, and they both laughed as they picked their way up the grassy bank. Then they turned and waited for the men to rig the bridle to the heavy rope and pass it up the riverbank.

"What do you think an Indian attack is like?" Decatur asked.

"Bloody," Jack said.

"You've been in such a fight?"

"No," Jack admitted. "But I've read much about them. There are histories about the old Indian attacks back east that are downright grim. In Pennsylvania a schoolhouse was attacked by Pontiac's maniacs and the schoolmaster shot dead and nine of his pupils killed and scalped. In Ohio, eight adults and two children were butchered at Big Bottom on the Muskingum River. The Indians always seem intent on getting to the women and children."

"Then it is good we have neither," Decatur said. "What seemed the most effective weapon against the Injuns?"

"Diplomacy," Jack said.

"Fat chance of that with Orton in command," Decatur said. "He'll just get a sour look on his face, put his hands behind his back, and begin to pace and talk to himself."

Then Decatur puffed out his cheeks in imitation, and Jack laughed.

"Are you scared?" Decatur asked.

"Some," Jack allowed.

"Have you ever shot anybody?"

"No," Jack lied.

"I wonder what it's like," Decatur said. "I think about it sometimes, and imagine some desperate situation where I have to take quick and sure action, and my aim is always true. Oh, I'm sometimes wounded, but not too badly, and then everyone tells me how brave I was and how grateful they are for me saving the entire company. But I know it can't really be like that."

"Could be," Jack said, sitting in the grass and lacing his boots. "I don't know. I expect heroes are made more through luck than courage."

Decatur sat in the grass and pulled on his boots.

The boys had been detailed to scout for the cordelle gang, because Decatur had the sharp vision and because nobody could best Jack's accuracy or range with his rifle. Jack wanted to be a hunter, but Orton said they needed their gunsmith at the boat—and because Jack had no experience in tracking or field dressing. What Orton didn't say is that he considered Jack and Decatur the most expendable of the men, because they were the youngest and had the least experience.

Jack stood, taking in the grassy meadow behind them and the riverbank ahead. The meadow was three hundred yards wide, and the grass was too short to hide a man, but the serpentine bank ahead was a series of brush-choked cuts and ravines.

"What do you think?" Decatur asked.

"Cate, we need to worry about the bank ahead," Jack said. "If I were with the Arikaras, and I wanted to attack, I'd hide in one of those deep cuts, let the cordelle gang pass, then unload when the boat drew even. So one of us needs to range ahead, while the other watches his back."

"You watch first," Decatur said. "We'll swap in a mile or so."

Decatur scrambled ahead, and Jack walked carefully behind, keeping an eye on his friend and the grunting and cursing cordelle crew. The going was slow, and the cordelle crew had the worst of it, because of the difficulty hauling the heavy rope over the broken bank. Their pace had slowed so that Jack expected they would make only four or five miles that day.

Then Jack smelled something odd coming from up-river, and he put his fingers in the corners of his mouth and whistled to draw Decatur's attention. But the boy had already smelled the same thing—a burning, sickening sweet smell, at once oily and sweet—and he was pointing to the river, where a twisting column of black smoke advanced toward them.

Then Jack saw the source of the stench.

It was a pirogue, smaller than a keelboat, drifting downstream and turning sluggishly in the current. The upper part of the boat was on fire. The stern was filled with water and was nearly at the level of the river, and the bow was thrust upward at an unnaturally sharp angle. One side of the boat was bristling with arrows, and two bodies hung over the side, the fingers of one trailing in the water.

Suddenly Jack was so scared he could hardly breathe.

Orton was shouting orders for the cordelle gang to return to the boat and the pilot was leaning on the steering oar to turn the *Jefferson* away from the flaming pirogue, but could not because the craft was still captive to the course determined by the tethered line. Then Orton shouted for the crew on board to throw a grapple on the pirogue and bring it close because the men might still be alive.

At the stern of the boat, where they had deposited the elk, the hunters watched with concern. Johnston unlimbered his rifle.

"Fools," Martin managed, his hand going reflexively to the testament in his pocket.

"You said a mouthful," Johnston agreed, his eyes on the bank. "The Rees are watching this just as sure as that fair-haired whore back at Westport who said she loved me was lying. Which direction you reckon they'll come from?"

Martin shrugged.

Johnston found a spot against the stern, facing the river, where the side of the boat protected most of him. He rested his rifle on the rail, then reached into his shooting bag and grabbed two balls, holding them in the palm of his right hand, while keeping the powder horn in his left, cupped beneath the fore stock of his rifle. Martin took up a position on the other side of the stern and made similar preparations for fast reloading.

"Where's that hook?" Orton asked, impatient.

A treble-hooked grapple was spun by one of the men and then released, and it traced a high arc over the water, with a light rope trailing behind it like a tail. The man's aim was true and the grapple banged down in the middle of the pirogue, and as it was pulled taut, it caught on the gunwale. As the rope was hauled in and the pirogue neared, Orton told the men to take up some poles and keep the burning prow turned away from the keelboat.

"These red niggers," a man at the poles muttered. "They're nothing more than animals. Look at what they've done to decent men. We'd give them what for if we had the chance, you can bank on that."

Of a sudden, the arm that was dangling over the side of the pirogue reached up and snatched the ash pole, pulling the man holding it over the side of the *Jefferson*. He lost his hat as he fell with a splash into the narrowing water between the boats, and the Arikara warrior that had been dressed as a wounded or dead white man stood with the pole in both hands. Then he brought the end of the pole down on the top of the man's bald head and the tip punched a neat hole in the skull.

Blood swirled in the muddy water.

The warrior shouted in either anger or exultation in his own language, his head thrown back and his mouth wide. Johnston leaned out from his spot at the stern to get a better angle and then fired. The warrior's shout ended as the ball shattered his front teeth and carried his brains out the back of his head.

"Whango," Johnston said.

The other Arikara who had pretended to be a fallen man was up now, bloody sleeves hanging from his arms, and he produced a pistol from his belt and took a shot at Johnston, but missed.

"We should have figured it out," Johnston, who was busy juggling ball and powder, called to Martin. "It's the way they hunt buffler, by wearing hides and sneaking in amongst the herd. They did the same to us."

Four warriors had been hiding behind the first two, and they were on their feet now, horn-and-sinew bows in their hands. The bows were drawn, nocked arrows on quivering strings.

"Cut the line!" Orton called.

The arrows released almost as one, finding their marks in torso and limbs.

The men on the *Jefferson* were sluggish with surprise and fear and tripping over themselves and the wounded to get to their weapons. One of the men brought an axe down on the line to the grapple, and it parted with a pinging sound. But the bow of the smaller boat swung sharply around and struck the *Jefferson* with a heavy thunk and a shower of embers.

"Push that boat away!" Orton cried.

Two rifle shots, and then three, came from the *Jefferson*, but to no obvious effect other than to create a cloud of smoke that shrouded the view. Some of the men put their shoulders into pushing the pirogue away, but another fusillade of arrows drove them back.

Six more Arikaras, who had been hiding in the water on the other side of the pirogue, were climbing up now and retrieving bows and trade guns from the bottom of the boat. Johnston leaned out from the stern, fired, and sent one of them back into the water.

"Whango," he said, as he began to reload.

"Swivel gun!" Orton shouted. "That means you, Mister Hollister!"

Hollister realized the gun had not been reloaded after it had been used to signal the hunters. Desperately, he began the time-consuming task of putting a two-ounce charge down the barrel, ramming it home, following it with a pound of musket balls, and cleaning and priming the vent.

"Prepare to repel boarders," Orton screamed, his belt pistol in his hand. He walked to the edge of the cabin and fired his single shot into the pirogue, shattering the elbow of one of the Indians. Then he took an arrow to the chest, and remained standing for a moment in uncomprehending shock before falling and tumbling off the roof of the cabin into the water.

The warriors had now clambered up the side of the keelboat, bows and trade guns at the ready, and the one Orton had shot held a knife in his good hand. The men turned and fired into them, but it was difficult to aim a long gun while panicked at such a close distance. Several of their rifles went off, almost at the same time, but only one of the warriors fell.

On a high spot on the bank two hundred yards away, Jack and Decatur were watching the battle unfold.

"What do we do?" Decatur asked.

"Take your best shot from here," Jack said, going down on one knee so as to better steady his aim. "Then we reload as we advance and fire again and again."

The distance between them and the *Jefferson* was growing now that the cordelle was slack and the keelboat and the pirogue were both being carried downstream. The fire from the bow of the pirogue had now spread to the side of the *Jefferson*. With the smoke and the distance, it was difficult to find a clear target. Decatur fired first but missed his man. Jack breathed in and slowly exhaled, his sights hovering over the keelboat, and when a clear view of a bare chest of one of the Arikaras appeared, he squeezed the trigger. The hammer fell, the flint sparked the primer in the pan, and the rifle bucked against his shoulder, all in a split second. After the report, there was the odd ringing B flat note from the barrel.

The ball drove the warrior over the side of the boat into the river, and Jack knew that at this distance he didn't hear the shot until the second or so after the .50-caliber ball had found his chest.

"Let's go," Jack said, and Decatur followed him.

At the boat, Hollister had the swivel gun loaded now, and a glowing punk in his hand, and he tried to swing the gun around, but found it an awkward affair to aim the piece backward at a target so near the *Jefferson*. Not only was he almost looking down the muzzle of the gun, but the yoke of the swivel prevented the barrel from being declined enough to aim at the pirogue. So he climbed up on the prow, holding the wooden tiller at the end of the swivel gun to try to aim it, and touched the punk to the vent hole. The gun gave a thunderous roar, the shot cutting one of his own men to pieces and biting a watermelon-sized chunk from the side of the boat.

"Try killing the Rees and not us," Johnston said.

Then Johnston fired, missed a warrior, and cussed.

With no time to reload, it was hand-to-hand now on the boat, with knives and clubs. Johnston was in the thick of it now, using the butt of his rifle, and Martin was beside him, his belt knife already bloody, saying the Lord's Prayer without a hint of a stammer.

Then the slack cordelle snagged on a sawyer and went suddenly taut, jerking the bow of the keelboat around and throwing the flaming pirogue back out into the river. The *Jefferson* came to rest against a worry, a tangle of trees and driftwood and other debris at the end of a sandbar, and became stuck fast.

Now seventy-five yards away, and with his rifle reloaded, Jack stopped and tried for another shot, but it was difficult to get a clear shot because the fight was on the far side of the boat.

"Damn," Jack said. "Let's keep going."

"Looks like they're losing," Decatur said, hanging back.

"That means *we're* losing," Jack said. "Come on."

"Look," Decatur said. "The cordelle gang is lighting out."

Instead of rushing to the boat to help their comrades, the men on shore who had pulled the cordelle were now climbing up the bank to the grassy meadow beyond.

"Cowards," Jack said. "Come on."

Decatur shook his head.

"They're right," he said. "It's turned into a slaughter."

Decatur sat, his rifle across his knees.

"Get up," Jack said.

Decatur shook his head.

"Stay here with me, Jack. They're all going to die."

Jack felt his legs grow weak with the desire to sit. He knew that Decatur was likely right, that all hope was likely lost for those on the *Jefferson*, and that sacrificing themselves would make no difference. But then the lonely prospect of he and Decatur being lost on the northern plains, having to find their own way to the mouth of the Yellowstone, and probably being killed by Indians anyway—and knowing they had abandoned their comrades—was more than he could stomach.

"I'm a lot of things, Cate," he said. "I've lied when it suited me and cheated cards when I could. But I don't believe I'm a coward, so I'm going ahead."

"Don't leave me alone," Decatur said, grasping Jack's sleeve.

Jack shook him off.

"Farewell," Jack said.

Then Jack began running toward the boat, his rifle locked in his hands.

He had splashed across a shallow pocket of water to the sandbar where the keelboat and the pirogue were tangled in the worry when he heard a pitiful sound from behind him. He turned and saw one of the men from the cordelle gang standing on the bank, holding his stomach in, from which a stout spear protruded. Then the man toppled down and rolled into the shallow water.

On the bank behind him appeared an Arikara chief atop a grayish pony. The chief was old enough to have more than a few strands of gray in his long black hair, and the creases on his face were deep, but his brown eyes were clear and his back was straight. His attitude was that of a prince, if not a king, and his expression was one of indifference, if not disdain. He wore a buffalo hat with shining black horns, with tufts of something white at the tips, a porcupine-quill breastplate, and the bottom half of his face was blue with some kind of paint or grease. Both of his cheeks bore the pockmark scars of some long-ago sickness. There were beads and bits of bone tied in his hair. Around his neck was a wooden cross and a peace medallion. Jack knew it wasn't Standing Wolf, because the medallion was one of the many smaller ones. In the chief's left hand was a hooked eagle feather staff.

A dozen Arikara men then came forward to stand on either side of the chief. Their faces, too, were partially masked in indigo. Most of them had bows, some had spears, and a few had trade guns or better. The spears had blood on them, and Jack knew the cordelle crew had been killed up on the grassy meadow, where it had been easy work for the Arikaras because there was nowhere for the boatmen to hide.

Jack's rifle was still charged, but he knew if he raised it he would be dead before he got off a shot. One of the warriors began to raise his trade musket, but the chief held out his hand and stopped it. The chief then waited, curious to see what Jack would do.

Behind him, Jack could hear that the fight at the keelboat was reaching a crescendo. There were shouts and the sound of limbs being battered and broken, and the occasional rifle shot. He did not know which was getting the worst of it.

Jack knelt down and carefully placed the rifle on the gravel bar, then slowly got back up. He stood uncertainly for a moment, then looped his thumbs through his belt because he did not know what else to do with his hands.

The chief said something in Arikara to him.

"Sorry," Jack said. "I don't understand."

"Parlez-vous français?"

Jack said that he did.

"Then you will take a message to your *capitain* from Lightning Crow of the Sahnish nation," the chief said in French. "You will tell him there will be war between us for as long as the whites continue to trespass on our land. You come dragging your ridiculous boats filled with trash and poison, carrying the worst of men, those who carry disease, and others who are murderers and thieves. You make friends with our enemies the Sioux and the Mandans and have *l'audace* to expect our friendship. Tell him that if you continue to come, you can expect only death. Can you remember this?"

Jack told Lightning Crow he could.

The chief nodded, then raised his arm and gave the signal for his remaining warriors to retreat from the keelboat.

"What do they call you?" Lightning Crow asked.

"Jack Picaro."

"It sounds like a sneeze," the chief said. "All of your names are unpronounceable and mean nothing. Why do you not take your names from animals? Instead you name yourselves for what you do—this one is a blacksmith, that one makes barrels. Your names are like your religion— empty and unconnected to the earth or sky. What does your name mean?"

"A scoundrel, a rascal, a thief."

"Then I will remember your name."

"Why am I spared?" Jack asked.

The chief said it was because he said so.

"But why not him?" Jack pointed at the cordelle gang member with the spear in his stomach.

"He was a coward," Lightning Crow said, "and unworthy of my message. But you were running to join your comrades at the boat, where you would have surely died. And, my little thief, you shot well, from the top of the bluff there. Tell me, what kind of medicine does your gun have that makes it sing?"

Jack didn't know what made it ring. It shouldn't have— he had made no other rifle that struck a note like a bell when fired—but it must have been due to the combination of metals and how carefully the light barrel was mounted in the stock.

"It is the spirit in the rifle," Jack said.

"Ah," Lightning Crow said. "A ghost rifle."

"Your people know more about these things than mine."

Atop his horse, the chief looked over the river, past the burning keelboat and its dying men, to the far bank. Then he seemed to look to the horizon, and beyond, to the long-dead past.

"When I was a boy, after I survived the blister sickness that took my brothers and my sisters and left me with this to remind others"—he passed a hand over the scars on his face—"what I most wanted was a gun with which to take revenge. My village had not even seen a white man yet, but we had their diseases, and their horses, both coming from the Spaniards who left them on the plains to find us. But we had heard stories of the thundersticks, and the medicine they possessed, and I wanted such power for myself."

The chief paused. The horse shifted anxiously beneath him.

"That was thirty winters ago," he said. "I have seen many guns come and go, some that blew up in our faces and others that had a degree of power, but not until I heard your gun sing did I believe in the old stories."

The chief said something to his men.

"Thief, I must have your rifle."

Two blue-faced warriors came down the bank and advanced onto the bar, one with a trade gun and the other with a spear, and it was clear their intention was to take Jack's rifle.

"No," Jack said, putting his left foot on the rifle and drawing the elkhorn-handled toothpick from its sheath at his belt. "You'll have to kill me for it, and then who will there be to deliver Lightning Crow's message?"

"Any of the *waisachu* who survive on the boat will do," the chief said, using the general term for white men used by tribes on the northern plains. It literally meant those who steal the fat, but it could also be interpreted as those who smell bad because of what they eat.

The warriors spread out, one on either side of Jack, and they made small taunting sounds in the back of their throats. Jack turned his knife toward one, and then the other.

"Why do you resist?" the chief asked. "If I wanted your horse, I would take it. If I wanted your woman, I would have her. It is the way of the world. The rabbit cannot resist the wolf."

The warrior with the trade gun advanced, switched the gun to one hand, and reached down with the other for the rifle. Jack could feel his body readying itself for a desperate fight. His heart beat faster, his vision seemed more acute, and time seemed to slow. He forced a certain detachment, as if the events were happening to someone else, so that he could think clearly.

Jack kicked sand and gravel in the warrior's face, just as he was about to touch the rifle, making him flinch and rub at his eyes. Then he turned to confront the one with the spear, who was holding the shaft in both hands and seemed determined to stick the stone point into some fleshy part of Jack's anatomy.

Jack switched the toothpick back and forth in his hands.

The warrior lunged, aiming for a knee. Jack darted to the side, so the spear point found only air. The spear came at him again, and this time Jack was not quick enough to avoid the razor-like tip of worked flint from drawing a line of blood on his forearm.

Through his blue paint, the warrior smiled.

Jack gave a wicked smile back, then dropped the Damascus toothpick and fell to the ground. He grabbed the rifle with both hands, pulled the hammer back with his thumb, and from a crouching position aimed from the hip at the warrior who had the trade gun. He pulled the trigger, and the rifle barked and rang, putting a ball in the warrior's chest. The Indian staggered backward in surprise, dropping the heavy musket.

Then Jack turned, knowing the warrior with the spear would be on him in a moment, and used the butt of the rifle to knock the point away before it pinned him to the ground. Then he took an overhead swing and brought the butt down on the warrior's forehead, sending him reeling backward. Jack scrambled over to where the trade gun lay, picked it up, and shot the warrior with the bleeding forehead in the face.

He fell dead on the sandbar.

Jack stood over him for a moment, the heavy musket smoking from the barrel. Then he turned and tossed the gun wheeling into the river behind him.

Deliberately, Jack walked over and picked his knife and the ghost rifle from the ground. He put the Damascus toothpick in its scabbard. Then he took an oiled rag from his bag and brushed the sand and gravel from the action, wiped the blood and hair from the metal buttplate, and stood with the rifle in the crook of his arm.

Just an hour ago, he had been untested in battle against the Indians. Now, three Arikara were dead by his hand. It all felt dreamlike, equal parts nightmare and fantasy, but the undeniable fact was that he still lived, at least for a time.

"Damned if I'll die like a rabbit," Jack declared.

"You have killed two of my people for no advantage," Lightning Crow said. "The warrior you killed with that first shot—now, that was in battle. But these two dead? They were told to take the rifle but not to kill you. Their souls have been loosed upon the world, and their ghosts will be hungry. Their women will weep and tear their hair and slash their arms in grief. But, Picaro whose names means thief, it is all for nothing. For I will have the rifle."

Then the chief gave a signal and the rest of his warriors came down the bank.

Jack turned, the empty rifle in his hand, and ran across the sandbar and into the river toward the burning keelboat. A swarm of dark mud-colored *somethings* clustered on the deck of the boat and were dropping into the water or skittering down the worry, and it took Jack a moment to realize that these were the many hundreds of rats escaping the wreck of the ship. He could hear the Arakaras behind him, and even as he could feel their hands upon him, he could not get the image out of his mind of the big brown Hanover rats surging up from every hidden place in the boat. Then his pursuers pulled him back and forced him down into the water, while attempting to prise the rifle from his hands, and just when he thought his lungs would burst and he must drown they brought him back up, took the rifle, and there was a sharp blow to the back of his head and then he felt nothing and no longer thought of the rats.

8   *The Splinter*

It was twilight when Jack awoke, staring upward at the darkening sky. He was stretched out on a blanket and his aching head was bandaged and Decatur was kneeling next to him.

"I kinda thought you were done for," Decatur said.

"Sure I'm not?" Jack asked. "I feel real queer."

"Here, drink some water," Decatur said, offering him a tin cup.

Jack drank a few swallows, then pushed it away.

"Where's my rifle?"

"The Indians took it, Jack. You don't remember?"

Jack shook his head.

"What of the men on the keelboat?"

"They're dead," Decatur said. "All except Johnston. He took an arrow in the gut and he says nobody lives to tell about it. He's lying over yonder drinking whiskey and clutching Martin's good book. Says he'll seem to get better in the next day or so, but then the fever will come and kill him for sure."

Jack tried to sit up, but his head pounded and swam. He placed his shoulders back against the blanket.

"The boat?"

"Sank, most of it," Decatur said. "Some of it is still sticking above water, because it's tangled up in the worry, but it's all burnt pretty bad. If the company finds us before high water takes the *Jefferson* away, Johnston says the company will be able to salvage the swivel gun and some of the cargo from belowdecks."

"How do we know the rest of the company still lives?" Jack asked. "I don't think they would have just given them the pirogue."

"Wasn't from the *Yellowstone*," Decatur said. "Markings on it say she was part of Long's Expedition, which Johnston says was up this way two or three years ago. They must have lost her somehow, because Johnston don't remember hearing of any fights."

"Well, there's been one now," Jack said.

"Johnston says the company will send somebody downriver looking for us after a few days, when we don't catch up with the *Yellowstone*. It wouldn't be such a bad wait if there weren't so many people we knew dead around us."

"This is a helluva start for General Ashley's company. War with the Arikara, a burned keelboat, and most of its crew butchered."

"At least we're alive."

"You should start digging some graves," Jack said.

"We can do it together, as soon as you're able."

"No," Jack said. "I have to get the rifle back."

Decatur laughed.

"That rifle's long gone, Jack," he said, dismissively. "You could have your pick of twenty rifles on the boat that are no longer needed by their previous owners. Besides, that Rees chief that took it is probably ten miles from here by now, and only the wind knows in what direction."

"He has to call someplace home."

"Yes, and I'm sure the walls are lined with the skulls of foolish white men," Decatur said. "You killed those two blue-faced devils up close, but they was holding back because the chief wanted you alive to tell Major Henry what happened here."

"You seem to know a damn lot about it. Where were you?"

"I was watching, careful like," Decatur said.

"Then you know I could have used a hand."

"You were holding your own," Decatur said. "Damn, where did you learn to fight like that?"

"I didn't know I could," Jack said, "until I had to."

"Besides, I didn't know what you and the chief were saying," Decatur said. "For all I knew, you were making a peace treaty. I don't speak French like you do, or Spanish or whatever the hell it is that you talk in your sleep."

"Dammit, Cate," Jack said. "You had a loaded rifle in your hand. Why didn't you use it?"

"Yeah, but I kept my rifle, didn't I? No need for both of us to lose our hair."

Jack reached out a hand.

"Help me up," he said. "I must talk to Johnston."

Decatur had dragged some of the cargo out of the boat and onto the sandbar, a pile of disordered goods that ranged from kegs of nails and cans of turpentine to bolts of cloth and burlap sacks of beans. Johnston was resting against the beans, shirtless, breeches blood-soaked, his left hand wrapped around a six-inch stub of arrow shaft in his right side. His right hand rested on a jug of whiskey. Dead Martin's Bible and gun lay within reach.

"You done good, boy," Johnston said. "You sent two of them Rees back to their red Maker."

Three, Jack thought, if the first shot was fatal.

"We're weren't in the thick of it like you," Jack said.

Johnston nodded.

"Well, they got me, sure enough," he said. "I snapped the shaft of the arrow off, but I can feel the rest of it in my *boudins*, my guts, like the biggest splinter you ever had. What's wrong? Why're you starin' like that?"

"Sorry," Jack said. "Never saw an arrow in anybody before."

"You'd best get used to it," Johnston said, grimacing. "That is, if you aim to spend any time in these parts."

"Did you know the Rees that attacked us?"

"Know them like personal?" Johnston asked. "Hell, I ain't been to their lodges for dinner, but I know of them, if that's what you mean. If that chief was Lightning Crow, which I'm pretty sure it was—"

"It was him."

"Well, he ain't your regulation redskin. He's one mean animal, and smart, and has had a bad case of wanting to put white men in the ground ever since the smallpox left his face like that when he was a kid. But he's never killed more than one or two before, during the usual business of stealing horses and such."

"Where does he call home?"

"Hard to say," Johnston said. "The Rees and the Mandans and the rest tend to move villages when the mood strikes them, or when something bad happens. Last I knew, Lightning Crow lived in a village up near the mouth of the Cheyenne River. Damn, boy, why all the questions? I'm suffering here."

"You reckon he's headed back to his village or will he go on raiding?"

"Don't rightly know," Johnston said. "This was no ordinary raid. The point was to kill, not to steal horses or guns. So I guess it depends on whether old Lightning Crow still has his mad up."

"I aim to go after him."

"That's the dumbest idea I ever heard, even for a Spaniard."

"I'm not Spanish," Jack said. "Can you draw me a map?"

"I have an arrow in my frickin' guts. What do you think?"

Jack was silent.

"Fetch dead Martin's powder horn over here, and use your knife to sharpen me a pencil," Johnston said. "I'm going to do this quick, because I'm almost too drunk to draw."

Jack brought the horn and a sharpened pencil and Johnston started sketching on the yellow horn.

"This here is the Missouri River," he said, drawing a curving line that looked like an Indian bow. "This lower point is where we met the Kiowa to trade, and the upper one is the Cheyenne River. Beyond it, way up here, is the mouth of the Yellowstone."

"What's the scale?"

"Do I look like a goddamned Mason or Dixon?" Johnston asked. "I'm doing the best I can, from my recollection, and with a Ree arrow in my gut. But I reckon these two points are about three hundred miles apart, as the crow flies."

Johnston made another line, as straight as he could, and put an arrow at the top.

"This here is north."

Then he made some curvy lines branching from the longest line, indicating rivers that joined with the Missouri.

"The Rees mostly live in villages between the Cheyenne and Cannonball Rivers, here," Johnston said, jabbing his finger at the spot. "Now, you know you're getting close when you come across some abandoned villages. Some of 'em have been empty a long time. Move through them and try not to get spooked. Don't take anything. On the other side was where Lightning Crow had settled, last I knew. About here."

Johnston drew an X that was closer to the Cannonball than the Cheyenne.

"How far a journey?"

"I don't know. I never made it from here," Johnston said. "But I reckon you could do it in a fortnight, if you don't get kilt along the way. But it don't matter, because once you get there, you'll be kilt for sure."

Jack nodded.

"Why shouldn't I take anything from the dead villages?"

"It's bad medicine," Johnston said. "It just ain't done."

"But the Rees steal horses, don't they?"

"Son, that's different. Horses is warfare. We're talking about *wakan* here."

Jack didn't understand, but he didn't say anything.

"Take Martin's rifle," Johnston said. "I busted my stock all to hell on a Rees's skull. It's a decent gun, but it don't pack much of a punch. It's only .45 caliber. But, that's good enough for elk and Indians. Martin liked it because you can carry a third more lead and powder for the same weight as a fifty. But it ain't big enough for buffler."

Johnston closed his eyes against the pain.

"Listen up, boy."

Jack nodded.

"Whatever you kill to help you survive," Johnston said, "you be sure to thank it. Whether it be an elk or whatever else you kilt, you give thanks, because it was them and not you that died."

"I will," Jack said.

"What the hell is so important about that rifle of yourn?" Johnston asked, eyes still closed. "Let it go. They're like women—you can always buy one or steal another."

"There's no other rifle like this one."

"Then it must be love," Johnston said. "Suit yourself, boy."

Johnston took a labored breath.

"If by some miracle you make it to any of the villages along the river, whether it's Cree or Mandan or any other red nation, you will find plenty that is strange. Their women are lusty, and their buffler god says they must be given to strangers. Do not offend them by refusing. There are men who have made the trip upriver just to visit those villages, to lie with the daughters of the nations, and help them bring the buffs. Hell, I have done so myself."

"Was it worth the trouble?" Jack asked.

"Son," Johnston said. "Life is trouble."

Jack smiled.

Then Johnston bellowed and cursed in pain, the spit spraying from his cracked lips. When he was finished hollering, he put his head back and tried to slow his breathing.

"What can I do?"

"Skin me and make a lady's private toy out of my hide,"

Johnston said, and managed a laugh. "But for now, I'd sort of like to know where the damned trade point is. If it's lodged in bone, nothin' to be done. But if it ain't, I'd like you to push it through."

Jack knelt and looked at the stub of the arrow in Johnston's hand.

"I don't think there's enough sticking out."

"Use a ramrod," Johnston said. "Use a ball puller to thread into the shaft."

"But the pain," Jack said.

"Hell, it's already fearsome," Johnston said. "If we leave it in there, it will fester and I'm a gone beaver for sure. But if you can push it through, that would at least be something. I hate the idea of it stuck inside me."

Jack nodded and took the ramrod from Martin's gun and unscrewed the tip on the ball end, revealing a small worm screw.

"Better drink some more of that," Jack said.

Johnston took several long drinks and then splashed some of the whiskey over his wound. He yowled in pain like an animal, balled his fists, and pounded them into the sand on either side.

"That's just for starters," Jack said. "You sure?"

"Do it, dammit," Johnston said. "Do it before I lose my nerve."

"Cate," Jack said. "Get that coil of hemp over there."

"Why?"

"Just do it."

Jack took the rope and cut a couple of four-foot sections with his knife.

"I'm going to have to tie you up," Jack said, "or you will beat the hell out of us before we're done. I reckon we'll also have to gag you so you don't bite us. Cate, get some cloth and stuff in his mouth."

Once Johnston's hands were tied, his ankles bound, and a scrap of burlap stuffed in his mouth, Jack rolled him over onto his side. Johnston's eyes went wide and he screamed into the burlap.

"All right," Jack said. "I reckon I can probe better with the ramrod attached as a tiller, so here we go."

Jack held the broken shaft of the arrow still while threading the ramrod into it. Johnston began to buck.

"Keep him from squirming," Jack said, "or else this arrow's going to come out his mouth."

One he was satisfied the shaft and the ramrod were one, Jack began to wiggle the arrow. Johnston screamed again in the burlap, his face went purple, and his eyes pleaded for Jack to stop.

"I don't feel it stuck on any bone," Jack said, then looked at the angle of the ramrod and tried to judge the trajectory of the arrow through Johnston's body. "I don't believe it'll get the kidneys on the way through, so let's try. I think I can push it through. So I'm going to count to three. You understand?"

Johnston shook his head furiously, managing to spit out the gag.

"No!" he screamed. "For the love of Christ Jesus get your hands off that shaft! Spare the rod and spoil this child!"

Jack held the ramrod in both hands, and leaned in close to get more leverage. Decatur was crawling over Johnston, trying to pin him to the sand, but was having a hard time keeping hold of him.

"One!" Jack said, and got a better grip on the rod.

"For God's sake!" Johnston cried. "Let go of that hickory!"

"Two!"

And then Jack brought his weight to bear on the rod, and the shaft slid into Johnston's gut so far that he had to release one hand to get a better grip, and all the while Johnston was cussing and screaming and calling him a liar and worse. Then Jack pushed again, and there was an awful sound like tearing meat.

"Whango!" Johnston cried.

The bloody iron point of the arrow emerged from Johnston's lower back.

"There it is," Jack said.

Johnston was quiet now because he had passed out.

Jack unscrewed the broken arrow from the ramrod and drew the rod back through the hole. It came free from Johnston's stomach with a soft sucking sound.

"I'm going to be sick," Decatur said.

"Do it someplace else," Jack said, splashing the last of Johnston's whiskey over the wounds. "After you're done puking, find some clean cloth and some sugar and pack his wounds."

Decatur staggered over to the water and began to retch.

"Farther away," Jack called. "Dammit, Cate. Hold it for another twenty yards, won't you?"

Jack scooped up a handful of sand and used it to scrub the blood and gore from his hands, then walked upstream of Decatur, knelt, and rinsed them in the river. Then he pulled his shirt over his head, cupped water in his hands, and splashed it across his neck and his bare chest. When he was done, he remained on his haunches, looking at the river. His shadow was long on the water, and he knew that it would be dark soon. It would be a summer kind of dark, all soft and warm, but it would still be impossible to travel in country he didn't know.

"Start a fire," Jack called. "We'll cook up some elk steaks."

"What about the Rees?"

"They already know we're here," Jack said. "We need food and rest, and you have graves to dig tomorrow. High up on the bank, where the floods won't get them. Mark the graves with stones and put the names of the ones you know on them. It will keep you busy until the boys from the *Yellowstone* come for you."

"Please, Jack. Won't you stay?"

"I can't."

"It's just a rifle."

"It's my fortune," Jack said.

What he couldn't tell Decatur was that in the stock of the ghost rifle was the brass disk miniature escapement that was the secret to the water-powered barrel boring machine. Work had been so difficult on the keelboat that he was afraid he would accidentally break the chain and the disk would disappear into the river, or that someone would steal the disk one night while he was sleeping on the crowded deck, assuming rightly that it was of some value. So whenever he had a spare moment and could find a spot away from others, he undid the screws to the brass patch box with the compass rose design set into the stock of the rifle, revealing the unfinished maple beneath. The chiseled and carved rout for the patch-box inset had been made just as carefully as the rest of the rifle, even though nobody was ever likely to see it; the lines were smooth, symmetrical, and matched the box perfectly. Jack found that the *lauburu* disk was slightly smaller than the diameter of the circular part of the patch box, but that the route was too shallow. So he worked for several days in a row, using the tip of his Damascus toothpick, to deepen the route until it finally accepted the disk. Then he carved a near-perfect circle from the branch of a maple tree he found on shore, which covered the bottom of the patch box, hiding the brass disk. There was still room in the box for a stack of greased patches, made from blue-and-white striped ticking. The carving away of an additional half-inch of maple beneath the patch box would not weaken the stock, because the river maple was hard and the stock was thick on the other side, because of the depth of the cheek rest.

Jack had thought it the perfect hiding place.

Somebody would have to empty and dissemble the patch box before they had a clue something was hidden beneath. If he could recover the ghost rifle, the brass disk was almost sure to still be hidden in the stock.

"I have to go," Jack said. "Tonight I'll write in dead Martin's Bible the message from the chief. You can take that to Major Henry, and tell him I aim to see him at the Yellowstone River. But, come sunshine or thunder, I'm gone by first light."

9 The Pack

It had taken several hours for Johnston to die. He never woke up, and as he slipped closer to death, his breathing became increasingly ragged. He seemed about to rouse once, because he coughed and moaned, but his eyes did not open. Before he finally expired, his body shook with spasms, and his breathing took on a peculiar rattling quality. And then he wasn't breathing at all.

Decatur spread a blanket over him and said a few words from dead Martin's Bible. It ended with, *"Do not let your hearts be troubled and do not be afraid."*

After, Jack and Decatur ate elk steak beside the fire.

Jack used the point of his toothpick to trace the lines the hunter had drawn in the powder horn. Then he took some of the black greasy residue from around the breech of dead Martin's .45-caliber rifle and rubbed it into the lines, darkening them, and then he wiped away the residue. The result was a fair imitation of the scrimshaw a sailor might have made from the tooth of a whale, but instead of a scene from life at sea, it was a map of the sea of grass that led into the uncharted heart of the Arikara nation.

Decatur fell asleep by the fire, turned on his side like a child.

Then Jack sharpened a pencil, opened dead Martin's Bible to the blank page inside the front, and by firelight wrote nearly word for word the message from Lightning Crow. When he was done, he read it over, and added a message to Major Henry: *I am sorry that I have not delivered this message in person, but I have gone after my rifle, which was stolen by the 'Ree chief. If I am not killed in the endeavor, I will see you and the rest of the company at the mouth of the Yellowstone.—YOS, Jack Picaro.*

Then Jack flipped to the back of the Bible, to the last page of the book of Revelation, and used his knife to neatly cut the page out. The chapter concluded at the top of the page with four short verses. The rest of the page was blank.

Jack propped the book on his knees, to make a flat surface, and below the last word on the page—*Amen*—he began to write.

14 April, 1822

Dearest Abella,

I regret that you have received no word of me these many weeks. It may be some months or even a year before this letter reaches you. My spirit is broken with sorrow because I was the cause of the terrible accident that took the life of your brother and my best friend, Aristide. I hope that someday you will find it in your heart to forgive me, because I will never forgive myself.

Presently, I am on a dangerous adventure to make my fortune, so that I may return someday to St. Louis and make such amends—to your uncle,

*to the law, and to you—as wealth allows. No
amount of specie, I know, will restore me in your
affections, but I hope that time and love might do
what gold cannot. It is my dearest wish that we
could be as we were before and, if you will have
me, marry and make our way in the world together.
If not, then I wish you happiness.*

Eternally, Jacques

*P.S. I am sending this message back to St. Louis
with a trusted friend, one who knows me as Jack
Picaro—as do all the company. You may trust
Decatur to arrange delivery of a reply, if you wish.*

Jack read the letter over and hesitated over the word
"affection." He crossed it out and wrote "love" in its place.
Then he folded the page twice, and held the square of
paper in his right hand for several minutes, staring at a portion of cryptic verse from John the Apostle . . . *may enter
in through the gates into the city. 15 For without* are *dogs,
and sorcerers, and whoremongers, and murderers, and
idolators, and whosover loveth and maketh a lie.*

Jack cast the thin page into the fire, where it was instantly consumed.

Jack did not sleep and left at the first blush of dawn,
while Decatur still slept, the Bible with the message for
Major Henry on the ground next to him.

In Jack's fringed possibles bag he stuffed the things he
had scavenged from the wreck of the boat: a full pound of
.45-caliber ball—just over 100 rounds—in a leather sack,
an assortment of flints, some iron needles and an awl,

some candles, a tin cup and a bag of coffee, a fire steel, a ball starter, a turnkey screwdriver, an oily rag, some patch material, and a tinderbox. The horn he wore slung over his shoulder was full of black powder, which he reckoned was just about enough to match the amount of lead he carried. He had a slouch hat, and a bedroll rolled into a tube and thrown across his back, and inside the roll a few pounds of the cooked elk meat, and some bread and cheese he had found.

As he walked into the prairie, the sun arced across a nearly cloudless sky. The land was rolling hills and grass, with cottonwoods and scrubby cedars lining the streams and creeks, and as he walked plagues of grasshoppers fled from his approach. Moths and butterflies floated over the prairie, and the meadowlarks and other birds were too many to count. On far hillsides, he often spotted antelope, but they kept a respectful distance, always beyond the range of his rifle as he traveled.

He kept his course by watching the sun and estimating where it would set, and trying to keep a bearing of about 30 degrees to the right of that spot. At first it seemed strange and a little frightening to be walking alone in an ocean of green with the dish of the sky above. He couldn't remember the last time he had been truly alone for any length of time, because during this flight from Missouri there always had been instances of asking somebody for some favor, or talking his way out of suspicion, and then on the keelboat there had been no privacy at all. By noon on the first day, however, he had begun to appreciate not having to speak to others or deal with their expectations, and slowly the ability to hear himself think returned, as when he would work on a particularly challenging mechanical problem at the gun shop. But the only work here was to place one foot in front of the other, try not to stumble over some dead wood or a rock hidden in the grass, keep an eye on the sun, and imagine what might be the best strategy to adopt when he finally caught up with Lightning Crow.

But, as time passed, the practicality of developing a strategy was pushed out of his mind by the sheer size of the prairie and the variety of creatures that lived there. The air here was clean, better smelling than that of the muddy river and certainly better than the stinking keelboat, and there was a satisfaction in simply breathing. As the sun finally met the horizon he stopped, at the edge of a clear-flowing stream, and set up camp beneath a cottonwood. He didn't make a fire because he didn't want to announce his presence, but he had plenty to eat. He ate several chunks of the bread, because it would go bad first, and then some of the cheese and the cold elk meat. He ate his fill and washed it down with cupfuls of water from the stream and wondered if this was the kind of place the Indians took the beavers that would be turned into stacks of pelts and traded for bad whiskey, cheap iron tomahawks, and other truck. Then he spread his bedroll and stretched out, his hands behind his head staring at the sky but with dead Martin's rifle within reach. The sky went a kind of blue he had seen before in paintings, and the evening star was the first to appear, twinkling like a beacon in the west.

He realized he was satisfied, for the first time in many long months.

Oh, he knew he was not permanently satisfied—there were still the matters of the rifle and his broken indenture and the murder of his best friend—but for the present, he was content. He vaguely missed cards and more sharply longed for liquor and women, but those were pursuits that came with civilization, and to be free of civilization might be worth the loss. Then he thought of Abella, and his feelings for her were not so easily dismissed; he suffered from a mixture of shame and loneliness and a desire again to see her fine-featured shape and hold her yielding body against his. But these feelings he managed to drive out of his mind with the thought that, in time, and once he had made his fortune, all could be set right with her.

Then he slept.

He woke in the middle of the night to the sound of something cautiously moving in the grass on the opposite side of the stream. The sky had clouded up now and it was dark in the deepest way. His hand went to the rifle and he sat up. Although he looked hard in the darkness for what was making the sound, all he saw were spots. Then, in the distance, some coyotes began to yip and talk to each other, and they made so much commotion it was difficult to hear anything subtle.

The feeling that he was at the mercy of something that could not easily be seen or heard made the hair on the back of his neck rise. Was it an Indian or an animal? He thought of the mangy huge bear with its great teeth at Clark's museum. Jack put the rifle aside, fumbled for his possibles bag, found the flint and steel inside, and took a pinch from the tinderbox. Then he struck a spark, several times, until he had ignited a ball of grease and tinder. He did all this with a maximum of fuss and noise, hoping to scare away whatever had been lurking in the dark.

He held the wick of the beeswax candle against the small blue flame, and when it had caught, blew out the grease and tinder ball. He cupped a hand behind the candle, to better throw the light ahead of him and to shield it from his sight. On the other side of the stream a pair of pale eyes were reflected in the candlelight, two pale glowing dots in a broad face. It was a timber wolf, and in the flickering candlelight Jack could tell it was a big one. It must have weighed as much or more than Jack did—150 pounds. The wolf opened its mouth like a dog, revealing a row of white teeth and a lolling pink tongue. It cocked its head, taking in the scent of the elk steaks that were bundled in a cloth near the bedroll.

"Go!" Jack said.

The timber wolf growled, a sound that began low and rose in pitch, competing with and then surpassing the idle chatter of the coyotes. The howl seemed impossibly long. When the howl finally ended, the wolf shook its head, snarled, and bared its teeth.

Jack drew the rifle to him with the hand not holding the candle, and the wolf's head swiveled as it took in the movement. Now Jack see could that other pale eyes glowed behind the snarling wolf, the rest of the pack, waiting to see what the leader would do.

"Git!" Jack shouted.

The big wolf lowered its head and pawed the ground, as if in indecision. Then another wolf tried to slip past, its nostrils wide with the small of the elk steak, and the big wolf turned on this rival in an instant. They fought furiously, biting and pawing, tumbling in the grass and splashing down into the stream.

With the candle in one hand and the rifle in the other, Jack backed away from the bedroll, putting some more yards between himself and the fight. Then he watched as the big wolf rose up on its hind legs and advanced on the rival, its forepaws slashing and teeth snapping, seeming for a moment to fight almost as a man does. The rival yelped in pain as the big wolf snapped away a chunk of flesh and fur from behind an ear, and then the fight was over. The defeated wolf ran into the grass, and the big wolf remained for a moment, turning its head toward Jack and fixing him with its glowing eyes, its muzzle bloody with the other wolf's blood.

Then the big wolf turned and walked slowly away, and the eyes of the pack winked out in pairs as they turned to follow. Jack held the candle for a moment longer, then blew it out.

Now, even the coyotes were silent.

10 *Village of the Dead*

In the next week Jack reckoned he must have crossed a hundred miles of prairie. Using the sun and the map on the powder horn as guides, he continued in a northwesterly direction, one foot in front of the other. His feet swelled until his boots were difficult to remove at night, and the blisters on his heel and toes burned like fire. His feet bled, staining his socks and seeping through the stitching of his boots, and while he slowed he never stopped walking.

Sometimes it seemed as if he was walking endlessly over the same patch of ground, because one rolling hill of grass looked much like another to him. He was still glad to be alone, but each day's travel—which began at dawn and did not end until there was barely enough light to pitch camp—left him a little more weary than the day before. He was also hungrier each day than the one before. The bread had gone first, followed by the cheese. He had thrown aside the elk meat on the morning of the fourth day because it had begun to putrefy. For the next day he had nothing to eat, and although he saw a deer and two antelope within killing distance, he did not shoot because he was afraid the report would summon enemies. On the next day, he tried the grass he had seen the animals eat, but it soured his stomach, and he threw up what little he had eaten. The back of his head still ached from the blows he had received from Lightning Crow's men, and the throbbing was worse as he leaned forward on his knees and retched.

On the morning of the seventh day, he decided he must kill the next animal he saw. It was a pronghorn, standing on a hillside below the rest of a small herd. As Jack approached, the herd began to move up the hill and over the crest, but this antelope that was lower on the slope had tarried for some reason, and in a moment, Jack was sitting in the grass, his elbows on his knees, and dead Martin's rifle in his hands. The antelope was 150 yards away, turned three-quarters in the opposite direction, and Jack chose a spot just behind the ribs he reckoned would take the ball into the heart and lungs. He squeezed the trigger and the hammer fell and sparked the pan, and there was a fraction of a second's lag before the main charge went off.

Jack stood in the drifting smoke.

He watched as the antelope bounded up the slope and over the crest. He expected the animal to drop immediately. Surely, Jack thought, the target was mortally wounded and had used the last of its life in one burst of energy. But when Jack had trotted over to the hillside where the animal had stood, there wasn't a drop of blood anywhere on the grass. When he topped the hill, he saw there was no sign of any creature, living or dead. He had made a clean miss with dead Martin's gun.

Jack cursed the gun loudly and fully, holding it in one hand and shaking it as if it were a living thing that would understand the chastisement. He wanted to toss the gun as far as he could throw it, but did not. When the rage subsided, he lowered the muzzle and brought the gun close to his right eye, examining the rear sight. The leaf was centered on the top of the barrel, the elevation screw was set properly for middling ranges, and the dovetail mount did not move when he pressed his thumb against it. Then he put the butt of the rifle on the ground and examined the front sight, which was a blade of brass pinched by an iron wedge in the octagonal barrel and set back from the muzzle by an inch and a half or so. The sight must have been jarred during the battle at the keelboat, because the wedge was nudged about a sixteenth of an inch to the left in the dovetail groove.

Now Jack cursed himself. He had checked the lock and the pan when he had loaded the rifle, but had only glanced at the front sight. He should have looked more carefully, because the small fraction of an inch that it had been jarred had caused him to miss the antelope by yards.

He sat down on the hillside with the muzzle across his lap and used the edge of the flint steel to hammer the wedge that held the front sight back into place. He centered it as perfectly as he could by eye, and he judged he could do little better even if he'd had a rule to work with, and while it would certainly be better, there was no guarantee that it would be in the exact right place. To do that, he'd have to shoot at paper and make adjustments, but he didn't have the paper and did not care to bang about repeatedly until the Arikaras found him.

After reloading the rifle, he continued on, expecting to see more antelope, but for the next three or four miles there was nothing but empty grass. He was so hungry his stomach churned, and all he could think about was food, even though he knew that men had survived for weeks without food when forced to. "But I don't want to be one of them," he said aloud.

In another mile, he came to a creek that was bigger than any he'd crossed yet, but still not broad enough to be called a river. He got his tin cup out of his bag, knelt on his heels, and scooped up some water. It was clear and good. He drank some more, then splashed some water on his face. He hadn't shaved since leaving the keelboat and he was surprised at the wiry beard that had taken root. He had shaved every day for his adult life, and the feel of the beard was alien to him, as if he had become someone new. Then he rose and, the water still dripping from his face, waded in the creek.

His boots left clouds of mud swirling in the water. The water was colder than he expected, and deeper, and with each step the creek came up over his calves and then his knees. He gave a little cry of surprise as the cold water reached his balls, and he held the rifle over his head for fear that he would step into an even deeper hole. But in a few more steps he could feel the sand and the gravel rising beneath his feet again, the cold recede from his private parts, and soon he was on the other side.

"That will wake you up," Jack said.

He had taken to talking to himself in the last few days, and the longer he was alone, the more frequently he did it. When he wasn't talking, sometimes he would hum tunes he remembered from childhood, and at other times he would softly whistle. Sometimes it would be a song, and at other times it would be imitating the cry of some bird or the sound of the wind in the grass. Sometimes he would launch into a spirited lecture about the art of making weapons, jabbing his finger into the air as if making a point before a room full of apprentices. "The Secret of Steel," he would thunder, "is also the secret to forging the character of men." And he would rehearse this lecture over and over until he knew every word was true. And at other times, when he had been walking and the gears of his mind were idling, he would surprise himself by simply whispering, "Abella."

He was glad the day was warm because the cold from the creek still clung to him, and when the sun went behind a cloud, he shivered. He stopped and peeled off his wet trousers and hung them on a scrubby bush on the sunny side of a low hill, and then pulled his shirt off and placed it on the ground to sit on. He wished he had brought some water with him from the creek, so that he would dare a small fire and brew some coffee in his tin cup, but back at the keelboat he could find no canteen or skin that had not been punctured or burned. Some coffee might help fight his hunger. There were yellow and red berries on the scrubby bush. He tasted one, but spat it out because it was bitter.

He sat cross-legged for a long time, trying not to think about food, and finally out of boredom he lay back on his elbows and turned his face up to the cloudless sky. A buzzard was wheeling overhead, making its way slowly to the northwest, and Jack watched it and tried to calculate how far away it was. Six or seven hundred yards, he decided, and the distance increasing with each lazy circle. As the buzzard continued its journey to the horizon, Jack noticed for the first time some bumpy hillocks beneath the bird. When he looked more closely, he realized that they were too regular to be hillocks at all, and he could see masts poking up above some of them, with fur or rags fluttering in the breeze. The hillocks were lodges.

It was a village.

Jack made himself small and remained still, looking for any movement, but saw only the fluttering things. He sat watching until his trousers were nearly dry, then he dressed and began walking slowly toward the village, dead Martin's rifle in the crook of his arm.

As he approached the village, he encountered a flat-topped mound, and as he climbed it the earth crunched and crumbled beneath his feet, like slate. As Jack topped the mound, his right boot sank into a soft spot and he nearly tripped. At first, he thought it was a den of some kind, and he hoped it was a home for rabbits and not rattlesnakes. But as he pulled the boot out something with teeth came with it, and he stood staring at it for a moment before he realized it was a human jawbone. He squatted and peered into the hole and saw a broken skull, many pieces of shell, a few beads, fish heads, and scattered teeth of various sizes. As he looked over the mound, there were the domes of other skulls peeking up through the dirt, along with mussel shells, and ribs, broken stone tools, vertebrae, long bones, and corncobs that crumbled to dust when touched by his boots.

He realized he was standing on a midden pile that had, in its last use, been a mass graveyard. The idea spooked him. He imagined the desperate last days of the village, with the dead being thrown on the community rubbish heap. Had this been a Mandan village or Arikara? He feared what Lightning Crow's reaction would be to his accidentally crushing the skull of one of his relatives beneath his boot.

He whispered a prayer to St. Ignatius and also to the goddess Mari.

As Jack made his way down the mound, he found other skeletons, full length upon the ground and with scraps of clothing, their bones bleached by the sun and made delicate by the passing of the seasons, and these dead appeared to have died where they had fallen. Jack had the feeling that their sightless eyes were watching him as he picked his way among them, careful not to crush any more bones underfoot.

As he left the mound of bones and trash behind, he could see more of the village spread out before him, and instead of the five or six round lodges he had spied from beneath the scrubby bush, he realized there were many dozens of them. The lodges were all arrayed around a broad flat spot that must have looked like a parade grounds once, but which now was choked with grass and weeds. The village was as dead as the burial ground had been, and perhaps had been for years.

With the exception of a bigger lodge on the other side of the parade grounds, each lodge was of the same size— about forty feet across—with a framework of timbers providing the structure for which the earth and sod had been laid. Each lodge had an entrance that faced the center of the village, and each of these entries were deep and lined with timber, including a porch-like awning that provided shade in summer and kept the rain and snow away from the doorway in winter. There were poles set in the ground on either side of the entrances, and from the top of the poles were the fluttery things that he had seen from the top of the graveyard hill. He recognized animal skins and bits of cloth, but he did not know what they meant.

In the center of the plaza was a strange kind of circular fence, made from cottonwood planks that extended to nine or ten feet high, and tightly bound by rope. Its purpose puzzled Jack, because it wasn't big enough to hold any kind of animals or much else—at most, it was eight feet in diameter, and there was no door or gate. He approached the bundled fence cautiously and, when he peered through a crack in the weathered planks, the mystery deepened, because the only thing the fence contained was a cedar pole in the center.

As he walked about, Jack realized the front side of the village was hugging the bank of a river. Jack did not know the name of the river, and it was not indicated on his powder horn, but he could see the tops of trees and hear the rush of the current and see the glint of water far off, as the river curved back north.

He walked over and stood in front of the largest lodge, which was like the others in everything but size and shape. This lodge was twice as large as the others and more oblong. This was the lodge of a chief, and as Jack planned to eventually confront a chief where he lived, it would be good to know what was inside.

A pair of crows sat on one of the four supporting timbers that protruded from the top of the lodge, and they watched as Jack approached. They shifted about on the weathered wood, pointed their beaks first this way, and then the next, tilting their heads for a better view. Finally, one of them gave a brief cry and took flight, followed by the other.

He stepped beneath the portico and into the lodge, pausing just inside the dark doorway. He could feel the cool air of the lodge on his face and hands. There was a timbered screen just inside the doorway, and he followed this to the right to emerge in the interior of the lodge, which except for a hole in the roof above was all darkness. He waited for his eyes to adjust, and gradually the interior took shape. They floor was packed earth, and there was a raised, long-cold firepit in the center of the lodge, surrounded by four timbers that went to the roof and were wrapped in animal skins—bison, antelope, elk, bear. There were stalls built of wood and thatch around the edges of the lodge, and the biggest of these, on his right, had evidence of having been used as a stable for one or two horses. The other stalls appeared to be sleeping areas, with chairs and mats made of reeds. One stall on the far side was apparently some kind of altar, with beads and rocks and other things arranged over a large upright stone. To Jack's left was a latticework of willow branches, and from these branches were laced the blackened and shriveled skins of what had once been pumpkins and squash. There were also clusters of gourds, and some of them had been shellacked and painted with birds and turtles.

In the earth floor there were cache pits, and Jack squatted and removed the wooden lid of one, revealing what had been left of a store of corn and beans being corrupted by time and rodents. In its day, Jack thought, this would have been a comfortable place to spend the winter—and he thought of William Clark. In the center of the top of the lodge was a square hole to allow smoke to escape, and through this streamed a shaft of sunlight, illuminating a jumble of reeds and bones near the edge of the firepit.

These must have been the most important seats in the lodge, an arrangement of reed backrests facing the firepit, opposite the entrance, where the chief held council and received visitors. And here, Jack saw, the chief of the village remained. His buckskin-adorned skeleton was draped over the biggest backrest, a rotting feathered headdress nearby, the rib cage on the backrest but the skull on the ground with jaw agape, as if laughing at the smallpox that had killed him. His black hair was piled nearby, and still contained bits of shell and bone. Near one skeleton arm was a buffalo shield, decorated with eagle quills and antelope hooves. Near the other arm was a long medicine pipe with a cedar shaft and a red bowl carved in the shape of a bird.

On the earthen floor, where it had fallen, was an oval gorget of hammered copper that had once swung beneath the chief's neck. It was tarnished green and blue with age, but when Jack held it in the light, he could see a pattern of square crosses and dots at the edges. In the center was etched a grinning coyote with six legs.

"Why six legs?" Jack asked.

Jack wondered why the lodge had not been looted. He had heard on the keelboat that the Indians were superstitious and would quickly disassociate themselves from talk of death, would not speak the names of the dead, and would not remain where death had been. But here Jack saw not superstition but practicality—it only made sense to get far away from the pestilence, and quickly.

"What was your name?" Jack asked the chief. "What was your village called? Did you kill many warriors in battle? How many wives did you have, and what became of your children?"

The only answer was the sound of the breeze in the grass outside.

Jack coveted the pipestone bird, but his gambler's instinct told him to be careful. The bird might be too important to steal. It was the same with the objects on the altar: there were odd black rocks, beads, shells, elk horns, antelope hooves, and leather bags presumably full of power.

He picked up one of the pitted black rocks and found it strangely heavy, and knew it contained iron or other metals of some kind, then put it back.

He turned away from the altar.

"Chief, I am powerfully hungry," he said. "Is there anything in your lodge fit to eat? No, I thought not."

He walked back to the skeleton and stared down at the pipestone bird, and the desire to possess it grew. It would be a simple matter to snap the cedar stem and slip the bird into his bag. He knelt, and his hand reached out for the pipe, but then he heard one of the crows scolding him from overhead. He looked up and saw the pair of birds walking nervously around the edge of the smoke hole, thirty feet above him.

"You're right," he told the birds and withdrew his hand.

Then he looked over at the coyote gorget.

"Would you blame me for taking this?" Jack asked the crows. "It's copper. I might be able to use it for some small repair to a lock or other device. And the coyote amuses me."

The crows were silent.

He picked up the gorget and the leather string attached to the ends fell to pieces. He blew the dust away from the etching of the coyote and then used some spit on the ball of his thumb to reveal more. The coyote with the six legs stood on the tips of its many paws with the hair on its back bristling and its tail erect, as if it had been charged with lightning.

Jack slipped the gorget into his bag and looked back up at the smoke hole. The crows were gone, but he glimpsed a great white bird flapping past far overhead, and he took it for one of the river birds that scooped up fish. Suddenly cold, Jack longed for the warmth of the sun.

He left the lodge and made his way past the strange fenced object in the center of the village and left the village in the direction he had come but detoured around the midden pile. When he was a mile clear of the village, he paused and jerked a long whang string from the fringe of his possibles bag and threaded it through the holes in the gorget. Then he slipped the copper crescent over his head and tucked it beneath his shirt. The copper wasn't strong, but it might be enough to slow a trade point or deflect a flint before it pierced his windpipe.

11 *The Storm*

Jack continued walking, using the horn as a guide, and for the next three days came to no more villages, living or dead—and no more game. In one meadow, he found an unmistakable sign of where a buffalo herd had passed. The moist earth and grass had been kneaded into mush, there were several circular places where the beasts had lain and rolled, and there were dozens of nearly fresh buffalo chips the size of dinner plates. He considered following the herd and taking a calf with dead Martin's rifle, but the tracks led to the south, in the opposite direction of Lightning Crow's village. Surely, Jack told himself, he would come upon more antelope or perhaps deer, and then his fast would end.

As the day wore on, he would occasionally spy a rabbit bounding ahead of him, but unless he could find one sitting still it would be a waste of powder and ball. A shotgun was needed to take such small game—or a snare, which he did not know how to make—and even if he could find one obliging enough to remain still enough to be shot, there wouldn't be much left from the .45-caliber round. But no larger game presented itself.

The days grew hotter and, as he grew weaker, he took to walking only in the early mornings and the late afternoons. At midday, he would find whatever shade was available—a bush, a rock outcropping—and sleep.

When he was walking, he was in a stupor, and his reactions dulled. When he did by chance jump a deer that had been sleeping in the grass, he was so slow bringing the rifle to his shoulder that the animal was gone before he could get his sights on it. Realizing he had missed his opportunity again, he wondered how long it would be before he was on his hands and knees trying to catch field mice to eat.

On the fourth day after leaving the village of the dead Jack encountered the river again, as it had looped back into his path, and as he stood on its curving bank, he consulted the powder horn and concluded it must be the Cheyenne. Surely, he must be close to Lightning Crow's village now. As he made his way down the bank to a sandbar nestled next to the bank, on the outer curve of the river, he startled three deer who were standing ankle-deep in the water, drinking. It was a doe and two fawns, and in an instant, he had dead Martin's rifle upon them, but he hesitated. If he were too near Lightning Crow's village, the shot would surely summon the Indians, and he was too weak to put up much of a fight. He cursed, lowered the rifle, and sat down to ponder his predicament.

Looking out over the river, he could see the dorsal fins of some fish as long as his arm working in the shallows, and he desperately wished he had taken some fishhooks and tackle from the boat when he had the chance. He could use his knife to carve some hooks from some twigs, but without any type of line, it would be wasted effort. Then he thought of the awl he had in his bag, and he set about finding the thickest and straightest piece of driftwood with which to make a spear.

After some searching, he found a river maple branch and used the Damascus toothpick to remove the twigs and smooth down the knots. It was reasonably straight and about an inch in diameter. The awl was double-pointed, with a crooked tang in the middle, and he drove one end into his newly made spear shaft. He used several pieces of whang leather tied around the crook to secure it to a couple of notches carved in the shaft. Then he plunged the awl end of the shaft into the shallow water for a few minutes to thoroughly soak the leather, and then he let it dry in the sun. As the leather dried, it made the knots tighter than Jack could have ever managed by hand.

It had taken hours to make the spear, and by the time Jack was done, it was near dark. Leaving his rifle, bag, and boots on the bank, Jack walked out on a curving sandbar and watched for the green and red fins of the carp that were feeding in the shallows. With the first one he tried to spear, he made the mistake of placing a foot partially into the water, and the fish nearly jumped out of the water getting away. With the second, he kept his feet on the sand but allowed his shadow to cross the water, and the carp swam away. But with the third, he took his time and crept slowly out onto a narrow spit of a sandbar, next to where one of the carp was working, and was careful to keep his feet out of the water and his shadow behind him. The fish worked back and forth in the channel, sucking things from the bottom, sometimes coming nearer and then moving farther away. Jack waited. When it was almost too dark to see, the fish moved close to him, and Jack slowly cocked the awl spear behind his head. When the fish revealed all of its dorsal fin and six inches of scaly back, Jack struck, driving the point of the awl into the thick part below the carp's backbone, and then he leaned on the shaft to drive the point of the awl through the fish and pin it to the bottom. The fish jerked fiercely for many minutes, pumping its blood into the river, and then gradually the spasms slowed and then stopped. Jack knelt and shoved his fingers into the carp's mouth and dragged the fish up onto the sandbar. Then he unsheathed his toothpick, gutted the fish, threw the offal into the river, and carried the carcass back to the bank.

With his knife and hands, he dug a hole about a foot across in the soft earth of the riverbank, packed it with driftwood, and used his flint and steel and the tinder to light it. He sliced steaks by making several straight cuts through the carp's backbone and sides, and he laid these on top of a lattice of twigs over the hole. He knew fire was a risk, but he could not stomach the idea of eating the fish raw. The blaze would be small and the night would make it difficult to see the smoke. The thought of having hot food and perhaps a cup of coffee was enough to ease his caution.

He boiled the coffee in the tin cup alongside the fish, handling the cup gingerly with a piece of cloth so as not to burn his fingers. When he ate, there were many soft bones, but he chewed it all and swallowed and was grateful. The coffee was thick with grounds but was strong and hot. He ate all of the flesh he had carved from the fish, even the parts that still had coppery scales clinging to them, which he had to spit out or use his fingers to remove from his mouth. Then he made more coffee, and drank that, being more careful this time to sip and keep the grounds in the bottom of the cup.

When he finished the meal, he smothered the fire, then climbed the bank and found a spot beneath a cottonwood tree to spread his bedroll and sleep. He was tired, and he felt the pull of the earth like a weight. Free from hunger, he was asleep quickly. In his dreams, he was back in St. Louis, first gambling with Aristide at The Grackle and then talking to the whore named Chelley, and Bledsoe was throwing the knife to split the apple between her legs, and as the knife struck, he realized it was not the whore at all that held the apple but Abella. Bledsoe had missed, and Abella had taken the blade in her womb. She lay dying on the filthy puncheon floor, curled up around the handle of Bledsoe's knife Biter.

Abella looked up at Jack and asked him why.

Jack woke in a sweat. He sat up and threw the blanket off, staring into the darkness and listening to the sound of the wind in the leaves. For the first time since leaving the keelboat, he wished for some company. He tried talking to himself, but the sound of his own voice in the darkness was disquieting. Eventually, he stretched out again and slept.

An hour before dawn Jack was jolted awake by a peal of thunder that rattled the leaves of the cottonwood and shook the ground beneath him. He sat up, disoriented, until it began to splatter rain, and then he scooted back against the trunk of the cottonwood, drew his knees up, and pulled the blanket tight around him. It was a wool blanket, so it retained warmth even when wet, but it did nothing to keep him dry. The blanket was dull gray except for a muted band of red on one end and blue on the other, meant to appeal as a trade good to the Indians of the Upper Missouri.

Soon it was raining in sheets. Water began puddling beneath him, and he shifted to try to find a better spot, and eventually he sat on his heels. He pulled dead Martin's rifle to him, wrapped the oiled rag around the lock, and then put his possibles bag on top of that, in an attempt to keep moisture out of the pan.

Then the rain slacked and it seemed to Jack the storm had nearly passed. He was gathering his things, about to go looking for a spot on drier ground to get a last bit of sleep in before dawn, when it began to hail.

It started small at first, about the size of peas, knocking leaves and twigs from the cottonwood and collecting in pockets on the ground. Then the hail grew in size and intensity, and when a stone the size of a marble bounced from the trunk of the cottonwood and hit the back of his head, he huddled under the blanket for protection and scooted back beneath the tree.

There was a brilliant flash, and his surroundings were captured for a moment in unnatural detail before plunging again into darkness. The lightning had been close, because it took only a second or two for the thunder to come and rattle Jack's teeth. Then another bolt of lightning struck, just thirty yards away, in a blast of sparks and a shock wave that made Jack cover his head with his hands. When he dared look, he saw the bolt had split a tree like the one he sat under, leaving the trunk a splintered and smoldering stub. When Jack realized he held dead Martin's rifle upright in his hand—a length of iron that was a serviceable lightning rod just inviting a strike—he released the gun as if it had bitten him and allowed it to fall. Then he crawled away a distance and made himself as flat as he could, his face pressed against the cold mud.

By dawn, the storm had passed.

Jack rose wearily and began to collect his things from where they had been scattered in his panic. He was still cold, and he shivered while he worked. All of his possessions were soaked, except for some of the contents of his possibles bag and the powder in his horn. Dead Martin's rifle was of particular concern, because water dribbled out of the barrel when he picked it up. When he put the action at half-cock and lifted the frizzen, he saw the powder in the pan had turned to a kind of mush.

"Dammit, Jacky," he said. "This is what comes of your cowardice."

He would have to pull the ball and empty the load from the barrel, clean the pan, somehow dry and oil the breech and all of the small and hidden parts in the lock. It would have taken only twenty minutes or so at his workbench in St. Louis, but here in the mud it would take hours. The sun and air would do the drying.

With shaking hands, he searched inside the possibles bag until he found the turnkey screwdriver. Then he went to a log that was flat enough to place the rifle on, with the lock facing up. Kneeling, he began the disassembly. By the middle of the morning he had the rifle back together, and he fired a couple of loose half charges, tamped only by a patch, to help dry the breech. The charges made soft sizzling sounds and produced only embers and blue smoke. Satisfed, he wiped everything down with the oily rag and, after a few minutes' wait, loaded a full charge, seated a patched ball, and primed the pan.

He made his bedroll, gathered the rest of his things, cut the awl from the end of the spear and threw it back into the possibles bag. He looked at the sun, orienting himself to north on the map etched into the powder horn, and set off walking once again.

12 *How Like Wolves*

Jack reasoned that if he kept the river on his right, and kept in a northerly direction, he would soon reach the village where the hunter Johnston had last known Lightning Crow to live. By trying to keep the river in sight, he found himself being led astray as it made a great horseshoe bend. It seemed shorter to cut across a series of low hills and pick up the river on the other side, as the map on the horn suggested. So he changed course and walked until nightfall, and there was no sign of the river. The grassy hills had gradually turned into rock-strewn hills, and he realized that there was nothing on the powder horn map to help him find his way.

He slept beneath a clear sky on one of the rocky ledges, and as he slept the hunger returned. He woke ravenous. The morning was bright and clear, and there was no wind, and the hill was covered with grasshoppers and other insects.

He caught a bright yellow and green grasshopper in his right hand and studied it, debating on whether he could eat it. The hopper squirmed and felt like a tiny machine against his palm, angular and sharp, with trapped wings trying to beat. The large black eyes were set in a face that resembled a horned and armored mask. He watched the tiny jaws work back and forth and eventually produce something that looked like tobacco on his hand. Disgusted, he crushed the insect with his thumb, threw the remains away, and wiped his hand on his trouser.

"Maybe today I will shoot something," he said.

He continued walking in the direction he reckoned was north, but by midday had seen no sign of the river. The rocky hills had again yielded to grass, but grass that was heavier than that which he had passed before. Some of the grass reached above his head, and at times it felt like trying to find his way out of a green maze. As he walked, he tore off some of the broad blades of this different grass and folded them in his mouth, but after a bit of chewing all he could taste was bitter, and he spat the mess out.

He could not now remember how long it had been since he left the boat. Had it been two weeks? Three? The back of his head no longer ached, but the rest of him did. He was tired, no matter how long he slept, and the drudgery of walking grated on him. His feet had toughened so that they no longer bled, but he no longer walked with purpose. It was hard to remember in which direction he had been traveling. His pace slowed and the amount of distance he covered diminished and he found himself longing to simply lie in the grass and be still. He passed within easy shooting distance of game—an antelope, a doe with fawns—but no longer had the will to lift the rifle.

Then, one clear morning when the sun rose like a burning bush in the eastern sky, he woke and realized he was no longer hungry.

He remained on his back, and swiveling his head to take

in a world that shimmered and shone and seemed newly created. He could smell the rain coming in from some distant plain and hear the small birds twittering in the scrub nearby and feel the warmth radiating up from the ground into his back and thighs. He marveled that he had been so worried about things when all had worked out as it should.

He was still there, on his back in the eternal moment, when the sun dipped toward the west and delirious, he could hear the sound of God walking in the garden in the cool of the day.

And the Lord asked, *Where is thy brother?*

"I don't know," Jack replied, turning his face to the ground. "Am I my brother's keeper?"

What hath thou done? the Lord asked. *The voice of thy brother's blood crieth unto me from the ground.*

"It was an accident," Jack cried. "I didn't mean to kill Aristide."

And now art thou cursed from the earth, which hath opened her mouth to receive thy brother's blood from thy hand, said the Lord. *When thou tillest the ground, it shall not henceforth yield unto thee her strength; a fugitive and a vagabond shalt thou be in the earth.*

"My punishment is greater than I can bear," Jack said and sobbed.

And then he felt the spirit of the Lord walk past.

Jack sat up and rubbed the tears from his eyes with the palms of his hands and, dimly in the back of his mind, the thought began to grow that he had lost his reason.

Tillest the ground.

He knew he was on the verge of madness, but in his unraveling mind there was still a dim spark. What did it mean?

Tillest the ground.

He was so tired that he feared he could not rise, but he forced himself to his feet, and stumbled the few yards to the scrubby bushes, from which the birds had long flown.

He drew the Damascus toothpick from his belt and began to stab madly at the earth around of the bushes, loosening the earth and cutting through the tangled roots, then he tossed the knife aside and began to claw with his hand and fingers. Soon his fingertips touched some cold and wiggling thing, and he popped the grub into his mouth, still wiggling, and chewed it to pulp. If it had a taste, it was overpowered by the texture of it, the feel of its many tiny legs, and the squishing-popping sensation between his teeth. He chewed, then swallowed, and went back to the dirt to dig with his hands for more.

It was summer and the season for beetle larvae to turn into grubs, and there were many more in the rotting leaves and earth around the roots, sightless and white and wiggling. He ate several handfuls of the grubs and then slumped to the grass.

He spent the night there, where he had eaten the grubs, and did not move even when a light rain came. In the morning, he pulled his knife from the dirt, wiped it on his trousers, and put it in his scabbard. He walked over to where dead Martin's rifle was, next to his blanket. He cleaned the damp powder from the pan and measured a fresh charge from the horn. Then he gathered his things, slung his bag across his shoulders, and set off with the rifle in the crook of his arm.

That afternoon Jack crested a hill and saw a broad meadow, where three hundred yards away were a small herd of bison, slowly moving black-brown oblongs on a sea of grass. His heart hammered against his ribs as he crept along a limestone outcropping to get a better vantage. In a break in the rocks he made himself comfortable, shouldered the rifle, and rested his left elbow on a stone as a brace.

He brought the hammer to full cock, nestled the rifle stock against his cheek, and looked over the iron sights to pick a target.

The bison were arranged in an arc below him, with a cow and her calf closest to Jack. He sighted on the calf, placing the front blade sight in the notch of the rear sight. He adjusted for elevation but not wind, since not a blade of grass was stirring in the meadow below. He was almost ready to squeeze the trigger when the calf turned, his head down but pointing toward Jack, presenting a narrow target. But the cow was still broadside to him. He swung the barrel slightly to the left, sighting on the cow, adjusting for elevation, and squeezed the trigger.

The rifle bucked against his shoulder.

Peering through the haze of smoke, he could see the cow still on her feet, as before. How could he have missed? "Damned sights," Jack said under his breath as he quickly withdrew the ramrod and went about the business of reloading. None of the animals seemed to have spooked or even taken notice of the sound of the rifle, as they were still in their relative positions in the herd.

Jack had just finished tamping down the ball and was withdrawing the rod from the barrel when he saw the cow sink to her front legs. It took another second or two for the rest of her to fall, but when she did, he could see the dust billow up from her coat.

"Ah," Jack said.

As Jack walked down to the meadow, the herd barely moved, their heads down and their tails switching occasionally at flies. As he grew closer, the calf and some of the cows began to move off, but a bull hung back, his head lifted and nostrils sampling the air. Sunlight glinted from his black horns. The cow, which was less than half the size of some of the bulls, was probably the biggest animal that dead Martin's .45-caliber rifle could be expected to take. Jack sat on his heels for a few minutes until the bull forgot about him and moved off to join the harem at the far end of the meadow.

Standing over the carcass, Jack marveled at the size of the cow. She must have weighed 800 pounds. He could now see from the hole in her hide that he had hit her lower than intended; he had aimed behind the shoulder, but the ball had entered a bare patch of skin just behind the elbow. The shot must have pierced a lung, because blood had sprayed from her nostrils and splattered the grass with her last breaths.

The smell of the blood was metallic and reminded him of fresh beef, and his mouth began to salivate. There was a mountain of meat in front of him, but how to get to it was a puzzle. He placed a hand on the rough hide, feeling how thick it was beneath his fingers, and how warm still.

"Thank you," he said.

It was going take some time to carve out some meat from the shoulder or the hump, and he wanted meat now. He went to the animal's massive head, grabbed one of the horns, and with difficulty turned the head so that the tongue slipped from one side of the mouth. The tongue was broad and pointed, banded mostly black on top, and pale pink elsewhere. He grabbed hold of the black tip and stretched the tongue six or eight inches, then used the knife to cut and saw it away. The skin of the tongue was rubbery, but the inside was tender, and he used his teeth to tear small chunks away. He chewed slowly, so as not to choke, the tongue in one hand and his knife in the other, the rifle in the crook of his arm, his sunken eyes scanning the edges of the meadow for trouble. The sound of the shot would have carried for miles.

After eating the tongue, Jack was thirsty.

He took the tin cup from his possibles bag and drove the Damascus toothpick into the neck of the cow, releasing a torrent of blood. Jack filled the cup and drank. It was warm and thick and tasted of salt and copper and iron. He filled another cup and drank it down, then stood with the blood dripping from his brushy beard and surveyed his kill.

He had a mountain of meat, and although he knew he could not carry all of it—it would take three or four men to do so—he aimed to pack up as much as he could. It would be easiest to take the meat from the exposed shoulder or flank, but he was curious to see where inside the creature the ball had stopped. The tongue and the blood had given him strength, and he aimed to use some of it.

Jack unslung his bag and placed it on the ground, then rested the rifle on top. Then he pulled his shirt over his head and tossed it next to the bag. The Damascus toothpick in hand, and the copper gorget shining warm in the sun, he leaned over and drove the point just below the ribs, then used both hands to draw the sharp blade through the tough hide, slowly exposing the guts.

They did not spill out as he expected, and he had to make another cut to make a flap in the cow's side, then reach in and grasp the ropy intestines with both hands and pull them out. They had an oddly sweet smell, like fermenting grass, and he knew from hearing Martin and Johnston talk that the hunters called them *boudins* and gobbled them raw or roasted them slowly over a fire. But his stomach was already tight with the tongue and the blood, and he could stand to eat no more. Eventually, the cow's intestines made a pile on the ground as big as he was. To get the rest of the vitals out, Jack had to duck inside the carcass to get up under the rib cage and cut away with the toothpick.

The knife had the wrong blade for this kind of work, but Jack had no other option. He had to sharpen his knife with a stone every five or ten minutes, and this slowed his progress, but he eventually dragged the liver and the heart and lungs from the cave of the ribs, his knees slipping in the blood and gore. The heart filled both of his hands, and he saw a hole in one side where his ball had pierced it. There was no exit wound in the heart, so he cut it open and found his misshapen ball in one of the chambers.

"Lucky shot," he told himself.

Now that he had the animal gutted, he began to laboriously peel the hide back from the ribs and shoulder. The work was exhausting. He had to use both hands and all of his strength to free even a few inches of hide, then cut through the sinew with the knife, and repeat the process. When he had exposed the cow's bare shoulder, he cut away twenty pounds of meat. He placed the meat on a strip of hide that he had placed faceup on the ground, a distance away from the rounded offal pile. He also put the heart and the liver on the hide.

Then he caught something from the corner of his eyes, several dark shapes slinking in the shadows at the edge of the meadow. At first he thought they were men, perhaps an Arikara war party. Or it could be some stragglers from the buffalo herd, which had slowly moved off to the north, with the exception of the calf, which stood unmoving in the meadow. Then Jack saw one of the shapes loping over a rise in the meadow, a hundred yards away.

It was a timber wolf, drawn by the scent of blood. There were other wolves behind it, but they were quick, and Jack could not count how many. At least six. Then the wolves stopped, and the leader stood on its haunches staring at him, waiting.

Jack looked at the sun, and realized there was only about half an hour of daylight remaining. He reached for his rifle, intent on killing the leader. It would be an easy shot. He didn't know if it was the same wolf he had seen before at the creek, but shooting the boldest one might drive the others away.

As Jack got into position, sitting on the ground, his elbows resting on his knees and the rifle leveled, the lead wolf bolted in a direction Jack had not anticipated. It was making a run for the calf, and the other wolves were close behind. By the time the calf had turned and began to run, the pack was upon it, snarling and biting. The calf bleated in terror and tried to kick them away, but the wolves were too quick. The pack clustered under the calf's throat, sharp teeth ripping at the soft flesh, and Jack could see a spray of crimson in the late-afternoon sun. It took the calf several minutes to die, and all the while the wolves were ripping away chunks of flesh from its neck and shoulders.

Jack sighed and surveyed the hundreds of pounds of meat that remained on the cow. He knew now he should have killed the calf because it had all the meat he would need and more, for less work. He had not known the cow was so massive when he had taken the shot, because the distance had deceived him. But now he had to abandon the kill or be prepared to fight the wolves for it that night.

And he knew the wolves would win.

He put on his shirt, stashed the twenty pounds of buffalo meat wrapped in hide into his bedroll, and slung the possibles bag over one shoulder. He rested the rifle over the other shoulder, with the cold steel barrel touching the back of his neck. He took one last look at the pack as it feasted on the calf. "How much like wolves are men," he said. The leader of the pack raised its head and stared back with pale eyes, unafraid.

13 *Broken Hand*

Jack followed the rock outcropping from where he had shot the buffalo cow to the north, out of the meadow and into the edge of a broken country with low hills and many more rocks. He spread his blanket up against one of the limestone chunks and slept deeply until just before dawn, when he awoke with a dream fresh in his mind.

In the dream, he had been flying.

He did not know how he could fly, because in the dream he was himself and not a bird, but somehow he could sail high over the twisting Missouri River with its many sandbars. It was daylight in the dream, and he was so high that he could survey hundreds of miles of the river. But his vision was sharp, and he could see the wreck of the *Jefferson*, charred and still half-submerged up against the unyielding worry. There were the graves of the men killed during the fight up on the high bluff, two dozen bed-sized mounds with a cedar post driven into the earth at the head of each grave, and the name of the occupant scratched into the wood. One of the graves had the name "Johnston."

His mind moved up the river to the mouth of the Missouri, to the mouth of the Yellowstone, where stern-faced Major

Henry was supervising the men in building a fort there. There was already a palisade on three sides, and a blockhouse, and swivel guns mounted on a platform. Smoke was rising from cooking pots, and men were lounging about, laughing and smoking clay pipes and playing cards, and Decatur was there, as well.

Then he went all the way down the river, past Westport, over the high bluffs at Lohman's Landing in the middle of the state of Missouri, and then to where the shining water joined the Mississippi. Bloody Island was just a little ways south, and then St. Louis. He hovered over the city like a cloud, looking down at the riverboats and the landing and the warehouses and the business district and his old haunts, the taverns and brothels. He could see people moving along the streets and at the riverfront, but try as he might, he could not find Abella.

He woke and thought about the dream while it grew light enough to travel. Then he gathered his things and set out, and although he was still weak, his mind was sharp and he knew his strength would return. He wanted to find a place where he could rest up for a couple of days, someplace that had shelter where he wouldn't be sleeping in the open, and maybe a hidden place to build a fire, and with water nearby.

Jack followed the low broken hills to the north, and the limestone outcroppings became more common and larger in size. The land was still prairie, but was a rougher kind of prairie than the tall grass he had passed through, with lower grass and many prickly-looking plants with blue and yellow flowers. He passed box canyons and potholes filled with water, where he lay on his stomach and drank.

About midday he drew close to a limestone outcropping that stood on a promontory overlooking a creek that meandered below. From one angle, the outcropping looked to Jack like a ship riding the crest of the hill, its prow in the wind, but after he had crossed the creek and began climbing, it seemed more like a many-turreted castle. When he reached the top of the hill he stood staring up at the cracked and fissured limestone walls, which rose a hundred feet above him. He climbed into one of the fissures in the limestone and followed it inside the outcropping, hoping he could find a spot to build a fire, shielded from his enemies. He had followed the passage about twenty feet into the limestone bluff when he discovered an opening at the base of the limestone faces, a half-moon of open space above a pile of smaller rocks, and chat that had fallen from above, threatening to hide the entrance. The opening was about two feet high, and Jack knelt and peered into it. He could feel a breeze on his face.

It was a cave.

He pushed himself into the opening, his rifle beside him. He had just gotten his chest and shoulders in when he found himself pitching headfirst in the dark down an incline of slippery clay. He landed in a jumble on a pile of rocky debris at the bottom, but broke neither himself nor the rifle.

The shaft of light coming from the mouth of the cave illuminated a spot on the opposite wall, and here the limestone was smooth and unweathered and a uniform beige color—and covered with drawings. In the spot of sunlight there was a double-humped animal of some kind, with round eyes and long ears and slender horns that went straight up from its head and resembled a harp. The animal had a calf below it, nursing. The animal didn't really resemble a buffalo, or anything else Jack had seen, but was more like the drawings of Egyptian oxen that he remembered from a picture book of the Bible times.

Around the strange animal were rows of carved antelope hooves, and to the left of that a sly coyote-looking figure like the one on the gorget. Around the coyote were stick figures that looked like men with upraised arms and hands with three fingers, and there were dots and crosses around them. Near that was a community of human handprints, fingers splayed, outlined with some kind of brick-colored dust or pigment sprayed around them.

Jack moved closer to the handprints.

He counted sixty-four hands, both left and right, all of adult size. He placed his own right hand in a handprint on the wall, wondering who had touched the stone before him, and how long ago it had been, how they had made the outline. He brought his other hand up to his mouth and softly blew, as if blowing pigment around his other hand. The outline his hand was in was about the size of his own hand, matching the contours of his own except for one detail— the artist's little finger had been badly broken and had healed bent. Jack looked at this telltale sign of individuality and smiled, for he had learned something about the maker.

As his eyes adjusted to the gloom, Jack could see the cave was about forty feet long and twenty feet across, its floor strewn with broken chunks of limestone. On one side, the ceiling sloped down to the floor and, on the other side, it seemed to disappear upward into a natural chimney.

Every flat surface in the cave was covered with art.

There were many more animals that resembled the two-humped cow, and more coyotes, antelopes, deer and elk. There were more human beings with triangular bodies and uplifted, three-fingered hands. Or perhaps, Jack thought, the hands didn't have three fingers at all, but perhaps were holding something instead.

Jack didn't know the significance of the cave, but it obviously held some special meaning for the Indians who had left their strange pictures on the walls here. Were these maps? Drawings to honor the dead? Or the cave might be a church, he thought, or perhaps a type of monument to historical events known now only to the artists.

Then he saw the offerings left at the base of the walls, beneath the drawings. There were shells, beads, tobacco, trade points, and copper bells. There were others who knew of the cave, even if they did not know any longer the stories it told.

And it was not a place they should find Jack.

This wasn't a place to stay long, but Jack was seized by a desire to stay just long enough to leave his own mark here. He unsheathed the Damascus toothpick and found a patch of wall beneath a drawing of a cat with ridiculous long teeth. In a few minutes, he had used the tip of the blade to scratch into the rock the following:

JACK PICARO—1822

He spent a few moments admiring his handiwork, and added the *lauburu* beneath.

Then he climbed the slope back to the entrance, sinking his fingers and the toes of his boots into the clay for purchase.

When he emerged back into the daylight his hands and clothes were smeared with the reddish-brown clay, and it was caked in his hair and beard.

After washing himself as best he could in the creek below, he found a tight corner of the box canyon through which it flowed. Jack used deadwood and brush to build a lean-to against a rock wall. Then he made a circle of the flattest rocks he could find and, in the center, piled a mound of sticks. He lit some tinder by sparking it with the flint and steel, cupping the glowing tinder in his hands and blowing as if breathing life into it, and then lighting the twigs and tending them carefully until he could add larger pieces of wood he'd gathered. Then, he put a couple of chunks of buffalo meat on the tines of a forked branch he'd cut from one of the small trees near the creek, and sat cross-legged while roasting his supper.

After he ate, and had some steaming coffee from the tin cup, he stripped off his clothes and went down to the creek and washed himself. The dirt and dried blood and crusted sweat poured from him in rivulets. He scrubbed his face in the water and used cupped handfuls to rinse his hair. He sharpened the blade of the Damascus knife on a stone and then trimmed his beard, pulling on great tufts of hair and cutting it free. He didn't remove all of his beard, but trimmed it back so that it did not feel so wild.

Then he beat his shirt and trousers on the rocks, rinsed them out in the creek, then placed them on branches to dry in the wind. He did the same for his socks. Then, naked, he picked his way back to his shelter to lie down on the blanket to tend to his rifle. There was clay in parts of the lock, and it had to be cleaned away so as not to interfere with the fall of the hammer or the movement of the frizzen.

When he was finished with the rifle, he would sleep. It was still daylight, but it was the middle of summer and the coming night was short. He was so weary that he would have to sleep during the day, as well. This hidden corner of the box canyon was the safest place he was likely to find where he could eat and rest until he was ready again to travel.

In the morning his clothes were dry, and he dressed and slipped on his boots. He started another fire in the little round cooking pit and made coffee and this time spitted some of the liver with the shoulder meat. While he waited for his breakfast to roast, he sat with the powder horn in his lap and looked at the map Johnston had drawn and wondered where he was in relation to any of the landmarks the old hunter had indicated.

The only thing he knew for sure was which side of the Missouri he was on.

He set out at dawn of the next day, deciding on a course that was due west. By midday he had left the broken limestone hills behind him and once again entered familiar tallgrass prairie.

In a week he left the tall grass behind and came to a broad meadow. Beyond the meadow, on the horizon, there rose the tips of some curious purple clouds. He walked for another mile before he realized these unmoving purple clouds were not clouds at all, but mountains. He had traveled much farther west than he had imagined and had gone beyond the map on the powder horn, for these peaks were unmarked. He would have to turn now and head back in the direction the sun rose, and hope he picked up a river again that would lead him to the Missouri. But Jack stayed looking at the western horizon for a good half hour. The mountains must have been fifty or a hundred miles distant, but the line of them spread across the western horizon stirred a feeling in him that Jack was unaccustomed to.

It was awe.

14 *Star*

Jack lay on the crest of the hill with his cheek against the rifle stock, sighting down the barrel at a pronghorn standing on a rock a hundred yards away. The hammer was at full cock, and his finger was lightly brushing the trigger, waiting for the right moment to send the ball to its target. The antelope was shuffling a bit on the rock, its head swiveling this way and that, and Jack thought that perhaps the wind was shifting and the animal had picked up his scent. Then the animal remained still for a second, and Jack was about to fire when he heard another shot ring out across the rolling hills, followed by a clear ringing sound— a perfect B flat note. The antelope bounded off unhurt and Jack sank down into the grass, making himself small, his heart thumping

It was the ghost rifle.

The report had come from somewhere in the direction he was facing, the northeast. He had a good view from his hunter's perch, but had seen nothing moving on any of the hills except antelope. But a rifle could be heard from two or three miles away, or more, depending on the wind.

Jack had stayed in position for a minute or more,

pondering whether it was best to follow the sound now or wait, when another ringing shot echoed across the hills. It was about the right amount of time to reload and shoot again when one was in no hurry, so he guessed that Lightning Crow—if he still had the rifle—was not fighting. If he was hunting, he was aiming at different animals instead of trying to send a second ball into a wounded one.

He placed a twig in the direction he believed the shot had come from.

In another couple of minutes there came a third shot.

Jack placed another twig beside the other.

He heard no more shots in the next twenty minutes, so he stood and looked over the grassy hills and tried to find a landmark on the horizon. There were just more hills, fading away to blue in the distance. He could spy no peaks or promontories. It was approaching midday, and the sun was high and bright in the sky, offering little help to set a course by.

He began walking, trying to make as straight a line as possible over ground in which little was straight, and although he wanted to run because he was so close now to the ghost rifle, he forced himself to watch and to move carefully because he was seeking an enemy who was cruel and smart and would be fighting on his home ground. What was Jack's plan when he finally confronted Lightning Crow? To recover the rifle. That was as far as he could think it through.

Jack had only covered a little more than a mile when he heard the rifle sing again, and this time it sounded much closer. It could have carried on the wind, because it was blowing from the north and he was walking into it. In another two minutes, there was the sound of the rifle again, and then about the same period after, another shot as before. Then, nothing more.

All of the shots had sounded uncomfortably close.

Jack looked for high ground.

There was a rounded knob high on a hill to the northeast, and he made for that, beginning in a quick walk that was nearly a run. But then he became anxious and he did a flat-out run of the last couple of hundred yards up the slope, and he dropped to his knees, panting, at the top.

In the meadow below stretched a great herd of buffalo. There must have been five hundred animals in the herd, and many of them were wallowing in the grass and kicking up dust, and because he was downwind he could smell the stink of them.

He had a good vantage point and he kept low, so as not to present an outline against the sky. The herd stretched a mile across the meadow, and Jack's eyes darted from one cluster of animals to another, looking for anything that would give him a clue to the rifle shots. Then he noticed a half-dozen animals on the ground, with others milling about them, on the eastern edge of the herd. A hundred yards beyond these animals he saw the hunting party. There were half a dozen of them, and although he could tell they were standing next to their horses, they were so far away he could see no detail and did not know if Lightning Crow was among them—or if, in fact, the tribe was even Arikara.

Then he saw a puff of blue smoke from the group and he counted the seconds until the sound of the shot reached him.

Three and-a-half.

Jack knew that it took sound five seconds to travel a mile—this was common knowledge among sailors and soldiers and hunters and gunsmiths—so that meant the hunting party was roughly three-quarters of a mile away. It was a good distance from which to stay and watch and to develop a strategy. It didn't matter whether Lightning Crow was among the band or not. Jack intended to have the rifle back.

Now Jack noticed that in the distance behind the hunting party was a larger group of Indians, all in buckskin, and he imagined it was an entire village that had turned out to help with the hunt, perhaps to skin the animals and harvest the meat.

Jack had been studying the hunting party so intently that he did not hear the sounds of moccasins behind him. What he did hear was the rattle of beads and the rustle of buckskin, and when he turned, he saw the warrior rushing at him, a buffalo shield in one hand and a wicked-looking trade tomahawk in the other. It was a pipe tomahawk, an odd combination tool that offered peace or war, and as the sun shone from the curved metal blade, Jack had no doubt which its owner intended.

The warrior was a young man with fringed buckskin trousers, long black hair greased back, three eagle feathers bristling from the back of his head, and many beads around his neck. His face was painted with red circles and white streaks of lightning and there was a band of black around his eyes, like a mask. The tomahawk, which was held high in his right hand, was looped around his wrist by a leather thong.

Jack swung the rifle around, but the warrior was moving fast, and he used the edge of the buffalo-skin shield to knock the barrel aside. Jack dropped the rifle and struck out with his left boot heel, kicking the warrior's right leg from beneath him and causing him to tumble forward. Jack jammed his left forearm against the shaft of the tomahawk, just preventing the blade from cleaving his skull, and he and the warrior rolled over, locked in an embrace that seemed all ankles and elbows. They landed disentangled in the grass, on their backs, a few feet from one another. The tomahawk had been knocked from the warrior's grip, but it was still on the loop, so he drew it to him while Jack was unsheathing the Damascus toothpick.

Jack lunged and drove the point of the knife deep into the warrior's right forearm. The Indian grunted but did not scream, his fingers still working for the shaft of the tomahawk. Jack turned the knife until he could feel the blade skitter against bone, and the fingers went still. Jack used his left hand to snatch the tomahawk, snap the thong, and fling the weapon away.

The warrior's other hand was still grasping his shield, and he brought it up hard against Jack's jaw, knocking him backward. But Jack kept his grip on the knife. As the blade slid out of the forearm, it trailed a welling ribbon of blood. Jack stumbled and got to his feet. The warrior was now between him and the rifle.

"Parlez-vous français?" Jack asked.

The warrior gave no indication he understood.

"Español?"

Still nothing, but at least the warrior paused.

"English!" Jack screamed. "Do you at least speak English?"

The warrior frowned, annoyed at being shouted at.

"You aren't with Lightning Crow, are you?"

The warrior advanced and gave a couple of swipes of the shield, making Jack take a couple steps back. Jack lunged with his knife, but the point didn't make a dent in the hardened skin shield.

The warrior smiled. He brought his right forearm to his face, smearing blood across his mouth and cheek. Jack retreated a few more steps, and the sole of his right boot found the tomahawk.

"Ah!" he said, and he kept his eyes on the warrior while kneeling and then coming up with the tomahawk in his right hand. "I wish we could understand one another, so then we could talk this over instead of trying to dash each other's brains out."

The warrior said something in a language Jack had not heard before.

"You're probably saying what you're going to do with my body after you kill me," Jack said, and he kept talking because he saw it annoyed his opponent so much it distracted him. "Well, if I was you, I'd give up on roasting me over a fire, because I've gotten a little tough over the summer. I'd wait until winter when I've grown fat and lazy in Major Henry's fort."

Jack swung the tomahawk in a big arc overhead, knowing that it would be an easy counter with the shield. The warrior brought the shield up, and the blade of the tomahawk went beyond the shield and the shaft struck with a sharp crack on the edge. Then Jack jerked backward on the shaft as hard as he could, and the curved lower point of the tomahawk dug itself deep in the webbing in the back of the shield. The warrior's eyes went wide as he struggled to shake the blade away, but it was stuck fast.

Holding the Damascus knife in his off hand, Jack pulled the warrior toward him. He thrust and the Indian countered with his free arm, the one that already had the wound, and again the slender blade made a deep gash. Jack pulled the knife back and then struck again, and once more the Indian took a deep cut, this one in the heavy muscle on top of the forearm, near the elbow, a wound that now made the arm of only marginal use.

Jack could feel the warrior losing strength, or perhaps will, and knew that in just a few more thrusts the knife would find vitals or guts. The warrior knew it too, because he released his grip on the shield and turned to run. Jack dropped the tomahawk and ran after him.

The warrior paused to pick up the rifle, but Jack was too close behind, so the Indian could only brush his fingertips over the stock. Then he continued running and, because it meant his life, managed a burst of speed that increased the distance between them by twenty yards.

Then the warrior fell to his knees and in a clear voice began to sing. Jack could not understand any of it, but from the warrior's stony face and the passion with which he sang, he knew it must be a prayer or a final statement of some kind. The warrior swayed and moved his arms as if telling a story. Then he scooped up some dirt and grass and threw it in the air, like a buffalo pawing the earth.

Jack stood, leaning on his knees, trying to catch his breath.

The entire fight had lasted no more than three minutes but, Jack thought, that's the way of the West. There's long period of boredom or starvation punctuated by an extreme danger and physical activity. Three minutes ago, he was going about his business and then he was in a desperate fight, and if things had gone a bit wrong, or if he had been just a bit slower, it would be all over, and he'd know if there was anything on the other side of this life or not. Now, it was this Indian warrior who reckoned he was about to have the big question answered for him.

"So this is your last rites," Jack said, sheathing the Damascus blade.

The Indian kept singing and was now swaying back and forth.

"What do you say we call it even?"

The warrior's voice had gone low now, solemn sounds that may have indicated—what? His spirit animal speaking to him? The thunder? The voice of his god?

"Stop that," Jack said. "I don't aim to kill you."

The warrior closed his eyes, but kept singing, and held his arms aloft with the palms up.

Jack stepped forward and put his hand on the top of his head.

The singing stopped.

"Look here," Jack said. "Let's figure out some way to parley."

The Indian was looking down, his face filled with sadness.

"Look, you ought to be happy," Jack said. "I'm glad I didn't have to shoot you, because that would have warned old Lightning Crow or whoever has my rifle down there about me watching."

Jack pointed toward the hunting party.

The warrior gave a knowing look.

"You're not one of them, are you?" Jack said. "You're a scout, maybe, for another tribe? Old Johnston said the Rees had many enemies and few friends. Were you planning to steal horses?"

The warrior said something in his own language, punctuating it with many hand gestures, and once looking into the sky and making a circle, but it was all lost on Jack. Then the warrior looked back down at the ground, dejected.

"You put up one heckuva fight," Jack said. "You damned

near had me, and I'll be hurting and walking funny for a few days."

Then the warrior was on his feet and lunging at Jack with a trade knife he had hidden in his moccasin. Jack jumped back, out of the way of the point of the stubby fat blade.

"Hey, what're you doing?"

The warrior advanced, the knife held in his left hand in front of him, his bleeding right arm held close to his side, his face grim, his eyes on Jack.

"This is ignorant," Jack said. "You're not even using your fighting hand."

Again, the warrior slashed with the knife, and Jack stepped to the side, narrowly avoiding the point. They did this two more times, and the last time the knife traced a thin line of blood on top of Jack's left forearm.

"Damn you," he said, and drew the Damascus blade.

The warrior lunged again.

Jack sidestepped and grabbed his opponent's wrist. Then he stepped in close, his boots touching the Indian's moccasins, and with his right hand grabbed the palm that held the knife and bent it backward over the wrist. The warrior let out a yell and tried to pry Jack's hand away with his injured arm but couldn't. The hand was bent nearly double back over the wrist, and the Indian fell to his knees, trying to relieve the pressure. Jack pulled the captured wrist toward him with his left hand and used his right to put even more pressure on the palm. The Indian's fingers went weak, and the blade drooped in his hand.

Jack took the knife.

He drove a knee into the kneeling warrior's chin, knocking him backward into the grass. The Indian struggled up to his hands and knees, spat out a couple of shattered teeth, and staggered to his feet.

Again, he came at Jack.

Jack slashed the trade knife into the warrior's throat.

It wasn't a deep cut, because the blade was dull, but it was deep enough to have nicked the warrior's windpipe, and he stood with his eyes wide and his hand clasped to his throat.

Jack dropped the trade knife and took the Damascus toothpick from its sheath. He stepped forward and drove the slender blade into the warrior's chest, just right of the sternum, and he could feet the blade skitter between ribs and find the heart. Then he pulled out the blade, and the warrior fell. He spent his last few seconds of life stretched out in the grass, on his back, looking up at the sky. He had a word on his bloody lips, but Jack did not understand it.

"I never seen anybody so determined to die," Jack said.

Jack wiped the Damascus blade on the grass and returned it to its sheath, then picked up the trade knife and looked at the blade. It was cheap, with a wooden handle held on by rivets, but he could sharpen the blade, and it was broad enough to be good for skinning.

Jack walked back and picked up his rifle and the horn and found his possibles bag, which had spilled its contents onto the ground. He put these wearily back in the bag and added the cheap knife. Then he searched a bit and found the pipe tomahawk and slipped it into his belt behind him.

He glanced over at the dead warrior.

"I wish I knew what tribe you were," Jack said. "And if there are more like you about."

He walked over to the dead man and stared at brown eyes that did not stare back.

"You're one humiliated savage now," Jack said. "And the only way out of it is for you to give me your horse. I figure you didn't walk here, not with your hair greased back like that and your feathers arranged and your paint on. No, you had to ride here, after maybe trailing me for a spell. Took your chance when I was stretched out on the hill there spying on the hunting party that has the rifle that rings like a bell."

Jack scratched the underside of his beard.

"You must have been alone, or else your friends would have come to help you, and I'd be done for instead of you," Jack said. "But I don't know why you decided to keep fighting after you started your song, because I was ready to call it a draw at that point. Pride, maybe?"

Jack sniffed.

"I suppose you leave a woman behind you and maybe some children," he said. "Was it worth it? Did your pride mean that much to you? Was it that important to come back with my scalp on your tomahawk? I reckon so."

Jack took one of the painted eagle feathers from the warrior's hair and examined it.

"I wish somebody could explain any of your damned etiquette about fighting to me," Jack said. "It was a damn sight more clear during the fight at the keelboat, because intentions were clear. What could I have that you could want, other than my rifle?"

Jack put the eagle feather in the bag.

"I'll take this," Jack said. "And your horse, when I find it."

He paused.

"I have taken your life and I thank you for it."

Jack followed the hillside down and around the bottoms of a couple of low hills, the way he guessed the Indian had to have come to keep from being seen. There was a trickle of water at the bottom of the hills and this led to a copse of scrubby trees.

Tied to a tree branch was a buckskin pony. It, too, had war paint—the circles and lightning bolts and a red handprint on its shoulder.

"Glad to see you are alone," Jack said.

Jack walked gently up to the horse and put a hand on its neck and untied the halter rope from the branch with the other. The horse was a mare, and the Indian had ridden her bareback, with only a halter rope and a knotted bit. She had been in at least one previous fight, because there was a healed arrow wound on her shoulder.

Jack patted her neck. She seemed to have a sweet disposition and did not mind Jack's touch, even though he was a stranger and smelled of blood. She was a fine strong horse, about thirteen hands high, with good teeth and clear deep eyes. She had white socks and white stars across her forehead that reminded Jack of a constellation.

"I don't know what you were called before," Jack said, "but I shall call you Star. How does that suit you?"

The horse pressed her nose against his chest.

"So it shall be," he said.

It occurred to Jack now that everything of value he now owned had been acquired because its former owner had been killed, by him or by others.

15 *The Secret of Steel*

The next morning Jack rode north, to where he had seen the hunting party. The buffalo herd was gone now, leaving only acres of trampled grass and hundreds of buffalo chips. The hunting party had also left little behind, just nine spots in the grass that were dark with drying blood and some bits of bone and offal. Much of it must have been cleaned during the night by scavengers, but still there was very little left. Jack wondered to what uses the Indians could make of so much of the buffalo.

Jack urged Star onward with just the touch of his heels, and she responded by moving forward at a steady but unhurried pace. She was an easy horse to ride, even though Jack had never ridden bareback before. He first tried putting his blanket on her back, but found it to be a slippery proposition that put him on the ground. After a bit of practice, he found reasonable balance by riding more forward than he would have in a saddle, his knees touching Star's withers. Soon, he saw the wisdom in not having to deal with sixty pounds of tack and the time it took to rig up. But still, it was uncomfortable and did not offer places to tie gear. There were also no stirrups to put your weight into and he fell often before getting the hang of squeezing his knees to keep his balance.

Sitting a few feet higher was a welcome change from being on foot, because he could see farther and sign was easier to spot. But the hunting party and its party of attendant helpers were easy to follow because they plowed a furrow across the grass and, in the muddy places, left prints of animals and humans and drag marks of the long poles of the travois.

By noon of the second day he could see the dust the group was leaving a mile or so ahead. Not burdened with a few tons of meat and bone and hide, he was traveling faster than they were, and he didn't want to crowd them too much. They probably wouldn't have scouts trailing behind—who would attack a group of that size?—but he didn't want to run the risk of bumping into a straggler.

Jack followed at an easy pace, roasting buffalo meat at camp and drinking strong coffee, sleeping well in the cool of the night. Then his coffee gave out and he had only water from creeks to drink, but he didn't mind so much because it was summer and the season suited him. He was glad he had never picked up the habit of smoking, like every other man on the keelboat, because he did not want always to be reckoning when his next opportunity to light a pipe would be or compulsively measuring how much tobacco he had left. He missed whiskey, but he did not miss the endless nights of drinking and the fuzzy headedness of the days after. He had enjoyed the easy conversation that went with drinking, and he would have welcomed a companion to talk to, and it was a worry that he could not seem to stop talking to himself. If he craved anything, it was more food—a variety of food, in this case, especially cakes and pies—and women, always. He often thought of Abella

in the way that men think of women, and it made his
hunger sharper.

By evening of the seventh day the group had forded a
stream at a shallow place, and after Jack had looked over
the mud with its many tracks and drag marks, he urged
Star into the water, which barely came up over her socks.
Then Jack lifted his eyes to the far bank and eased Star to
a halt.

Beyond the far bank, he could see a wooden fence and
the tops of many lodges, with smoke trailing from the
thatched roofs and little bits of colored cloth and fur hanging from the tips of the lodge poles. He could also hear the
village now, the laughs and shrieks of children absorbed
in some game, the percussive sound of wood being shaped
with an axe, the sound of horses milling in a corral.

He was much too close.

Jack had pulled gently on one side of the halter to turn
Star when an Arikara woman appeared on the far bank.
She had long black hair, a wooden crucifix that swung between her bare breasts, and she wore a buckskin skirt and
had a basket of crab apples under one arm and her eyes
were to the ground, looking for more that had fallen from
the trees.

Jack remained still and put a calming hand on the horse's
neck. There was a chance the woman, intent on collecting
crab apples, wouldn't look up if he didn't move. Then Star
shuffled her hooves in the water and backed away, giving
a snorting sound of disgust as a snake serpentined across
the water away from them. It was a bull snake, and harmless, but Star hated it just the same, and snorted her dis-
pleasure.

The Arikara woman looked up.

Her eyes met Jack's, and Jack did the only thing he could think of.

He waved.

The woman dropped her basket and shrieked, then pointed and began talking very fast. He heard the sound of others rushing forward, and he had only a few seconds to make a choice: would he stand or would he run? Running would just prolong the inevitable. He would be hunted down and dragged back to the village no matter what happened, either alive or dead, and he preferred alive— and rested, with his wits about him.

He put dead Martin's rifle in the crook of his left arm, with the barrel pointed behind him, and sat a little straighter in the saddle as a crowd of Indians gathered on the opposite bank. They were women and children, and a few old men, but Jack knew the warriors would soon follow.

He nudged Star gently forward, and she walked across the stream and then struggled a bit as she climbed the soft earth on the other side of the bank. Once on top, Jack saw there was a trio of warriors rushing to greet him, and they all held bows or spears. They didn't have the blue face paint he'd seen at the fight at the keelboat, but they resembled in action and dress the warriors he had seen there. He lifted his eyes as they approachcd, because even in the far West, locking eyes with a stranger was an invitation to trouble. He kept his head up, gazing at the cluster of lodges ahead.

The warriors shouted questions and commands in their own language, but Jack ignored them and kept riding. One of them reached for the bridle, but Star snapped at his hand. The women and children laughed.

Jack allowed himself a smile.

As he continued on, the warriors kept scolding him and shaking their weapons, but they did not hurt him. They fell in beside him and trotted alongside.

The village was protected by a deep ditch and a stockade fence, and Jack rode Star over the plank bridge over the ditch and through the open gate of the fence.

As he neared the center of the village, he saw evidence of great activity caused by the hunt. Buffalo hides were stretched out and were being fleshed by women with flint knives, in preparation for tanning, and there were strips of meat and intestines and tails hanging from racks. There were also fires built beneath bison stomachs that had been made into cauldrons, and there seemed to be a kind of stew simmering in each of them. In other piles were hooves and bones, and some women were cracking open buffalo skulls with stone mallets and scooping out the brains with their hands.

On other platforms, higher than Jack's head, pumpkin and squash and other vegetables were drying in the sun. Much of the pumpkin had been sliced and woven into strips. There were also stalks of corn, heavy with ears, piled atop the platforms. The cornstalks had been braided together, making neat bundles.

In the center of the plaza was another peculiar wooden circle of cottonwood planks, like the kind he had seen at the village of the dead, except the ground around this one was well-tended. An old man stood in front of the structure, a spear in his hand, making sure that Jack did not ride too close.

Jack reined Star to a stop in a clear spot, away from the fires and the hide working, but facing the biggest lodge. Out of the lodge came Lightning Crow, in moccasins and fringed buckskins, and with the beads and the bits of bone in his hair, but with no signs of rank. He had been surprised by the unexpected visitor. Behind him, one of his wives carried his warbonnet and a beaded robe, but he pushed her away.

Lightning Crow took ten long seconds to look Jack and his horse over, then threw his hands up wide in disbelief. He spoke sternly to the warriors, and in a moment, they had pulled Jack down from the saddle and relieved him of the gun. He tried to fight them off, but more had joined now and his arms and legs were being held down, and they beat him with the butt ends of their spears and aimed kicks at his ribs. They removed his left boot, and then his right, took his knife, and then pulled off his shirt to reveal his bare chest.

They stood staring at the copper gorget.

The warriors released him. Jack sat up, wiping the blood from the corner of his mouth where he'd been whacked with a spear shaft. His ribs also smarted, but he did not think any were broken.

The crowd parted as Lightning Crow approached.

"Is this any way to treat a guest!?" Jack asked in French.

"You are right," Lightning Crow said in French. "In our plaza, even our enemies may expect to pass safely, to parley, to conduct business. This is the custom of all peoples along the river, and it protected your captains Lewis and Clark. And it is the only reason my warriors have not killed you."

"They have treated me roughly."

"You frighten them," the chief said.

Lightning Crow walked forward, knelt down, and examined the gorget.

"What is this?"

"Sorry," Jack said. "It's been weeks since I talked to

another human creature that understood what I was saying. You'll have to forgive me while I marvel at the sound of it."

"It is from our cousins," the chief said. "From the tribe whose name we do not speak. They no longer walk the earth, but the Dancing Coyote held great power for them. You have stolen it."

"I didn't steal it," Jack said. "It was given to me by the chief."

"This is a lie."

"How could I take anything from the People Whose Name Is Forbidden?" Jack said. "Such things must be given. Otherwise, only calamity would follow. The chief—"

"Do not say his name!"

"If you insist."

"How could you speak his language?"

"We communicated plenty, through signs and gestures, and we got along right well," Jack said, switching to English. "You might say we became brothers, this dead chief of yours and me, and if you don't believe me you can go to the devil, because you damn sure could speak his name if you wanted to."

"En francais, s'il vous plait."

"I could not understand him," Jack said, in French. "He spoke a language I do not know. But he showed me his name by drawing symbols on the floor of his lodge, in front of his great firepit."

"You are lying," Lightning Crow said.

"I suppose you could say it was the ghost of the chief," Jack said, "but he appeared to me as real as you are now and invited me into his lodge. He showed me the things on his altar, the strangely heavy black rocks and the beads and the shells and things in leather bags that I could not open.

And we smoked the medicine pipe and he made a present of this gorget, which I was happy to receive."

Lightning Crow snorted.

"And he also gave you this pony?"

"You know better than that," Jack said. "This pony belonged to a different people. I don't know what nation exactly, but I brought along something to show you. Can you hand me that bag?"

The chief nodded and the bag was returned.

Jack took out the eagle feather and handed it to the chief.

"Blackfoot," the chief said. "A confederation of cowards. This feather is from one of their warriors. He was a long way from home. It represents victory in battle, but from them it might have meant counting coup on an old woman."

"Then he did it four times," Jack said. "I only took the one feather."

"You," the chief said, "took this from a Blackfoot warrior?"

"Well, he was reluctant to part with it. And I don't think he was used to fighting old women. I had to kill him, of course, but then he was trying pretty damned hard to kill me. Then I took his pony."

The chief looked skeptical.

"I did you a favor," Jack said. "He was spying on your hunting party, and I don't think he meant any friendly visits. He would have surely gone back and told his friends where you were."

"Why were you watching our hunting party?"

"I heard the sound of a rifle," Jack said. "Sounded familiar."

"I still think you lie," the chief said.

"There's the pony and the feather."

"Stolen, most likely," the chief said.

"Now, I can understand stealing a pony—that's an affair of honor, and practical. But why would I take a feather?"

Lightning Crow looked at him with eyes like dark stones.

"If you smoked the pipe with—with this chief who cannot be named—then describe the pipe to me."

"The stem was about so long," Jack said, holding his hands about eighteen inches apart. "It was cedar, I think. Had leather wrapped around it as sort of a handle, and some beads handing from the stem. The bowl was not a kind of stone I've seen in these parts. It was red and smooth, and it was shaped like a bird."

The chief said something to his warriors in their own language.

"Get up off the ground," the chief said.

"Sure," Jack said, rising. "But it seemed a moment ago that's where you wanted me."

Jack stood and dusted off his trousers.

"Think I could have my shirt back?"

The chief spoke again to his warriors.

"And the rifle?"

The warriors brought dead Martin's rifle and Jack's shirt to the chief. Lightning Crow cocked the hammer, held the rifle aloft, and fired it. Then he handed the garment and the rifle to Jack.

"Fair enough," Jack said. "And my knife?"

The chief issued another command, and the Damascus toothpick was passed forward. The chief looked at it for a moment, testing its heft, and then handed it pommel-first to Jack.

"Obliged," he said, replacing the knife in its sheath.

"We will care for the horse," the chief said. "For now, until we decide whether or not to kill you."

"Mighty kind of you," Jack said.

The chief peered at Jack's face, then put a hand beneath his jaw and lifted his chin. Then he tugged on the side of Jack's beard.

"Have you always had this hair?"

"No," Jack said.

"Then why do you seem familiar to me?"

"I was at the keelboat."

"Ah, the foolish one who talks too much," the chief said. "You all look alike to me once you grow this absurd fur on your faces. Did you deliver my message?"

"No, because you took my rifle," he said. "But I wrote the message down, and made arrangements to get it to Major Henry. I put it down on paper, word for word, just as you said."

"The message was unheeded," Lightning Crow said. "They are building a fort."

Jack said that was their plan all along.

"Say, I don't want to be rude," Jack said. "But how exactly are you going to decide whether to kill me?"

"We will pray on it," the chief said.

"Your God or mine?" Jack asked.

"We worship the same Creator," Lightning Crow said, then shook his head in sadness. "But you come from a savage people. You leave destruction in your footsteps. Your hearts are hard and your ears closed to the words of Jesus. Your lives are filled with strife instead of grace."

"I saw some of your grace down at the boat," Jack said in English.

"Be careful, I understand more than you think," the

chief said, then turned toward the lodge and motioned for Jack to follow. "Come, you will be treated as a guest until the matter is decided."

That night, Jack took a portion of meat and corn from the wooden bowl that was offered by the young woman who knelt beside him. She had long braided hair and wore a beaded dress, and she covered her smile when he looked at her. The food was wrapped in a corn shuck, so as not to make one's hands greasy, and the boiled meat had an odd tang to it.

The lodge was like the one Jack had seen in the Village of the Dead, but this one was warm and lived in. There was an altar here, too, but instead of the rocks and other objects there was a wooden crucifix, two candles in silver sticks, and rosary beads.

Jack was sitting on the other side of the firepit from Lightning Crow and was part of a circle that included twenty men. Most of them had gray in their dark hair. There were women, too, at the edges of the circle, and everyone was watching as an old man to the right of Lightning Crow made some kind of speech. Jack could not understand a word of it, but knew the tone perfectly well—here was an interloper among us. He may as well have used the word *rogue,* his affect was so like that of Uncle Guy. What shall we do with him?

The girl who had brought him the food returned in a few minutes, placed a hand on his shoulder, and leaned down so that her lips were close to his left ear.

"My father, Lightning Crow, has asked that I translate," she whispered in English.

"Why does he not translate in French to me?"

"He must remain apart," she said, "in order to be fair. Would it be acceptable that I translate for you?"

"Yes," Jack said. "And kind of you."

The girl folded her legs beneath her and continued to whisper in his ear.

"The man talking is the peace chief of our village," she said. "He is urging caution when it comes to you. You are a white stranger who claims to have visited with the spirits of our dead cousins, the People Whose Name Is Forbidden, and before that you were one of the men on the boat who someone talked my father into sparing your life. But if Lightning Crow saw wisdom in allowing you to live before, perhaps that remains the best counsel. Unless, of course, you are a demon."

"So I'm on trial?"

"Not the same," the girl said. "This is a council circle. The white man's courts are straight lines about punishing people. This is a circle in which the elders consider what is justice for both the victim and the one who has caused offense, and what is best for the village."

"So they seek the truth."

"There is not one truth," the girl said. "Every person sitting here has their own truth, and combined they make up the world. Each person may speak their truth. The chiefs then decide. The chiefs lead us because they are trusted. When trust is broken, they are replaced."

"I'm not so sure about there being more than one truth."

"My father would say the only truth is Jesus."

"What do you say?"

She put a finger to her lips.

"What is your name?"

"Sky," she said. "Now, let me listen."

The peace chief was still talking, and Sky was translating, but Jack could not concentrate because of her nearness. Their bodies were not touching, but he was keenly aware of how close her shoulder was to his, and her elbow, and her cheek. Sometimes, when a particularly important point was made, her hand would press against his thigh.

"Now it is the war chief's turn to speak," she said.

A man of indeterminate age with a face that bore the scars of many desperate fights leaned forward, staring into the fire, as if seeking his words in the flames. Then he began to speak, and when he did it was so loud and so deep that Jack could feel his voice reverberate in his gut.

"Under the leadership of Lightning Crow, the village has gone to war to kill the whites until they give up and retreat from our land," Sky translated slowly. "This has been the path we have set our feet upon, and it is one that will lead to victory. If *wakan* is with us, then it will be our victory. If not, then we will go the way of nations before us, our name known only to the wind. We were once a great nation, but our numbers have withered since meeting the whites. The time when victory was ours for the taking was many winters ago, before any of us were yet born, before the horse and iron and Jesus came and changed us forever. Yet, we are men and we must now fight as we see fit."

The war chief paused.

"So then, our choice is a simple one. We do not argue about whether this white man who talks without thinking is from this world, or the next, or whether he has received a gift from the chief of the People Whose Name Is Forbidden, or if he has stolen it. It does not matter if he killed one of our Blackfoot enemies or how he came to have the pony with the stars on her forehead. It does not matter that Lightning Crow took from him the rifle which sings. We must do as we have sworn."

The war chief looked around the circle, staring into each face. His eyes came to rest on Jack.

"We must kill the white man," he said.

Sky did not translate this last.

"What's he saying?" Jack asked.

"It's no good," she said. "He wants . . ."

"That I should die," Jack said. "I can guess that much from his stare."

Except for the crackling of the fire, there was silence in the lodge.

"May I speak?" Jack asked.

In a low voice, Sky asked a question of her father. Before he could answer, several others spoke up, including some women at the edges of the circle, and Lightning Crow urged them to silence by holding up his hand.

"They fear that if you speak," Sky said, "you will ensnare them in lies."

"Tell them I won't plead for my life," Jack said. "Tell them I want them to know the truth of iron and steel, of which there is only one universal truth, and I am tonight its speaker."

Sky translated.

Her father listened.

The war chief objected loudly, but Lightning Crow held up his hand. Then he spoke to Sky, but Jack could not read the expression on his face.

"He says you may speak," Sky whispered.

Jack began to rise, but Sky grabbed his sleeve.

"You must not stand," she said. "It is not allowed."

"I will stand," Jack said. "If I am to be sentenced to death, then I will receive the news as I have lived—on my feet. Tell them."

Haltingly, Sky translated.

Her father simply stared.

"I am a stranger in your nation," Jack said, standing. "My home is far across the sea, farther even than the white men against whom you fight. I am among them, but not of them."

Sky translated, struggling to keep up.

"You have never heard the name of my nation, for even though it has existed since the dawn of time, for the last thousand winters we have been ruled by others, the Romans and the Spanish and the French. But we survive as a nation, like you, because of our love for freedom. A nation of such individuals can never be defeated, even though its individuals be scattered to the wind. And so it is with your people. A thousand generations may pass, but still you will find one another. Is this not so?"

Sky asked the question.

Lightning Crow motioned for him to continue.

"These things you already know to be true. But what you do not know is the secret of iron, which I have carried from my antique land." Here Jack allowed himself a smile, because he had read his Shelley. "In my village of Carcosa, near Eibar, where the finest weapons in this world are made, every boy is taught the secret of iron when they come of age. I will share it with you, as it was shared with me."

Jack paused to allow Sky to catch up.

There was no other sound in the council chamber than her voice, because even those who weren't looking at

Jack were listening intently. When Sky stopped, there was silence.

"Just as iron is transformed to steel, through being hammered and folded a thousand times in a forge of unbearable heat, and being quenched in the freezing water of the mountain, so too are individuals tempered by life," he said. "We begin as iron, soft and malleable—"

Sky tripped over the translation of the word.

"Flexible, easily influenced and shaped."

She translated.

"But as we make our way through the world we are tested, and if we persevere and are purified, then we become hard like steel—stronger, sharper, and taking great pressure without breaking. While iron is useful, the tools that are most useful are made of steel. So it is with people. Most of us are yet iron, but we aspire to be steel."

He waited for Sky to catch up.

"That is the secret of iron to steel, as handed down countless generations in my family. But there is one lesson more, and that is the danger of allowing impurities to remain within the steel."

Jack reached down and grasped a flaming stick from the firepit, blew it out, and regarded the smoking, charred end. Carefully, he ran the thumb of his right hand up to the charred end, knocked loose some of the carbon, and caught the flakes in the palm of his left hand.

"This blackness, this is what makes steel possible," he said. "It is essential. Without carbon, there can be no steel. This charcoal is like the challenges we face in life—it is essential for our growth, but unless we can eventually purge it from our souls, it will poison the steel. The steel will still be sharp, but it will be brittle and will break instead of retaining its shape."

Jack tossed the stick back into the fire, which received it with a bloom of embers.

"This is why we have rituals—the sacred pipe, the rosary, the drawings made in secret caves from where the world began—to purge ourselves and our nations of these impurities, so that we may be strong but not brittle, wise but not arrogant, fair but not cruel."

Jack rubbed his hands together and looked down at his blackened palms.

"You will do as you wish with me," Jack said. "You are many, and I am but one. But I will tell you this: A nation that loves freedom but denies it to others will break. A village that loves life but kills because it can will fracture. That is all I have to say."

Jack brushed the ashes from his hands and sat down.

16 *Flute Song*

When the council ended there was no verdict, as Jack had expected. Instead the members simply drifted away, and no decision was the decision.

Jack would live by default. For Lightning Crow to have agreed with Jack, Sky explained, would have meant shaming war chief and his supporters, so the reasonable thing to do was simply to ignore Jack.

Jack was prevented from sleeping inside the village that night, so made his bed by the river. At dawn, Sky came to him. Her hand briefly touched his shoulder as she knelt beside him, and Jack thought it was as light as the touch of a butterfly.

They sat on the blanket, watching the sunlight chase the fog from the surface of the water. Neither said anything for a long time. Jack thought about the speech he had made the night before, and how Sky had translated, and about how the speech seemed to have changed him, even if it had not convinced anyone else. What kind of steel was he turning himself into, he wondered? Would he eventually break? Or had he already broken? Jack stole guilty glances at Sky and studied how the morning light bathed her bronze face and illuminated her brown eyes. It reminded him of paintings he had seen as a boy, when warm light seems to emanate from the subjects. She smiled when she realized he was looking at her, revealing nearly perfect white teeth, with the exception of a chipped incisor.

"Stop staring at me," she said.

"I can't," Jack said. "What happened to your tooth?"

"I broke it biting the last boy who looked at me as you do."

"Honestly."

"I chipped it on a stone that was hidden in some pemican. Is it ugly?"

"No," he said. "It is endearing."

She play slapped him.

"I have something to tell you," Sky said. "My father says you have until the dark of the Green Corn Moon. Then you must leave."

"How long do I have?"

"Two weeks," Sky said. "The moon was full seven days ago. We are already into August, I think. It is sometime difficult to reckon our moons with your months. But I spent some time thinking on it last night. Yes, I am sure it is August or nearly so."

"That hardly seems long enough," Jack said.

"Oh?" Sky asked. "Long enough for what?"

"To get to know one other."

Sky frowned.

"Do not be so sure that I want to know you in that way," she said. "You made a fine speech last night, but even the blue jay can imitate the hawk. You have not convinced me of what you are. I think of you as the Chief of the Village of the Dead, and it frightens me."

"Because of this?" Jack touched the copper gorget.

"That and other things," she said. "You mentioned the cave where the old ones drew their souls on the walls, and you shouldn't have known about that, either. No, don't tell me. I don't want to know."

"All right," Jack said. "So I have two weeks here. But I might just want to leave earlier. Can I take my horse?"

"He will allow you the Blackfoot pony."

"And my rifle?" Jack asked.

"You already have your rifle."

"Not dead Martin's rifle," Jack said. "The one your father carries."

Sky shook her head.

"He will never part with the ghost rifle," she said.

"I will have it back."

"You will die trying to take it," she said. "How can you be so wise one night and so foolish the next morning? You almost had me convinced you are one of the human beings. Are you one of Trickster's animals instead?"

"Who is Trickster?"

"Coyote," Sky said. "He is one of the makers of this world. He is clever but reckless, he breaks rules, he puts others in danger. He is always hungry and is given to stealing and chases after women. He is often killed but comes back anyway."

"A rogue," Jack said.

"It is nothing to be proud of."

"We have something similar in the Old World," Jack said. "Stories told down from parent to child through the generations. The rogue is Reynard the Fox. He has many adventures, and his archenemy is his uncle, Isengrim the Wolf."

"How can a wolf be an uncle to a fox?"

"They are tales told by simple folk," Jack said, "and the

animals in the stories are human-like and have familial connections."

"In our stories," Sky said, "there are often women who take animals as husbands, or who are themselves both animals and human beings. Coyote often addresses the other animals as brother or cousin. So that does not seem so strange."

"You are Christian," Jack said. "Yet you speak of these other stories."

"My father is Catholic," she said. "He was particularly fond of a priest, Toussaint, who came up the river before I was born. And so is his village, mostly. But the old ways die hard. They speak to me in a way that the god of ink and paper does not. Others feel the same. So the village is caught between the worlds."

"As am I," Jack said. "I find myself praying to both Jesus and our old goddess, Mari, in desperate times. It is discouraged by the church. But I do not care."

There was a pause.

"I like talking with you," Sky said. "It makes me feel less alone."

"You cannot imagine when I was in the wilderness how I yearned for someone to talk to," Jack said. "I eventually began talking to myself. I feared that I was going mad."

"You are quite mad, I think," she said. "But not in that way."

"I was told of strange rites in many of the villages along the river," Jack said, cautiously. "That the women of the villages lay with strangers."

"The *Okipa,*" Sky said. "It is a ritual for bringing the buffalo. It is mostly the old men, the bull chiefs, who fuck the young wives who are offered by their men, or sometimes offer themselves."

Jack could not hide his shock when Sky used the common term for intercourse. She laughed.

"Why do you flinch when I say the word?" she asked. "It is one of the first words in English I learned as a girl, because it was the most common word I heard from the white Americans who came to visit my father. If they weren't using it to describe the act itself, then they were using it to season their language, and it was as natural to them as saying *the* or *it*. When the priest came—the one who taught me my letters—he forbid me from saying it. But it seems silly to use substitute words for the act, don't you think?"

"My culture is different."

"It seems oddly childish," she said. "Like your substitute words for making water and—"

"Yes," Jack said. "We have euphemisms for death as well. Gentle people do not die, they 'shuffle off this mortal coil.' The phrase comes from the greatest of the English storytellers. You said you can read?"

"I read poorly," Sky said. "Our only book is the Bible. I have seen pieces of newsprint, used to wrap some trade object in, but I can tease no meaning from it. My gift, since I was a child, was the sound of language. As more Americans followed your captains Lewis and Clark up the river to trade, my father required a way to communicate with them. Few spoke French, and he was too old to learn a new tongue."

She brushed the hem of her beaded calfskin dress.

"When I was a child, my father had me sit at his knee as he received every party that came. Some spent the winter. There was plenty of time to learn. It wasn't difficult."

"What did you think of the men?"

"They were men, like others. Some took winter wives.

It was allowed if the women agreed. But my father killed two of the traders for touching me against my will. It started a war. It took a lot of ponies and beaver plews to settle."

"Will your father kill me?"

"There would be no need," she said. "Because if you touch me after I object, I will kill you myself."

"Fair warning," Jack said. "Why are you not married?"

"How do you know I'm not?"

"Are you?"

"That is none of your business."

But she laughed.

"What of your mother? Where is she?"

She shook her head and put a finger to her lips.

"So the woman who is with your father is not your mother?"

"She is not," Sky said. "This other person who we are not speaking of was captured by my father from our cousin enemies the Mandans. I do not remember my mother Red Buffalo Woman, because I was a child when she became a person we no longer speak of."

"She was a captive?"

"Yes, a slave," Sky said. "War is about women and horses, is it not? I am told she was beautiful and clever and that a white man named John Evans spent some time with her before your captains came up the river. This man Evans was from a people across the sea, the Welsh, and he had a strange belief the Mandans were some branch of his family, many generations ago."

"I know of him," Jack said. Evans was known in St. Louis and had made a map that Lewis and Clark used to find the Mandan villages. "But the captains were unconvinced as to the theory."

"We did come from the south and east, many winters ago," Sky said. "From the Gulf. We came up the Mississippi and then followed the Missouri, over many winters."

"Why?" Jack said.

"Because the Great Spirit told us to."

"Would you like to see the states someday?" Jack asked. "St. Louis, perhaps?"

"No," she said. "This is my home."

"It is good to have a home," Jack said. "I would go home, if I could."

"To St. Louis?"

"No," Jack said. "My grandfather's house across the sea. But I cannot return. It is too far and I am no longer a child. I must make my place in a country that I can call my home."

"Here?" Sky asked.

"Perhaps," Jack said. "It is a fine land."

"In summer," she said. "In winter, too. The living is harder, but the beauty is beyond words. Will you stay for the winter?"

"I have only two weeks," Jack said.

"There are other villages," Sky said. "You are young and handsome and it will not be difficult for you to find a winter wife. Or two."

"Why not three?"

"You would probably have to find sisters to make that work, and one of them is sure to be unpleasant," Sky said. "So I would not be so greedy if I were you, Jack Picaro."

There was another silence as they looked out across the river, which had changed character and had now become glittering diamonds in the sunlight. From downstream, there came a strange sound, a low warbling note that at first Jack thought must be some bird. Then a flutter of notes followed, and Jack recognized it as music, but unlike anything he had heard before.

"What is that?" Jack asked. "I've never heard that key before."

"It is a flute," Sky said. "Someone is courting."

"Ah," Jack said. "Lucky devil. Perhaps I will learn to play the flute."

She looked at him, her face suddenly turned serious. She brushed a shock of black hair from her eyes to behind her right ear and gently shook her head. The sunlight was streaming behind her, and it illuminated the tip of the ear, bright and warm, and made a brilliant halo at the crown of her head.

"Choose your song well," she said. "Do not make me guess its meaning."

Sky rose.

"I must return," she said. "The day has begun and there is much to do. The gates to the village will be open now and the plaza full of activity. Come and eat when you are hungry, and tend your pony. It is only at night that you must remain outside the walls."

Jack lingered by the river, stretched out on his blanket, his hands behind his head while looking at the clouds. The flute music continued for another half an hour, the sliding and sometimes bent notes drifting in the air, sometimes playful and at other times wistful. Then the music stopped, and Jack could hear the low voice of a man and the sound of a woman giggling.

Jack packed his things and then walked upriver to give them privacy. He walked along the bank, searching the trees, until he found a silver maple of suitable size. He had made flutes as a boy, and had learned a few Basque tunes from his grandfather. The flutes his grandfather played were the traditional three-holed pipes called *txirula,* which imitated the singing of birds, but Jack had learned to make flutes in the French style, simple instruments that could be used to play melodies across two octaves.

Jack searched below the maple until he found a stout limb that had been knocked from the tree in a storm, some months past, and which was dry and had lost all of its leaves. He found the straightest part of the limb, un-sheathed the Damascus blade, and hacked about a foot of it away. He ran his hands over the resulting stick, testing it for straightness, and felt dryness of the meat of the wood with a thumbnail. Satisifed, he put the cylinder of maple in his bag, picked up the rifle and bedroll, and walked toward the village.

Surrounding the village were many fields of corn and squash and beans, and Jack was careful to thread his way around and through the crops as he approached. It was this produce that would be hung to dry in the lodges or stored in underground caches, like the ones he had seen in the Village of the Dead, that would allow Sky's people to survive even the harshest winter.

Jack found a flat rock to sit on just outside the stockade gate, then took out the maple stick. He used the awl and the Damascus toothpick to begin hollowing out the interior of the maple stick. But after an hour of work he had made less than an inch of progress, and his hands were sore from the work. As the inhabitants of the village passed by, they laughed, not bothering to hide their condescension.

"Dammit," Jack muttered to himself. As a boy, he had access to his grandfather's tools to make his flute. Neither the awl or the thin knife were suited to the task. He was considering using the ramrod of dead Martin's rifle in some fashion, perhaps using the ball puller to begin a pilot hole, when he looked up and saw the old man he had seen before standing guard in front of the sacred ark looming over him.

"What?" Jack asked.

The man said something Jack didn't understand.

Then the old man offered him an object.

It was a cord drill, a stick with a string wrapped around one end, a round flat stone in the middle to serve as a counterweight, and a tip made of a flint projectile point.

"Ah," Jack said.

He took the drill, put the point in the hole he had started in the maple stick, and pulled one end of the cord to spin the shaft. Jack lost control and the thing tipped over.

The old man sat down and motioned for Jack to hand the pieces over.

He pressed the maple stick firmly into the ground, then held it in place with the soles of his feet. Then he carefully aligned the bit in the hole, grasped each end of the cord, and gently pulled while exerting enough downward pressure to keep the drill in place. The shaft spun as the length of cord played out, and then the weight kept it spinning as it reeled the cord back in. The old man tugged again, and the operation was repeated, but a bit faster. Again, and bits of maple were spraying up from the work.

The old man stopped and looked at Jack.

Jack nodded his understanding.

"I am grateful," Jack said.

The old man handed the work back, then stood and walked back into the village. Jack started working with the drill, as the old man had demonstrated, and after a few fumbling starts, began to get the hang of it. In a few minutes,

he had drilled another inch, and had to stop to clear the
chips and sawdust. In another hour, he was finished with
hollowing out the maple cylinder, then smoothed the outside and began to measure where the holes should go by
placing his hands in a playing position and noting where
the tips of his thumb and finger fell. He marked where
each should go with the tip of his knife. The drill then
made short work of drilling these holes. Then he used the
knife to shape the mouthpiece and carve a window above
that, and used a scrap piece of wood on the stopper to fit
beneath it.

Jack put down the knife, positioned his fingers on the
sound holes, and softly played a D major scale, up and
down. The stopper would need adjustment, some of the
cuts needed smoothing, and the intonation was imperfect
on one or two notes. But even though it was rough, the
flute played as expected. Jack found an unexpected satisfaction in having made something again from scratch, and
he realized that for a few hours he wasn't thinking about
the past or the future, but was here in the present.

He slipped the flute in his possibles bag, brushed the
shavings from his legs, and stood. He shouldered the bag
and walked toward the plaza, carrying the unloaded rifle
in the crook of his arm. The old man was not at his cus-
tomary spot, guarding the sacred ark, so Jack left the drill
on the ground next to the fence. He also left the iron awl
with the drill, as thanks.

That evening, he made a fire and sat by the river on his
blanket and toyed with an old tune on the flute. It was a
Basque love song that he had known by heart since child-
hood, and it began with the line, *"My love enchants me."*
Jack alternated playing the melody and singing the verses.
When he reached the last line—*"In the rain we parted on*

the road to Bilbao, but still I feel my heart beneath your loving hand"—he was aware that Sky was watching and listening.

"Is this your song for me?" she asked.

"It is an old song from my land," he said. "All of the old songs are full of parting, of sorrow, of loves that are never to return. Let us create a new song."

She sat beside him.

"My people have a tradition of spontaneous song," he said. "It is called *berstsolaritza,* and there are musicians who improvise poetry to commemorate any occasion and set it immediately to song."

"And you are skilled at this?"

"All Basques are poets at heart," Jack said.

"And what kind of song would you write for me?"

"We will start with a melody," he said. "Most Basque music mimics the sound of small birds, high piping like that heard in the morning, but that will not do here. Oh, your song will start with bird sound, but it will be a lower and richer sound, full of knowing, and perhaps one heard at night."

"But not an owl," Sky said. "I am frightened by them."

"No, not an owl," Jack said. "A loon. It will begin with a low and plaintiff call, a loon calling for a mate at the water's edge, like this."

Jack played a melody that was a near-perfect imitation of a loon's call, a question repeated twice. Sky smiled.

Jack lowered the flute.

"Where are you, my love?" Jack sang, making up the words as he went along. "Just yesterday we were together, beneath the warm sun. Now the night lasts forever."

Jack smiled.

"Comes the answer," he said.

He played a response to the first phrase, using all of the same notes with the exception of a final, declarative note at the end.

"I am here, my love," he sang. "Watching for you in the mist. I yearn for your dark eyes and the sweetness of your kiss."

Sky looked away.

"That rhyme was too easy," she said.

"All right," he said. "It's your turn. Give me the next line."

"No," she said.

"Do you not like my loon song?"

"Loons are beautiful," she said. "Your song is silly."

"Then why are your eyes wet?"

Jack reached out and touched her cheek. She grasped his wrist and kissed his palm, her tears falling into his hand.

"We will break each other's hearts," she said.

He drew her to him.

"We may not," he said.

"We will because we betray our people," she said. "My father is at war with yours because he blames them for most of our suffering. And he is right, except for his madness that inflicts its own suffering. And you would dishonor your dead friends from the boat, because it was my father that led the attack."

"Have I caused any of your people's suffering?" Jack asked.

"No," Sky said. "Not personally."

"Did your hands kill any of the men on the boat?"

"No," she said. "But the killing of your people was done for my sake."

"Did you ask it?"

She shook her head.

"Then we betray no one," Jack said.

He kissed her neck.

"Do you want me?" he asked.

"Very much," she said.

He slid his left hand up her thigh and felt the dampness and warmth there. She removed her dress and threw it aside. Her breasts were full and round, and her smooth skin glowed in the firelight. She reached over, took his head in her hands, and kissed him fiercely.

"Now you," she said, breathlessly.

He kicked off his boots and wriggled out of his trousers and pulled off his shirt, popping some of the stitching in his haste. He was on his knees before her, but proud, and the places beyond his face and arms, where the sun usually did not reach, were a ghostly white. She reached a hand out and put it on his chest, feeling the muscle and bone beneath her palm.

"How different we are," she said.

"Yes," Jack said.

"You must promise me one thing," Sky said.

"Of course, I love you," Jack said.

"No," she said. "Do not speak of that yet. Instead you must promise to never take up arms against my father. For us to couple there must be peace between our families."

"But he will not hesitate to kill me if he can justify it."

"I will discourage him," Sky said. "But you have already made up your mind to kill him if you must to get that damned rifle back. This you must not do, because even if you succeed, you will perish at the hands of those who would avenge him. Then your friends will come to avenge your death. And so it will go."

It seemed an unequal bargain to Jack, but the urgency

he felt allowed no time to negotiate. The depth of her desire seemed to match his own. Her breathing was quick and shallow, and her shining eyes searched his face with expectation.

"Yes," he said. "I promise."

She roughly pulled him down on top of her.

17 *Twelve Villages*

In the plaza the next morning, the women were still working on fleshing the hides, boiling meat from the bones, preparing hooves and horns, making sinew into cord, or doing a dozen other things with the buffalo harvest that Jack barely understood.

The old man was again standing with his spear near the odd circular fence in the middle of the plaza, and Jack asked him in English and French to explain what it was all about, but the old man did not understand or pretended not to understand the questions. He remained staring impassively until Jack became bored and walked away.

He found Lightning Crow sitting cross-legged outside his lodge, watching his wife work on a buffalo hide. In his lap was a femur from the buffalo that he had split open to reveal the marrow, and he was using a thin wooden spoon to dip it out and eat it. The ghost rifle was beside the chief, on an antelope skin, along with a powder horn, a patch knife, and other small items.

Jack sat down next to the chief, and began a conversation in French.

"What is in the cottonwood ark?" Jack asked.

"It is not for you to know," Lightning Crow said. "But it is part of the old religion. Many of the Sahnish villages have given it up. But the old man who guards it, Crooked Foot, and some of our elders insist on keeping the sacred canoe, even though our enemies the Mandans venerate it, as well. When Crooked Foot finally dies, we will take the canoe down and worship it no more."

The chief offered him the spoon to dip out the buffalo marrow.

"I've never had it."

"Eat," Lightning Crow said. "It is warm and fresh and one of the joys of the hunt. It is good for your blood and will make your sap run thick and strong. Take it."

Jack took the wood spoon and scooped out a dollop of the fat, creamy marrow. He put it in his mouth and was surprised that it was warm and rich and tasted like meat-flavored butter.

"It's good," he said, handing back the spoon. "Thank you. I will remember this delicacy."

"You would do well to study the ways in which the buffalo gives to us," Lightning Crow said. "When white men first come here, they kill our buffalo and take only the easiest meat. They do not give thanks, and it is only when they are truly hungry that they abandon their wasteful ways. But some never learn to give thanks."

"I was hungry and killed a cow," Jack said. "My ignorance and weakness caused me to be wasteful. But I was grateful for the tongue and meat and blood I did have."

"There is enough in the world for the wise," Lightning Crow said.

"Is there enough here for both the whites and your people?"

"For fools and the greedy," the chief said, "there is never enough."

Jack tried to think of a reason why keeping the rifle would be impractical for the chief.

"What will you do when you run out of lead for the ghost rifle?"

"The keelboats bring lead and powder," he said.

"Do you have a mold for making rounds?"

"I will trade beaver plews for one. It is not an uncommon bore, about as big as half the distance from the first joint of my thumb to the tip. Fifty-three, I think, as your people say."

"It is exactly half an inch," Jack said. "A fifty. Its power leads you to think it larger. I will trade you the Blackfoot pony and my lesser gun for the ghost rifle."

"No," the chief said.

"Then tell me how many ponies I will need."

"It is not for trade," the chief said.

"Others will want it," Jack said. "It may not be for trade, but what warrior could resist the chance to fight you for the rifle that sings? You know the power of the rifle. Think of the buffalo you killed with it—could any other gun in this village or any other reach out so far or hit so hard? It is the thunderstick you dreamt of as a boy. Its reputation will spread. Others will want it."

"Speak no more of it," the chief snapped.

"Then let us change the subject," Jack said. "What do you know of a Crow warrior named Standing Wolf?"

The chief shook his head.

"Wolf Standing Like a Man fears nothing," he said. "He is war chief of one of the secret societies of the Crow and is keeper of the sacred bundle. The Crow are a nomadic nation who live north of the Yellowstone River and make their home on the prairie in tents made of buffalo hides. They are jealous of the earth lodges peoples and have sometimes raided us for ponies and women."

"Does he have a peace medal, one of the larger ones?"

"The captains gave many peace medals," Lightning Crow said. "They are as common and as worthless as ticks on a dog. The Sahnish did not like the captains, because they were cheap and brought nothing of value to trade, like the French and the English did. I do not remember what kind of peace medal Wolf Standing Like a Man possesses."

"How old is he?"

The chief shrugged.

"It is hard to say. Few have seen his face and lived."

"Have you fought him?"

"Why do you ask so many questions about this man?"

"I heard his name once," Jack said.

"You are foolish to ask of him," the chief said. "Sometimes talking about a person will summon the individual— or his spirit animal. Wolf Standing Like a Man has no mercy, and, if he comes, he will kill you."

"Because he hates whites so?"

"No," Lightning Crow said. "Because he hates everyone. He is like a rabid wolf, biting and snarling, infecting all he touches with a sickness that punishes and eventually kills."

"I have known men who were the same," Jack said, thinking of Moses Bledsoe.

The chief scooped up the last of the marrow, spooned it into his mouth, then tossed the bone aside. After he had swallowed, he wiped the fat from the corners of his mouth with the back of his hand.

"Your interest in my daughter is unwelcome," he said.

"You have turned her head with your words. You are a kind of poison, and the good book warns against fornication with strange women."

"I've read the book," Jack said. "Old King Solomon seems to have done all right for himself. Can you think of a wiser king? Or wealthier? He had seven hundred wives and three hundred concubines. A thousand women for one man. That's quite a lot of strange women. And yet we speak admiringly of the wisdom of Solomon."

"Solomon was punished for his sin," Lightning Crow said. "His foreign wives caused him to break his covenant with the Lord and caused ten of the twelve tribes of his kingdom to be scattered to the wind."

"What about the ways of your people?" Jack asked. "What of the ceremony that brings the buffalo? Old men sleeping with the young wives of the village does not seem so different to me, nor does the practice of allowing traders to take wives for the winter. Will the kingdoms of the Arikara and their enemy cousins the Mandans also be scattered?"

"Perhaps," the chief said. "It is not for us to know."

"There are some that say your people are a remnant of those lost tribes," Jack said. "What do you believe, my chief? That the Arikaras are among the sons of David and somehow crossed the sea after the fall of the kingdom?"

"I have often pondered this," the chief said. "The Sahnish nation consists of twelve villages, each with its own government. That is a strange similarity. But we did not come from across the sea."

"From where, then?"

"We came from deep in the earth below us, and Corn Mother created all life and caused it to move to the surface. After encountering many obstacles, the Sahnish finally arrived at a beautiful land, and Corn Mother taught the people how to live and how to pray. When she died, she left the corn plant behind to remind us that she would always be with us."

"Where is Jesus in this story?"

"Corn Mother was *his* mother," the chief said. "Sometimes, you are very stupid."

"I know many who would agree."

"You make my head ache," Lightning Crow said. "You now have three days to leave here. I grow tired of you and want you gone sooner than later. That is enough time to make yourself ready for your journey. You are to remain sleeping outside of the village walls. By the third morning from today, if you remain, you will be killed."

"That doesn't seem very Christian."

"My counsel is to leave my daughter alone and begin preparing your pony and yourself," the chief said. "You may pack some beans and meat. We will give you enough for a month. If you use it sparingly, it will last until you rejoin your Major Henry upriver."

18 *The Mad Wolf*

In the plaza, Jack made his way beneath the platform on which rested the corn and the other produce, and as he did so he was nearly knocked over by a dog that was running all out for the rear gate. There were usually many dogs milling about the plaza and around the lodges; the Arikara did not keep them as pets, but as a work animal and a food supply. The larger dogs could be harnessed to drag a travois on journeys, and all the dogs could be boiled and eaten.

Then Jack heard the screams of women and the cries of children, and the sounds of a vicious dogfight. Then there was the sound of a shot, with a familiar ringing tone after. Jack made his way toward the rear gate, the one that led to the cemetery on the hill behind, and he passed many families who were shutting themselves up in their lodges. Some individuals were climbing the drying racks to get above the ground. A few warriors were running toward the gate, spears and bows in hand.

He passed Sky, running for her father's lodge.

"What's happening?" Jack asked.

"Come with me," Sky said, motioning with her hand.

"I heard the sound of my rifle," Jack said. "Who's attacking?"

"Nobody," she said. "It's a wolf."

"In August?" Jack asked. He thought wolves were only a danger in the winter months, when game was scarce.

"It's mad," Sky said. "Have you seen my father?"

"No," Jack said.

"Come, don't let it bite you. It is a long and painful death."

"I will be all right."

Jack was charging the rifle from the powder horn.

Sky was facing him, but walking backward.

"Go," Jack said. "Run!"

"Find my father."

She turned and ran as Jack drove home a patched ball with the ramrod. He was walking forward as he did this, and now his angle had changed and he could see the wolf fighting with one of the dogs, both of them on their hind legs. There was a dead dog on the ground, its throat torn out. The wolf was not a big wolf, but its coat was ragged, and flecks of foam sprayed from its bloody mouth.

One of the warriors stepped forward and threw his spear, but it narrowly sailed over the back of the wolf and landed in the dirt. The other warrior had his bow drawn, but now the wolf was twisting and turning, locked with the dog it was fighting. The archer hesitated, waiting for a better shot.

Jack primed the pan.

The wolf got the head of the dog in its jaws, nearly tearing off an ear, and the dog yelped and began to run away. Confronted now with two rabid targets, the archer chose the dog and sent an arrow into its chest.

The wolf growled and stood with its legs planted wide

in the ground, snapping and biting at the air. The archer had another arrow nocked now and was at full draw. Suddenly the wolf bolted, leaving the arrow to strike the ground where it had been a fraction of a second before.

Jack had the rifle to his cheek and the hammer at full cock, swinging the barrel to put the sights just in front of the running wolf, when it went behind a corner of a lodge, blocking his shot. Jack cursed, partially lowering the rifle so as to have a broad view. He heard cries and screams behind the lodges, and the sound of people running, and then a boy of fourteen or fifteen shot out from between a pair of lodges, the wolf close after him. Jack did not think he had ever seen anyone run as fast. Just as Jack thought the wolf was about to sink its teeth into the backs of the boy's legs, the boy leaped up and grabbed a crossbeam of one of the drying racks and pulled himself up, the wolf's teeth missing his heels by inches.

Then the wolf ran straight for the archer.

"He's presenting too small of a target," Jack said to himself. "Wait for it."

The archer pulled the arrow back and stood his ground, but Jack could see his hands quivering. Then he loosed the arrow too soon, while the wolf was still thirty yards away, and the arrow missed widely and flew past to bury its point in the post of the drying stand the boy had taken refuge on.

It was the last arrow the warrior had.

He drew back the bow like a club.

In what seemed as one motion, Jack had dead Martin's rifle up and drew a bead on the wolf and pulled the trigger. The *ker-chow!* of the ignition seemed to take forever, and his senses were so overcharged he imagined he could see the ball in flight. The ball took the wolf just below the eyes, smashing the skull in two, and the wolf fell in the dirt, its legs still jerking for a moment in a running motion. It was scarcely a yard away from the archer.

"Whango," Jack said.

The archer turned to look at Jack in amazement.

"*Merci beacoup,*" he said.

"Was anyone bitten?" Jack asked.

The archer pointed to a spot along the fence near the rear gate.

The old man with the spear who usually stood in the center of the plaza, in front of the sacred ark, was dead on the ground, his throat bloody and some of his intestines leaking out of his stomach. His spear was twenty yards away in the dirt. There was blood and fur on the tip of the spear.

Lightning Crow was sitting on a cottonwood plank with his back against the rough fence, staring ahead with vacant eyes, clutching one hand in the other. His right hand below his wrist was bright red with blood. The ghost rifle was on the ground nearby.

"Crooked Foot was the first to know what was happening," the chief said, in French. "He came running and fought the wolf with his spear. He did not kill the animal, but he allowed some of the women and children to get to safety. He was an old man, and an elder of the Sacred Ark Society, and will be remembered for his courage."

"He was also kind," Jack said.

"A weakness, yes," the chief said. "At least the old man drew blood."

"Did you have an opportunity to shoot?"

"I missed," he said.

"It would have been a difficult shot," Jack said, kneeling beside him. He put down dead Martin's rifle and peered at the mangled hand. It was gushing blood and the two smallest fingers were missing.

Sky came and sat on the other side of her father, brushing his graying hair back from his face.

"Do not touch the hand," the chief said.

"I won't," Sky said.

"Or the fingers if you find them."

"They may be in the mad wolf's stomach," Jack said.

"The animal was so quick, it went into some of the lodges," the chief said. "It attacked Turtle Woman where she lay, but it could not bite through her buffalo blanket. It chased some children in the next lodge, and when it came out, that's when I confronted it. The wolf was too close and too fast. The power of the rifle did not save me."

"It is made for range," Jack said. "You would have needed a shotgun."

"I thought at first that I could not have missed," the chief said. "That perhaps the wolf was not a real wolf, but a spirit animal, or a man turned into an animal. But when I saw your shot bring it down, I knew the wolf was real."

The chief looked down at his hand.

"I can still feel my fingers," he said. "I wonder if they wiggle in the dead wolf's stomach?"

"I hope they did not taste good," Sky said.

"Why did I not foresee this in my dreams?" the chief lamented, shifting on the cottonwood plank. "It is certain death for me. You must tie me to a post so that when the madness comes I cannot injure anyone or spread the sickness. Or, you must allow me to walk into the woods with my knife and not return."

Sky looked at Jack.

"There may be a chance," Jack told her in English. "It's

not certain, but it is what I learned once from a doctor in St. Louis. But I must have your consent."

"Yes," she said.

"Then fetch me the trade tomahawk that's hanging beneath the drying rack yonder," he said. "Do not let your father see it until you hand it to me."

She shuddered with fear.

"It is the only way," Jack said. "And it must be done quickly."

She nodded, and stepped away.

"You share secrets with my daughter in front of me in a tongue I cannot understand?" Lighting Crow asked. "That is disrespect for the dying, and from the both of you. You have turned my daughter against me."

"Lightning Crow," Jack said, "We must speak plainly. There is a chance that you may be spared death, if we act quickly. But this chance depends on the amputation of the bitten hand."

"Amputer?"

"The hand must be cut away."

Sky returned, carrying the iron axe behind her.

"I will die anyway, snarling and snapping like the wolf," the chief said. "I think I would rather my four souls enter the next life with two hands instead of one. Go tell my wife, Elk Woman, to lay out my burial things."

"Wouldn't it be better to live and not to die?" Sky asked.

Lightning Crow looked at her with eyes that were heavy with shame.

"What kind of warrior would I be with only one hand?" he asked. "I would be incomplete, like a broken blade. I could not shoot an arrow or fire a rifle or even hold the medicine pipe properly. Others would have to do the things for me that warriors should do for themselves."

"A chief must lead," Sky said. "That's all."

"No," Lightning Crow said. "I am ready to die before the madness turns me into a beast. Load a short gun for me and place it in my good hand."

"I have never asked anything of you," Sky said. "I have known my place as a daughter. I have embraced your silly religion and negotiated countless trades for you and did not protest when you declared a war against the whites that will only mean our defeat. And I have never once said a word even though I know you killed my mother, your captive, in a fit of jealous rage. But I ask you this now. Take the chance that is offered."

He tilted his head back against the fence.

"I have asked Jesus to forgive me for slaying Red Buffalo Woman," he said. "It is why I cling to the book that the priest brought. But now I see that instead of asking God to forgive me, I should have been asking you, my adopted daughter."

"Take the chance offered," Sky said.

"No," the chief said, holding up the mangled hand. "I will not risk madness."

"I do not forgive you," she said. "I may never forgive you."

Lightning Crow let his three-fingered right hand drop on the plank to his side while he left reached for the wooden cross around his neck. He rested the back of his head against the fence, closed his eyes tightly, and began to pray.

"Notre Pére, qui es aux cieux . . ."

Sky looked at Jack.

Jack nodded.

She passed him the tomahawk.

"Bury the fucking blade in his heart," she said in English.

Jack got a good grip on the ash handle, then took two quick steps forward, to add force to the blow. The tomahawk came down in a sweeping arc.

"Pardonne-nous nos offences . . ."

The heavy curved blade severed the hand just above the wrist, with a sound that was like that of sticks being snapped off inside a wet sack, and sank into the cottonwood plank below. Lightning Crow looked over in disbelief at the severed hand on the ground. He reached for it with his remaining hand, but Jack kicked it away before he could reach it.

Sky picked up the severed hand before the dogs could get to it.

"Now what?" she asked. "He'll bleed to death."

"Tie up the stump with some cord to slow the bleeding," Jack said, jerking the tomahawk out of the plank. "Then we have to cauterize the stump. Stoke the fire in his lodge so we can heat this until the head glows red hot. But your father may still bleed to death."

"I'm undecided if that would be a good thing," she said, handing her father's disarticulated hand to a warrior.

"Burn it," she told him.

"No!" the chief said.

"Yes, burn it," Jack said.

The chief was sitting upright, watching as his blood wet the dirt around him. He was strangely calm, breathing normally, and listening to the conversation with indifference.

"Let's get us some help to carry him over while you're making up your mind," Jack said.

Sky looked around.

"No!" she shouted at the archer, who had an arrow

drawn and was aiming for the middle of Jack's back. He had watched in alarm as Jack had swung the tomahawk and severed the hand. "He's trying to save his life," she said in their language. "Put that down and come help us get him to the lodge."

"Do not touch me," the chief said.

Sky was kneeling beside him, wrapping the stump in layers of cloth.

"I told you not to remove my hand."

"It was necessary," Sky said. "Who is my father?"

"I'm your father."

"Adopted. That's what you said. Who sired me?"

"Leave him be," Jack said.

"No. This is the one chance I have to know the truth," she said, tying an angry knot in the bandages, already heavy with blood. "If he dies, I'll never know why he killed my mother. And if he lives, I'll never again have him at a disadvantage."

The archer and a handful of other warriors moved forward to carry Lightning Crow to the lodge. Sky held up her hand to stop them.

"Tell me," she said. "Who made me in my mother's womb?"

Lightning Crow stared at her.

"It was the French priest, Toussaint," he said. "The one who gave me this."

He touched the cross around his neck, and then gestured at the world.

"But why kill Red Buffalo Woman? So she lay with a priest and became full with child. It is the way of our nation. It was a gift—the strange man's power is transferred to you. Did she want to leave with him?"

The chief shook his head while the archer and the others helped him to his feet.

"Then what was her offense?"

"She beguiled him and encouraged his wickedness," he said. "His shame was great, but the sin was hers."

19 *Banished*

Lightning Crow slept beneath a pile of buffalo robes near the fire while Elk Woman sat beside him, watching. The stump of the chief's right wrist was on top of the buffalo robes, wrapped tightly in skins. The lodge was layered in bands of bluish haze that still smelled slightly of burning flesh, and from the smoke hole overhead a shaft of morning light cut through the bands of smoke like a spear. Sitting on a backrest on the other side of the chief, Jack watched as the oval of sunlight traveled across the earthen floor of the lodge as the sun climbed higher. Sky was asleep, her head resting against his shoulder.

Jack listened to the sound of Lightning Crow's breathing, satisfied that he was out of immediate danger. But it would be another two weeks before it would become apparent whether he had contracted rabies. When the chief finally roused, he asked for water.

Elk Woman held a bowl of water to his lips, and he drank.

Jack gently shook Sky awake.

"How do you feel?" Jack asked.

"Tired," the chief said.

"It will take some time to recover from losing the hand," Sky said.

"Have you come to hate me?" the chief asked.

"How can I hate you?" Sky asked. "It seems I hardly know you. Besides, it is not the place of the disobedient daughter of a disobedient slave woman to express emotion."

Elk Woman, who did not understand French, remained silent, but knew from the tone of Sky's voice that she was being disrespectful. She frowned to show her disapproval.

"Your disrespect is unbecoming," Lightning Crow said, then drank more water. "But I will allow it, trusting that it will pass in time."

"As you wish," Sky said.

"Are you in much pain?" Jack asked.

"This," the chief said, holding up the bandaged limb, "is of no consequence. The madness may kill me yet, so I have made some decisions for the survival of the village."

Lightning Crow removed the wooden cross from his neck and weighed it in his left hand. His fingers closed over it and held it tightly against his palm while he spoke.

"The first is that the war with the whites—and their allies, our cousin enemies the Mandans—will continue, but with added ferocity. The second decision is that should I indeed leave this world, my wish is for the war chief to lead the people. He will become keeper of the village's sacred bundle."

"No," Sky said.

"War requires a general, not a peacemaker."

"You may yet live," Jack said.

"In which case I will continue to lead, even with one hand," he said. "And I will be a better general. We have grown soft and lazy with the gifts of the white man. It should be a time of victory."

"The boat was not victory enough?"

"It was only a taste of victory," Lightning Crow said. "My third decision is this." He tossed the wooden cross into the firepit, where it flared and burned with unusual intensity.

"Jesus teaches forgiveness," he said. "But there is no room for forgiveness in my heart, only vengeance. Until war is over, I will have only one religion, and that is the doctrine of the knife and the gun. No mercy will be found in my heart."

"This is unwise," Sky said.

"My last decision is this," the chief said. "You, Jack Picaro, must leave this village. You have brought us nothing but bad luck, you have turned my daughter's head until it sits backward on her shoulders, and your careless talk of wolves summoned a mad one to our gates. I should have killed you at the first chance I got, back at the boat."

"Please," Sky said. "Father, don't."

"When must I leave?" Jack asked.

"Now," the chief said, and his head dropped to the folds of the buffalo robe. "No more words from you as you exit my lodge. You must never return to the village, upon pain of death. And the next time we meet, outside these walls, I will kill you and put your scalp on a pole atop my lodge."

Jack stood.

"Don't," Sky said, trying to pull him down.

He walked out of the lodge. It was still early, and there was little activity, except the usual milling of dogs and the sounds of wood being thrown on the ground. In the center of the plaza, the archer and another warrior were tearing apart the sacred ark, plank by plank. They had half of it down, revealing the inside.

Jack walked over and looked.

In the center was a pole, about the height of a man, painted bright red.

"That is all that was inside the canoe," Sky said, now at his shoulder. "A single cedar pole that is Lone Man—Lucky Man, to the Sahnish—who stood in the middle of the great waters at the beginning of time and created this world. It is all passing now."

Jack nodded.

"You must leave, and quickly," Sky said. "Lightning Crow is asleep now, but when he wakes, he will give the order and his men will kill you if they find you here or near the gates. Gather your things and go to the corral and get your Blackfoot pony. I will be waiting at the front gate to say good-bye. Now, hurry."

It took Jack ten minutes to gather dead Martin's rifle and the possibles bag and find his pony in the corral at the rear of the village. His Damascus knife was in its scabbard, and he carried the iron tomahawk behind him, the handle looped beneath his belt. He slipped the halter on Star and swung up on her back.

He rode through the village at an easy pace, watching the crimson and gold of dawn bloom in the eastern sky. The men had the sacred ark completely disabled now, and although they had treated the cottonwood planks roughly, they were gently removing the cedar post. He nodded as he rode past, and the archer nodded back.

Sky was waiting at the front gate. In one hand she held some bags of corn and squash, tied with cord. In the other she had a long gun, and it took Jack a moment to realize it was the ghost rifle.

"Why?" Jack asked.

"Because I must," she said. "It is the only thing of value I can give you in farewell, and it is the only thing I can take from Lightning Crow that will strike at his heart. I may kill him yet, but this is enough for now."

Jack slung dead Martin's rifle across his back from a rope tied to the barrel and the waist of the stock. Then he took the ghost rifle while Sky slung the bags of food over the horse's neck. He thumbed open the door to the patch box, shoved aside the squares of patch cloth, and turned the stock to the light to peer inside.

"What are you doing?"

"Checking that the rifle still has power."

Nestled beneath the hinge, he saw the rim of the brass disk.

"Thank you, Jesus and Mari," he whispered.

"My father's shooting bag is in the sack with the squash," Sky said. "It has powder and the lead balls for the gun."

"I am grateful beyond words," Jack said. "Won't he punish you?"

"He will beat me," she said. "But not kill me, I think."

"Will we ever see each other again?" he asked.

"I don't know," she said.

"Then come with me."

"I cannot," she said. "My father and his warriors would spend their last breaths tracking us down in order to kill you slowly. They would make me watch, and that is something I cannot do."

"My affection for you is deep," Jack said.

"Speak not," Sky said, tears spilling down her cheeks. "It only makes things worse. But there is love in my heart for you, as well."

He leaned down and they kissed.

"Winter is not far off," she said. "Your path must be upriver, to where Major Henry and the fur company are building their fort on the Yellowstone. It is at the edge of the Crow territory. The journey will take three weeks. On your way, you will pass the biggest of the Mandan villages, at the mouth of the Heart River, where your captains wintered years ago. Return there during the Moon of the Long Nights. If it is to be, you will find me there."

Jack touched her cheek.

"When you hear the loon's song," he said, "think of me."

"I will think of your bad poetry," she said. "Now, go!"

Then he urged Star forward, following the trail over the ditches and past the fields where the corn had been harvested, leaving only stubble.

PART THREE
THE CONVENT

20 *The World Is So Large*

The narrow bed in which Abella Rapaille lay bleeding was in the garret of the stately brick Sacred Heart convent building, near a gable in the barnlike ceiling of unfinished wood. The window in the gable was open and Abella could feel the August breeze on her clammy face and, if she focused her eyes, see a patch of sky and the gilded cross on the steeple of the church that fronted the convent.

The Rapaille family had contributed heavily during the construction of the convent, and had even loaned the Sisters of the Sacred Heart two slaves, until the sisters could buy their own. The convent building was just three years old and was one of the few brick buildings in the city of St. Ferdinand de Florissant, on Coldwater Creek, a few miles northwest of St. Louis. It was built in the Federal style, which added a certain authority to the structure.

The sisters had come up from New Orleans to establish the convent and eventually a school. Some of them had sought refuge here from France, where the religious order was sometimes derided by the anti-Catholic Republic as the Whores of the Sacred Heart. The convent mother, Sister Rose Philippine Duchesne, was fifty-three years old, had been born at the foot of the French Alps, and now had a face scarred by smallpox. She believed it her duty to bring the word of Jesus to the native tribes in the American interior, but her assignments thus far had largely to do with educating and caring for the girls of the wealthier French Catholic families.

In fulfilling this duty, she assigned one of the other sisters to visit Abella once a day, and the sister always brought a relevant Bible verse as a topic of conversation. Past lessons were about how a woman's pain in childbirth was part of the suffering brought into the world by sin. But today's catechism was about the redemptive power of faith and the promise of life everlasting.

"I'm dying," Abella said without inflection.

She had difficulty concentrating, and it sometimes seemed as if she were standing beside the bed, looking down at someone else whose black hair was plastered on her forehead, whose eyes were sunken in dark sockets, and whose bedsheets were ever stained crimson across her thighs.

"We are praying for you," the sister said. Her name was Beatrix, she had been born in St. Charles, and she was a small young woman with a face that seemed perpetually pinched. Abella thought her French crude and always insisted, in the days she was still able to insist on anything, that they speak in English. "Dr. Muldridge has been summoned and we expect him shortly. But there is little he can do."

That is what the good doctor always does, Abella thought. *Little.*

"And Aristide?"

"Your brother is away."

Abella nodded.

"Yes," she said. "I had forgotten."

"Please, don't talk. It's better if you rest."

"Is there any word of Jacques?"

Sister Beatrix hesitated.

"Your Uncle Guy forbade us from speaking of him."

"My uncle has disowned me," Abella said. "I am a stranger to my family. Please, of you know something of Jacky, tell me."

"There has been no news," Sister Beatrix said.

She did not say that Jacques Aguirre was believed dead these many months, having last been seen in a distressed state and making enemies of a cruel keelboat man named Bledsoe at a riverfront tavern in Carondelet. Bledsoe, too, had disappeared, and it was assumed that he had fled after murdering Aguirre on the trace, and perhaps after wrecking the Rapaille gun shop downtown.

"Will I be permitted last rites?" Abella asked.

"No," Sister Beatrix said. "Father has considered it, but feels your sins are too grave. You have also not been properly disposed to receive the sacrament of communion."

"Oh?" Abella asked.

"You seem unrepentant," the nun said. "You have brought disgrace to yourself and your family, you have dishonored God, and yet you remain unrepentant."

"I repent of having injured others and I admit to disobedience," Abella said. "I regret making unwise choices. But I do not repent of having loved, and I will not denounce Jacky."

The nun folded her hands.

"Water," Abella said. "Please."

"Of course," the nun said, and poured a cup from a white porcelain pitcher on a stand. "Can you hold it?"

Abella nodded.

She took the cup and brought it to her cracked lips, sipping a little. The water felt curious as it went down, like it was a living thing curling about inside her. She had the sensation again of standing beside the bed, watching herself drink from the cup. This made her loosen her grip, and the cup sagged, spilling water down her chin and throat.

Sister Beatrix took the cup and put it back on the stand.

"How funny it all is."

"What is?" the nun asked.

"This," Abella said, motioning with her hand. "Here I am flat on my back in this bed with blood seeping from my wound, and there I am in my favorite blue dress looking down at myself."

"Your mind is playing tricks," Sister Beatrix suggested.

"No," Abella said. "I think I'm seeing it all clearly for this first time."

"Would you like to pray?"

"For what?"

"Forgiveness," Sister Beatrix said. "For your sin."

"What is my sin?"

"You know as well as I do," the nun said, putting a hand to her well-covered bosom. "You have lain with a man—"

"—Jacques," Abella said. "And many times I have lain with him."

"Yes, this Jacques," Sister Beatrix said. "You surrendered to the iniquity of the flesh, and have borne children without sacrament of marriage, and now you are paying the price for it."

"I thought I was paying the price for a difficult birth," Abella said. "As many women do."

"Your guilt is heavy," Sister Beatrix said, and she got down on her knees beside the bed and clasped her hands together, her rosary entwined in her fingers. "Pray with me now for God to lift the burden."

Abella reached down and grasped the nun's wrist.

"Pray for my health, but do not pray because you think me guilty," Abella said. "For I feel no guilt."

Sister Beatrix rose and crossed herself.

"My children," Abella said. "I want to see them."

"That is unwise," the nun said. "They are to be taken."

Abella laughed, and she saw the Abella in the blue dress laugh with her.

"What kind of attachment can a dying woman form?" she asked. "Not a lasting one, at least not on this side of life. Bring the children to me. I want to hold them and say farewell."

"I hope they do not inherit their mother's insolence or disbelief," Sister Beatrix said.

I hope they do, the Abella in the blue dress said. *But it is not insolence, it's stubbornness. And it is not disbelief, it's pragmatism.*

The nun turned, walked down the hall, and went down the stairs.

In a few minutes a young slave and wet nurse named Portia came holding a baby in each arm. The infants were small, just two days old and had been delivered in the middle of the night by a midwife who smoked a clay pipe and spoke only Creole French. She had left a poultice to apply to help with the bleeding, but after she had left the sisters had thrown it away, worried that it was the work of the devil. When Abella's bleeding worsened, they blamed her sin, rather than an internal hemorrhage.

"Are you strong enough to hold 'em?" Portia asked.

"Yes," Abella said.

Carefully, Portia placed the boy in Abella's right arm

and the girl in her left. But Portia remained hovering just in case the mother was suddenly taken by weakness.

"They are so tiny," Abella said. "And the world is so large."

The boy was quiet in her arms, his wide eyes blinking and his fingers working. But the girl was more restless, kicking her feet, and was taking in great breaths, preparing to cry.

"They'll be all right, miss," Portia said. "They came early, but I've seen babies smaller than this grow up to be right strapping lads and healthy little ladies. I've been sweet on a lot of children in my time, and I'll be sweet on these too, until . . ."

"Where will they go?"

"I don't know, miss," Portia said. "It's up to Master Guy."

The girl infant was crying now, her open mouth revealing pink gums.

"Will you tell them their mother loved them?"

Portia's eyes filled with tears.

"Oh, they will know that."

"They will not unless someone tells them," Abella said. "You must promise me you will tell them, and find someone to keep telling them until they are grown."

"I don't know, miss," Portia said, tears running down her cheeks.

"You must," Abella said, and her other self in the blue dress insisted as well. "Because they will not know otherwise. You must tell them who their father was, and that he was brilliant despite his flaws. You do know of Jacques Aguirre, yes? Good. And you must tell them I had no regrets in having them, and that I would sin a thousand times over to bring them into the world, and that no child so loved is illegitimate."

Portia was looking down, where her tears were falling on the rough floor at her feet. She was thinking of her own children, two by her slave husband and a third by one of her masters.

"Does that go for all children?" she asked.

"All children," Abella said, and then realized what was being asked. "Of every color."

"I will, miss," Portia said. "I promise."

The girl was crying louder, and now her brother was crying, as well.

Good, the Abella in the blue dress said. *We can go now.*

"Take them," Abella said. "Please."

Portia took them carefully from Abella and, once they were in her arms, she gently began swaying to soothe them.

"What shall we call them?" Portia asked.

"Their names, of course," Abella said drowsily.

"But we don't know," Portia said. "You haven't named them."

The Abella in the blue dress rolled her eyes in impatience.

"The sisters wouldn't let me," Abella said softly. "They said their new families will give them names. Tell me, are they going to a good family?"

"I don't know, miss," Portia said.

But Portia did know. The uncle had arranged to send the children to a struggling French family, who had a farm northwest of St. Louis, in exchange for a hundred silver dollars for himself and ten to the convent. Even though indentures were increasingly rare in the states, Guy Rapaille clung to the ways of the Old World—and regarded Jacques Aguirre's broken indenture as a debt the bastard children must pay.

Portia hesitated, then clasped her hands.

"To hell with what the sisters say," she said sharply. "You must give them their names. Otherwise, you won't know them in the beyond, and they won't know you. It doesn't matter what anybody else will call them—the names you give them will always be their real names. Please, miss, have you thought about their names?"

"Oh, I know their names," Abella said. "The girl is April, like the ship Jackie came to America in."

"And the boy?"

"Augustus," Abella said. "For the month of his birth."

"April," Portia repeated, smiling. "And Augustus."

Then the Abella in the blue dress reached out and grasped the other in the bed firmly by the hand. *Time to go,* she said, pulling her upward toward the open gabled window and the blue sky beyond. *Do not be afraid. Follow me.*

By the time Dr. Muldridge ascended the stairs to the garret and knelt by the bed, Abella had been dead for half an hour. Muldridge stood, removed his hat, and was still standing over the bed in reflection when Aristide burst into the room.

"Abella!" he cried.

His boots were like thunder on the garret floor.

He fell beside the bed, looking in horror at the darkening stain in the bedclothes. He took his sister's cold hand into his own, trying to rub some life into it. "No, no, my poor sister," he said. "I saw you just a week ago and you were in fine health, the babies still weeks away. I would not have run the errand down the river to Cairo had I known."

"They were early," Muldridge said. "The midwife was called, I'm told, but could not stop the bleeding."

"Could you have stopped it?"

Muldridge shrugged.

"Such bleeding is vexatious."

"You stopped my bleeding," Aristide said, placing the palm of his right hand on his shirt, over the spot where the ball from the dueling pistol had entered his chest.

Aristide had been found at daylight on the morning after the duel, washed up on a stretch of muddy bank just below the landing, by some black fishermen who were about to run some lines for catfish to supply the former governor's dinner table. They thought he was dead, but Muldridge had detected the slightest of pulses. By some presumed miracle, the ball had narrowly missed the heart and lungs, and without striking an artery had lodged against a rib in Aristide's back. Muldridge had removed the ball from the rear, and for two weeks Aristide fought a fever brought on by infection, but within months had fully recovered, with the exception of a cough that was prompted by bad weather.

Aristide sat on the floor beside the bed and buried his face in his hands.

"She was seventeen," he said.

Muldridge placed a hand on the sobbing man's shoulder.

"She is with the saints now," the doctor said.

"What of her children?"

"Ah," Muldridge said. "Twins. Sadly, they did not survive."

PART FOUR
THE MOUNTAINS

21 *Major Henry*

Jack reached Fort Henry just as the first flakes of snow were falling from a gunmetal-blue October sky. The fort was a sorry-looking blockade building and a collection of lean-tos surrounded by a palisade, with swivel guns at the corners overlooking the river, where a single keelboat was tied. The fort did not look nearly as fine as he had seen it in his dream. Instead, it looked hastily constructed, and with little regard for level or square.

Jack was wet when he rode up to the gate, because the fort was on the north bank of the Yellowstone, and he had come from the south. He had found a place to ford and then swim the horse just upriver, but crossing had soaked his buckskins and his moccasins. Halfway through from Lightning Crow's village to the fort, he had stopped at the Mandan village on the Knife River that Sky had spoken of. He was welcomed there, and he ate well and rested for a day. Because his boots were nearly split open at the seams, and his cloth trousers torn and frayed, he had gladly traded dead Martin's rifle for a jacket and breeches of fringed buckskin, two pair of fine moccasins, a buffalo robe, and a hat made from the fur of a fox.

When the sentry above the gate spotted Jack as he approached, he called out a warning to come no closer bearing a rifle. Indians, he said, must come unarmed to trade. Still thirty yards out, Jack took off his cap of fox fur and waved it over his head.

"It's a white man," Jack heard the sentry call.

"Of what nation?" The question came from Major Henry, behind the walls. Jack recognized his gruff voice.

"I'm an American," Jack called.

"What's your name?" the sentry asked.

"Jack Picaro."

The gate swung open and Jack rode in.

A dozen men of the company clustered around. Jack looked for Decatur, but did not see him. Major Henry was standing off to one side, his hands behind his back, his top hat askew, taking the measure of the man he had hired back in Washington County when he had presented himself with a letter of introduction from William Clark.

Henry was forty-five years old. His cheeks were covered in a week's worth of beard stubble, and tufts of gray hair escaped from beneath his hat, but his bearing was formal, giving the impression of an aristocrat who had fallen on hard times. He wore a long black coat with brass buttons with the checkered handgrip of a pistol poking from one of the pockets.

"Gunsmith," Henry said, "we haven't seen you in five months. We chalked you up for dead. But I see the boy we knew is gone, and in his place is this full-bearded man in buckskin on a fine Indian pony."

"I wasn't coming here without my rifle," Jack said, sliding down Star's side to the ground, the gun in his hand. "It was some bother to get it back."

"Some bother indeed," Henry said. "You disobeyed standing orders to stay with the boat."

"With respect, sir, the boat was half burned and half sunk, and there wasn't anybody of rank left to give any orders," Jack said. "Did Decatur give you the message from the Arikara chief Lightning Crow?"

"He did not."

"Where is Cate?"

"Gone," Henry said.

"He went back home?" Jack asked.

"That's not what I meant, son," Henry said. "Decatur is lost."

Jack watched the snowflakes swirling down and resting on the hats and heads and shoulders of the men around him and could think of nothing to say.

"He was retrieved from the bank of the river near the wreck of the *Jefferson* by a search party sent downriver," Henry said. "He delivered over the Bible with your message. On the party's ascent, they held over for three days at the Mandan village. Decatur went hunting on the morning of the second day and has not been heard of since and is presumed dead."

Jack was surrounded by men, but he felt more alone than ever.

"He was a friend," Jack said. "I will miss him. But I do not think he was suited for the wilderness."

Henry cleared his throat.

"I must agree," Henry said. "After his rescue, he was reported to have said that he wished he'd stayed home."

Jack blinked back tears.

Henry nodded and awkwardly put a hand on his shoulder.

"Such is the risk for men of action."

"Homesickness?" Jack asked.

"Dying far from home," Henry said

Jack nodded and scanned the interior of the stockade.

"There seems to be more truck here than was loaded on the boats when we left," Jack said. "There's a forge yonder, and smithing tools. More swivel guns. The iron screw for the press that squeezes the plews into bundles."

"General Ashley came, with a boat loaded with food and the things he thought would be most useful," Henry said. "It is the second supply boat he has sent. The first, the *Enterprise*, of some seventy-five feet in length, was barely out of the states, in Pawnee country, when it sank. It was being cordelled upriver and its mast caught a heavy branch of a low-hanging tree, and it tipped and swamped."

"Anybody drowned?"

"No," Henry said. "But we lost ten thousand dollars in boat, supplies, and trade goods. General Ashley borrowed enough on credit to replace the boat and its contents."

"It is a nearly unimaginable fortune," Jack said.

"If the Rocky Mountain Fur Company does not succeed," Henry said, "we are ruined. General Ashley returned downriver immediately after delivery of the goods, so as not to risk the new boat being damaged by ice. He has left us the *Yellowstone* for a time. Ashley will return in the spring, with more men and more supplies, and we will load them up with plews."

"The *Yellowstone* is not big enough for all of us to return downriver."

"No," Henry said. "And it will have to go downriver soon, to keep from being damaged by the ice, and to load supplies for the return trip."

Jack was uncomfortably reminded of Cortés burning

his ships on the shores of the New World so his men would have no choice but to conquer or die. As a bound man, he had found his only freedom in books, and he read everything he could borrow or steal—especially books on history, geography, and metallurgy. He has also read poetry and fiction, when nothing else was available.

"This evening, come see me at my table upstairs," Henry said. "We will eat and you will tell me of the country you've seen and the situation with the hostiles. I'll wager you didn't trade for that pony—or for the rifle, either."

Major Henry's quarters were in an end loft of the blockhouse, elevated from where the company ate and slept, and there was a window that, when the shutter was open, had a view of the river. Tonight, the leather-hinged shutter was closed tight against the bitter wind blowing from the north.

In the center of the loft was a long table with a dozen chairs around it, with a chair reserved for Henry at its head. But tonight, just Henry and Jack sat at the table, with light provided by a pair of candlesticks. The table was laden with elk and buffalo roast, corn and beans, a wedge of cheese, and a loaf of crusty bread.

There was also an open bottle of red wine.

Henry pulled the pistol out of his pocket and placed it with a clatter on the table. He unbuttoned his coat but did not remove it, as it was cold in the blockhouse. Then he poured a pair of tin cups full of the wine and pushed one toward Jack, who sat to his right.

"To your health," Henry said.

"À votre santé," Jack said, and they clinked cups.

Jack took a drink and sighed in satisfaction.

"I had forgotten the taste of wine," Jack said.

"This comes from Sauternes," Henry said. "I have a few bottles set aside for special occasions. Your prodigal return merited uncorking one."

"I'm glad you think so," Jack said. "Tell me, how does the trade go? Have you collected many bundles of plews?"

"Hardly any," the captain said, putting his cup on the table. Jack waited for explanation while the major fished for a briar pipe in his jacket pocket. He brought it out and packed it carefully with tobacco taken from a leather pouch. He took one of the candlesticks and tilted the flame down to light the pipe, sucking with his cheeks.

"There's been a change in our way of doing business," Henry said. Then he puffed on his pipe and expelled a great cloud of smoke. "James Monroe's government in Washington, at the urging of my old friend William Clark, has passed a new law that forbids us from selling or trading liquor to the Indians. This law went into effect in August, but Ashley brought the news of it."

"Then the venture is over," Jack said, tearing off a piece of bread and slicing a bit of cheese. "The Rocky Mountain Fur Company is out of business."

"Business has changed for all of us," Henry said. "Now, instead of relying on the Indians exclusively to bring beaver plews to posts like this one, we are going to have to have to trap the beaver ourselves. It is something the majority of our men have no experience with. They will have to learn, and learn quickly, because they are latecomers to the game."

"But you're not," Jack said.

"No," he said, shifting in his chair. "I was in the fur business with Manuel Lisa, years ago, along with Chouteau and Clark. We were the original Missouri Fur Company. Since Lisa's death two years ago, it has been reorganized by Joshua Pilcher into this new venture. Then there is the American Fur Company, which is Astor's, and is reaching into the upper Missouri from its bases in the Northwest. And all of this competition for the hide of a rodent."

"With fortunes in the balance."

"The demand in Europe and Russia is insatiable," Henry said. "And there are new markets for beaver pelts opening in China."

"I heard in St. Louis that the best beaver pelts come from where it is high and cold," Jack said.

"Pilcher is in the best position, because he has a post far up on the Bighorn River, which is the gates of the Rocky Mountains. Despite our name, we are yet on the plains here."

"I saw mountains, in my wanderings," Jack said. "Although what range I know not. I was lost, out of sight of the river."

"It was summer," Henry said. "A forgiving season."

"I do not see how we can compete with Pilcher and the others," Jack said. "These men are experienced, they have already established themselves in the best locations, their relations with the tribes are superior—and they will know how to trap beaver. If this was a game of cards, I would fold and cut my losses."

"That I cannot do," Henry said. "I have staked what little money I have on this enterprise, as has General Ashley. The alternative is to return to St. Louis in shame and in debt. We must succeed or perish in the attempt."

"No matter what," Jack said, "we are stuck here for the

winter. Here or the Mandan village. The boat is too small to take all of us back and, even if we left now, we will be trapped if the ice comes early."

Jack had finished his wine, and Henry poured him more.

"I want you to scout and trap for me," Henry said. "So that you may be an example to the rest."

"I know nothing of trapping."

"You have had a summer in the wilderness to teach you how to survive on your own and to parley with the tribes," Henry said. "You've already demonstrated that you can survive on your own in hostile territory, which is the primary consideration for a good trapper. You can learn how to trap, from some of our older men and the Mandans below river. They are welcoming and will teach you."

"I have been to their village," Jack said. "I know."

"We have plenty of steel traps," Henry said. "I will send some of the men to help you scout, perhaps young Wilks. Or, there's a one-eyed nigger named Shephard who joined the company when we were a week above Westport."

"I'm a gunsmith, not a scout."

"We already have a blacksmith, and he will do to mend whatever guns need it," Henry said. "But you, boy, I need you to trap. Our challenge now is considerable more difficult than the one presented to us when we left St. Louis in the spring. For morale, we must demonstrate that it is a challenge that can be mastered and that promise of fortune still holds."

Jack stabbed the elk steak with a two-pronged fork, cut off a generous slice, and plopped it on his plate.

"What's your plan?"

"A new system," he said. "Using our own trappers is a

start. We will still trade with the Indians, but they will not be anxious to part with their plews if we can't offer them spirits. Trade knives and brass bells are just not as enticing as popskull whiskey. Beyond that, we'll have to reckon a better way to get our plews to market."

"More forts?" Jack asked. "More boats?"

"The best plews are taken in places our boats can't go," Henry said.

"In the mountains," Jack said.

"And in the ice," Henry said. "You are free to roam and find new places to trap. The rest of the company will winter here. You will rejoin us before spring, and then we will head west, into the mountains."

"I would like a fortnight to consider it," Jack said.

"You have a day," Henry said.

"I was hoping for a rest."

"Outside the walls of a Mandan lodge," Henry said, "there is no rest in winter. What can you tell me of the Crees you encountered?"

"The village led by Lightning Crow intends to continue his war against the whites. He has burned his symbols of Christianity and abandoned their old ways. Their new religion is war itself."

"But this is just the one village?"

"It is a large village," Jack said. "And I fear the passion for war will spread to the other twelve. We are safe for the winter, because the Sahnish people sensibly do not like to war in the cold. They will wait until spring."

"And the Indian pony you ride?"

"Taken from a Blackfoot warrior who ambushed me," Jack said. "I killed him and took his horse. He was along and far east of the normal range for the tribe, so I do not think we have to fear a Blackfoot attack, not yet."

Henry said that was a bit of welcome news.

"When General Ashley came," Jack asked, "did he bring any news of St. Louis?"

"He had quite a lot of say about politics."

"That is all?"

"As I recall, yes," Henry said. "Why do you ask?"

"I . . . I am homesick for news of my family."

Jack could not tell him that he wanted to know if there was news of the fugitive Jacques Aguirre, so he substituted homesickness. But as he did, he thought of Abella, and then he was indeed homesick.

"Aren't we all," Henry said. "But Ashley mentioned nothing about Picaros or any other family. I think if you had a relative who had shuffled the coil, word would have been sent upriver. So I would not worry, gunsmith."

"Yes," Jack said. "That is a comfort."

"Now," Henry said, spooning food onto his own plate. "Tell me what you found in the wilderness?"

Jack took a sip of wine.

"I have found a place in America to call home."

"And do you know what it will take to keep it?"

Henry stared at him as a schoolmaster looks at a boy who has not learned his lessons. He reached his right hand deep into his pocket, brought it out with his fist closed.

"These," Henry said, opening his hand. In the palm were a cluster of lead balls for the pistol. "These come from my mines in Washington County. They are cast from good Missouri lead, and many of them will end up buried in the hearts and skulls of our enemies."

Henry spilled the balls onto the table, and they rolled

in a dozen directions, clinking against plates and the cups of wine and the brass trigger guard of the pistol. Some of the balls fell from the edge and bounced across the plank floor.

"Nothing but force ever kept anything worth having," Henry said.

22 *Reunion*

Jack walked down the stairs into the big open room of the blockhouse with Major Henry's words still ringing in his ears. He did not want to believe them, but in his heart he feared it was true. The source of all the trouble he had known in the world was because somebody wanted to take something from him that was precious: his freedom, his rifle, his life. All of his hard work and strife seemed impotent in comparison.

"You," somebody shouted as Jack's moccasins touched the floor.

Moses Bledsoe was pointing an accusing finger at him from across the room.

"I saw you ride in, but I didn't recognize you under all the beard and long hair and buckskin," Bledsoe said. "But then I looked again and thought, perhaps. But when I heard you talk, I was pretty sure of it. That's a downright strange accent you've got there. It ain't French, and it ain't Spanish. What is it?"

"Creole," Jack said.

"No, I don't think so. I've heard plenty of Creole, and you don't sound like them."

"Then you've never been to my parish," Jack said.

Jack stopped and looked at Bledsoe as if seeing him for the first time.

"We don't know each other," Jack said.

"But I think you do know old Moses Bledsoe. I think we're old friends."

Bledsoe reached behind him and drew a ten-inch knife from the sheath at his belt. Jack recognized the knife as the one Bledsoe had called Biter and used on the apple between Chelley's legs at The Grackle.

"What's your name, stranger?" Jack asked.

"Moses Bledsoe. And yours?"

"Jack Picaro."

"No, I don't think that's right." Bledsoe advanced, the knife held loosely in his right hand. "But there's really only one way to be sure. I aim to scrape all that fur off your face and have a gander."

"You're mistaken," Jack said, putting a hand on the hilt of the Damascus toothpick. His rifle was across the block-house, rolled up in his blanket where he had found a place against the wall to sleep. "And you've been drinking. I can smell *that* from here."

"I may have had a little sip," Bledsoe said.

"I think you've had the whole jug. Go sleep it off."

There were thirty other men in the blockhouse, lounging about some rough wooden tables in the center of the room, and gradually they left their seats and opened a space between Jack and Bledsoe. The men now stood near the wall, their arms crossed or leaning against posts, some of them smoking clay pipes and others whispering to one another.

"Oh, no," Bledsoe said. "You always was a smooth talker, but your tongue ain't going to get you out of this one. You cheated me at cards, and I have a strict rule about killing liars and cheats."

"I don't think Major Henry would approve of fighting in the blockhouse."

"There he is," Bledsoe said, indicating the railing above Jack with a jerk of his head. "Why don't you ask him?"

"What's the trouble?" Henry asked, leaning on the rail.

"No trouble," Jack said.

"This one ain't who he claims to be," Bledsoe said.

Henry sighed.

"Half the men in the company are known by different names in the states," Henry said. "It doesn't matter what a man did back home, as long as he pulls his weight here and is loyal to the company. He does that, and I don't care if he's the bloody Prince of Darkness in Pennsylvania."

"Me and him have history," Bledsoe said.

"I don't give a good goddamn," Henry said. "You'll do no fighting inside the walls. You have a score to settle, you do it outside the gates—and you do it with your fists, not knives. Every man in the company is to be treated with respect, no matter what their life was in the states."

"Equal?" Bledsoe asked. "Including criminals?"

"Picaro is charged with no crime here."

"Well, what about color?" Bledsoe asked. "You're saying that nigger in the corner is the equal of a white man?"

He pointed his knife at a young black man sitting on a barrel, one of his legs drawn up. He was resting his hands on the raised knee and was watching Bledsoe with an unreadable expression.

"Every man in the company is equal to every other, rank notwithstanding," Henry said. "Shephard does his share. He has an equal stake."

"Let's see him produce his letters of manumission."

"There is no need," Henry said. "Shephard joined the company in Pawnee country, upriver of Westport. He is a free black."

Bledsoe glared, still holding the knife in his hand.

"It ain't right," Bledsoe shouted. "It's ag'in the Bible and the state legislature."

"We are far beyond the laws of any state," Henry said. "There is no slavery here. And there is no God on the Upper Missouri except for good Missouri lead."

There was silence in the room.

"Do I need to make myself any clearer?" Henry asked.

Bledsoe cleared his throat.

"Your nigger better not bump elbows with me at the dinner table."

"Sheath that blade," Henry said.

"And what if I don't?"

"I'll shoot you dead where you stand," Henry said. "I can always find another man to pilot the keelboat."

Bledsoe looked up and saw that Henry now had his pistol in his hand.

"All right," Bledsoe said easily. "No trouble. If this shaggy critter says he's a stranger, then right as rain, that's what the lying sack of horseshit is. But there will come a time when we're outside the gates and we will see what is what, sure enough."

Bledsoe returned Biter to its sheath.

"Let's go now," Jack said. "While your words are fresh in my mind. It will add to the enjoyment of beating the filthy words out of your mouth. Come along, out the gates and in the snow."

"Picaro," Henry called. "Stand down."

Jack could feel the men watching.

"Major Henry is right," Jack said, taking his hand from

the hilt of his knife. "It wouldn't be a fair fight. You're too drunk. We'll wait until you sober up so you only have stupid as a disadvantage."

"I need some air," Bledsoe said. "It's become a mite foul smelling in here."

Bledsoe sauntered across the room to the door, turned, and went through it backward with his eyes on Jack. The door slammed after him, but did not close, and the snow swirled in.

"Latch that door," Henry said. "Let him cool off a bit."

Jack walked across the room to where the black man sat. He had a leather patch over his left eye, which made him seem a bit piratical.

"Damn," the black man said. "This is a reunion. I haven't seen you since the last time we didn't see each other. You've changed a bit since I saw you throwin' something I didn't understand into the muddy old river."

"Hello, Quarles," Jack said. "It looks like the runaway has found his new land."

"It weren't easy," Quarles said. "You?"

"The same."

Jack held out his hand and they shook, then they thumped each other on the shoulders.

"Major Henry has asked me to scout for new places to trap beaver," Jack said. "Clear to the front porch of the Rockies, maybe further. Are you of a mind to come with me?"

Quarles smiled.

"I might could be talked into it," he said. "I've grown tired of the scenery here."

23   *Shadow Heart*

Jack knew they were being watched.

They were a month from Fort Henry and had followed the Yellowstone up the Bighorn, which led into the mountains. Jack didn't know exactly where they were, but the air was thin and the snow was somehow drier than it was down on the plains. They were in the mountains, but there were higher mountains still to the west, stony peaks that the snow curled from like steam escaping a kettle. Jack kept adding to his powder horn map so that they could at least find their way back to where the Yellowstone joined the Missouri. About the only thing Jack knew for certain, however, is that they were deep in Crow country.

Jack had suspected for several days that they were being followed, but he wasn't sure until he was thigh-deep in freezing water baiting a trap in a creek below a beaver dam. The dam was a sturdy woven contraption of sticks and branches, causing high slack water above it. The traps were set below the dams, in shallow water. The chain that held the trap was secured in deeper water by a sharpened stick driven into the river bottom. Then the trap was baited with a branch marked with castoreum, a yellowish liquid that came from some glands near the ball sacks of the bull beavers, and was used to mark territory. The castoreum was carried in a horn, like a small version of a powder horn with a stopper. The branch that had been dipped in it was set upright in the shallow water, above the trap. A curious beaver, standing in the water to investigate a stranger's scent on a stick, would be unlucky enough to step on the trigger of the trap, springing its jaws shut on its foot. The chain in deeper water would prevent the beaver from making for the shore, where it could chew its paw off to escape. Usually the beaver would drown fighting the trap—a prolonged affair because a beaver can stay submerged for fifteen minutes without drawing a breath. If the chain was pulled from the bottom in the struggle, then the location of the five-pound trap and the drowned beaver would be marked by the stick floating on the surface.

It was mid-afternoon and Jack was setting the last of six traps for the day, which he would run early the next morning. Jack was barefoot in the snowmelt-chilled water and naked from the waist down, and although he could barely stand the cold, he could force himself to do it for the ten minutes it took to set a trap. Although others wore their breeches and moccasins into the water, it didn't make sense to Jack, because instead of being cold for just a few minutes, you would be miserable for the hours it took to dry your clothes, even if you had the luxury of a fire. Better to let most of the water drip off you and then change into dry breeches and moccasins.

Eighteen-year-old Jonathan Wilks was on the bank, his rifle beside him, and he was supposed to be watching out for Indians but he was shivering too violently to be of much use. Quarles was back with the horses, a quarter of a mile upstream, where they had made camp.

Something was in the snow-covered brush only a few dozen yards away from Jack. He heard whatever it was more than saw it, because when he glanced in that direction, all he could see was a thicket heavy with snow. But he could feel eyes on his back, as sure as he felt the cold water numbing his leg bones.

Jack stoppered the bait horn and stood up, trying to act as natural as possible. His rifle was leaning against the trunk of a tree at the water's edge, thirty yards away. He had a pistol in his belt, but that would not do much good against a Crow war party.

"This is a helluva way to make our fortunes," Jack called to Wilks, talking casually to show to whoever or whatever was watching he wasn't afraid. "Wading in ice water and setting iron traps and using beaver spunk to catch critters that have done us no harm. If we were smarter, we'd find an easier way to make our way in the world. But this way of life does have its rewards."

"What are you talking about?" Wilks asked, trying to stop his teeth from chattering. "Hurry up so we can get back to camp. I'm not sure I'll ever warm up until about July."

"Just look around you," Jack said. "This is the most beautiful country I've ever seen. The mountains have the plains beat all to hell. I said look around you, Wilks. The kind of creatures you find in these hills are a sight to behold. There's every kind of creature. Some of them are even two-legged."

Jack was wading cautiously to the bank.

"You know, the old-timers thought beavers had whole societies, like men do. Thought the dams were gathering places where the beavers held a kind of parliament and debated various issues of beaver politics and then voted.

Newspapers carried stories about it. It was a damned foolish notion, but probably no more foolish than me here in the water with just this popgun in my belt and dipping my pecker in the water. Get your own piece to hand, Wilks."

Alarmed, Wilks sat up.

"The curious thing about the beavers is that they mate for life," Jack said. "I wonder what happens when we take just one of them and the wife or the husband is left behind. Do they die of loneliness? Speaking of dying, you'd best be looking sharp."

Wilks picked up his rifle.

"Whango," Jack said.

As Jack climbed up on the bank, there was a tremendous shaking in the thicket and a kind of bawling growl. He jerked a pistol from his belt and held it in front of him. The pistol was .45 caliber, had an octagonal barrel, and was among the supplies allotted to him by Major Henry.

A small bear emerged from the thicket, a cub, with thick tawny fur. It shook its dish-shaped head and shuffled forward on feet that seemed too large for such an animal. It had a stubby snout and a face that seemed to be perpetually smiling.

"Collect yourself," Jack said, putting the pistol back in his belt and snatching up his moccasins and his breeches and the ghost rifle. "Let's be out of here quick."

"It's just a little bear," Wilks said. "And I hate bears."

Wilks brought the rifle to his shoulder.

"Don't," Jack shouted. "That's not a black bear, it's brown—"

Wilks fired, hitting the bear in the belly. The bear sat heavily down and bawled in pain, its eyes wide with terror.

"You idiot," Jack said, "That little bear is a grizzly, and it's calling for its mother. The sow can't be far behind."

"How was I to know?" Wilks asked.

"By paying attention," Jack said, pulling the pistol from his belt. "Every time we've come across a grizz we've given it a wide berth, and I've given you the whys and what fors."

Jack aimed at the cub's head. He fired, silencing the cub by putting a ball down his throat. The little bear collapsed in a heap of bloody fur.

"I should have put that ball in you," Jack said. "We need to put distance between us and that sow. Head out now. Go!"

At the camp, Quarles was reclining on a blanket beneath a canvas tarp, watching a boiling kettle that held corn and beans and a little elk meat. A clay pipe was in his mouth, the bowl upside down, the smoke curling away on the breeze over his shoulder.

Jack strode into camp, leaned his rifle against a tree, and placed a dead leaf over the muzzle to keep snow from falling down the barrel. His face was grim and he glared at Wilks as he walked into camp.

"What's the trouble?" Quarles asked.

"Wilks shot a grizzle cub," Jack said.

"Why would you do that?" Quarles demanded.

"It looked bigger than it was," Wilks said. "I hate bears. I didn't know it was a grizz—we've seen all kinds of bears, and some of them are brown and ain't grizzlies."

"I told you what to look for," Jack said. "The shape of the head, the long snout, the short ears, the hump on the back for grown ones. But I guess you won't know for sure until it rips your face off and has it as a snack."

"Now, Jack," Wilks said, putting his rifle across a snowy

log and taking a seat next to the fire. "You were acting all buggy like there was Indians about, so I was a little spooked anyway, what with all your talk about getting my piece to hand and so forth."

"I'm unconvinced there weren't Crows about," Jack said. "I had the feeling, you know, of somebody watching. It wasn't just the bear. It was something else."

"You're just superstitious," Wilks said. He had his tin cup out. "Is this stew ready?"

"It's ready if you can eat your beans uncooked."

Wilks made a face.

"I'm only superstitious when I'm gambling," Jack said. "What my feelings are telling me are things my mind can't get a grip on to put into words yet. It might be a sound or a smell or the way some snow lays near a log somebody has stepped over a day before."

"I've never seen any of that," Wilks said.

Quarles looked at Jack and smiled broadly.

"This one's going to be somebody's else's stew," Quarles said. "I hear the Crows they take their enemies alive and cook 'em up in a big pot. More tender that way."

"You're just trying to scare me," Wilks said.

"Yes, that's right," Quarles said. "Maybe scaring you will wake you up so you can learn and not get all of us killed."

Jack found a capote and threw it over his shoulders. He hadn't time to fully dry himself from the creek before pulling his clothes on, and now that he was sitting, he was getting chilly.

"What do you reckon the month is?" Jack asked.

Quarles shrugged.

"I tried to count the days since we left the Yellowstone,

but I've lost track," Jack said. "We went down to the nearest of the Mandan villages and spent a couple of weeks with them showing us how to trap beavers, and then we set out for the Bighorn River. I reckon it is the last of November or the first of December?"

"The nights are pretty long," Quarles said. "December for sure."

"I think we've scouted enough," Jack said. "We've got bundles of beaver plews on our packhorses to show for it, and plenty of new territory to tell Major Henry about. Let's think about going back downhill."

"Suits me," Quarles said. "Those Mandan maids do like me."

"I'm ready," Wilks said. "Tired of being cold all the time."

Jack nodded.

"This week, then, we'll head back," Jack said. "Now, how about some coffee?"

Quarles nodded, found a pot, and walked over to a patch of clean snow and scooped it up. Then he put it by the fire.

"Look here," Jack said to Wilks. "You're not a bad sort. I know you're strong enough, because I saw you do more than your share of work at Fort Henry. I know you're not an imbecile, because you can understand lessons and had done right well until we started into the mountains. So what's happened? Why have your brains suddenly dribbled out your ears?"

Wilks shrugged.

"You'd best figure things out," Jack said. "The higher we are, and the farther from the mouth of the Yellowstone, the less forgiving things become. A mistake on the plains means you maybe break a bone and are laid up in some warm lodge with a winter wife until you heal. You break something out here and you can't hunt or fend off enemies and it means you'll either freeze to death or become a scalp hanging from some warrior's lodge pole."

Wilks crossed his hands over his knees and rested his chin on his forearms.

"My mother had a dream," he said. "I didn't think much of it at the time, but when I told her I was going west with Ashley's company, she said she had a dream in which I was killed in the snow by an animal with thick fur and huge claws. It's been on my mind since we came to the mountains."

"It was just a dream," Jack said. "And mothers will say anything to keep their sons at home."

"Did yours?"

"No," Jack said.

"I'm afraid I'll never see her again," Wilks lamented.

"Jack's right," Quarles said. "You can't put any stock into any dreams other people have, just your own. Your dream was to come west to seek your fortune, and here you are. Don't let fear rob you."

Wilks nodded.

"You'll feel better with coffee and food in your stomach," Quarles said, looking at the pot. "Damn, but it takes longer to boil water up here. How high do you reckon we are, Jack?"

"I don't know," he said. "Not that high, maybe. The peaks beyond look fearsome, and we're not even close to where the trees stop growing."

"Do you get the entire set of traps out?" Quarles asked. Jack said he did.

"What are we going to do, then?" Quarles asked.

"If we didn't have the traps out, I'd say we should put

some miles behind us come morning," Jack said. "But the traps are five dollars apiece. That's thirty dollars down there in that creek."

"That's a winter's worth of ordinary wages," Wilks said.

"And Major Henry will take it out of our shares," Jack said.

"That's a lot of money," Quarles said.

"But you can't spend money if you're dead," Jack said.

Tiny bubbles clung to the bottom of the pot, and Quarles reckoned it was close enough. He threw a handful of coffee into the water. Many long minutes later, the coffee was churning in the boiling water.

"There's something cheerful about the smell of coffee," Jack said.

"When you're cold," Quarles said. "Other times, I'd prefer tea."

"What do you think about that stew?" Wilks asked. "Done yet?"

Quarles nodded.

"We're talking about nothing to avoid making a decision," Jack said. "Let's have it done with so we can set a course. What's your votes?"

"What's yours?" Wilks asked.

"Leave," Jack said.

"Stay," Quarles said. "We break camp at first light, take the horses with us, and two of us stand guard while the other snatches up the traps. Then we make a run on up the mountain and find some more peaceful country to scout."

Wilks was kneeling in front of the kettle, dipping out stew with his tin cup.

"Damn, that's hot," he said, using his sleeve to grasp the handle.

"What say you?" Quarles asked.

"Thirty dollars," Wilks said. "That's ten dollars each, and a powerful lot of money. I've never had ten dollars in my pocket before. You're right, my mother just had a dream. Let's stay."

"All right," Jack said wearily. "But Wilks, you're the one who retrieves the traps. Quarles and I will stand guard."

The creek was eerily silent at dawn. The slack water was covered by a thin sheet of ice, and in the channel where the water ran it barely made sound, just a soft liquid whisper. A thick fog had descended overnight, muffling sounds and giving the landscape a dreamlike appearance.

Jack was standing beside Star, bridle in hand, the pistol in his belt and the butt of the ghost rifle resting on his right thigh. He could barely see Quarles on the other side of the creek, just thirty yards away, holding the reins to the other horses. There were the two ponies that Quarles and Wilks rode, and another three packhorses, laden with beaver pelts.

Quarles had his rifle beneath his left arm.

"Do you see the dead grizzle cub?" Jack asked.

"No," Wilks said from the far bank.

"Wasn't it just about there you shot it?"

"I don't know," Wilks said. "A little farther down, maybe."

"Put your rifle where you can get to it right quick," Jack said.

"It's on the bank," Wilks said.

"Gentlemen," Quarles said. "To business, please."

"I'm going to leave my clothes on," Wilks said.

"Just get into the water and find the traps," Jack said.

"The first two are right in front of you. I can see the branch I dipped into the critter spunk right there, in front of you."

Jack waded in, a stout limb in one hand.

"Mind the trap," Jack said. "It may not be sprung."

Wilks probed with the limb, felt the trap, then reached down and pulled it out of the water. It was sprung, but there was nothing in it. He threw it up on the bank near Quarles.

"The next one should be just downstream," Jack said.

"I don't see a branch."

"Look for the stick, then."

"Aha!" Wilks said, seeing the stick floating on the surface, anchored by the chain. He pulled up the trap and a drowned forty-pound beaver it held, and he pitched both to the bank.

"Good," Jack said. "Farther downstream now. Keep going."

"I don't see it," Wilks said.

The fog was getting thicker, seeming to roll down from the tops of the snow-laden trees. Jack had a hard time making out Wilks's shape moving through the water, and now could not see Quarles at all.

"I have it," Wilks called.

Jack heard the heavy sound of another trap and its beaver being pitched to the bank.

"That's half," Jack said. "Why don't we call it quits? We've cut our losses to five dollars apiece."

"No, I see one more," Wilks said.

Jack heard sloshing in the water, and then the rattle of an empty trap being thrown onto the bank.

"You're doing well, boy," Quarles called. "Just two more."

Jack was staring into the mist that shrouded the creek,

his eyes unblinking, and he could feel the wet mist on his eyeballs. He tried blinking the discomfort away, but somehow it made it worse. He shifted his rifle to his left hand and wiped his eyes with the back of his right.

"How far do you think the last two are?" Wilks called, his voice distant.

"Twenty yards downstream," Jack called.

"I'm farther than that."

"You've passed them," Jack said. "Come back this way."

"This fog is getting thick as cotton," Wilks said.

"The water must be damned cold," Quarles called. "There's no use wading around blind. Come on it."

"Wait, I found one," Wilks called.

The horses Quarles held began to shift and snort.

"Damn," Wilks said. "The chain is caught beneath a log."

"Leave it," Jack said.

"I about got it."

"Get out of the water, boy," Quarles said quietly. "Now."

Jack heard something moving on the opposite bank, then the sound of sheaves of snow falling from the trees. He dropped Sky's bridle rope, knowing she would stay until he came for her, and ran down to the water's edge with his rifle at the ready.

"Come easy to the sound of my voice," Quarles said. "But don't run."

"The water's too deep," Wilks said, and Jack could hear the splashing sound of each of his quickening steps.

"Don't run," Jack shouted.

Then there was the sound of a deep animal roar that raised the hairs on the back of Jack's neck. There followed the sound of furious splashing. Wilks screamed, and the sound of the scream echoed from the mountains on either side.

"Help me!" Wilks cried.

There were more growls and splashing and then Wilks was screaming in terror. Jack ran down the bank toward the sound of the terrible fight. He could hear the horses on the opposite bank trying to bolt and Quarles cursing and struggling to hold them.

Jack could dimly see a dark form through the fog. He splashed into the creek, and, as he grew closer, he could see the bulk of a sow grizzly hovering over something in shallow water. Blood was splattered in every direction, and the bright red contrasted sharply with the white snow on the banks and the logs and the places on the creek where there was ice. The bear had the boy's head in her mouth and a front paw on his chest. Jack could see her long claws were sunk into Wilks's ribs and her yellowed fangs were holding his face like a vise. The sow shook Wilks like a rag doll. His skull popped and cracked under the pressure. The sow dragged him up onto the bank, then used her claws on him, chunks of flesh being thrown behind her. When she stopped, half of Wilks's face was ripped away, but he was alive, and his one remaining eye gave Jack a pleading look.

Jack had the rifle to his cheek, but from this angle he didn't have a chance of killing the bear. She weighed at least four hundred pounds, and even a .50 caliber ball would just lodge in layers of fat before it hit anything vital. He needed a clear shot at its muzzle.

"Sweet Jesus and Mari," Jack said.

Then he silently asked for Saint Ignatius to forgive him.

He lowered the rifle and pulled the pistol from his belt, took offhand aim, and fired. The ball struck Wilks in the center of what was left of his face, killing him instantly.

Jack replaced the pistol in his belt and shouldered the rifle.

"What's going on?" Quarles shouted. "I can't see a damned thing."

"Move the horses," Jack said.

"What about Wilks?"

"Dead."

"You need me?"

"Move the horses," Jack said. "Now, before the bear goes after them."

The sow was rolling Wilks's body over with her paw. Then she sank her fangs into the small of his back, popping the ribs like sticks. The bear opened its mouth wide and gave a rumbling low roar that Jack could feel reverberate in his gut.

Jack began stepping carefully backward, keeping the rifle high. He had almost reached the bank behind him when the bear swiveled her head around to look at him.

Jack stopped.

The bear gave Wilks's body a last slap with her paw, rolling it back into the water, then turned to face Jack. He did not move a muscle, not even to blink. The bear rose and began to lumber toward him, opening and closing her mouth and making odd jaw-popping sounds. Blood dripped from her muzzle.

The bear stopped just thirty yards away.

"Don't," Jack whispered, drawing a bead on her muzzle.

He knew the bear was faster than he was, so there was no use in making a run for it. If she decided to close the distance between them, she could do it in a few seconds, and would make a harder target. Jack had a spent pistol in his belt and only one shot from his rifle. There would be no opportunity to reload. It would be best to take the shot now, when he had the best chance of dropping her on the spot, but Jack hesitated. He hated the thought of killing the bear, but knew it was necessary; the Arikaras said a grizzly that had eaten human flesh would not be satisfied with anything less and became a kind of were-animal that could decimate a village.

Still, Jack hesitated.

The muscles in Jack's forearms began to quake.

The sow swiveled her head, keeping her eyes on Jack. Then she extended her shoulders and lowered her rump, getting ready to charge.

Jack pulled the trigger. The ball shattered the top of her muzzle. The bear took a few wild steps toward him, closing half the distance, then collapsed in the water. The waves of her fall lapped at Jack's moccasins as her blood spilled into the creek.

Jack climbed up on the bank and sat down.

He looked up at a sky he could not see through the fog. "*We* are the animals," Jack screamed. "God damn us all."

Then someone laughed behind him.

Jack turned.

In the fog was a Crow warrior in antelope skins on a white horse, almost blending into the fog. The Indian was tall, and the horse was large, so the effect was like looking up at a statue. The left sleeve of his antelope-hide shirt had six black bars, each signifying an act of bravery in battle by counting coup against an enemy—touching them in battle while he himself was unarmed. He cradled a trade gun in his right arm, and Jack could see a brass dragon curling around the screws that held the lock. There were brass tacks like rows of eyes running down the stock.

The warrior wore a wolf's-head cape, with the upper jaw and barred teeth projecting out over his forehead like the bill of a cap. The warrior's face was painted white, except for the lower half, which was smeared with black, giving the impression of a jawless skull.

At his throat was a four-inch bronze disk. Jack could see the impression of clasped hands beneath a crossed medicine pipe and tomahawk. It was a Jefferson peace medal.

"You're Standing Wolf," Jack said.

"I am Wolf Standing Like a Man."

He spoke English.

"Why haven't you killed me?" Jack asked.

"I must wait," Standing Wolf said. "I have seen you in my dreams for many months, coming closer, crossing the rivers and the prairies to reach the Crow nation here at the base of the great mountains. We fight, in my dreams, but never in fog like this. We are between worlds. Now is not the time."

"Glad to hear it," Jack said.

"My warriors and I have tracked you for many days."

"We're not looking for a war," Jack said. "We're just scouting beaver."

"Crossing our land without our leave is an act of war."

"Didn't realize how far we'd strayed," Jack said.

"You whites," Standing Wolf said. "Always making excuses for your bad actions, smiling like a fox while you take the beaver from our streams and the food from our mouths."

"We will pay for what we have taken."

"The boy has already paid," Standing Wolf said. "He was foolish, and cousin bear taught him the final lesson."

"It is the final lesson that comes to us all," Jack said.

"Balls," Standing Wolf said. "Some go to the spirit world

as ignorant as the day they entered naked and screaming into this one. They deserve our scorn, not our sympathy."

"Every man's death should remind us of our own."

"You speak as you do in my dreams," Standing Wolf said. "In riddles. What are you called in this world?"

"Picaro. What am I called in the other?"

"Shadow Heart."

Jack laughed.

"Well, I have not dreamed of you—but I have heard of you," Jack said. "All the way down the river at St. Louis I heard stories about you. And the chief of the Arikara, Lightning Crow, spoke of you as well."

"Bah! Lightning Crow is an old woman with all of his . . . *this*."

Standing Wolf mocked making the sign of the cross.

"No longer," Jack said. "Lightning Crow's only religion now is killing. He makes war on the whites. He killed many of us on the river."

"Too late he finds his balls," Standing Wolf said. "He has been the lapdog of the white traders for too long. But I heard of the fight at the boat, and will admit that floating warriors down among you beasts in your own small boat was clever."

"He has sworn to kill me," Jack said. "But he is afraid of you."

Standing Wolf smiled with satisfaction.

"I am glad the mad wolf bit him."

"He thinks you sent it," Jack said. "Or that I summoned it."

"Both true."

"You scare many," Jack said.

"Good! They should fear me. And you?"

"I am not afraid," Jack said.

"Not while you possess the ghost rifle," Standing Wolf said. "I know it from the bell-like sound it makes. But when we meet again, and I kill you, I will have it."

Standing Wolf turned his horse and disappeared into the fog.

24 *The Nail*

The fog lifted by mid-morning, and Jack found Quarles a mile down the creek. He had managed to keep the horses together. Jack slid down from Star and handed over Wilks's rifle.

"How bad was it?"

"Talking about it won't make it any better," Jack said. "There was a Crow war party about, too. I didn't reckon we should make a gift of the boy's rifle."

"Where are the devils now?"

"Gone," Jack said.

"I damn near expired of worry," Quarles said. "I couldn't leave the horses, so I just stayed here, figuring you would find me if you were still alive. If I hadn't seen any sign of you by morning, I was going to take my leave."

"As you should," Jack said.

"What of the body?"

"Too cold to dig a grave," Jack said. "So I sank him in the creek with stones. Seemed better than allowing critters to scatter his bones."

"You kill the sow?"

"Yes," Jack said.

"Take the claws?"

"Didn't feel like taking a trophy from the bear that killed the boy," Jack said. "Let's not tarry in this part of the world. There's a shadow here I'd like to be rid of. What say we see how far down the mountain we can make it in the daylight that remains?"

Two weeks later, Jack and Quarles rode into Fort Henry with their packhorses laden with pelts behind them. The snow was two feet deep outside the walls but had been trampled to a muddy crust inside. Smoke curled from a stovepipe above the blockhouse, and Jack longed for the warmth of the fire while he tended to Star and the horses; his bones ached from the cold, his joints were stiff, and his eyes felt burned by the bitter wind. But most of all, he was hungry.

"What do you suppose they have for supper?"

They were standing outside the door to the blockhouse, trying to knock as much snow and ice off their clothing and from their hair as they could before entering.

"Whatever it is," Quarles said, "it's going to sit right with me."

"What are the chances of cobbler?"

Quarles shook his head.

"You do go on about food more than anybody I ever knew," he said. "And there's damn little chance of cobbler here. When Major Henry made his speech about there being no God on the Upper Missouri, he should have added that there ain't no cobbler, either."

Jack swung open the door and walked in, his eyes adjusting to the gloom. There fire wasn't well drafted, and the room was blue with smoke. There were a dozen men sitting at the tables or sleeping on blankets near the walls, hacking and coughing, and they barely looked up at the pair.

"Somebody should tend that fire," Quarles said.

"Tend it yourself," somebody called from the corner.

"I will, then," Quarles said.

"What's the matter here?" Jack asked.

"Winter," the man who had told Quarles to tend the fire himself said. He was sitting against the wall with his blanket drawn up to his chin. "The temperature hasn't been above freezing here in over a month. All of us here been sick with the grippe or worse. I haven't felt like moving in three days. The blockhouse has become the infirmary for the company. Everybody else is out working or trapping."

"Stop your complaining," Major Henry said as he descended the stairs. "I'm sending you out to work tomorrow, because that's the only remedy. Goddammit, I've told you men about this stove."

Quarles was crouching in front of it, trying to adjust the damper.

"Well?" Ashley asked. "Did you two find beaver?"

"Sure enough," Quarles said. "*Beaucoup* beaver."

"There are many nutria," Jack said. "Far up in the mountains along the creeks that feed the Bighorn. It's Crow country. But it's ripe for trapping. Better plews than around here. We've brought back bundles to show you. Rich, thick pelts."

"Good," Henry said. "Where's Wilks?"

"That boy did not survive an encounter with Old Ephraim," Quarles said.

"Killed by a grizzly?" Henry asked.

Jack nodded.

"I will have to write a letter to his mother," Henry said.

"I would be grateful if you could share some details of his demise. It has been my experience that relating the circumstances offers the bereaved a sense of relief."

"There aren't many details I can share," Jack said.

"Then are you sure he's dead?"

"I am," Jack said. "I saw his body, and there were only pieces of him left. That fact is not likely to bring comfort to his mother. But he died doing his duty in retrieving traps, so you could write that." Jack then told Henry about the Crow war party, but stopped short of describing the conversation with Standing Wolf.

"Do you have a map of this new territory?"

"On my powder horn," Jack said.

"Bring it up and I will add the details to my map," Henry said.

"We would like to eat first," Jack said. "We have been traveling rough and eating pemmican for the past two weeks. Is there be something hot to eat?"

"Beans and cornbread," Henry said. "Some cheese."

"Any fruit?"

"No, sadly." Henry said. "Some of the men have scurvy."

"So that means there won't be any cobbler?"

"That's a novel idea," Henry said.

The pair began to walk up the stairs behind Henry.

"Not him," Henry said, nodding at Quarles.

"But I thought we was all equal here in the company," Quarles said. "You said so yourself. It was a good speech, made finer by being delivered with a pistol in your hand."

"Shephard, I said you were an equal member of the company down there, on the floor of the blockhouse," Henry said. "Not upstairs in my quarters. You'll get your supper, but you'll have to eat it downstairs. You may be a free nigger, but you are still a nigger."

Jack paused.

"Go on," Quarles told him. "Ain't no use making a fuss. We all want cobbler we can't have."

In half an hour, Jack pushed his plate away while Henry was still drawing in pencil on the map he had spread out on his side of the table. Jack reached for the jug on the table and poured himself half a cup more.

"Easy with my whiskey," Henry said.

"Major," Jack said, "I promise I won't waste a drop."

Henry peered at the powder horn.

"Now what is this symbol here?" he asked. "This little mark that looks like a cross."

"That's where Wilks died," Jack said. "I don't know the name of the creek, or even if it has one. But you can follow the line down to where it joins the Bighorn, there, and where the Bighorn joins the Yellowstone."

"I have the part of the Bighorn here," Henry said. "Your orientation seems quite good. Have you had some experience with mechanical or navigational drawing before?"

"Some experience," Jack said. "If I'd had a compass and a sextant, it would be more exact. We'd also know how high those peaks are to the west."

"The sextant is on the boat with Ashley," Henry said.

"Have there been any more hostilities with the Arikaras?" Jack asked.

"The Rees have been quiet," Henry said. "A harsh winter discourages all combatants and gives them time to prepare for new campaigns in the spring. I expect no trouble, not yet. Of course, they will have to be punished for the attack on the *Jefferson*."

Jack took another sip of whiskey. It was truly bad whiskey, but by the second cup had improved to be simply bad.

"With your permission, I would like to descend to the largest of the Mandan villages until spring," Jack said.

"To what purpose?" Henry asked. "The prospects of trapping around the Knife River seem poor in comparison to the Bighorn."

"The men here are in no shape to trap in the mountains," Jack said. "You have other parties out, scouting other locations, but until we are resupplied, we are unprepared to take beaver in any organized way. We should also tread carefully on Crow land before arranging some sort of agreement."

"I sense there's more," Henry said.

"I need a rest," Jack said. "And I would rather take it with the Mandans than remain here. Their lodges are warmer and their company more pleasant. Apologies, sir."

"Then go," Henry said. "You've earned the rest."

"And I'd like to take Quarles with me."

Henry sighed.

"Yes, take him," he said. "You may take one of the dugouts. But be prepared to board General Ashley's boat when it comes upriver in the spring, and to resume your duties as a trapper and scout. Otherwise, you forfeit your share."

"What of my horse, Star?"

"Your Blackfoot pony will be cared for in the stables here," Henry said. "So will the horse that Quarles rides. Both will be here when you return. You have my word on it."

Jack and Quarles slipped the heavy wooden canoe into the Yellowstone River at dawn the next day, their paddles breaking thick sheets of ice near the bank before they reached a clear channel of moving water. The sun was rising like an ember behind folds of snow clouds in the east, but there was no wind, so the morning was pleasant. They soon reached the Missouri River, and as they crossed over to the opposite bank, to avoid a series of sandbars that had built up where the rivers met, they paddled near a flock of mallards. Alarmed, the flock moved as one, noisily splashing and flapping in the air. They climbed effortlessly, dark silhouettes against the pewter sky. Once they were out of range of any gun, and higher than any tree, they set their wings and wheeled sharply, looking for a safer patch of calm water.

"What a handsome sight," Quarles, who was in the front, called over his shoulder. "Do you know what this feels like?"

Jack knew.

"Freedom," he said.

Carried along with the current, they made thirty miles a day. They stopped only at night, when they spread their blankets on sandbars in the middle of the river and pulled their buffalo robes around them. They kept their rifles beneath the robes, to keep them handy and free of frost, and in the mornings and evening they cooked and ate the catfish they caught with hook and line.

On the third day, Quarles spied a flock of geese in shallow water on the near side of a bend they were approaching. They stilled their paddles and allowed the canoe to drift within rifle range, then Jack shouldered the ghost rifle, took careful aim at the largest goose, and killed it from a hundred yards with a ball to the head.

"Whango," Jack said.

That night they had roasted goose for dinner.

"Is it Christmas yet?" Quarles asked.

"Not yet, I think," Jack said. "A week before, perhaps."

"Well, I've never had a finer Christmas dinner," Quarles said. "Here we have all the goose we care to eat, we have a fine spot on this bar to watch the sunset, and I have tobacco for my pipe. What about you?"

"Not the finest," Jack said. "That would have been at my grandfather's stone house, where the table was stacked high with food and there were many sweets. But I will admit that this is mighty pleasant."

"Ain't nobody trying to lift our hair," Quarles said.

"Amen," Jack said.

"What's your dream?" Quarles asked.

"How's that?"

"What do you wish for most in life?"

"Same as most men," Jack said. "Riches. Women. Food."

"If you have the gold, then you have the food and the women," Quarles said. "You are not like most men, Jack, and I doubt that you desire the same thing. What is it you want most?"

"Freedom," Jack said. "I would say that money buys it, but we have it now, on this patch of sand in the middle of a cold river many hundreds of miles from white civilization."

"We're free for a time," Quarles said. "At least until we rejoin the company."

"It is others that make us less free, whether their chains are of iron or forged from expectations," Jack said. "We cannot live without others, and yet each relationship makes us a bit less free."

"I have known real chains," Quarles said. "And the whip. You are my friend, Jack Picaro, but you speak nonsense."

Jack smiled.

"There are things about me you do not yet know," he said.

"Do you think our friendship makes you less free?"

"No," Jack said. "We expect the same of one another: trust, help when needed, good conversation."

"Then who makes you less free?"

Jack thought for a moment.

"I do," he said. "Oh, I blame others quickly enough. But I'm my own jailer."

"Damn," Quarles said. "You might become a human being after all."

"There are many who would argue against that being a noble ambition," Jack said. "But I will allow that my thinking has changed some since coming west."

"You plan on staying west?"

"If there's a home here for me," Jack said. "I have unfinished business in St. Louis, but yes, I intend to remain here, at least until I'm ready to return to the Basque country to die."

"Well, I'm here until the peculiar institution of slavery is abolished," Quarles said. "And that may mean I'm here for good. I don't know where my people came from in Africa, so I guess that means I'll be buried far from my ancestral home. But I have everything I need here. Everything except a woman."

"That can be remedied."

"It has to be the right woman," Quarles said. "Pretty but not vain. Strong-willed but not stubborn. Intelligent but not arrogant."

"You might be searching a while."

"That's all right," Quarles said. "I can wait."

"I could never wait," Jack said. "Not for women, not for luck, and not even for breakfast. That's one thing about this country. It teaches you patience—or will kill you trying."

Quarles laughed.

Jack looked at the sky.

"We'd best enjoy the fine weather while we can," Jack said, "because a storm has come stealing from the north."

By dawn, the temperature had dropped far below freezing, and the snow came in sheets whipped by the wind. The river was whitecapping, and when they set out in the canoe, they found the wind always driving them to the southeast, making it difficult to paddle hard enough to avoid the many sandbars ahead of them. Often, they simply dragged the canoe over a bar to the next stretch of water deep enough to paddle, but it was laborious because the dugout weighed two hundred pounds and the water was cold on their feet. Jack had stripped off his moccasins and was going barefoot, but eventually he had had enough. By mid-morning they had made less than two miles, so they decided to drag the canoe high up on a bar, turn it upside down, stretch a canvas tarp to one side, and wait until the storm had passed.

"This may not be such a pleasant Christmas after all," Jack said.

"We're still free," Quarles said. "So it's fine with me."

Jack lay beneath the tarp, listening to it buck and strain against the ropes holding it, and when he closed his eyes, he was back on the three-masted barque *April* as it made its way through a storm in the mid-Atlantic. He had been eleven years old, and although he had been fishing with his grandfather in Bay of Biscay, he had never been at sea before, and the storm had frightened him badly. The *April* was a British merchant ship and had sailed from Weymouth, where his grandfather had deposited him after sailing the fishing boat up the French coast and then across the English Channel. Spain was in a civil war created by the abdication of the king, and France had taken advantage of the chaos by invading the Iberian Peninsula. On April 14, 1808, the French emperor Napoleon Bonaparte had come to the Basque Country, making his headquarters in Bayonne, and had pressed for the installation of his brother, Joseph, as the Spanish monarch. Bonaparte had also sought to rebuild his military with the use of Basque arms makers, including Jacques's grandfather. Portugal and England were drawn in to the conflict, as well, and the Basque country—perched between France and Spain—had become the crossroads of the war. Tens of thousands of soldiers flooded the villages. Although Napoleon promised the Basque a protectorate, many did not trust him, and Jacques's grandfather's property was taken because of his refusal to make arms for the little corporal. With Jacques's parents dead of typhus, which the grandfather blamed on the rats that followed the soldiers, and his fortune gone, he did the only thing he could to get Jacques to safety, and that was to take the sailboat to England and pray they were not intercepted by a French warship. At Weymouth, Jacques's passage could only be granted by agreeing to an indenture of five years in America. The grandfather was too old to accompany Jacques, so they embraced on the wharf at Weymouth.

"You are Basque," the grandfather had told him. "You will always be free, no matter what others say. You have learned well your lessons in my workshop, and you will use your hands and your mind to earn your fortune. You are no longer a boy, but not yet a man. Much trouble lies ahead of you. But when you are a man of consequence, and Bonaparte is dead and these wars are over, you will remember our family's good stone house."

"You will be waiting for me?" Jacques asked.

The grandfather grasped him gently by the shoulders.

"I am sixty-nine years old," he said. "I will be in the honest Basque earth by the time you are a man. No, don't cry, because I have lived a full life. Always remember me and our time together. Keep me in your heart."

During the first part of the crossing, Jack was desperately seasick and afraid of French privateers and kept a lookout for sails on the horizon, when he wasn't puking in a bucket or over the rail. The tension in his stomach eased somewhat after passing the Azores, but then the sheer size of the Atlantic made Jack feel an insignificant speck in an unfeeling universe. The passage lasted eight weeks, and Jack spent much of it huddled atop a hatch cover on deck, listening to the pop and groan of the canvas, the creak of timber, and the sigh of the wind until he slept. His sleep was filled with lessons from his grandfather's workshop, and he began to dream of boring machines with clockwork mechanisms.

The *April* had left Weymouth in the last week of June, hoping to reach America before the hurricane season, but a day out from Philadelphia, a storm that had blown up from the West Indies battered the ship. Jack tried to ride out the storm in his berth belowdecks, but the feel of the ship pitching and rolling around him instilled a terror of being trapped in the hull and drowning. He ventured above and, holding tight to a rope rigged around the hatch, stared in disbelief at the mountain of waves that topped the ship's sixty-foot masts. As he watched, he heard a terrible splintering sound, and the foremast toppled. The tip of the mast and its yards dragged in the water as the crew desperately tried to free it by cutting its rigging away, but the *April* rolled heavily onto her starboard side. The sea rushed over the rail and nearly swept Jack back down the hatch to the guts of the ship, but he held fast to the line. Although drenched with water, he could feel the ship wallowing in the trough between the waves. The crew cranked her rudder hard around, trying to get her bow into the next wave, but it was too late, and tons of water crashed once more on the *April,* and she remained with most of her copper-sheathed port side out of the water. He could hear the screams of the other passengers belowdecks, some of them crushed by shifting cargo, others up to their chests in cold and rising seawater.

Jack prayed to Jesus and Mari and Saint Ignatius to spare him from drowning.

Then the waves shifted, and the *April* spun in the trough and her foremast was suddenly on her port side, acting as a sea anchor because it was still attached by some rigging. The drag was enough to right the ship, and the crew managed to sever the remaining lines. The *April* had lost a mast and most of its rudder, and had shipped a lot of water and could not take much more, but for the moment she was still afloat. The reprieve was short, however; it was now night, and the storm not yet spent, and the *April* was driven upon the rocks just off Cape May, at the mouth of Delaware Bay. Her hull was stove in, and she sank in less than a minute, taking 163 of her passengers with her. Jack and about one hundred others managed to scramble over the side, and those who were not dashed to death on the rocks finally made the beach. When Jack was found, so too were the letters of indenture in his jacket. Although the *April* was lost, her owners would enforce the contract—and that would lead to extensions and new indentures, terms that were compounded when Jack discovered women, drinking, and gambling in his late teens.

When Jack awoke on the bar on the Missouri River, his right hand was stretched out beyond his blanket and his fingers were in the wet sand. He believed for a moment that he was again on the beach at Cape May, and he bolted upright and began to scream for someone to help.

"Jack!" Quarles shouted. "You're dreaming."

"There are people on the rocks," Jack pleaded. "You must help them. There has to be some way to reach them. Their limbs are broken and their heads are bloody. The rest went down with the ship."

"Wake up," Quarles said.

Jack stared at him. He was shivering as if he had just been pulled from the North Atlantic.

"It's me, Shephard Quarles."

"*Merde!*" Jack cried. "What a nightmare."

He was still shaking.

"It's all right," Quarles said. "You're safe."

Quarles put his arms around Jack's shoulders and hugged him tightly. The move so surprised Jack that he attempted to pull away, but Quarles would not allow it.

"Don't," he said. "Just be still."

Jack quit struggling.

"This is the only thing that will convince you you're safe," Quarles said. "I could keep saying it, but you wouldn't believe it. But the touch of a friend, now—that has the power of truth in it. When our hands are filled with each other, they can't hold guns or knives or do any other evil."

Jack stood it for another twenty seconds, then slapped Quarles on the shoulder.

"That's enough," he said. "I'm in my right mind now."

"Good," Quarles said. "Because you smell bad. Like fish and grease and old sweat. It wouldn't hurt you to bathe every now and then."

"And you think you smell good?" Jack asked. "I've

been downwind of you in the canoe since we left Fort Henry."

Jack paused.

"I have been evasive when asked about how I came to America," Jack said. "I misled people. I said I was of noble birth, and that I fled here to escape gambling debts. The truth is that our house was broken by Bonaparte and that I was a refugee, sold into indenture for my passage."

"At least you know where you came from," Quarles said. "I don't even know the year of my birth."

It was still snowing, but the wind had stopped howling, and the snow had slowed to lazy swirls. Jack poked his head beyond the tarp and looked for the sun, but the sky was shrouded in gray clouds.

"What time of day do you reckon it is?" Jack asked.

"Afternoon," Quarles said.

"Should we set out?"

"We're short on daylight," Quarles said. "An hour until the sun sets, I reckon. I don't care for the thought of hauling this heavy dugout up on another sandbar and setting up camp all over again. We're here for the night, Jack."

"All right," he said.

Quarles took out his clay pipe and filled it with tobacco, then took a stick from the fire beside him and held it beneath the upside-down bowl. He sucked some flame into the tobacco, then threw the stick back into the fire and exhaled smoke.

"That nightmare," Quarles said. "Did it come from something real?"

"It was a long time ago," Jack said. "Something from when I was a kid. That's why I discard my clothes when I run the traplines. The feel of wet clothes against my skin reminds me of it."

Quarles nodded.

"The things that happen to us as children remain with us," he said. "Have you ever found a tree that has a nail in it? Well, it's like that. Those old rusty fears are driven into us as children and they become trapped as we grow. They never leave us, not even the day we are cut down."

25 *Moon of Long Nights*

Two days later, in clear but cold weather, they reached the series of Mandan and Hidatsu villages above the mouth of Heart River. The Indians had placed round bull boats over the smoke holes at the tops of the lodges, to keep the snow out, but canted the boats a bit to allow smoke to escape. The snowy banks of the river were filled with women and children, working or playing, and many waved as Jack and Quarles glided past in the canoe, using a stroke of the paddle every twenty feet or so to keep the nose pointed in the right direction.

"How many people live here?" Quarles asked.

"Several thousand, counting all the villages together," Jack said. "More than in St. Louis. The captains spent the winter of 1804 here."

"We didn't pause here long on our trip upriver," Quarles said. "Major Henry was worried about reaching the Yellowstone before the snow. And he made most of us stay on the boat, worried that we would get too settled here."

Shortly they left the Missouri at the mouth of the Heart River and clung to the west bank, which soon brought them to the largest of the Mandan villages, Mitutanka. The village was built on a high bank, fifty feet above the water, and Jack could see the tops of many dozens of lodges. As they paddled into slack water that was below a cut in the bank, which served as the village's river access, Jack was surprised find, among the many large double canoes, one of the company's keelboats anchored there. Sheets of ice floated past.

"They should have been far downriver by now," Quarles said. "I wonder what is the matter."

"Ho, the *Yellowstone!*" Jack shouted.

An old man who was repairing a willow-reed fish trap on the shore shook his head.

"Nobody home," he said in English.

"Where'd they go?"

The old man pointed up the bank at the village.

They beached the dugout and dragged it far up on the bank, then turned it over so it wouldn't fill with snow and ice.

Rifles in hand, and with blankets over their shoulders, they climbed the slope to the village. In many ways, Mitutanka resembled the village of Lightning Crow, but was larger and had not just one ceremonial lodge, but several, all facing the plaza. In the middle of the plaza was a well-tended cottonwood plank corral, and Jack guessed there would be a lone cedar post in it.

As Jack and Quarles walked across the plaza, none of the Mandans gave Jack a second look, but several stopped to stare and point at Quarles. The children laughed and the women giggled, and one young woman ran forward and thrust her hand toward Quarles, stopping a few inches from his head. She was talking rapidly.

Quarles stepped back.

"What's she saying?"

"Don't know," Jack said. "But I think she wants to touch your hair."

"All right," Quarles said, and leaned down so she could feel the top of his head. The woman ran her fingers over his hair, laughed in delight, and began talking rapidly again.

"I don't understand," Quarles said.

The woman held her fingers beside her head like ears and pawed the snow with a moccasin.

"She thinks you're part buffalo," Jack said.

"I've been called a lot of things," Quarles said, "but never that."

"It's a good thing," Jack said. "The buffalo are their world. About everything they do connects with the buffalo in some way, and they think the bulls are especially powerful medicine."

Quarles made a snorting sound, and the woman ran off, giggling.

"I thought you could speak to these people," Quarles said.

"Only if they know French," Jack said. "Or English or Spanish. I picked up a few words of Arikara when I was with old Lightning Crow, but the Mandans speak a different language. It doesn't even sound like Arikara."

"Well, they seem right friendly," Quarles said.

"They see us as allies," Jack said. "And merchants."

"Where do we introduce ourselves?" Quarles asked.

"We find the chief or some of his headmen," Jack said. "There will be a bit of business and speechifying, and the pipe will be passed around, and they'll want some gifts."

"What kind of gifts?"

"The dugout and some blankets," Jack said. "Balls and powder. What we can spare."

"Looks like some civic types lounging outside that lodge over there," Quarles said, indicating a trio of older Mandan men sitting against buffalo-robe-covered backrests. "You think they're important enough?"

"They just might be the town council," Jack said.

They had taken three steps in the direction of the headmen when a woman shouted Jack's name from across the plaza. Sky was standing with her hands clasped in front of her, wearing a white dress decorated with porcupine-quill beadwork and a fox cape around her shoulders. Her head was bare and her dark hair shone in the winter sun.

"Hold this," Jack said as he gave his rifle to Quarles.

He ran across the plaza and picked up Sky by the waist and wheeled around with her, while she looked down smiling and held his face in her hands. When he lowered her, they kissed, but after she put a hand to her lips.

"Your beard," she said. "It is even thicker."

"I will trim it," he said. "Or shave it off, if you like."

"I am pleased to see that you have survived," she said. "And that you remembered where and when to find me."

"How could I forget?" Jack asked.

"Men do," she said. "Was there much trouble in surviving?"

"Some trouble," Jack said. "At other times it was just dull. Mostly, I have been cold without you."

"This is my lodge," Star said. "It is warm. It was my mother's lodge when she was captured long ago by the Arikaras, but now that she has died and I have come home, it is mine again."

"Wasn't there someone living here?"

"My aunt, Antelope Woman," Sky said. "She still lives here, but it is my lodge. Ours is a matriarchal society, Jack. The lodges and the clans are handed down through the women."

"So you are Mandan now?"

"I am Sky," she said. "This is my lodge. That is enough."

Jack motioned Quarles over and introduced him.

"You speak English," Quarles said.

"As do you," Sky said. "A black man. Somehow, I expected you to speak another tongue."

"I only have one."

"You will be popular with the women."

"Why is that?"

"Because you are special," Sky said. "You have the spirit and the strength of the buffalo. My aunt and the other old women tell stories of a man that came with the captains a generation ago, a black man named York, who made many girls happy. But the old stories say he was most suited to life with our enemies the Crows, far up the river against the mountains. They say he had a Crow wife."

"A winter wife?" Jack asked.

"No," Sky said. "An all-year-long wife, and children."

"To whom he had to say farewell."

"It is not the farewells that break one's heart," Sky said. "It is the never having saids. I see you have managed to keep possession of the rifle I stole back from Lightning Crow for you. Has it served you well?"

"It has," Jack said.

"One day you will have to tell me the secret of the brass disk."

"I will."

"What's she mean?" Quarles asked.

"There's a . . ." Jack began, but stumbled on his words, trying at once to tell the truth and also conceal the location of the disk beneath the patch box. "It's a tool I used in making the rifle."

"So those are the men we are to meet?" Quarles asked.

"Not unless you want to learn how to trap eagles," Sky said. "They are the elders of the Eagle Society. They instruct the young men in making the pits and the bait and how to lie in wait for the eagles and then spring out and wrestle them into submission. The birds fight fiercely. Many of the young men lose fingers and eyes."

"You are having a joke at my expense," Quarles said.

"No," Sky said. "Eagles are trapped in that way. Have you not seen all of the eagle feathers in the hair of our warriors and used to make the bonnets for the chiefs? Did you think we climbed the trees along the river and stole them from their great nests?"

"I hadn't thought of it," Quarles said.

"Where's the crew of the keelboat?" Jack asked.

"Drunk, mostly," Sky said. "They are scattered about in various lodges. They drink and sport all night and sleep all day. Their leader is a large and uncouth man whose name sounds like a wound."

"They were not supposed to tarry here," Jack said.

"It does not appear they are in any hurry to leave," she said.

Jack shook his head and cursed.

"Let's not confront them," Quarles said. "They outnumber us, and I am not anxious to continue the argument from the blockhouse."

"What do you think Major Henry would have us do?" Jack asked.

"Let's wait until spring and ask him."

Jack scratched his beard.

"All right, Sky. Show us who to talk to here to be invited to stay a while," Jack said. "We are tired, and I am anxious to spend a warm night with you."

"You will bathe, first," she said. "Come along, I'll take you to the lodge of White Fox. He is the son of White Coyote, who was chief when the captains came. You have gifts? Good. He will feed you both, and you need to give something in return, but not anything too fine—or too cheap. Bullets are an insult, but those blankets will do."

That night, Jack bathed naked in the river where the keelboat was anchored. He dunked his head several times beneath the clear and cold water, and he came up gasping each time. Finally, he pulled himself shivering up onto the deck of the keelboat and threw a buffalo robe Sky had given him around his shoulders. He balled his clothes under his arm.

"Who's there?" a voice called from the cabin of the boat.

"It's me, Jack Picaro."

"Hell, I nearly shot ye," a sleepy voice said. "Weren't you in the mountains?"

"I'm back now," Jack said. "Who am I talking to?"

"Snypes. Bledsoe sent me down to keep guard of the boat so the heathens don't rob us or steal it. Are you alone?"

"Yes," Jack said.

"Are you on company business?"

"No," Jack said.

"Good," Snypes said.

"Where were you earlier?" Jack asked.

"Oh, the old man who fishes keeps an eye during the day," Snypes said, coming to the door of the cabin. "We just have to worry at night. What the hell are you doing? You're going to give yourself the pneumonia by getting all soaked like that in the middle of winter."

"You won't get sick if you don't wear wet clothes," Jack said. "What's the boat still doing here? You should have made your way down to Pawnee country or even Westport by now. Major Henry will not be pleased."

"Well, the major ain't here," Snypes said. "Bledsoe's in charge."

"He won't be, once Henry learns of this."

"Yeah, Bledsoe is kind of thinking that we don't need the major anymore. Figures we can do better on our own than the major ever could do for us. So you might say we've become an independent arm of the Rocky Mountain Fur Company."

"Or you might say you're stealing the boat. Where is there to go?"

"Ole Mose says we can go all the way to New Orleans if we like."

"It's possible," Jack said.

"You going to join us?"

"I'll have to talk to Bledsoe first," Jack said.

An hour later, Jack stood in front of a polished brass mirror that hung from a pole in the earth lodge shared by Sky and her aunt and by the light of a candle he regarded his appearance. He was on the other side of the lattice that separated the lodge into two rooms, but he could hear Sky and Antelope speaking in Mandan, and he knew they were talking about him because occasionally they said his name. He let the buffalo robe fall from his shoulders and adjusted the mirror as he took in all of himself. He barely recognized the man who stared back.

His hair was past his shoulders and his beard was bushy like a hedge. His face and hands were brown as leather, but the rest of his body was pale and roped with muscles that he had never had before. His biceps were deep, and the muscles in his stomach and sides rippled when he turned. His hands and his face were covered with small cuts and a few scars, and he could not remember all of the injuries that had caused them. The only thing that seemed the same were his eyes, clear and blue, as if staring from behind a mask.

With the Damascus toothpick in hand, he began to cut away tufts of hair from his head.

"Stop that," Sky said, coming up behind him.

"I honed the knife," he said.

"You're making such a mess we would have to smear your head with bear grease to keep you from scaring children," Sky said. She took the knife from him and gently tested its blade with her thumb. It drew a thin line of blood.

"I have never held a knife so sharp," she said.

"It is good steel," Jack said.

She gathered the hair at the back of his head in her fist and used the knife to trim it away. Then she repeated the process, moving around his head, removing the hair that covered his ears and fell into his eyes. Then she spent some time on some final cuts, using her fingers to comb his hair.

"I cannot do the beard," she said. "Mandan do not have hair on their faces."

Jack took the knife and began removing tufts of his beard. She placed her hands on his waist and peered over his shoulder at the mirror, watching him work. When he deemed it was short enough, he used a brush and some water to whip up some shaving soap in tin cup, then brushed the lather over his face. He had borrowed the shaving soap from the keelboat, along with a straight razor, and now he stropped the blade on his belt, which hung from the pole below the mirror. He scraped the razor across his cheek, and it made a rasping sound and left a speck of blood.

Jack frowned.

"What's wrong?" Sky asked.

"It's not sharp enough," he said. "Hand me my knife."

She handed him the Damascus toothpick, and he experimented for a moment to find the right grip, and finally settled on pinching the blade between the thumb and forefinger and resting his palm on the hilt. He turned his cheek to the mirror and slid the blade down to his jaw.

"That's better," he said.

He wiped the knife with a rag, then shaved the rest of his face.

Sky reached around and touched the strip he had just shaved.

"Why are you so interested in this?" Jack asked.

"It is fascinating," she said.

Soon Jack had removed all of his beard except for a well-tended moustache and a patch on his chin and at the sides of his mouth. Then he splashed water over his face and saw that he was indeed the man who had fled St. Louis nine months before, just a little older and more rugged and a bit worse for wear.

"So this is the face that Jack Picaro keeps hidden," Sky said.

"It is the face of the man I was before I became Jack Picaro."

"We are in the process of becoming," she said. "What was your name before you were yourself?"

"Jacques," he said.

"And your surname?"

"Aguirre."

"I do not know the word. Is it French?"

"No, it's Basque. The language of my people."

"What does it mean?"

"A prominence, something elevated . . ."

"A mountain?"

"Yes, I suppose," Jack said.

Sky smiled.

"It fits you," she said.

"No longer. I am wanted by that name back in the states."

"Why?"

"I broke a contract," he said. "And I killed a man."

"It means nothing here," Sky said. "Men kill other men. For horses, for women. To acquit themselves in war. It is a sickness that men share."

She put her arms around him and kissed his chest.

"And women?" he asked. "What sickness do they share?"

"Men," she said. "And sometimes women. But my only sickness is for you."

Then she ran her hands through his hair. She produced a buckskin tunic and slipped it over his head. It reached down to his knees. Sky said his old clothes would have to be beaten against the rocks, stitched up, and maybe even doused in sage smoke before they were fit to wear again.

Then Sky draped the buffalo robe over his shoulders and they walked around to the main part of the lodge to sit with Antelope Woman.

There were only a few logs burning in the firepit, but there were glowing coals spread wide and deep. The screen that separated the main room from the entrance, and the plank door, also helped to shut out the wind, as did the three feet of earth on the walls and ceiling. Compared to the cold and drafty blockhouse at Fort Henry, the earth lodge was a welcome bit of civilized living and was as cozy as any hearth in St. Louis. Sky had hung the ghost rifle, Jack's possibles bag, his pistol and the knife and the powder horn, from a peg on one of the poles behind the firepit.

Antelope Woman was fifty years old and thin like a coyote, and her hair was gray. A scar ran from above her right eye and across her cheek to her jaw, the result of some long-ago attack, and Sky had told Jack it had been inflicted by Lightning Crow when he had stolen Sky's mother, Red Buffalo Woman. Antelope Woman had fought for her sister and had received a war axe to the face.

"My aunt wants to know if you are a crazy person," Sky said.

"Why does she ask that?"

"Because you have made an enemy of Lightning Crow and he has sworn to kill you. Only a crazy person would do that. She can see where some foolish people might call it courage, but courage would be teaching him a lesson by counting coup."

"Tell Antelope Woman I am the same kind of crazy she is," Jack said, then drew his forefinger from the eyebrow down to his jaw. "Tell her I am crazy for you."

Sky told Antelope Woman that Jack was indeed crazy, but the kind of crazy that is peculiar to some white men—crazy with pride and ambition. She also said that Jack was crazy because he was reimagining the event as somehow protecting her when all he wanted was his rifle back.

Antelope Woman laughed.

Sky laughed, too, then said something else in Mandan, and her aunt gathered her things and retreated to her sleeping corner.

"Can we hang a blanket for privacy?" Jack asked.

"There is no need," Sky said. "She will be asleep soon, and even if she isn't, she has heard fucking before. It is our way. She will ignore us."

"I hope I can ignore her," Jack said.

"If you're thinking of her while you're mounting me, I will stab you with your exceedingly sharp knife."

"You can try," Jack said, pulling Sky to him. "But I think only of you."

They kissed, and Sky ran her fingers over his face.

"Much better," she said. "It would have been scratchy here," she said, putting her fingers to her lips, "and else-where."

Jack rubbed his hand over his jaw.

"And you are younger than I thought."

"I am twenty-three. No, a year older. My birthday passed in autumn."

"I am twenty winters," Sky said. "You, I thought, were much older."

"Just how old did you think I am?"

"Old enough," she said. "Come. I have spread out the robes for us."

They undressed, and by the light of the firepit they

gazed at each other's bodies. Jack reached out and touched her breast, then her thigh. He could feel the warmth radiating from her body.

"I have dreamt of this moment since we parted," he said. "When I was in the mountains it guided me. When I was cold it warmed me. When I was lonely it comforted me."

"Will you never shut up?"

Sky placed her right hand over his mouth.

"There is a time to talk and then there is a time to live. Please, let us just live." Then she rolled him onto his back, straddled him, and guided him inside her.

26 *Biter*

"Jacques Aguirre!"

The bellow was so deep and full of anger that it seemed to come from a creature from a fairy tale, perhaps the giant that chased the boy down the beanstalk.

"Where are you, Jacques? I know you're in one of these anthills," Bledsoe shouted. "Snypes told me that Jack Picaro was here, so that means the lying sack of horseshit I used to do business with is here, too. Come out, Jacques. Come out, come out, wherever you are!"

"Jack, wake up," Sky said. They were still beneath the robes in her warm lodge. "That man with the ugly name is calling your former self. What does he want?"

Jack sat up.

"To kill me," Jack said.

Sky shook her head.

"How can one white man have so many other white men and red human beings and my adopted-father-who-is-dead-to-me want to kill him?" she asked. "What do you do to these people?"

"Rub them the wrong way, I suppose."

Jack pulled on the buckskin tunic and began to rise, but Sky grasped the tail of the garment and pulled him down.

"Don't," she said. "He's drunk. Let him shout."

"I must go," Jack said. "He will just keep shouting. It will be worse if I wait, because he will think I am afraid of him."

"Are you?"

"He's bigger than I am," Jack said, "and his knife is sharper. Yes, of course I'm afraid."

Jack got up and pulled on his moccasins. He took his belt from the pole beneath the mirror and buckled it around him, with the Damascus toothpick in its sheath. Then he tucked the .45 pistol in his belt.

"The ghost rifle is loaded," Jack said, nodding to the rifle that was next to the robes where they had slept. "If he kills me, then he will come for you. Don't give him the chance. Take a position inside the shadows of the door and shoot him in the middle of the chest."

Sky picked up the rifle and held it across her bare thighs.

"Why can't I shoot him now?" she asked.

"The men from the keelboat will be watching," Jack said. "I have to beat him face-to-face so they will show respect. If he is killed from the shadows before that happens, then they will kill us from the shadows at the first opportunity."

Sky nodded.

Jack walked casually out of the earth lodge and into the plaza.

"Aha!" Bledsoe cried. "There he is. And look, he's scraped the fur from his face. How are you, Master Jacques? Still shooting your friends? Is that why you have that iron in your belt?"

Bledsoe had a pair of calf-high hobnailed boots and striped wool trousers and a blue linen shirt that appeared to be stained with most of the meals he'd eaten in the past week. A stoneware jug with a ring at the neck was dangling from his left middle finger, and he occasionally hefted it over his arm and poured some in, or near, his mouth. Biter was in its sheath at the small of his back.

"You're drunk, Mose," Jack said pleasantly. "Why don't you call it a night and get some rest?"

"You're right," Bledsoe said. "I am drunk. Absolutely, gloriously, the monkey is out of the cage drunk. Have been, for the past three days. There was plenty of whiskey on the boat, and I aim to drink it all up before setting out downstream."

"To New Orleans."

"That's right. The boat will turn a handsome profit. Do you take issue with that?"

"Considering the boat and its cargo are the property of the Rocky Mountain Fur Company, I do," Jack said. "I am representing Major Henry and General Ashley in this matter, and you deal with me as you would them."

"When did you get so fastidious?" Bledsoe asked. "All of those boats me and my crew wrecked for you and all the shiny parts we stole—why, you didn't care as long as you had your precious iron and steel. But now you're changed."

"I didn't know what you were doing until that last night at The Grackle."

"Then you're dumber than I thought you were."

"Likely," Jack said. "Now, go find you a lodge and a couple of maids who are impressed with your bragging and sleep this thing off. We can talk this out in the morning."

"Just two?" Bledsoe asked. "I had three last night. At the same time. How many did you lay with? Just one?"

Jack was silent.

"She in that lodge?"

Bledsoe stumbled over toward the entrance. Jack stepped in front of him.

Biter flashed in Bledsoe's right hand in an instant.

Behind him, Jack could hear Sky bring the ghost rifle to full cock.

"You kill me," Jack said, "and it will be the last thing you ever do."

"No," Bledsoe said, laughing. "If I kill you, dying rough will be the last thing you ever do."

"Jack!" Quarles called from across the plaza. "How about some help?"

Bledsoe turned, stepping away from the entrance.

"Oh, look," Bledsoe said. "It's your nigger."

"Quarles is nobody's nigger but his own."

Bledsoe took another splash of whiskey and waved the knife at Quarles.

"Come join the fun," Bledsoe said.

Around the edges of the plaza, a crowd was gathering. There were many Mandans, with some of the boat crew scattered in clusters among them. Jack made a quick count—there were fifteen white faces, including Snypes.

"Stay put," Jack called to Quarles. He moved out into the center of the plaza, leading Bledsoe away from Sky's lodge. "I don't need any help just yet. But I appreciate your offering. Did you have a warm night?"

"I'm pleased to say I did," Quarles said. "Mighty warm. And it looks like you got all barbered up."

"Less hair to tempt the Crows," Jack said.

"All your big talk," Bledsoe said. "I bet you ain't never killed an Injun."

"You're the one who's full of big talk," Jack said. "Well, are you going to talk or are you going to fight?"

"Lose that pistol in your belt."

Jack walked over to Quarles and gave him the pistol.

"You sure about this?" Quarles asked.

"No," Jack said, "but I can't think of anything better."

"All right," Jack said, his hands spread wide. "All I have is my wits and this one knife at my belt. I'd say we were even, but I have you beat in the wits department."

Bledsoe laughed.

"I'm going to dig the wits out of your skull with the point of my knife."

"This isn't going to be as easy as scaring a young whore who did you no harm," Jack said. "But then, I suppose that's how you achieved gratification, by scaring girls who couldn't or wouldn't fight back."

Bledsoe approached, leading with his left arm, and Biter held firmly in his left hand. Jack drew the Damascus blade with his right hand but held it low, and led with his right leg, hoping to jam Bledsoe and not give him an opportunity to get close enough to slash his stomach open. But even though Bledsoe was drunk, he was steady on his feet and cautious.

Jack needed him not to be cautious.

"Maybe we should find an apple and have you hold it between your legs?"

Bledsoe grunted in anger and lunged, but it was a clumsy move, and Jack bobbed out of the way and then jammed his right knee against the outside of Bledsoe's knee, causing the big man to trip and roll on the ground. The crowd, including the boat crew, laughed.

As Bledsoe fell, Jack took a swipe with the toothpick. It split open the filthy shirt, and Jack could feel the tip of the knife skipping along Bledsoe's rib cage. It wasn't a deep wound, but blood poured down his side.

Bledsoe got to his feet, swearing.

"Looks like you're bleeding," Jack said.

"You was lucky," he shouted.

"If this were a duel," Jack said, "we'd say satisfaction had been achieved because you've been blooded. What do you say? You give up, no hard feelings?"

"I'm going to cut open your chest and eat your heart."

"I've got five dollars," Quarles shouted. "Two-to-one odds on Jack!"

"I'll take that bet," one of the boat crew said.

"And me," said another.

"Put me down for Jack," Snypes said.

"You traitor!" Bledsoe shouted, then spat.

"Sorry," Snypes said. "It's how the wind blows."

"Maybe it was a mistake to fight me drunk," Jack said.

"Shut up," Bledsoe said and charged again.

He was swinging Biter in wild arcs, and Jack could not duck fast enough. Once the knife drew blood across his right cheek, and another time it cut into his upper arm.

Bledsoe paused and looked at the blood on Jack's face and arm.

"The wind changes," Bledsoe said, changing Biter to his left hand.

Then he came straight at Jack again, and this time he was ready for the feint and instead drove Biter's point like an arrow toward Jack's throat. Jack got his right arm up just in time to stop the thrust, but he could not match Bledsoe's force, and he felt his moccasins sliding backward on the dirty snow.

Bledsoe drove him all the way back against the sacred ark, and when Jack's shoulders touched the cottonwood planks, he could hear the Mandans muttering their disapproval. Jack's own knife was pinned in his right hand, which he could not move because his right forearm was keeping him from being immediately skewered. Jack drove his left fist again and again into Bledsoe's ribs, but it felt like punching a slab of beef and had no discernable effect. Biter's wicked tip came closer and closer to the hollow just below his Adam's apple.

The cottonwood planks behind him began to crack.

Jack dropped the knife from his right hand and caught it imperfectly in his left, most of the handle out of his grip. Then he choked up on it and drove the knife upward into Bledsoe's arm, severing muscle and tendon at the elbow. The arm dropped, the knife with it, and Jack slipped out to the side. Bledsoe stumbled, clutching his bleeding arm, and then crashed through the cottonwood planks, revealing the cedar post within.

Some of the Mandans began to shout.

"Oh, to hell with you heathens," Moses said, getting to his feet and knocking the cottonwood planks aside. As he climbed out, the heel of his hobnail boot kicked the cedar post, knocking it askew.

"Give it up," Quarles called. "He's ruined your arm."

Bledsoe roared with laughter.

"I can still kill the bastard with one hand."

Two old Mandan men rushed forward. They had blankets and what looked like a bundle of sticks and other awkward things with them. They shoved Bledsoe out of the way, and one of them held a blanket up while the other began to straighten the cedar post and reassemble the planks.

"Now you've done it," Jack said. "You've violated their Holy of Holies."

"It's a bunch of pagan sticks and trash," Bledsoe said. "A chamber pot of a religion for ignorant turd eaters."

"They take Lone Man serious," Jack said. "It's bad medicine for you."

Bledsoe picked up Biter with his right hand. He flipped the knife in the air and caught it by the hilt.

"I'll tell you what's bad medicine," Bledsoe said. "I'm sober now. And I'm right-handed. Remember?"

Bledsoe weighed the knife in his hand.

He drew back for a throw, as Jack had seen him do before. Fifteen feet separated them, which was too far to try to rush him and too short to try to run. But he had to try. With the Damascus toothpick in his right hand, Jack crouched and made ready. He expected to take Biter in the chest, but perhaps he could reach Bledsoe's throat before dying.

Then Jack saw something he did not immediately understand.

Bledsoe dropped the knife behind him, and his face went slack. He looked down and saw the flint point of a spear sticking upward, having sliced its way through his private parts and emerged just beneath his belt. The spear was held by one of the old Mandans who had rushed to cover the ark canoe.

"We are not an ignorant nation of turd eaters," the old man said in English, then he twisted the spear, bringing Bledsoe to the bloody snow beneath him.

Bledsoe screamed in pain, his face to the sky.

The other old Mandan then brought a triangular iron war axe down on Bledsoe's head, splitting his skull.

The crowd gave a collective groan.

Jack looked away.

He sheathed the Damascus blade and walked across the plaza to Quarles, where he took the pistol and put it in his belt.

"I thought you were in trouble there for just a minute," Quarles said.

"For just a minute," Jack said, "I thought I was dead."

"Pay up," Snypes said as the others grumbled. "It was last man standing."

"We're going to have to do something about the arm," Quarles said. "You're bleeding badly."

"It can wait."

Jack took a few steps into the plaza, then turned and addressed the crowd.

"Men of the Rocky Mountain Fur Company," Jack said, with force. "You are hereby on notice that theft and mutiny will not be tolerated. But I am authorized as the agent of General Ashley and Major Henry to grant amnesty to all those who are willing to resume their regular duties and swear fidelity to the company. That means getting this keelboat downriver to St. Louis quickly and safely. Those of you who are willing, step forward."

Jack was making up most of the speech, but he thought the company would forgive him if he could save the keel-boat.

Snypes walked over and stood by Jack.

"Who else?" Jack called.

"How do we know you'll keep your word about amnesty?"

"You are in no position to bargain," Jack said. "But

should you not wish to rejoin the company, you have the option of awaiting trial."

"And just who will be our jailers?" one of younger men asked. "I count three of you, if you can count Snypes. We outnumber you five to one."

"Look around you," Jack said. "You are surrounded by five thousand Mandans. I believe they can hold you until spring and the general arrives to convene a trial."

Sky was standing in front of her lodge, ghost rifle in her hand.

"Mountain Jack Picaro is right," she said in English. "You have given offense to my people because of your behavior. They will gladly make you captive—or teach you the same lesson as the one whose name sounded like a wound."

"It wasn't our fault," another of the men said. "It was Ole Mose. He was powerful mean and wicked, and there was no arguin' with him. We wanted to do right, but we couldn't."

"I'm sure General Ashley will be glad to hear it," Jack said. "And be advised that Bledsoe was mistaken in his belief about my identity. I am, and always have been, Jack Picaro."

"Mountain Jack Picaro," Quarles said, smiling.

The rest of the men began to step forward.

"Jack, you make some fine speeches," Quarles said. "But you're short on planning. I know these men, and none of them can steer a keelboat. Nobody but Bledsoe in this group could. And you damn well know that even if we could, neither of us can go downriver."

Jack cursed softly.

"Do you mean it about the amnesty?" a voice called.

"Yes," Jack said.

"Who is that?" Quarles asked. "I think everybody is accounted for."

"It's me, Jack," said a young white man who made his way through the Mandans watching. "Don't you remember? It's me, Decatur."

"Cate," Jack said.

Decatur was wearing buckskins and was carrying the same rifle Jack had last seen him with at the wreck of the *Jefferson*.

"Henry told me you were lost and probably dead," Jack said. "That you went hunting and never came back."

"I ran away," Decatur said. "Just long enough for the boat to go on upriver. I've been here in the village since. The fight with the Arikara made me afraid. But the Mandans have been kind to me. I do my share by bringing game. But I want to go home."

"Then you shall," Jack said.

He stepped forward and shook his old friend's hand.

"Can you steer the boat?"

"Downriver, I think so," Decatur said. "I would be no good going upriver, but I can manage the other way. There's ice, I know, but not too much yet."

"All right, then," Jack said. "Cate, you have a chance to redeem yourself. Gather the crew and get the *Yellowstone* ready. It's early in the day—if you can be on the river by noon, you'll be that much farther downstream come nightfall."

Decatur nodded.

"But what about Bledsoe? Shouldn't we bury him first?"

"Take a look," Quarles said. "There ain't nothing to bury."

Jack and Decatur turned and looked back toward the

ark canoe. There was the bloody stain in the snow, and the many footprints and other markings in the snow where the fight had taken place, but Bledsoe's body was gone. The Mandans had already carried it away.

Only Biter lay in the snow, as if washed clean by the winter sun.

27 *Many Crows Died*

The winter snows grew deeper and the wind more bitter. Beyond Mitutanka and the other villages along the Heart and Missouri rivers, the world became a vast frozen landscape, a white crusted blanket that seemed to stretch forever. As the weeks passed and became the worst winter in Mandan memory, both firewood and food grew scarce. Much of the short days were spent in scouring the river-banks for fuel, and Sky labored many hours chopping limbs from trees along the bank that had burst from the cold and fallen, or wrenching driftwood from the snow and ice. There was no easy wood to be had, because the villages had long ago used it up. Rats that had come up-river with the keelboats and had previously confined themselves to the midden piles at the edges of the village had now grown bolder and more voracious, and had invaded the lodges in search of food, which they found in the caches of beans and squash. What was ordinarily an inconvenience, of having to ration food a little more strictly in order to reach spring, had now become a necessity. Antelope Woman spent her time obsessively measuring the diminishing amount of beans and squash left in the lodge and chasing the rats away with a club. The dogs that were ever-present around each Mandan lodge quickly began to disappear, until there were none left to pull the travois in the spring.

All of the dogs had been eaten.

Jack and Sky spent the long nights happily enough under the robes in her lodge, but the mornings brought the sting of cold and the pang of hunger because of the cold firepit and the empty larder. What had once been a warm and happy lodge increasingly began to resemble a cold hillside cave where the inhabitants were increasingly reluctant to move. Even the crows, which ordinarily topped each of the lodges and kept up a raucous chorus, became silent. Most of the crows had left, seeking a more hospitable environment. Those that did not fly away, as Jack discovered one clear and bitterly cold morning, would never leave; when he ventured outside the entrance to climb up and adjust the bull boat atop the lodge, he found two crows motionless in the snow, frozen to death.

"I must hunt," Jack said when he returned inside.

"You will have to go far," Sky said. "There are five thousand human beings living in the space of a few miles, and they have already hunted all the animals that can be found close by. There's not even a rabbit to be found outside the villages."

"I'm not going after rabbit," Jack said, checking the contents of his shooting bag. "I will settle for nothing less than a nice fat elk. We need many pounds of meat or we will not survive the winter. The rats from the ships have grown large while we starve."

"I will need a horse," Jack said.

"There are no more horses," Sky said. "Most have either been eaten or have frozen to death. There may be a few in the lodges with their people, but nobody will loan you their horse, if they have one."

"Then once I find game," Jack said, "I will make a sled."

"What if you find no game?" Sky asked.

"Then you and Antelope Woman will be able to last a little longer on the food you have," Jack said. "I am always hungry and eat more than my share. My plan makes sense. You must see the truth of this."

"I cannot stand the thought of staying in this cold lodge without you," she said. "Let me go with you. I can help pull the sled, like a dog. I will be no more trouble than a dog, I promise."

"No," Jack said. "This is your home, and Antelope Woman needs you. Besides, you cannot help be more trouble than a dog, because I could not bring myself to eat you."

Jack took the dancing coyote gorget from the bag.

"Remember this?" he said. "Here, take it. It's too much for me to carry."

He slipped the gorget over her head. She flipped the back of her hair over the rawhide with a stroke of her hand, and with her other hand adjusted the gorget on her chest. Then she began to cry.

"Don't cry," Jack said. "Your tears will freeze."

"Let them freeze."

Jack put on all of the clothes he had, beginning with his buckskins and ending with a buffalo cape. He placed his pistol in the belt, put the Damascus blade in its sheath, and threw his possibles bag over one shoulder. Then he picked up the ghost rifle and put on his fox-skin cap.

"You look like a bear," Sky said.

"I'm as hungry as one, for sure."

They kissed.

"I will count the days," Jack said. "Tell me honestly how long you and Antelope Woman can hold out with the little food that is left."

Sky shrugged.

"It takes a long time to starve," she said. "But freezing to death is quick."

Jack nodded.

"Start tearing apart the wood inside the lodge and burning it," Jack said. "You don't want to take the beams holding up the roof, but you can start undoing some of the lattice work and pegs and so such. It won't last long, but it will last a little while."

Sky looked unhappily around the lodge at the things she could burn.

"I will bring firewood on my sled, along with meat. If I have to go where nobody has hunted yet, then there will be trees as well as animals there. I have the hatchet, and a length of hemp rope."

She nodded.

"We will count the days together," Jack said. "Expect me in seven days. That's two days out, two days of hunting and gathering wood, and three days to drag it back. If I am not back in a week, then do not expect me to return, and do what you must to survive. But now the first thing you do is to take the dead crows outside and bring them in and eat them."

"They will call this the winter the crows died."

"And rats, if you can catch them."

She hid her face in her hands.

"Don't," Jack said. "You must keep your eyes wide open."

"I know," she said. "Please, do not lecture."

"I cannot stand farewells, so I will simply leave now," Jack said. "Do not say good-bye. Say . . ."

"Good hunting, my love."

28 *Dreams Fighting*

Jack left the village and walked into the plains and low hills to the west. On the first day, the weather was cold but clear, and he could turn and look at his tracks stretching back behind him for miles and miles. Sometimes he would run across other tracks—elk, antelope, wolves—but he did not see any other living animals except some hawks and an eagle, high in the sky above. The brightness of the snow and sky seemed to jab at his brain through his eyes, so he rubbed some of the grease he used on the rifle lock beneath each eye. He sheltered for the night beneath a rock out-cropping along a creek that was frozen over, sleeping with his back against the rocks, and when he woke in the morning the snow was falling like spilled flour from a leaden sky. He continued on, walking across the creek and up the bank and over the next hill, but looking behind him, he could no longer see his footprints. The snow had covered them.

The snow continued heavy that morning, and then the wind picked up and blew it into his eyes, making him wince and cuss. But he continued west, until the snow was too deep to continue. It was up to his thighs, making every step an awkward stride with an uncertain landing. To the south was a lone bare tree standing atop a hill, and he turned and made for the solitary landmark. When he finally reached the maple, he threw himself at its base, exhausted. But he only allowed himself to rest a few minutes, and then began to pull branches down to where he could hack them off with the trade hatchet. The ice cracked and showered him as the branches bent, and several snapped before he could find two that had limbs long enough for his needs. He had to make a pair of snowshoes, or travel would be impossible as the snow grew deeper.

From two green branches, he made two large hoops, and then used lengths of whang leather to lace across them and squeeze them into oblong shapes. His hands were cold, and he often had to blow on them or put them under his armpits for the feeling to return. He put more branches across the middle of the hoops, then tied them in place with more whang leather until there was no more fringe to his shirt or bag. The result only somewhat resembled the shoes he had seen; instead of sturdy and perfect ovals with a point end, these were slight and misshapen. But when he jammed his moccasins beneath the strips of leather-wrapped crossbars and took a few steps, he was gratified to find they worked, keeping him atop the snow. He gathered his rifle and other things, wrapped his hands in strips of wool, and set off again to the west, with the wind and snow blowing in his face.

Nightfall found him in the middle of an expanse of featureless and snowy plain. Too tired to move another step, he dropped to his knees and used his hands to scoop out a snow pit, just big enough to hunker down in, and he put the fraying snowshoes over his head. Now motionless, he began to shiver uncontrollably and could not sleep. Far off, he could hear wolves calling to each other. He could not remember how many days it had been since he had eaten, and he knew that if he didn't eat soon, he would die in the snow, and the wolves would find his body and scatter his bones. He tried to think of pleasant things—of Sky, his grandfather's stone house, the taste of sweets, the bloom of good whiskey in his gut, the feeling of a winning hand—but his mind retreated behind a white fog.

When dawn finally came, it was just a dull pink in the east behind the clouds. Jack was still awake, his eyes stinging with cold and his teeth chattering. He roused himself from his trance and lifted himself from his hole to find more than a foot of snow had fallen during the night and was still falling. He could not see to the horizon.

"Jesus and Mari," he said.

Then he spied some dark spots on a nearby hillside. He squinted, trying to make them out through the driving snow. There were half a dozen of them, at least, and they were shaped like buffalo. They were out of range, but perhaps the storm would provide him enough cover to get closer. He jammed his feet into the snowshoes, grabbed his rifle, and set out in a crouch, going slowly and keeping low to the ground. Luckily, the wind was in his face. It took him half an hour to get close enough to where he did not think he could miss.

The buffalo had not moved, and now he could see there were two bulls, four cows, and several calves. Jack slipped off the snowshoes and sank to his knees in the snow, keeping his rifle up and level. He pulled the hammer to full cock and sighted on the closest bull, then stopped because his hands began to shake. He left the rifle on the snow and shoved his hands under his belt to his groin, warming them for thirty seconds, then again took up the rifle. The bull was now fully broadside to Jack. He was close enough to see the tuft of fur at the end of the bull's penis sheath. Jack aimed at the deepest place in the animal's chest and pulled the trigger.

The powder in the pan fizzled impotently.

"Oh, no," Jack whispered. "No."

The powder had become wet.

Working quickly, Jack emptied the pan, using his fingernail to flick away residue from the touchhole, and refilled the pan with the fresh powder. Then he extended the barrel, cocked the hammer, and sighted again on the bull.

The rifle rang with lead and fire.

The bull raised its head, as if it were confused, and sniffed the wind. Blood was splattering on the snow beneath it from the wound, but still it remained standing. Jack drew the pistol from his belt, cleared snow from the muzzle, and aimed it at the bull's eye.

Before Jack could fire, the bull dropped.

"Yes," Jack said. "Yes, yes."

The other buffalo moved off over the hill.

With the pistol still in his right hand, Jack began trudging through the snow, half expecting the bull to spring back to its feet. The animal's eyes were unfocused, and Jack could see no breath coming from its nostrils, just the steam rising from the blood on the snow beneath it. Jack reached out with a moccasin and gave one of the bull's horns a shove. The head rocked slightly, but that was all.

Jack threw his head back and let out an exultant and primal cry.

Then he turned back to the bull.

"I am grateful," he said.

He was shivering badly and he could no longer feel his

fingers and toes. The snow was falling heavier now, and the wind was growing stronger.

Jack drew the Damascus blade and plunged the tip in the bull's neck and with unfeeling hands ripped far enough down the tough hide to begin a rivulet of steaming blood. He caught a handful of blood and then washed his hands with it, and did it again. The blood made his hands feel prickly with heat, but he continued until he could work his fingers and feel them flexing.

Then he took the knife and opened up the bull's stomach. The intestines poured out onto the snow, and he snatched up a length and bit into it raw. It tasted faintly of grass and was both salty and sweet. He tore the rubbery chunk away, chewed it and swallowed, then ate more.

The storm was a full-blown blizzard now, and Jack could not see more than ten yards in any direction. He wiped a bloody hand across his bloody face and surveyed his situation. Then, his mind made up, he flung off the buffalo cape and kicked off his moccasins. Then he pulled off his buckskins and every other stitch he wore. He gathered his clothes and other things and placed them on the cape— the rifle, the pistol, his bag. The knife he kept in his hand.

He turned to the bull and grabbed an armful of intestines and dragged them out onto the snow. Then he used the knife and made the cut in the belly longer, and pulled more of the guts out, until there was enough room to crawl inside. It was warm, like slipping into a hot tub of water.

The blizzard continued, but Jack did not care. Curled up in the body cavity of the bull, he slept as the storm raged around him. He could hear the cries of the wolves on the wind, and when they seemed to get closer, he reached out and found his pistol and drew it inside with him. Then their howls became more distant, chasing some other prey, and he forget about them and went back to sleep.

When he woke, it was night, and the storm had passed. He climbed out from inside the cooling body of the bull and stood, bloody and naked, surveying his surroundings. The sky was clear and the Milky Way glittered overhead, just as the snow around him glittered in the light of the full moon.

Jack dropped down to the snow, used it to scrub most of the blood and gore away, then he dressed. He hacked away more *boudins* and ate them, along with part of the liver. Then, unused to so much food, he walked a few yards away and threw it up. He kicked snow over it to hide the stink.

It would soon be the morning of the third day, and it would take Jack all day to butcher as much meat from the bull as he could and to build a sled from the branches of the maple tree on the nearby hillside. But then he would start back with the loaded sled and, with luck, return to Sky by the morning of the seventh day.

Then he heard the wolves, and they were closer.

A timber wolf could eat twenty pounds of meat in one day, and a pack could eat all the best parts of a bull carcass in just a few hours. Remembering his previous encounter with wolves, Jack knew a fire wasn't likely to deter them, especially if they were starving. Jack reloaded both the pistol and the rifle, secured the knife in its sheath, and climbed on top of the bull carcass and sat on the shoulder. The moon was still high in the sky and brilliantly illuminated the snowfield around him. He hoped the attack would come while the moon was still high.

An hour later he saw them coming from the north, the big male out front, breaking a trail in the snow, and the rest of the pack of a dozen spread out behind. He waited as the pack drew closer, drawn by the smell of a fresh kill, and when the big male in front was close enough that Jack could see its pale eyes in the moonlight, he shouldered the rifle and shot it in the chest. The wolf went down heavily, and the pack tumbled over itself as it paused for a moment, sniffing the body of their dead leader, then yawning and growling. Then the largest male remaining began to move forward, and the others followed. Jack was in the process of reloading but had not yet finished when this new leader sank its teeth into the bull's body cavity and tore away part of a lung, shining blue and leathery in the moonlight.

Jack aimed the pistol and put a ball into the top of its head.

"Whango," Jack said.

The rest of the pack scattered into the night. One smaller male lingered behind, eyeing Jack with caution, seeming to know who was dealing the fatal blows to the pack.

"Git!" Jack shouted. "Go on, git!"

The wolf trotted after the others.

Jack finished reloading the rifle, then did the same for the pistol.

He determined he would offer no thanks to the wolves he had killed, for they were threatening the meat that meant survival for himself and Sky and Antelope Woman. Gold or beaver plews or meat for the table, it was the way of the world, and Jack was determined to have his share.

Jack sat watching for another fifteen minutes atop the carcass, having heard or seen nothing except the cry of a barred owl in a tree far across the prairie. *Who,* the owl asked, *who cooks for you?* The moon was setting and the prairie was disappearing into shadow. It would be daylight in a few hours, and Jack was anxious to begin butchering the bull. At least he wouldn't have to worry about the meat spoiling before getting it back to the village.

Then the young wolf leaped at Jack from behind, knocking him from the top of the carcass and into the snow. Jack turned and tried to bring his rifle to bear, but the wolf was on him, a mouthful of teeth lunging at his throat. The wolf gnawed angrily on the breech of the rifle, which Jack had jammed into the animal's mouth. The wolf was also digging with its claws, and Jack could feel points slice through his buckskin to his chest.

Jack rolled, throwing the wolf off him, and when it made another lunge for his throat, he swung the rifle like a club and drove the butt against its jaws. The wolf yelped and withdrew a few steps, but circled and hunched down to attack again. Jack leveled the rifle and fired, but missed because the wolf was too close for a long gun. Jack dropped the rifle and looked for the pistol, but it had fallen too far from his reach. So he pulled the knife from its sheath.

"Come on," Jack said, motioning with his left hand.

The wolf sprang and sank its teeth into Jack's left forearm.

Jack drove the Damascus blade into the wolf's chest.

It died with its teeth still in Jack's arm.

Jack shook the animal away, then crawled over and washed the bite wound with snow. It was bleeding freely from multiple punctures. Jack cut a strip from the tail of his buckskin shirt and wrapped it tightly around the forearm, then opened and closed his fingers to make sure his hand still worked.

* * *

He picked up his rifle and returned the pistol to his belt and saw no more wolves that night. At daybreak, he stood on the buffalo carcass and looked for the nearest tree. On the slope of the hill, close to the base where there would be a rivulet between the hills in a rain, was a squat redbud tree, its branches thick and low to the ground.

Jack stuck the trade hatchet in the back of his belt, cradled his rifle, and trudged the hundred yards to the tree. He walked around the tree, seeing in his mind's eye which branches were naturally formed into the shapes he needed. There were two branches with gentle elbows that would make fine runners. The other branches he could shape to fit his needs. He began to work with the hatchet, and in two hours had hacked away most of the limbs of the tree and had the lumber he needed. The wood was dark, and the limbs were resilient and had not split in the cold. Jack believed he could make a serviceable sled from it.

"I'm grateful," he told the tree. "I hope you will survive, and in the summer your purple flowers will once again grace this hillside."

He carried the lumber back to the buffalo kill, where he laid the pieces out in the snow. Then he went to the hind legs of the animal and worked with his knife to cut away tendon and sinew for rope, and with this began to bind the sled together. He went back many times for more sinew. By midday the sled was built, and then Jack busied himself with peeling away the skin from the side of the buffalo and using his knife to slice out the best cuts of meat. He took the hump roast from behind the head, and the best parts of the brisket, the short loin, and the flank. The meat was more coarse than beef, and greasy. As he worked, he stacked the meat on the sled, packing it carefully. He used the hatchet and hacked away at the ribs, and piled them on the sled. He also took the tongue and the liver and the testicles, each of which filled his hand and weighed three pounds. When he judged the sled could hold no more—and he could drag no more—he covered the meat with the hide and secured it with sinew. He put his rifle and the pistol, and the hatchet and the possibles bag, on the sled, slipping them beneath the sinew.

He took the fifteen feet of hemp rope and tied each end to the curved portion of the sled's runner. He slipped his moccasins into the snowshoes, then looped the rope across his chest and began pulling the sled to the east. Jack did not know how much weight the sled carried, but he guessed it was 150 pounds, because it felt like he was dragging the body of a man behind him.

Jack kept his eyes on the eastern horizon and pulled. The work was not easy, but on level ground at least it wasn't unpleasant; even the slightest incline increased the difficulty, and threatened to tip the sled if he didn't pull it perfectly uphill, or use a hand to steady it on the downhill side. After an hour, he stopped to rest and to move the rope across to the other shoulder. He was drenched with sweat, and the muscles in his legs were trembling. His snowshoes were also falling to pieces, but he had no other wood for repair, and there were no trees in sight. He took the snowshoes off and jammed them on top of the sled and broke snow as best he could, pulling the sled behind him. In some pockets, he sank up to his thighs, and he felt like he was swimming through snow and pulling a raft behind him.

When darkness came, Jack did not know exactly where he was, because there were few landmarks from which to judge, but he estimated that he had only covered a fifth of the distance back to the village. Exhausted, he sat down beside the sled and rested his back against it. His back and shoulders felt as if they were on fire, and he could not feel his legs except for the quivering in his thighs and calves. There was an odd tingling in his feet, and when he removed his moccasins and wool socks, he saw the toes were purple and blistered. He rubbed them to try to warm them up, but the friction only made the prickly feeling unbearable. He put his socks and shoes back on, knowing that he was frostbitten.

The night was clear and cold and he kept his back against the sled and sat on a piece of hide, the rifle within reach. He was so tired that he could not immediately get to sleep, so he rested the back of his head on the sled and looked up at the winter sky. He did not remember seeing the stars so brilliant as he did now. Every so often a falling star would flare and spark across the northern constellations, and he marveled at the stark and unreachable beauty of things. He feared that he could not pull the sled all the way back to the village, but he did not know. The future—the next few hours, the next few days, the next few years—were as unknowable as the falling of the stars. He only knew that he had to try, and when dawn began to lighten the rim of night, he again set the rope across his chest and began wading through the snow.

He kept walking in the direction of the dawn until the sun was a full three hands above the horizon, then he had to stop and rest. He scooped some snow in his hand and put it to his mouth, sucking out the moisture. Ahead of him was a flat stretch of prairie that seemingly had no end. Then he turned to look at his tracks behind him.

Three riders were approaching.

They were two hundred yards away, following the sled tracks, and Jack could tell from the way they sat their ponies that they were Indians. They seemed to be in no hurry.

"Jesus and Mari," Jack whispered. "Let them be friendlies."

Jack threw off the rope and stood on a runner of the sled and waved his right arm over his head in a slow greeting.

There was no response from the riders.

"So be it," Jack said.

He drew the possibles bag from the sled and slung it over his shoulder and turned the handle of the hatchet toward him, where it would be easy to grasp. He retrieved the pistol, checked the action and the pan, and placed it in his belt. Then he hunkered down behind the sled with his rifle, watching them over the top of the mound of meat.

"Maybe you don't want to fight," Jack muttered. "Maybe you just want to parlay. It would help if I knew what nation you are."

At a hundred yards, Jack knew they were Crow warriors. All of their faces were painted black and white, two had rifles and the other a war club, and the tallest one held a beaded coup stick with a hoop covered in antelope fur, from which fluttered red and black bits of cloth. The one with the coup stick also had white buckskins beneath his robe, a porcupine-quill vest, and a face painted to resemble a skull with no jaw.

"Standing Wolf," Jack said.

His heart began to bang against his ribs.

He took two deep breaths and took stock of his situation. Three against one was never good odds, but Standing Wolf made his chances even worse. Jack was in no position to bargain; whatever they wanted, whether it was the ghost rifle or the buffalo meat, they would simply take after they killed him. He could shoot first, but if he killed Standing Wolf from a distance, without knowing his intent, the other warriors would bide their time until they could inflict a long and painful coward's death.

The three warriors separated, with Standing Wolf in the middle and the other two riding long to flank.

Jack drew the pistol, checked the powder in the pan, pulled the hammer back to half cock so it wouldn't accidentally go off, then placed it back in his belt. He kept his hands where the Crows could see them as they approached. The two warriors stopped thirty yards on either side, and he could now see their faces were lightning streaked. One had a white bolt across his face, and the other had the reverse. Both had scalps hanging from the halters of their ponies.

Standing Wolf approached on his white pony, the coup stick held high.

"Shadow Heart," he said. "Am I dreaming?"

"Hard to tell sometimes," Jack said.

"It is a clear day," Standing Wolf said. "The omens are good. Today we fight, and I will have the rifle that sings—and your hair woven into my pony's mane.

"I'm kind of partial to my hair," Jack said. "And the rifle. But I don't want to fight you, Wolf that Stands Like a Man."

"Ha!" Standing Wolf said, with so much vehemence that it made his pony shift with alarm. "So you refuse to fight?"

"I cannot fight you," Jack said. "I am tired and can no longer feel my toes."

Suddenly Standing Wolf dug his heels into the pony's side and it bolted forward, and as he passed Jack he reached out with a leg and kicked him in the chest, sending him sprawling in the snow. Jack fought to catch his breath.

Standing Wolf slipped down from his pony and in a moment was reaching for the ghost rifle, which leaned against the sled. Jack got to his feet and charged, and they both went down, Standing Wolf dropping the coup stick. Jack drove his right fist into Standing Wolf's mouth, smearing the paint. Then Jack felt Standing Wolf's foot as it drove into his groin, and he doubled over, heaving onto the snow.

Standing Wolf again reached for the ghost rifle.

Jack pulled the pistol from his belt.

Standing Wolf wheeled, kicked the gun out of Jack's hand, and slapped him in the face with the palm of his hand.

"Ha!" Standing Wolf cried. "I have counted coup!"

"Then it's over?" Jack asked, touching his fingers to the trickle of blood at the corner of his mouth. "I thought I hit you first."

"You don't understand," Standing Wolf said, picking up the coup stick.

"But I have the paint from your face on my fist," Jack said. "Isn't that coup? And shouldn't there be some rule about the stick not touching the ground?"

Standing Wolf frowned.

"Be silent," he said. "We are not done. Fights often begin with the counting of coup. And coup is not a blow meant to injure, it is a harmless slap meant to humiliate."

Standing Wolf threw the coup stick to the Black Lightning warrior, who had ridden in close while the pair rolled and fought. Then Standing Wolf went to his pony and retrieved the brass-studded trade gun with the dragon curling down the side of the lock.

Jack reached for the pistol.

"Don't," Standing Wolf said.

"I thought we were still fighting."

"First I want to know why you pull a sled over the snow like a dog," Standing Wolf said. "It is very peculiar. We watched you for a long time this morning and could make no sense of it. Is this some kind of penance?"

"No," Jack said. "The people of Mitutanka are starving. The food is for Sky Woman and her aunt, Antelope Woman."

"They are your winter wives?"

"Sky is. For a winter and more."

Standing Wolf spat.

"I do not approve," he said. "People should marry within their tribes, or at least take captives of the same color. All of this mixing is weakening all of our nations."

"You're wrong," Jack said.

"I will kill you."

"You can kill me, but it still won't make me wrong."

"Why should I care if the Mandans are starving?" Standing Wolf asked. "They live in holes in the ground and cannot follow the buffalo as the Crows do. They should give up Lone Man and the old ways and become a tribe of horse warriors instead of farmers who keep a few horses to drag their travois."

"You should care because of the stories that will be told."

"What stories?"

"That Standing Wolf had it in his power to spare the lives of enemy women and children who were starving during the Winter the Crows Died and did not," Jack said. "It is conduct unbecoming a chief—or a warrior. To be fierce in battle and fair in judgment is what all men should aspire to."

"So what do you want?"

"Give me a horse to take the meat to the village," Jack said. "And then I will come back and fight you, and you can kill me if you can."

"You ask for too much," Standing Wolf said and smiled. "If I let you go, you will disappear downriver and then I will have to follow you all the way to St. Louis to kill you."

"And kill Captain Clark as well?"

Standing Wolf stopped smiling.

"What do you know of the captain?"

"He sent me to kill you," Jack said. "And to bring him the peace medal."

"You are lying."

"You know I speak the truth."

"What does he say about me?"

"That you are neither dead nor alive," Jack said. "That you can change your shape at will, and that you were old when he first met you, but that you would be younger now. And that he fears you and stays awake at night waiting for your shadow to cross your door."

"Damn him to his white God."

"Clark is your father."

"No, he is not my father," Standing Wolf shouted, shaking the trade gun at Jack. "You understand nothing about human beings. You are as you were in my dreams, alien."

"Then tell me what I do not understand."

"The man called York was my father," Standing Wolf said. "My mother was the daughter of the Standing Wolf that Clark betrayed, and he was indeed a war chief with a fearsome reputation."

Jack asked how Clark betrayed his grandfather.

"With his words," Standing Wolf said. "There were many speeches with fine words and talk of friendship, and admonishment about stealing their horses, but he did not understand the ways of our people. *'Your Great White Father will be very sorry to learn of the Crow stealing horses from his captains who he sent to do good among his red children along the Missouri waters.'* Balls! Then he promised us trinkets and trade if we allowed the whites to build a fort in our country. Clark was on his way back down the river, after crossing the mountains and reaching the great water to the west."

Standing Wolf paused.

"My grandfather knocked the ashes of his medicine pipe on Clark's boots and cursed him to dwell forever in the land of uneasy dreams. Then my grandfather declared that Clark did not visit the Crow nation at all, but that it was just his malevolent redheaded ghost."

"But there is no question that York was there."

"I am here, aren't I?" Standing Wolf shouted. "York was admired for his courage and his honesty and was adopted by the tribe and participated in the sacred Sun Dance. He hung from the lodge poles from eagle talons driven into his skin, he dragged buffalo skulls behind him, he blew the whistles and danced until he had a vision of freedom. He wanted to stay with the tribe, but the captain's ghost demanded he leave. He did not understand he was a member of our tribe and not a slave."

Standing Wolf threw his head back and looked at the sun.

"That is why my grandfather swore to kill the captain," he said. "And that is why you have visited me in my dreams, and why we have sworn to kill each other. It is my duty until York returns to us. Tell me, does he yet live?"

Jack cleared his throat.

"Clark believes he has died of cholera."

Standing Wolf let out a mournful cry.

"Never am I to see my father," he said. "Except in my dreams."

Standing Wolf took a deep breath.

"Now we must fight," he said.

"I will not fight you," Jack said.

"You must, you're sworn to it."

"Only if you agree to carry the meat to the village," Jack said. "Then I will fight and hold nothing back. I promise. If I win, then your warriors are to let me pass with your horse. If you win, and I am dead, then you are to deliver the buffalo meat."

Standing Wolf spoke to his warriors in their language. There was a bit of back-and-forth, and then they nodded.

"Agreed," Standing Wolf said. "Shall we begin?"

Before Jack could answer, Standing Wolf was swinging the butt of the trade rifle at him. Jack ducked, then scrambled ten feet away into the open snow. He had the pistol in his right hand and the Damascus toothpick in his left.

Standing Wolf had ducked on the other side of his pony.

"Come on," Jack said.

Then Standing Wolf got on the pony's back and went forty feet away, then circled around and came back at full speed, hanging onto the horse's mane and pointing the trade gun beneath the neck of the horse. Jack could see the bobbing muzzle of the gun, and he dropped to one knee to make himself smaller. Then he saw the flash of flame and heard the *zip* of the ball as it narrowly missed him. The muzzle blast from the gun was still ringing in his ears as Standing Wolf leaped down from the pony and rushed toward him, a flint knife in his right hand.

Jack met the flint with the Damascus blade, and sparks flew until the stone knife was stopped by the brass hilt. Standing Wolf jumped aside, fearing the muzzle of the pistol, and slashed twice with the flint, but narrowly missed each time. Jack spun and swung the heavy muzzle of the pistol against the back of Standing Wolf's head, which made a terrible *thunk* sound. Standing Wolf lost his grip on the flint blade and went sprawling in the snow. He searched in the snow for the flint but could not find it, and he lost just enough moments to allow Jack to come back around and kick him in the face, bloodying his nose.

Jack pointed the pistol at Standing Wolf's chest.

Standing Wolf gave a scream and sprang like a cat, throwing Jack backward into the snow. As Jack fell, he threw the Damascus toothpick behind him, but held tight to the pistol. Standing Wolf grabbed his right arm in both hands and began to twist. When Jack would not let go, Standing Wolf lowered his head and began biting his arm.

With a yelp, Jack dropped the pistol. It landed muzzle-down in the snow, the butt sticking up. Standing Wolf snatched it up. He stood and pointed the pistol at Jack's chest.

"Don't," Jack said.

"Now it is over," Standing Wolf said and pulled the trigger.

Nothing happened.

"Balls!" Standing Wolf shouted.

Jack was backing away toward the sled.

Standing Wolf pulled the hammer back and Jack heard it click into place.

"Don't pull the trigger," Jack said. "The barrel is—"

He saw Standing Wolf's finger tighten on the trigger.

"—packed with snow."

Jack threw his hands in front of his face as the pistol exploded in Standing Wolf's hand. A chunk of iron went sailing by Jack's right ear, and something struck him in the left side with enough force to spin him to the ground. Jack put his hands to his side and saw blood, then looked over at Standing Wolf.

A screw had embedded itself in the brow above his left eye, and there were various pieces of metal and wood peppering his face. His right hand, which he still held in front of him, was wrecked, with the fingers dangling by pieces of flesh, and a piece of the splintered walnut grip was driven deep into his palm.

The blast had fractured the pistol at the welds of its octagonal barrel, the flat pieces either blown away or peeled back. The breech plug had been driven backward out of the pistol, and the smoking breech and its tang were now embedded in a hole in the shattered porcupine-quill vest.

Jack simultaneously heard a rifle shot and felt a ball splatter into the snow beside him. He spun to see the Black Lightning warrior holding the smoking trade gun with the dragon lock and the brass tacks. Jack grabbed the ghost rifle from the top of the sled and shot the warrior in the chest, knocking him off his horse, and sending the trade gun into the snow.

The White Lightning warrior had his war club raised and was riding in a circle, preparing to charge. Jack began to reload, and suddenly the warrior turned his horse in the other direction and rode away to the west. The retreating warrior still presented an easy shot after Jack had the ball seated and the gun primed. He took careful aim at the center of Black Lightning's back, then paused and lowered the rifle.

Jack leaned the rifle against the sled and plucked his knife from the snow. Then he walked over to Standing Wolf, who now had slumped to his knees.

Jack looked down at the blood around Standing Wolf and noticed there was another trail, one that led over to the sled and back. Then Jack saw that he himself was bleeding from the left side. He lifted his buckskins and saw blood welling from a hole beneath his ribs. A piece of the ruptured iron had torn away a chunk of flesh but had hit no bones.

Standing Wolf was staring at him with a dull eye.

"This should have ended different," Jack said.

Standing Wolf attempted to speak, but could not draw enough breath.

He reached for the breech plug with his left hand, trying to pluck it out of his chest with his fingers. He pulled it away from the shattered quills and the torn buckskin. Jack could see the shimmer of bronze beneath. Standing Wolf grasped the rawhide string around his neck and pulled the medallion from beneath the vest. He stared at the dented bronze circle in his left hand for a moment.

"Look," Standing Wolf said. "Our blood mingles in the snow."

"We all bleed the same color," Jack said.

"Here," Standing Wolf said, holding out the medal. "Kill me and take it back to the captain. I am blind in one eye and crippled in one hand, and now await death. This is what has happened many times in my dreams, and I was foolish to believe that I could change my fate."

"I do not think the eye is blinded," Jack said. "There is a piece of metal in your skull above it, and the eye is swollen and filled with blood, but you might keep it."

Jack knelt, grasped the peace medal, and used the knife to sever the rawhide around Standing Wolf's neck. He held the medal for a few moments, looking at the profile of Jefferson. The president had a self-satisfied look on his face, and his long hair was tied behind his head with ribbons. Th. Jefferson President of the U.S. a.d. 1801 was the legend. Then he turned the medal over and studied the shaking hands over the crossed tomahawk and peace pipe. Peace. Friendship.

"I do not want the medallion," Jack said, placing it back in Standing Wolf's left hand. "I will not kill you. The words that are written on it are not lies. They express a hope that may yet come true, in spite of our nightmares, and I will not take it from you."

Standing Wolf shook his bloodstained head.

"It has been a generation since the medal was given to my grandfather," he said. "And my father was a captive of the whites for all of his life, denied the freedom to live with his family and his adopted tribe. Why should we believe anything will change?"

"Because as long as we live," Jack said, "we are in the process of becoming. We must wake from these wicked dreams that keep us fighting one another and make a new dream for a new country. What is it that I hear the Indians say often? That all tribes are related in some cousinly degree. Our blood spreads in the branches of the great tree of life. It leads back to a time beyond remembering and forward to an age unimagined. So let us begin dreaming now of a time that we recognize there is only one great tree of life, when we repent of our offenses to one another and our cousins the bears and the wolves, and strive to live in harmony with each other."

"Words," Standing Wolf said. "Only words."

"It may not happen in our lifetimes," Jack said. "But just as you cannot build a machine without first imagining a purpose for it, you cannot achieve the future you want without first dreaming of it."

"We are not machines," Standing Wolf said, "and time is a circle. You might as well wish to change the seasons."

"The circle of time is broken," Jack said. "Life on the Upper Missouri is now driven by the price of hats across the sea. When these silly hats fall out of fashion, another commerce will take its place—buffalo horns, perhaps, or porcupine quills or the rocks beneath our feet."

Jack paused. He could not remember being so tired. He sank down and sat on the bloody snow next to Standing Wolf.

"For years I have tried to understand what it means to be an American," Jack said. "I come from the Old World, and my grandfather drove Old World ideas into my heart. So I have sought money, because it is the key to influence over others; I sought freedom, because I felt I had none; and I hurt others, because I myself was hurting. Now that the answer has come to me, it is perhaps too late."

"What is this answer?" Standing Wolf asked.

"To be an American is to be free to dream," Jack said.

"We are ensnared by our dreams," Standing Wolf said.

"Only when we don't know the dreams come from inside of us," Jack said.

"So many words," Standing Wolf said.

Jack began to laugh.

"Yes," Jack said. "But I will be a little better man tomorrow because of them."

"Your weakness disgusts me," Standing Wolf said. "I am your enemy and yet you will not kill me. I am ashamed for you."

"I have shame enough for us both," Jack said.

Jack reached out to touch Standing Wolf's face, but the warrior slapped his hand away.

"Let me remove some of the pieces," Jack said. "The screw in particular is quite deep."

"No," Standing Wolf said.

"You are badly wounded, even though the peace medal saved your life," Jack said. "You may still die of putrefaction or blood loss or a dozen other things. Come to the village and perhaps you can recover your health."

"And be your captive?"

"You would be nobody's slave."

"No," Standing Wolf said. "I will return to my tribe."

Jack agreed but said it was a foolish decision.

"There are two horses," Jack said. "I will use one to drag the sled to the village. The other is yours, and I will help you up onto it."

"No," Standing Wolf said. "Go, leave me. I will get on my pony myself. Besides, the coward who ran will be waiting ahead, and I will not let him forget his cowardice as we return to the tribe."

Jack stood.

"So you will no longer kill?" Standing Wolf asked.

"Not for profit," Jack said.

Jack took a last look around him before he gathered his things and tethered the Crow pony to the sled. Standing Wolf was still sitting, the peace medal in his left hand.

"When you recount this to your tribe," Jack asked, "what will you call it?"

"The Day of Dreams Fighting."

29 *The Messenger*

Spring came late to the Upper Missouri, and as the ice began to leave the river and the snow recede from the banks, Jack tarried in the earth lodge with Sky and Antelope Woman. With time, the wound in his side healed over, but he never regained all of the feeling in his toes. He was glad to see the Winter the Crows Died pass, but he wasn't anxious to return yet to the Rocky Mountain Fur Company. But one day in April, when patches of snow still clung to the prairies outside the village, a canoe came down the river paddled by a young trapper. He was twenty-three-year-old Jedediah Smith, and he had been sent by Major Henry.

"The men at Fort Henry are in pitiful shape," Smith told Jack as he sat in Sky's earth lodge with a bowl of roasted elk meat before him. "The winter was something fierce."

"We noticed," Jack said. "Anybody die?"

"That is an impolite question," Sky protested. "Remember, we do not speak of the dead."

"No, but plenty were sick," Smith said. "Things are better now, but Major Henry is worried. He sent me downriver with a message for General Ashley, who I am to intercept near the Grant River."

Jack reached for a bit of the elk, but Smith held up a hand.

"We must pray," he said.

Smith closed his eyes and clasped his hands together.

"Oh Lord, we your humble servants give thanks for these blessings," he said. "Give us grateful hearts and make us mindful of the needs of others. Amen."

Smith reached into the bowl and got a handful of chunks.

"Now can I have some of my own elk meat?" Jack asked.

"Of course," Smith said. "The Lord provides."

"Where're you from?" Jack asked. "I can't quite place your accent."

"I was about to ask you the same thing," Smith said. "I was born in New York and then my family moved to Pennsylvania when I was around ten. After, that we moved to Ohio. I knew the West was for me, and here I am."

"I'm from lots of places," Jack said.

"Where were you born?"

"You wouldn't know of it."

"Might."

"The Basque country."

"Between France and Spain," Smith said quickly. "I've had my lessons. I can recite some of the New Testament by heart and can keep accounts and know a little Latin, too."

"French or Spanish?"

"Nope," Smith said.

"Either would have been more useful," Jack said.

Sky smiled at Smith.

"This man is insufferable," she said in French.

"Henry sent you downriver by yourself?"

"Yep," Smith said. "But I was to collect you and Quarles if I could find you."

"Quarles is about," Jack said. "He's among the Hidatsa, just upriver. I'm not sure he'd like to be collected, however."

"Just following orders," Smith said. "The major knows you've had some experience with the Rees and could be of help."

"Help with what?"

Smith took a square of cloth from his pocket and dabbed his mouth.

"The message for General Ashley is to stop at the Ree villages on his way upriver and buy horses," Smith said. "He's also to bring as much food and other supplies as will fit on the boat. But mainly, Henry wants as many horses as he can get from the Rees."

"This is a bad plan," Sky said.

"Why?" Jack asked.

"Because the Sahnish burned the *Jefferson* last spring and killed all of the crew except two," Sky said.

"Sahnish?" Smith asked.

"That's what the Arikara—the Rees—call themselves," Jack said. "It means the tribe from which all other tribes spring."

"That attack was by a lone war chief," Smith said. "The major doesn't think the whole Ree nation is against us."

"I wouldn't underestimate the influence Lightning Crow has," Sky said. "The Arikara have been unhappy with the whites since their great chief, Ankedoucharo, died in 1806 after being convinced to travel to Washington to meet with Thomas Jefferson. The captains were reluctant to tell the Sahnish, so they kept the death a secret. A letter Jefferson sent back to the nation said Ankedoucharo had died of illness, but many were convinced he was murdered."

Smith laughed.

"That's ridiculous," he said. "Why would Jefferson murder the chief?"

"From their perspective," Jack said carefully, "it would just be a case of a white man killing a member of the Sahnish nation. It is not unheard of."

"The Sahnish would like the body of their chief returned," Sky said.

"Jefferson is a good Christian man," Smith said. "A bit unconventional, but a Christian still. He made a Bible that just contains all the red-letter things said by Jesus. But he excluded the miracles and such. I'm sure Jefferson gave this chief a proper Christian burial."

"For Ankedoucharo, there could be nothing more improper," Sky said.

"Since we're on the subject, my friends," Smith said, "Have you heard the good news?"

"All my damned life," Jack said.

Smith's eyes were roving over the interior of the earth lodge, taking in the firepit and smoke hole above and Jack's rifle hanging from a pole behind him.

"That's an unusual rifle," Smith said. "Short barrel. Hawken?"

"No," Jack said.

"What caliber?"

"Fifty."

"The ghost rifle is not for sale," Sky said.

"The ghost rifle?" Smith asked. "Why is it called that?"

"Let's talk of something else," Jack said. "Why does Henry want horses?"

"Business," Smith said. "Between the Blackfoot and the

Missouri Fur Company, we are being crowded for areas to trap along the easy places near major rivers. So horses are needed for the company to travel overland. Each man is to be a free trapper and roam about for the season. The company will sell the traps and other truck the free trappers need, and that will improve the profit."

"So the men of the company are to become a source of profit?"

"Yes," Smith said.

"Like the beaver?"

"Well, not like that," Smith said. "Nobody's going to get skinned."

"That's open for debate," Jack said. "So traps and horses and whiskey for sale to the trappers. Just like the company traded liquor to the Indians for the plews."

"It's clever business."

"Ashley is a clever man," Jack said. "But clever doesn't always win."

"He's lieutenant governor now of the state of Missouri, but I'll bet he's elected governor in the next election," Smith said. "I mean, being a military man and all. Brigadier general of the Missouri Militia in the War of 1812."

"And he's coming himself upriver?" Jack asked.

"Yep," Smith said.

"He should stay in Missouri."

"The call of business," Smith said. "The company has already suffered several grievous losses. Two keelboats lost and all the goods on board. The financial situation is dire."

"So Ashley's move is to double down?" Jack asked. "I'm not sure he has the cards showing for that."

Smith said he didn't know what Jack meant.

"Never mind," Jack said. "Look, you're free to rest here for a spell. But you'll have to start downriver alone to meet up with Ashley. I'm not of a mind to participate in this horse-buying exercise, and I'm not sure Quarles will want a part of it."

"So you're not coming?"

"I'll come," Jack said, "but when I reckon it's time."

"No," Sky said.

"I will miss your chipped tooth," Jack said.

"Don't tease," Sky said.

"Major Henry won't like you not coming now," Smith said.

"I thought we were all free trappers now. So I'm exercising a little of that freedom by not paddling into a disaster. And when you finally meet up with General Ashley, you'd best tell him to find the horses from some other tribe."

Weeks later, when snowmelt and rain had filled the river, Jack set out as a passenger on a double canoe headed south. There had been news, carried from village to village, that keelboats were coming upriver, but there had been no reports of fighting. But it was 170 miles from Mitutanka to the Arikara villages, and news traveled slowly.

Still, Sky was anxious about Jack leaving, and she asked him to stay. But Jack was desperately low on powder and ball, and there were other items the keelboat carried that he either needed or wanted. Chief among these was a Dutch oven, salt, cane sugar, and fine wheat flour. Sky had shown him a range of fruit that grew wild near the village, including apples and blackberries and the grapelike chokecherry. Jack was determined to have pie or at least cobbler.

The double canoe was a big boat, with a deck placed in between the two large hulls, and it was big enough for Jack to stretch out and rest his head on his bag during the trip downriver. Quarles could not be convinced to leave the Hidatsa village, saying he was content enough to allow Ashley to come to him.

Jack watched the river slide past, and it reminded him of how difficult the ascent was on the *Jefferson*. Just thinking of the cordelling and the poling made his shoulders and his feet hurt. It was just a year before, but now it seemed an unimaginably long time before.

It took eight days for the double canoe to reach the bend in the river where the Arikara villages were strung out on the west bank. Jack could hear the popping of rifles and see black smoke rising from the riverbank. The crew of the double canoe steered away from the villages, hugging the left channel. Jack could see a keelboat tied at the foot of the village, a couple of dead men on its decks. Next to the keelboat was a pirogue. But most of the fighting seemed to be up on the banks, in or around the villages.

As the canoe slipped past an island in the middle of the river, Jack spotted a dugout canoe hidden beneath some scrubby trees. Jack gathered his things and made a sign of thanks to the Mandan crew, and rifle in hand jumped from the deck of the double canoe into the shallow water. They told him in sign that he was crazy and that they were going far downriver before putting in.

Jack splashed ashore, made his way across the narrow island, and found Jed Smith with his rifle across a log, looking for targets of opportunity near the keelboat, which was a long city block away.

Jack settled down beside him.

"So I'm guessing the Arikaras weren't interested in selling any horses?"

Smith fired at a target that Jack couldn't see.

"Picaro," he said. "Things got mighty hot this morning."

"What happened?"

"The Rees attacked the keelboat first," Smith said. "The rest of the company was in the village, bargaining for horses, and they got ambushed, too. They've had us pinned down all morning."

"I see you managed to paddle away."

"The Lord was looking out for me," Smith said.

"How many are there?"

"Seems like the whole Arikara nation," Smith said. "One of the chiefs made a speech about the river being closed from now on to white traffic, and that's when all blazes broke loose."

"Was this chief Lightning Crow?"

"Don't know his name."

Unhurriedly, Smith began to reload.

"Was he missing a hand?"

"Yep," Smith said. "I just got bits and pieces of the speech from one of the other men who speaks French. He started out talking about that chief who had went to Washington and died, and then he talked about the white trappers plundering the beaver, and then he railed against the whiskey that's brought upriver. Then he said the Arikara were at war with the whites."

"I think I may have mentioned that to you sometime before," Jack said. "Did you tell General Ashley this?"

"He didn't seem to be in the mood to hear it," Smith said.

He took another aim at something else Jack couldn't see and fired.

"Would you stop?" Jack asked. "There's nothing moving over there for you to aim at. Save your powder."

"I keep thinking that I see something," Smith said.

"You stare at anything long enough, and your brain will

see what it wants to," Jack said. "Happens all the time in the mountains. You see enemies behind every rock. Have you been up in the mountains yet?"

"Nope," Smith said. "Not yet."

"It's an education," Jack said. "But there ain't no Latin."

"What do you think we should do?" Smith asked.

"Not stay here, for one thing," Jack said. "We're easy pickings once the Arikara figure out we're here. They'll paddle one of their big canoes over here with a half dozen warriors, and that will be the end of us."

"So we run?"

"Maybe," Jack said. "Tell me how many are with Ashley."

"Well, he has seventy all told," Smith said. "There's one keelboat that managed to get downstream when the fighting started that had about twenty men on it. There were another forty up in the village, some of them looking for sport, others engaged with Ashley trying to buy horses. Then there were about ten men on the keelboat you see."

"If there were as many Arikara attacking as you say," Jack said, "then the company up in the village most likely just hoofed it to the south, rather than try to fight their way to the boats. All the shots seem to be coming from that direction."

"What do we do?"

"We need to get the keelboat away before it dawns on Lightning Crow to burn it," Jack said. "He'll most likely be obsessed with capturing Ashley right now. So we slip across and see if there's anybody left alive on the boat, and we set off downriver."

They went to the dugout. Jack got in front, his rifle at the ready, and made Smith do the paddling. They shoved off from the island and pointed the bow upstream, with

Smith working hard to keep the current from sweeping them past the keelboat.

"Something's moving on the bank," Smith said.

"They're our people," Jack said.

As the dugout approached, a half-dozen company men ran down from the village, waving their hands over their heads. A line of Arikara warriors appeared on the bank fifty yards behind them. Most of them were armed with bows, which they drew back almost as one and released a flight of arrows as their targets reached the keelboat. The arrows hitting the side of the boat sounded like hail. Two of the company men were hit in the back, and one fell in the water while the other was dragged aboard by the others.

"They're going to get us all killed," Jack said.

Smith put the nose of the canoe against the side of the keelboat that was away from the village. Then he and Jack jumped up on the boat, took a position against the opposite rail, and fired. Two of the archers fell while a ringing B flat echoed across the river.

"Whango," Jack said.

"Return fire," Smith said calmly to the men.

The four men huddled against the rail brought their rifles up and shot back toward the village, but without effect. Then they fumbled as they tried to reload, the juggling of powder and ball suddenly seeming to be beyond them.

"Slow down," Jack said, ramming a ball home and then withdrawing the rod. "Take aim before pulling the trigger. Reload as if you have plenty of time. This your first time being shot at?"

"We were told the Rees would be friendly," the man nearest said.

"You were told wrong," Jack said.

"Think that swivel gun is loaded?" Smith asked.

"Maybe," Jack answered. "But they're more for show, in my experience. It's foolish to stay here and fight. We've got to get this boat into the current, or we'll all be skewered."

Smith nodded.

"Everybody hold for a moment until all rifles are charged," Smith said. "Then we're going to shoot, one at a time, every two seconds, to lay down some fire to cover the man who cuts the line."

"Who's the man?" Jack asked.

"You," Smith said.

"I thought you would ask for volunteers."

"You volunteered when you said we had to set the boat adrift," Smith said. "There's an axe there on the deck. You pick it up on your run toward the line and hack away quick."

Jack cussed but agreed he would do it.

"Go!" Smith said, firing his rifle.

Jack sprang from his position beside the rail and ran across the deck, snatched up the axe, and went to the bow. The thick rope was wrapped around a cleat and tied with an overly complicated and amateurish knot. Jack heard the next man at the rail fire.

Jack swung the axe, and the blade came down on the rope, taking a bite out of it, but not severing it. Then there was a lag in the firing, and as he drew back for another strike, he could hear Smith exhorting the next man in line to fire, that he was waiting too long. An arrow sailed in an arc toward the boat and buried itself in the deck near to Jack's left foot. Jack swung the axe again, and this time it severed the rope, and the boat lurched into the current.

The pirogue, which was tethered to the keelboat, followed.

Another rain of arrows came, but either fell into the

water or added to the bristling collection on the keelboat's cabin and deck. Against the rail again, Jack looked back toward the village and saw a lone figure riding his horse down to the riverbank.

It was Lightning Crow.

He was as Jack had seen the chief the first time, with the buffalo hat and the tufted black horns and the porcupine-quill breastplate. Beads and bits of bone were in his greased, graying hair. The bottom half of his face was painted blue. In his one good hand he carried a fierce-looking war axe, and the blade was red with blood.

Jack knew the bell-like sound of the ghost rifle had summoned him.

Smith, who was next to Jack, had finished reloading his rifle. He brought the rifle up and took aim at Lightning Crow, but Jack put a hand on his gun and forced the barrel down.

"Don't," Jack said. "He's daring me to shoot him."

"Then why don't you oblige him?" Smith asked.

"Because he is Sky's father," Jack said. "Or at least he once was."

"But he's the one-handed devil who started it all," Smith protested.

"He didn't start it," Jack said. "But he might finish this round of it."

Jack watched as the village receded, with Lightning Crow sitting on his horse as still as if he were a statue. Jack wondered if the old chief would think he was weak for not killing him, or whether he would believe instead that he had been shown mercy. But Jack wasn't sure himself which one it was.

"Look sharp!" Smith called.

Jack looked downriver.

"Get the poles," Jack said. "There's a spit of a sandbar we're going to have to push away from or we'll be in even worse shape than before, because we'll be stuck in the sand."

"Watch for hostiles," Smith said. "I'll take the steering oar."

"If you say so," Jack said.

As the boat neared the head of the bar, the men readied the poles.

"Don't wait too long," Jack said. "Start pushing now. This boat is heavy, and although it doesn't seem like we're moving fast, it has tons of momentum. It'll bury itself in the mud and sand in a second."

The men pushed, the ash poles bending with the strain, and Smith swept the rudder. The boat turned toward the deeper channel and the island glided past, the sand a whisper beneath the keel.

The men dropped their poles and sat on the deck, their shoulders sagging.

Jack looked at their faces. They were smudged with gunpowder, smeared in places with blood, and their eyes burned with fear and fatigue. Their clothes were suited to town, not the wilderness. A couple of them barely knew how to load and shoot their rifles, and one of them was pleading with Smith for whiskey. Were these the best men that St. Louis now had to offer? But then, Jack thought, he and Decatur looked hardly any better after that first fight with the Arikara.

"There's a wounded man yonder," Smith said. "Somebody tend to him."

At dusk, they found the other keelboat anchored in a patch of slack water twenty-five miles downstream. There were shouts and hallos from the other boat, and as they drifted alongside, lines were thrown and made fast.

Smith hopped over to the other boat. Jack hesitated.

"Come on," Smith said.

There were two dozen men on the keelboat, some of them tending wounds, others watching the near bank for signs of Arikara warriors.

"General Ashley?" Smith called.

"The cabin," came the answer.

Smith ducked through the open doorway and Jack followed.

William Ashley was sitting at a desk beneath a swinging lantern, studying a map of the Upper Missouri. He was a lean clean-shaven man in his late forties, and he wore his old Missouri Militia uniform, a sword at his side. Jack thought it would be appropriate if he had beads and bits of bone in his hair as well.

"Smith," he said. The Virginian accent reminded Jack of Clark. "You saved the other keelboat before the Rees could burn it. That is the only bit of good fortune in an otherwise rotten day. Who is with you?"

"This here is Jack Picaro," Smith said.

"General," Jack said.

"You're one of Henry's men," Ashley said. "I remember the name."

"I'm one of the free trappers," Jack said.

"How many dead have you?" Ashley asked Smith.

"Three dead and one badly wounded, not expected to live."

"That makes thirteen so far," Ashley said. "The shore party had the worst of it, and all of them are still not accounted for. I'm afraid Major Henry will not be getting his horses or his supplies anytime soon."

"He is a patient man," Smith said.

"There will be other tribes from which to buy horses," Ashley said. "The Pawnee, perhaps. But for now, we will spend a time gathering our men and then make our way back downriver some 160 miles to Fort Atkinson."

Ashley's finger traced the route on the map.

"It is the westernmost military post of the United States," he said. "There, we will enlist the aid of Colonel Leavenworth in punishing the Rees."

"Punishing?" Jack asked. "How?"

"By marching against them, of course," Ashley said. "The Rees have killed more than a dozen American citizens and have closed the river to traffic, stopping the fur trade. Leavenworth has three hundred troops under his command, and together with my brigade that will be more than enough to burn the Ree villages to the ground."

"All of them?"

"They have to be shown a lesson," Ashley said. "The villages are strung out along the south bank of the river, and if we allow any of them to stand, then we are risking another attack."

"Have you asked them what they want?"

"We set a price for the horses," Ashley said. "The interpreter said they were satisfied with it. Then the next morning they attacked."

"That's not what I mean," Jack said. "Have you asked them why they're angry?"

"It is their nature to be savage," Ashley said.

"They want the body of their great chief, Ankedoucharo, returned to them," Jack said. "He was unaccustomed to white civilization, became ill, and died back east, after a meeting with Jefferson. The Arikara would like his body returned. It would help restore their honor."

"They have no honor," Ashley said. "That was clear enough today."

"If President Jefferson had died on foreign soul," Jack asked, "is there any length the United States would not go to recover his body?"

"Smith, get this man out of my cabin," Ashley said. "He has been too long with these people who are trying to murder us."

"General Ashley did not seem to like you much," Smith said, handing another burlap bag of supplies down to Jack in the pirogue. "But I can talk to him and explain how much help you were in getting the keelboat free of the Arikara village. That might change his mind."

"No favors," Jack said. "I don't want to owe anybody anything."

"Well, you've more than earned this," Smith said. "There are thousands of dollars in goods and supplies in this keelboat, which you helped save, and we're giving you less than a month's wages."

"It's all I need," Jack said. "For now."

"You've got the pirogue just about fully packed," Smith said. "General Ashley will be unhappy when he finds the Dutch oven is gone."

"I'm not leaving without it," Jack said.

Smith glanced at the ghost rifle in the bow of the pirogue, with Jack's possibles bag and powder horn with his ever-expanding map of the Upper Missouri beside it.

"You're going to run out of room on that horn," Smith said.

"I keep finding new places," Jack said. "And I can always get a bigger horn."

"You going to make it upriver all right?"

"I reckon so," Jack said.

"How long are you going to stay with the Mandans?"

"Not so long," Jack said. "The villages are too close to the river, and the river has become too busy for my tastes. I aim to take Sky and find someplace farther west, maybe up in the mountains. Someplace where we're free to choose our own dreams."

Smith coughed and cleared his throat.

"Say, I might be able to help out your accounts receivables a bit," he suggested. "The rifle of yours—I've never seen one like it. And it rings like a bell! With a rifle like that, a man would have an edge over anybody who meant him ill. How much will you take for it?"

"I told you before," Jack said. "It's not for sale."

"I've got some silver saved up," Smith said. "I could let you have sixty dollars and my rifle to boot. No free trapper in the mountains could expect to make that kind of money in a season."

"No," Jack said. "It's not for you."

"If you say so."

"I do," Jack said, and held out his hand. They shook. "You are a peculiar man, Jed Smith, who says unpleasant things. You'll go far."

30 *The Spark*

Ten miles upriver, Jack saw a keelboat anchored in some slack water beside an island on the north bank of the river. The keelboat was about forty feet long, which was smaller than either of Ashley's, and Jack pondered why he hadn't spotted it on the drift down from the Arikara village. He could see a couple of men at the rear of the boat with rifles, and he knew they saw him because they held their guns at the ready.

"Hallo the keelboat," Jack said, releasing an oar and waving his hand over his head.

"Who're you with?"

"Ashley's brigade," Jack said. "Who're you?"

"Missouri Fur Company," one of the men said. "Come aboard."

Jack took the oars again and guided the pirogue to the side of the keelboat, then tossed a rope up. One of the men caught it and made it fast to a cleat. Jack grabbed his possibles bag and powder horn and slung them over his shoulder, grabbed his rifle, and took a hand to help him into the boat.

"You boys took some fire yesterday," the man said.

"Thirteen dead," Jack said. "More wounded. I was on

the boat that was cut free and drifted down yesterday. I didn't see this boat on the river."

"We were hiding over yonder, beneath the trees," the man said, nodded toward the bank. "We've been trying to divine the best time to slip upriver past the Ree villages."

"How many of you on board?" Jack asked.

"Eight," the man said. "Not enough to put up much of a fight, so we reckon we'll try to slip by in the dark, before the moon rises, if we can pole it. But it'll be tricky. The river's always tricky. Say, are we swapping names or are we going to be all mysterious? Mysterious suits me if you have a need for it."

"Jack Picaro."

"Joshua Pilcher."

"Mountain Jack Picaro," Pilcher said, slapping him on the back. "I'll be skinned. I've heard a lot about you, son."

"Some of it's true, I reckon," Jack said. "You own this outfit, I hear."

"Times like these I wished I didn't," Pilcher said. "We're headed far up the Yellowstone to resupply one of our trading posts. You're welcome to hop aboard, for as long as you want some company."

"We're competitors," Jack said.

"Hell, there's no competition here," Pilcher said. "We're just trying to get upriver without losing our hair. You know these parts as well as I do. The Rees are on the warpath here, and the Blackfoots are making trouble in the mountains. We need to watch each other's backs. Just leave the pirogue tethered behind. It will help keep our bow pointed upriver while we pole."

Jack nodded.

"Hey, Fontanelle," Pilcher called to a man forward. "Get

the boys ready to pole. I'll take the steering oar. We start now, and it'll be dark by the time we reach the Ree village."

"I'll help pole," Jack said. "Otherwise, you have an uneven number of men on one side."

"Suits me," Pilcher said. "There's a rack just inside the cabin to store that fine-looking smoke pole. Take the port side, if you would, and keep a lookout for hostiles. And after it gets dark, we'll have to move quiet and be careful of the snags and swayers."

Jack walked the tread around the side of the cabin and went to the bow, where he ducked into the fore doorway and placed his rifle in a rack with a half-dozen others. He kept the powder horn and his possibles bag over his shoulder, because if there was to be shooting, he didn't want to have extra items to grab. Then he said quick hellos to the other men and took one of the stout ash poles and waited for Pilcher's order. When it came, he fell in with the other three men on his side, walking the tread back and forth. As the boat moved forward, Pilcher lifted the anchor, and then scrambled on top to man the steering oar.

As the sun set, they were still poling, and as the dusk became night they slowed and kept a sharper lookout for hazards in the river. One of the crew, a man named Doherty, was smoking a clay pipe as he poled, a bobbing cherry-red coal going back and forth in the dark.

"Doherty," Fontanelle called. "Douse that pipe. That's like waving a torch to tell 'em we're here."

Doherty cussed and knocked the pipe out against the side of the cabin. The embers of the full bowl rolled down the wood and fell into the cracks in the wood.

"Want to throw some water on that?" Jack asked.

"This boat is so old and tough she won't burn," Doherty said.

Jack was about to object when Pilcher made a low whistle.

"Look sharp, boys," Pilcher whispered. "The biggest village is on the other bank. See anything moving?"

Jack peered across the dark water. He recognized the outline of the bank and the mound that was the village beyond. He saw no fires or smoke, and there was no movement. It was also quiet. He couldn't even hear a child cry or a dog bark.

"I don't think anybody's at home," Fontanelle said.

"You can't tell," Jack said. "The whole village may be lined up on the bank, watching us pass, and we'd never know it."

"Keep it steady," Pilcher said. "We need more miles behind us before we'll be safe enough to anchor for the night. Say, is something burning down there?"

"Nope," Doherty said.

"Check, would you?" Pilcher asked. "I get a whiff of something every now and then."

When the moon rose, two hours later, Pilcher declared they would stop. They anchored in the middle of the river, with a high bluff on the south side, and watched as the three-quarter moon climbed higher and bathed the water and the banks in silver light. Jack was sitting in the stern with Pilcher, and they were talking about the best places to build a cabin on the Yellowstone and Powder Rivers.

"I'd stay close to one of the outposts," Pilcher said. "My company or yours, it doesn't matter. You don't want to be so far away that you can't call for help."

Jack shook his head.

"I want to get as far away from everybody as possible," he said.

"Have you heard of Colter's Hell?"

"Heard, but never been there."

"It's on the Stinking Water River," Pilcher said. "About a hundred miles from where it joins the Bighorn. There're hot springs there where you can bathe comfortable in winter. When John Colter came back in 1808 and told folks about it, they thought he was lying."

"Then, you've been there?"

"No," Pilcher said. "But I've talked to enough who have. It might be a hazardous area for a white man. It's Shoshone country, and the Crows are close by."

"Might be worth the trouble to take a look," Jack said.

Pilcher sniffed the air.

"Fontanelle," he called. "Sure there's nothing burning? I still smell—"

An explosion ruptured the side of the keelboat below where Doherty had tapped out his pipe. The embers had been smoldering for hours and had finally burned their way through to the boat's store of black powder, where two hundred pounds of the stuff was stored in fifty small wooden kegs packed in straw. Water flooded the side of the boat, causing it immediately to list to port, while flaming pieces of the hull floated past. While only two of the kegs had exploded, the rest were now ignited and were belching flame like Roman candles, filling the cabin with flame and smoke.

"My rifle," Jack said.

He sprang to the aft doorway and opened it, but was driven back by a torrent of flame.

"She's going down fast," Fontanelle called.

"Anybody hurt?" Pilcher called.

"Two dead."

"Is one of them Doherty?"

"Nope," Fonantelle said.

Jack could feel the deck of the keelboat tip at a steeper angle. Water boiled up from the steps leading down into the cabin and lapped at his moccasins.

"Everybody ashore!" Pilcher called. "North bank! On the bar."

"My rifle is still on board," Jack said and started making his way to the bow. Pilcher grabbed his upper arm and pulled him back.

"You're going to either roast or drown if you go after it," Pilcher said. "I hear it's called the ghost rifle, and it'll make you a ghost unless you give it up now."

Pilcher released his arm.

"This keelboat is gone in about thirty seconds," Pilcher said he as walked over and released the knot that held the pirogue tethered to the stern. He threw the rope at Jack, who caught it in his left hand.

"You'd best get in your boat and start rowing," Pilcher said.

"What about you and your men?"

"We'll have to hoof it from here," Pilcher said, holding his rifle in one hand and climbing over the rail. "Take care of yourself, Mountain Jack. I hope we meet again under better circumstances. May you find a luckier rifle."

Pilcher jumped into the water, and he and his five surviving men made for the sandbar along the north bank.

Still holding the rope, Jack slipped off the stern and swam to the pirogue. The current was carrying him downriver of the anchored keelboat, amid some of the flaming debris. He pulled himself along the rope to the pirogue, then grasped the side and pulled himself flopping into the boat. Then he found the oars, put them in the locks, and began rowing back upriver, taking glances over his shoulder as the flaming keelboat disappeared into the river.

By the time he had rowed to where the boat had been anchored, there was nothing to see there except the reflection of the three-quarter moon rippling on the dark water.

31 *Medicine Owl Woman*

The day after the Missouri Fur Company keelboat burned and sank, a Lakota woman named Medicine Owl stood on a rock at the foot of the bluff on the south side of the river and carefully slipped out of her beaded elkskin dress. She folded the dress and placed it on the rock beside the black and red ribbons she had already taken from her hair. She had watched the night before as the keelboat had caught fire and sank, and she marked the location in her mind by remembering the location of a cottonwood tree on the opposite bank.

Medicine Owl was twenty winters old and had journeyed far from home on the advice of her village's medicine man. She had caused nothing but trouble in the village for the past year, bickering with her parents and refusing to take a husband in spite of her beauty. It was rumored that she would be happier being a *winoxtca*, a member of the women's soldier society, but Medicine Owl was unsure. Her mission, the medicine man said, was to look for a sign to heal her life, some vision or gift from Wakan Tanka.

As she sat on the bluff and watched the pillar of fire that rose from the keelboat, and then saw it extinguished in the muddy water, she felt the presence of the unspeakable power. She knew the boat would be loaded with all manner of weapons and goods, and she determined that in the morning she would swim out to where the boat sank and see if she could recover anything of value that the fire or the water had not ruined.

Medicine Owl dove into the water and swam easily out to where the boat lay beneath her. She looked around for a moment, her dark hair trailing behind her in the water, making sure there was no one watching her. She took several deep breaths, then held the last one. She jackknifed and allowed the weight of her legs to drive her beneath the water, and kicked hard until she felt the sandy bottom. She could feel the current moving her along, and she feared she had picked the wrong spot until her hands touched burned wood.

She opened her eyes and blinked against the green water. Medicine Owl could just make out the shape of what was left of the cabin and the hull beneath. Using her hand to pull herself deeper into the cabin, she felt among the cargo and other items that lay in a jumble. She grasped the handle of a pot and decided that would be useful, and with her lungs beginning to ache for want of air, reached out with her left hand to pull herself back up. But then her fingertips brushed something familiar.

It was the octagonal barrel of a rifle.

She dropped the pot and grasped the rifle instead. Pushing off from the wreck of the keelboat with her feet, she swam for the surface, which was just a dull brownish-green glow thirty feet above her. But it was a struggle with the weight of the rifle. She kicked hard with her legs and used her free hand to try to pull her up through the water, but it didn't seem as if she was making any progress. She could feel herself drifting with the current, and as her lungs began to burn, she kicked harder. But the more she struggled, the louder her body screamed for air.

She thought she would either have to release the rifle or drown.

Then Medicine Owl thought of the shame in either. She calmed herself and concentrated and coordinating her kicks with her free hand, swimming upward in short but determined bursts, and the greenish-brown light grew stronger. It got easier as she neared the surface, and finally her head broke the surface of the water, and she took in grateful lungfuls of air.

The current had carried her far down from where she left her clothes, but she was near a sandy beach and here the water was shallower. She swam a few more strokes, holding the rifle at her side, and soon her feet found the bottom. She waded ashore, her long black hair plastered to her breasts and her back, river water dripping from her body onto the sand. At least she was on the south bank of the river, and it wouldn't be too far a walk to the rock where she had left her dress.

She crossed her legs and sat down on the sand to rest, the rifle resting on her thighs. It resembled the kind of rifle she had seen the white trappers with, but this one seemed different. It had a walnut stock and a short barrel like the others, but it seemed more finely made. None of the rifle seemed to have been touched by the fire. She opened the patch box and peered inside, but saw only wet ticking. She snapped the patch box shut and examined the stock near the breech, which had what looked like bites from a wolf. Then she looked at the top of the breech and saw a curious stamp on the top, a kind of curved four-armed cross.

The rifle hadn't been in the water long enough to

damage it, but she knew it had to be cleaned and dried or else it would rust. The sun and air would go far in drying the outside. She would use the cotton ribbons that she tied her hair with to wrap around the ramrod and dry the inside of the barrel, and the bear grease she used to make her hair shine would protect it.

Medicine Owl stood, the rifle in her right hand.

Then she held it above her head and uttered a cry of exultation.

32 *The Cabin*

Jack closed his eyes and listened to the rustle and pop of the canvas in the breeze. There was the smell of rain in the wind, and of dirt, and the sounds of wild and living or once-living things—the cry of birds overhead, the groan and creak of wood, the rattle of distant thunder. The rhythm of his own breath was a familiar whisper, the sour stench of sweat from his own body a comfort. He was eternally hungry, and as he drowsed he thought of the shortbread pies filled with the black cherry jam he had eaten at his grandfather's table.

There would come a time, he swore to himself, when he would have his own great limestone house, and his own sturdy oak table, and there would be plenty of sweet gateau Basque spread out for all, in a country to call his own. Perhaps then he would find the courage to write Abella an honest letter. But for now, there was the cabin, nearly completed, placed on the side of a mountain overlooking the Stinking Water River. The work of building was exhausting, but when the cabin was done it would make a fine and warm winter home for himself and Sky, and the baby to come. When they grew tired of the cabin they could bathe in the hot springs, which Jack had found to be quite real.

As he lay drowsing beneath the tarp that covered the half of the cabin that was yet without shingles, another aroma came to him. It was the pleasant smell of roasting meat. Sky was busy making their dinner of elk steak, while Antelope Woman was busy fleshing the hide of the elk Jack had killed. But there was another smell, too, a sweet smell that filled Jack with anticipation. There would be wild cherry cobbler, freshly baked in the Dutch oven buried in the embers of the stone firepit.

PART FIVE
THE TOWN

33 *The Yellowstone House*

One day in September 1838, a boy stood in the doorway of a tavern letting his eyes adjust to the gloom. He held his cap in one hand and hooked the thumb of his other hand self-consciously under the strap of his frayed coveralls. It was mid-afternoon, and the Yellowstone House was un-usually quiet, or he would not have dared enter.

The tavern occupied the first floor of a limestone build-ing that was just around the corner from the courthouse in St. Louis, and its clientele was somewhat finer than that of the houses near the landing, which bristled with steam-boats and an ever-changing flow of humanity.

The boy walked across the oak floor to the bar.

"We have no work," the bartender said, barely looking up from his newspaper.

"I'm not after work," the boy said. "I'm looking for Mr. Jones."

"You have no business with him."

"No, not business," the boy said. "But I wonder if Mr. Jones would be kind enough to answer some questions for me about his experiences on the Upper Missouri."

"Do you have enough to buy a drink?"

"No, sir."

"Then out you go," the bartender said. "Don't make me come around this bar and kick your rear out the door. Can't you see I'm busy reading the news about Governor Clark's passing?"

"Everyone is talking of it," the boy said.

A man in his late thirties with thinning hair who sat at a table in the back of the tavern spoke up.

"What is it, Krueger?"

"This boy says he wants to talk to you about Ashley's Brigade and Governor Clark," the bartender said. "But I don't like the look of him or his manner. He's trouble, I can tell you that much."

"I'm bored," the man said. "Send him back."

"April!" the boy called. "He'll see us."

A girl in a fraying blue dress appeared in the doorway.

"You didn't say anything about a girl," Krueger said.

"Let them come," the man said. "They may be amusing."

The boy and the girl walked back, standing in front of the table. Both of them had long brown hair and blue eyes. The boy was quick and athletic, and the girl was thin and had unusually fine features. In better clothes, she could have passed for someone beyond her station.

"Sit down."

"Thank you," the boy said, and held a chair out for his sister. Then he sat as well. "You are Decatur Jones?"

"Yes," the man said. "I own the Yellowstone House."

"My name is Gus Aguirre," the boy said, the name still sounding strange on his tongue. "This is my sister, April."

"Are you twins?" Decatur asked.

"Yes, sir," Gus said.

"I thought so. How old are you?"

"Seventeen," Gus said. "Well, almost."

"We're sixteen now," the girl said. "We won't be seventeen for another year."

"What do you want to know?"

"We think you may have known our father," Gus said. "Jacques Aguirre."

"I've never known anybody by that name," Decatur said.

"You may not have known him by our last name," Gus said.

"This is nonsense," Decatur said. "I don't know anyone named Aguirre. What other name would he have used?"

"We don't know," Gus said, frowning. "We talked to Governor Clark—"

"You were admitted to see William Clark," Decatur said. "While he was ill and nearing death at the home of his son, Meriwether Clark. And you were allowed to speak to him."

"Well, no," April said. "Gus was not exactly admitted."

"I came in the middle of the night," Gus said. "And I sat with Clark and we spoke. He asked me if I had managed to kill the wolf and bring him the peace medal, and I didn't know what he was talking about. But then I asked him if he knew our father, and he said that yes, he had once, and that he had given him a rifle that was made to kill a ghost—a rifle that rang like a bell when fired. Clark sent him with Ashley's first brigade up the Missouri River to start a new life. He said he had written him a letter of introduction using a different name."

"What was the name used?"

"Clark could not recall," Gus said. "It was so long ago, he said, and the assault of age had made him dim-witted.

But he said he though it meant something like rascal or rapscallion."

"And he spoke of a rifle that rang like a bell?"

"Yes," Gus said. "He was very clear about that."

"The ghost rifle," Decatur whispered.

Decatur called Krueger to bring him whiskey.

"Can I have one, too?" Gus asked.

"No," Decatur said. "But you can have some bread and cheese."

Krueger brought a bottle of whiskey and a glass, and a plate with a loaf of bread and a wedge of cheddar. Decatur poured two inches of whiskey. He motioned for the twins to help themselves to the food. Gus let April take her portion first.

Decatur swirled his whisky in the glass.

"I knew your father as Jack Picaro," Decatur said.

April asked him to spell the last name.

He did.

"Picaro," Gus said, trying out a new name.

"We were friends," Decatur said. "I heard that rifle sing in his hands. He was the smartest and most stubborn person I've ever known. We were the only two that survived an attack on our keelboat by the Rees. The chief took his rifle and Jack nearly killed himself getting the rifle back, but he did, eventually."

"Do you know where he is now?"

"I haven't seen him in fifteen years," Decatur said. "We parted a thousand miles from here, at a Mandan village on the Upper Missouri."

Decatur held the glass up in a toast.

"Here's to you, Jack."

He drank half the whiskey before he put down the glass.

"He was in good health and his right mind then?"

"Yes," Decatur said. "But I have no way of knowing if he even still lives. It is a dangerous country. Many did not survive long. It was not for me, but I cannot escape the shadow of the adventure even after these many years."

"I wish I could have such an adventure," Gus said.

"Be careful with your wishes," Decatur said. "Perhaps Jack is dead and that is why you have not heard from him."

"It is not," April said. "It is because he did not know of our birth."

"He has not contacted your mother?"

"She died," Gus said. "In childbirth."

"I am sorry," Decatur said. "Where have you been living?"

Neither spoke.

"You must have been raised up somewhere," he said.

"We'd rather not say, sir," April said.

"We are what you might call runaways," Gus said.

"I'm someone your father called a friend," Decatur said. "You can confide in me."

"We were given as infants to a farm couple named Gilson up in Marion County," April said. "The living was harsh, and we were not treated as family. They had their own children. We were no more than property to them. But we thought it our lot in life. We didn't know any better until the old woman named Portia who had nursed us came one day and told us our real names."

"Augustus and April Aguirre," Gus said.

"Old Portia said we were of an age to understand these things," April said. "She said we must not ask our mother's family, the Rapailles, because they would be no help. But she heard Governor Clark might know something."

"That was six months ago," Gus said.

"And since?"

"Living as we can," Gus said.

"Stealing?"

"When we must," the boy said.

Decatur took another drink.

"What is your plan now?"

"To find our father," Gus said.

"You are too young."

"We are determined," Gus said.

"You will need money."

"We are working at acquiring what we need," April said. "Gus is good at gambling and pilfering and I can sew. Men say they will pay me for my attention, but I ignore them. We are saving our silver, and it won't be long."

"Do not steal," Decatur told Gus. "And you, April, must resist selling your company. I will help you both find a living. It is the least I owe to Jack."

"Thank you," April said. "But we are quite independent."

"And anxious to begin the search," Gus said.

"Why?"

"To know our place in the world, of course," Gus said. "And there must be a home waiting for us with our father in the West."

"You have very little chance," Decatur said. "Even if he is still alive, the trappers have left the river and gone ever deeper into the mountains in search of beaver. He may even have changed his name again, and then how would you track him?"

"The rifle," Gus said. "If we cannot follow the name, we will pursue the ghost rifle."